I0593821

path of the Half moon

path of the Half moon

VINCE BAILEY

IngramElliott

Path of the Half Moon
Copyright © 2018 by Vince Bailey

All rights reserved. No part of this publication may be reproduced, stored in a retrieval system, or transmitted in any form or by other means electronic, mechanical, photocopying, recording or otherwise, without the prior written permission of the publisher.

Published by IngramElliott, Inc.
www.ingramelliott.com
9815 J Sam Furr Road, Suite 271, Huntersville NC 28078

This is a work of fiction. The names, characters, places, or events used in this book are the product of the author's imagination or used fictitiously. Any resemblance to actual people (alive or deceased), events, or locales is completely coincidental.

Book design by Maureen Cutajar, gopublished.com
Cover design by H.O. Charles

ISBN Hardcover: 978-0-9990573-7-7
ISBN Paperback: 978-0-9990573-8-4
ISBN E-book: 978-0-9990573-9-1

Library of Congress Control Number: 2018953549
Subjects: Fiction—Historical. Fiction—Paranormal. Fiction—Suspense.
Fiction—Western and Pacific States. Fiction—Myth & Legends.

Published in the United States of America
Printed in the United States of America
First Edition: 2018, First International Edition: 2018

Dedication

I dedicate my inaugural novel, *Path of the Half Moon*, to my wife, Rita, who indulged my extended closed-door marathons, and who gently reined in my occasional excursion beyond the willing suspension of disbelief.

Author's Note

Path of the Half Moon is a historical fiction work, with the emphasis on fiction, although it was not always so. The writing process taught me what was vital to the tale. At the outset of telling the story, I was preoccupied with maintaining precise historical and geographical accuracy. In the age of seemingly infinite data stores and powerful search engines, little effort is required to discover, for instance, the high temperature on April 30, 1964, or the exact time for the sunset on any given date. During the course of writing, though, I began to feel my obsession with such exact minutiae was becoming restrictive and cramping my creativity. For example, the reader is given to understand that the phase of the moon is crucial in triggering the story's events. A search reveals that the very real massacre at Fort Grant occurred during a waxing half-moon. It followed the ghostly reprise of that atrocity should be enacted under that same phase. But it occurred to me that the story would be better enhanced if the moon were waning—getting darker, as the plot was darkening. After several of these conflicts in which creativity ultimately triumphed over historical precision, I all but abandoned my fixation on nit-picking accuracy with regard to historical and geographical details.

Consequently, though the Fort Grant massacre is a historically factual event, its actual location may be somewhat sketchy. Similarly, you won't find a town anywhere in Arizona called Jacobs Well. Its description, however, suggests a suspicious similarity to Mesa—where I grew up. State highway designations and even county names in the book may or may not be fictitious, depending on their consistency with the story.

This is not to pay short shrift to the historical background. Clearly, it is essential to the tale. This partial abandonment of strict accuracy, however, allowed me free rein to fabricate a world of shadowy places, actors, and actions that imitate the real, unhampered by the realities. Historical purists will certainly find a number of flaws in *Path of the Half Moon*, but I think casual readers will enjoy the creativity that imprecision allows.

path of the Half moon

Retrospectus
—a prologue—

Whatever is has already been, and what will be has been before;
And God will call the past to account. Ecclesiastes 3:15

Nachise awoke with a start at the low nickering of a restless horse disturbing the crisp quiet of the predawn air. The boy sat up and peered out through the open end of the canvas tent toward the ring of rocks that encircled a now-cold cook fire. No flicker of flame or gleam of ember blinked from those dead stones. But absent the hypnotic flames of hours past, he could see that the muted glow of a westering half-moon bathed the desert campsite outside in a ghostly luminosity that drew him away from any yen for a return to sleep.

The gentle whinnying died away at once, leaving only a vacuous stillness as if the very life's breath of the entire earth were held in abeyance. The neigh of an aroused nag among the herd was not a sound out of place, but set in stark contrast to this deathly silence it may as well have been a thunderclap. It was this suffocating quietness, not the horse's disruption of it, that troubled Nachise's awakening mind. Already at the tender age of eleven he'd learned that such buoyant stillness all too often presaged some sudden descent into calamity.

Stealthily, so as not to awaken his older half-sister, the boy pulled aside the warm wool blanket and slipped from the stale air of the canvas womb into the cool, clear phosphorescence of the world outside. He inhaled the aroma of damp earth and cast a narrow-eyed gaze eastward at a nascent glimmer. It was the slightest hint of a faint purple band clinging tenaciously to the horizon that subtly backlit the rugged silhouette of the Pinalenos range. The hunting party would be en-camped dozens of miles beyond that distant monument, already mounted and no doubt stalking their quarry in the predawn glow. He sighed wistfully because his manly spirit was very much with his father and the other braves of the Aravaipa clan, though he'd been left behind when they had departed two mornings before—passed over again with all the other boys who'd weathered fewer than twelve winters.

His dark eyes broke away from the premature herald of dawn, now scanning the sprawling basin floor that hosted the clan's fifty-six Army-issue tents for any sign of movement. No one was astir among the canvas shadows. The watch fire at the center of the camp, which had blazed forth with so much assurance at moonrise, had now decayed to a bed of dying coals. The toothless old veteran who had been named surrogate sentinel now watched only for the phantom intruders of his restive dreams.

Another outburst of whinnying from the scant string of ponies now drew the boy's attention westward to the opposite end of the camp where the few remaining steeds of the herd were sequestered together in a primitive corral. Nachise cautiously approached the post-and-rail enclosure fashioned from peeled mesquite boughs that he had helped to erect. Facing the overhead gleam of the descending half-moon ham-pered the boy's night vision, and Nachise strained in vain to catch sight of what might be bothering them. Perhaps it was merely a passing desert serpent, wending its menacing way among the horses' spindly legs that disturbed their hypnotic, half-sleeping state—or perhaps something similar, only worse.

Nachise suddenly recalled the coffee-colored boy he'd surprised along the trail at twilight last evening. It was clearly a fateful encounter but a brush that had been no threat. Quite the contrary, the young Apache boy held that chance meeting as a positive omen—a premoni-tion of some imminent reckoning, one that his father, Ezzymandias, had prophesied. No, the brown-skinned boy was not the source of the disturbance; this was something else—something, somehow . . . unfath-omable. He grasped now the source of his inner disturbance, for unfathomable, in Nachise's experience, was something unheard of.

Intuitive glimpses presaging everyday events were commonplace for the boy, and all of the clan members agreed that Nachise had inherited a shaman's sixth sense from his father. He could "see," for instance, the approach of a visiting pony soldier from Fort Grant an hour before hoofbeats could be heard in the camp; he could "feel" the nearing death of a clan member before illness or foul weather even set in. So it was this unusual failure to fathom what was out there in the near-darkness that stirred within him a sense of foreboding. Nevertheless, he felt a certain prescience in the glowing desert silence.

And in spite of his youth, Nachise also harbored an inborn sense of responsibility, one that adhered to the gift of seeing beyond the horizons of everyday perception. It was predictable, then, that the inkling of an unseen threat compelled the boy to set out to probe the perimeter of the camp. He simply *had to* ensure the security of the sleeping clan members in spite of his apprehension.

But after a few steps toward the corral, the cool sponginess of the clay beneath his bare soles reminded him that he was shoeless. For a thorough investigation of the perimeter he would have to venture beyond the campsite floor of rain-softened caliche soil, and into the brush where sharp granite stones and cholla thorns demanded proper footwear. He reluctantly returned back to the tent for shoes and breeches, regretting the necessary delay and hoping not to awaken his slumbering half-sister, Sika.

Now he was a man with a mission, and the mission made him more a man than the mere boy that he seemed to be. Obligation to the clan ran deep with each of its members. The clan was provider and protector, and all who were sustained by its collective power owed fealty to it. But this feeling of tribal obligation was multiplied tenfold in a boy whose destiny was to assume the role of chief from his father. In fact, he would gladly, even now, face any foe against any odds. He would freely forfeit his life, if need be, to protect the clan that was the anchor of his life.

He fumbled at the tent flap and groped in the darkness for his togs. And although he was as silent as a stalking puma, his sister, already awake, whispered from the darkness at the back of the tent.

"What is it, little brother?"

She used the diminutive as a term of affection, but it seemed to mock his self-endowed stature, and he resented it.

"It is nothing—only a restless pony. Go back to sleep." He spoke aloud, but more softly than her whisper.

"If it is nothing, then why does a restless pony merit your dressing before dawn?"

"I rise before dawn every day to get fish for breakfast," he said, much annoyed at her insolence. "You women only sleep until dawn when the braves are away."

"And you dance around the heart of my question, but your dancing does not distract me," she retorted, now in a voice that matched his.

"If you must know my every movement, sister, I plan to relieve myself beyond the corral once I have checked the herd." He was citing a tribal tradition never to defile the campsite. "I dress for the occasion," he added with a quiet chuckle as he pulled up his short leather breeches. Glancing at the spit he had assembled over the now-darkened fire pit, he noted that the two fish he had roasted for Sika were untouched. "I ate alone again last night," he observed drily. "You stayed at Fort Grant long past dark."

"Yes," she replied, "I waited for the arrival of the visiting Adjutant General and his wife to display our wares, much to our good fortune. I traded a trove of our silver jewelry for two sides of beef, two barrels of flour, five sacks of dried beans, and five jugs of oil."

"And where are these supplies you have traded our people's handiwork for?"

"They are to be delivered by wagon today," she returned. "Why do you ask?"

"Because the white-eyes are thieves of the worst kind. They steal with false promises."

"Of course, I only offered General Huish a small sampling of our jewelry last night. The greatest portion of our silver is still here with us. Besides, I have the word of the camp commander that a fair trade will be made, and he is a friend to our father," Sika said.

"And very friendly toward you, I have noticed," the boy quipped.

"It troubles me, little brother, that your malice for the soldiers has grown as of late. Does it so blind you that you cannot take some enjoyment from

4

our gain? The food we have traded for will allow us to prepare a home-coming feast for our braves when they return from the hunt."

"I for one will not eat the white-eyes' beef," Nachise sneered. "The hunting party will return with plenty of venison to feed our clan. We won't need the soldiers' handouts."

"You call it a handout when we trade fairly for supplies?"

"Look around you, sister," Nachise said. "We live in their tents on their land. We work in their fields and cut their hay. We sleep under their blankets and eat their cornmeal. They call us wards of the government, but we are little more than prisoners. Anything we get from them is a handout, so don't fool yourself into thinking that your trinkets were anything more than a token offering to ease your shame."

"Your resentment poisons your young heart, Nachise. You will waste your life harboring such hatred."

The boy glanced up, noting that the lambent light from the nesting moon rapidly diminished as the lunar orb slipped silently behind the veil of a solitary cloud. He grasped a three-pronged gig that was leaning against the tent.

"What I've wasted is my time with all of these worthless words. I will go to the river to fish after I secure the camp. Your chore is to build a fire so that we have some live embers for roasting when I return."

"The Apache people do not eat fish," Sika reminded him.

"Yes, but our venison is used up, and I would prefer to eat worms over the rations that the soldiers dole out to us."

Nachise strode purposefully away, westward toward the corral in the gathering gloom, brandishing the pole-gig like a warrior's battle lance. He closed the intervening stretch of bare ground in less than a minute. He found the dozen or so horses quiet but awake as he gently leaned his fishing gig against the fence, lifted the makeshift bolt, and slipped inside the gate. A pale gelding approached and nuzzled the boy's bare chest.

"What's all the fuss, boy?" Nachise whispered as he stroked the horse's muzzle. He scanned the ground in and around the corral, but the darkness was growing thicker by the minute and harder to pierce, even with his keen night vision.

Then, from somewhere distant and just at the edge of earshot, a faint ping like the sound of two river rocks colliding broke the silence. Nachise held his breath, straining to hear a repeat of the sound to locate its source. He thought again of the dark-skinned boy he'd met on the trail the previous evening. Could this stranger be the herald of emancipation the people had been waiting for? Ezzymandias had foretold that a strange young brave, neither red nor white, would one day appear to lift the clan from its curse: the shame of bondage to white-eyed soldiers.

There. Yet another faint ping followed by another. The sounds, now clearly coming from the west and slightly south, began to multiply and build into a barely audible but distinct rolling clatter. Horses' hooves— plodding, but nonetheless approaching!

Nachise rushed from the corral, hastily fastened the bolt, and reached for his gig. It was gone.

Quicker than a pit viper striking, a meaty hand shot over the boy's left shoulder and clapped over his mouth. From the right, the chilling touch of cold steel flashed across his bared throat.

"Don't you let out a squeal, little piglet, or I'll butcher you right here and now!"

The words, hissed more than spoken, came in Spanish, a tongue that Nachise knew quite well, though it was not native to him. The ape-like claw, redolent with the stench of stale tobacco, now firmly clamped over his nose and mouth. It made breathing, much less crying out, most unlikely. Besides, the biting edge of the freshly sharpened blade that pressed so tightly against his tender neck spoke volumes in the universal language of terror. The threatening whisper conveyed a brutal statement of fact more than a command.

But the intruder's suffocating grasp forced a weak reflexive retort from Nachise, a desperate little cry for mercy as the boy tried his best to gasp for air and hold fast to a tenuous grip on consciousness. Instinctively, the intruder slackened his grasp only enough that the helpless child was able to manage a single inhalation through spreading fingers.

Then came another voice, muted but not whispering. "This one's too old to keep. He'll hear. He'll remember. Kill him," came the other invader's words from somewhere near in the gloom.

"You are too quick to forfeit *my* prize—the one that you seem to have missed yourself, Patron. I think I'll just keep this one and take him back to Tucson," retorted the boy's captor in lowered voice. "He'll bring me a pretty penny down in Sonora. That's what I came here for."

"Silence! There is no time to argue. Kill him as I have commanded and attend to the mission," the other voice reverberated in the still air. "Kill him now, or I will do it for you!"

Nachise sensed the approach of the other voice in this last chilling phrase. Miraculously, the hand that gripped the boy's mouth went slack and the blade pulled away from his throat. Sounds of a struggle ensued, and a surge of adrenaline coursed through the boy's veins as he slipped from captivity and bolted like a flushed rabbit. He bounded for twenty yards or so and pulled up considerably short of what his instincts told him was a safe distance. With tribal fealty eclipsing self-preservation, Nachise steeled himself, faced the direction of the camp, cupped trembling hands around his mouth, and let out the alarm.

"RAIDERS! AWAKEN! RAIDERS! ARISE! RAIDERS ARE UPON US!"

His voice, rasping and somewhat muted from the lingering effect of the pressing blade, nevertheless pierced the still of the predawn hour. Nachise was only dimly aware of the menacing shadows of furtive figures that stole across his field of vision toward the slumbering camp, their stealthy strides muffled by the damp clay underfoot.

Buoyed by an exhilaration aroused by his own daring, the young brave drew in a deep draught of cool air, filling his lungs for another warning burst. But at the very split second that his voice engaged, a dull thud resounded through his skull, throwing up a wall of pain at the front of his face. His breath escaped in a gasp as a dozen blue-white sparks danced before his eyes for an instant. Then, as his knees went limp, a wave of smothering darkness swept him headlong into an ocean of absolute silence.

Early Warnings

Our parents warned us about Fort Grant, but they really had no idea. Actually, none of us had much of a clue, either, until Curtis disappeared. Besides, if you consider all of the surplus of nonstop, irrational warnings we were subjected to back in the early sixties, it's a wonder that fear of the Fort didn't get all but diluted in that pool of ravings.

For the entire time that I was growing up in Jacobs Well, I was regularly smothered with well-intended admonitions aimed at keeping me from straying too far afield when I wandered beyond the watchful eyes of my dear authoritarian mother and my likewise tyrannical father. We were a devout Catholic family, and so I naturally assumed that this wagging-finger syndrome was unique to our persuasion. Not so. Upon comparing notes with the admittedly wayward Protestant and Jack Mormon ruffians that I ran with, I found that all of my unruly friends were similarly attacked with a machine-gun barrage of identically ominous warnings from their own folks. And even though none of our parents socialized with the others, it was as if they were intuitively locked together in this cautionary conspiracy.

And while none of us put much stock in our parents' hysterical alarm about walking barefoot among the indigenous desert denizens, or swimming in the nearby canals, or staying out past curfew, there was one admonition that dramatically eclipsed our adolescent skepticism.

You better start straightening up, or they're going to ship you off to Fort Grant!

Okay, this terrifying, vaguely triggered threat was the only one that *really* hit home, mostly because we all knew that Fort Grant was an actual place. It was on our Arizona state maps at school. We were painfully aware of its purpose as the regional juvenile detention facility for the greater Phoenix area, as well as for Tucson. We also understood that it was a really bad place, and you didn't want to cross any lines that would get you "shipped off" there—even if it meant "straightening up," which was a similarly revolting alternative, though slightly less so.

Actually, my cohorts and I had for years tried to convince ourselves that the Fort Grant mythos was wildly exaggerated by our parents to help sustain their oppressive warning message over distances and durations. It was like some invisible cautionary tractor beam transmitted by our oppressive guardians that all delinquents evaded in blissful pursuit of our various avenues of mischief making. *Straighten up, or else it's the Fort for you!* Yeah, right.

But then, one fateful day in February, one of our ragtag numbers, Curtis Jefferson, inadvertently crossed that fuzzy line between a prank and a crime, and he was immediately snatched from our midst by the inescapable hand of the law. Our friend was whisked away to that God-forsaken outpost in the desert, and our colorful band of misfits was instantly rendered less so. Just as suddenly, the imminent threat of Fort Grant and reform school doubled—no, *quadrupled*—in gravity.

Now, for me, Curtis was the most magnetic character in our gang, no question. Oh, he was a bright kid, all right, with a bittersweet humor, a smile that could turn a funeral dirge into a bossa nova number, and a trove of musical chatter that could brighten even the dour spirits of the condemned. Clearly, Curtis possessed a wit that would bring cheer to the dreariest corners of a state-run depression ward. But those characteristics could readily describe any one of our clan of clowns. They were requisite for membership.

And no, it wasn't his physical prowess that made him a standout in our gang of toughs, although his natural ability and legendary performances in any number of athletic endeavors made him something of a celebrity in the student body of Jacobs Well Junior High. Curtis could sprint around the quarter-mile oval ten seconds ahead of the sweep-second hand of a Timex dial, broad jump into the next county, bench-press the rear end of a half-ton pickup truck, and hold a handstand on the parallel bars for a phenomenal five minutes without breaking a sweat—all the while maintaining that typically toothy Curtis Jefferson grin.

Nor did his athletic good looks particularly distinguish him. Well, except that he was a dead ringer for an adolescent version of Cassius Clay. This uncanny likeness resonated eerily with his boyhood dream to win the Olympic gold medal for boxing, as did his look-alike idol.

No, there was something more about this all-American kid that only his closest confidants knew about that made him delightfully unique: Curtis was a natural-born storyteller. He could expound for hours, quite literally, on some folktale or legend from his early childhood that would keep the rest of us spellbound for the duration.

Of course, part of the attraction was in the content. His stories were always laced with an intoxicating whiff of the supernatural. Curtis's mother and grandmother had brought him to Jacobs Well nearly ten years before from some place called Plaquemine Parish. I'm told it was, or possibly still is, situated somewhere along the swampy back roads of Louisiana. It's reputed to be a place where supernatural events are apparently still commonplace, and matters of the netherworld are openly discussed as fact.

But the standout story for my money, the queen mother tale of all his fabulous yarns, was the recounting of his harrowing experiences as an inmate at Fort Grant. Aside from the sheer volume of the fable and the factual way in which he related it, the personal value became a badge of honor. You see, he shared this legendary jewel solely with me. And while we did run with the same flock of black sheep during those late spring days back in 1964, we were never really close friends until that evening in late April, when I was able to coax the mysterious truth about his Fort Grant Reform School experience from his creative memory.

Looming

"There's no use in whinin' about it, Curtis," Sergeant Joe said. "At the very least, you put yourself at the scene. Besides which, we both know you were up to no good there."

The sergeant was guiding his Ford Galaxie 500 cruiser down an unpaved desert roadway, chatting over his shoulder with his juvenile prisoner in the back seat. A steel-mesh security grate separated the front seats from the back.

A suffocating wave of apprehension swept over Curtis Jefferson, boy-convict, as he sensed they were nearing their destination. It was a vague sense of loathing that was more prescient than Curtis could ever anticipate. It seemed as if something even more grim than the prospect of reform school awaited—something supremely sinister crouching at the end of this vacant desert artery.

"And on top of all that," the cop continued, "they had an eyewitness that identified you."

"Yeah, I admitted I was there, Joe, but I didn't start no fire. You know I wouldn't do somethin' that crazy."

José Garcia, aka "Sergeant Joe," was something of a patriarchal figure in the Jacobs Well community that was home to Curtis. Joe was a hard-nosed cop when he had to be, but a softer side of him frequently surfaced, as he seemed to gravitate toward befriending teenage boys. He umpired for the Little League and helped the parish priest organize a junior high track team. Curtis knew him as Freddy Moreno's uncle. Freddy was a good friend, and the warm inner sanctum of the Moreno house was something of a home away from home for Curtis and other members of his ragtag band of boys. Sergeant Joe would often stop by on his hours or days off and indulge in some touch football in the street with Freddy, Curtis, and all the neighborhood youths. He'd play "pass-only" quarterback on whichever side was on offense. He and the priest, Father Frank Cullen, even took turns giving Curtis some boxing pointers from time to time. At those times, José Garcia seemed like more of a friendly coach or mentor than a cop. Right now he was being a cop.

"I've known you for a long time, Curtis, and if it gives you any comfort, I believe you didn't set that fire," said Joe. "But just the fact that you were the only one spotted there . . . well, the juvenile court judge didn't buy your story, and his word is law—no two ways about it."

"Yeah, like I said, I wasn't the only one there. But I wasn't about to rat nobody out—at least not to nobody but you."

"Yeah, and with the name you gave me, you wouldn't have gotten to first base with that fairy tale."

"So you're sayin' you *don't* believe me, then?"

"I'm saying that what I believe or don't believe doesn't amount to a hill of *frijoles* with the court. So copping a plea was the best hand you had, Curtis."

"Some hand. You know, that low-life public defender said they'd go easy on me if I rolled over and copped to a no-contest. But *twelve months*, Joe—that ain't fair!"

"You need to forget about what's fair and make up your mind that you broke the law just by being where you didn't belong, and now you're paying the consequences—that's all," Joe growled. "We've been over all this before—now you just need to take your medicine and do what I tell you. If you follow my advice, you'll get through this just fine."

Joe glanced in the rearview mirror to make sure Curtis was paying attention before continuing.

"So, the whole time you're in there, just wipe that constant smile off your face, keep your eyes lowered, and shift that motormouth of yours into neutral—you hear?"

Curtis nodded: "The smile part will be easy."

But Joe wasn't finished: "And steer clear of any guys that want to buddy up with you. They've probably got motives you don't know about . . . and don't want to."

"Okay, Joe," Curtis grumbled, "is that it, or is there more?"

"Yeah, there's more. Don't ask a lot of questions when you first get there. Just try to figure things out for yourself." A brief silence ensued before Joe capped it off with a final admonition. "And for God's sake, try to stifle that world-famous imagination. It'll get you into nothing but deep shit at the Fort."

"Got it—don't smile, don't talk, don't pal, don't ask, don't tell, and don't dream. Can we breathe at this place?"

It was Thursday, the last day of February 1963—a little more than a year prior to Curtis's telling of his tale on a peaceful snake-hunting evening in a remote melon field. More on that, presently. Sergeant Joe was transporting Curtis from Jacobs Well to begin serving his term at the reform school. The police car weaved its way along a network of poorly maintained gravel roads in the desert, somewhere west of Safford and north of Tucson. The wheels chattered across the washboard surface. The sandy soil of the roadway still retained some moisture from a recent microburst, keeping the dusty wake to a minimum.

"Man, we are really headed down *Empty Street* to *Nowhere Central*," Curtis muttered. "Nothin' but rattlesnakes and centipedes for as far as the eye can see."

"Ah don't be so dramatic, kid."

The cruiser now slowed, as it was coming up on a long, low blinding-white stucco wall that jutted abruptly out of a gradual rise in the desert floor. Studying this, his first glance at the imminent place of residence for the coming year, Curtis felt a prickling on his skin. "Joe?"

"What is it?"

"I got a *really bad* feelin' about this place," Curtis whined.

"Well, it's not supposed to be a country club, you know."

"No, I don't mean just bad; I mean *creepy*, sort of."

"This is what I mean about those runaway fantasies of yours. You need to put all that weird stuff you've heard about the Fort away in an iron box and throw it in the river."

"What weird stuff are you talkin' about, Joe?"

"You know, the things all the jaydees around the neighborhood say."

"Jaydees?"

15

"Juvenile delinquents. That's what us cops call you teenage vagrants—jaydees."

"Anyway, back to the 'weird stuff,' Joe."

"I just mean all the talk about strange happenings and stuff at the Fort. You've heard the stories, I'm sure."

"Oh, *this* is a real comfort, man."

"Look, all I'm saying is if you do see or hear anything out of the ordinary on your stay down here, just put it out of your mind. Youngsters like you with an overactive imagination tend to dream things up while they're in the cooler—supernatural things, I mean. Just keep your head focused on realities, and the nightmares will go away."

"Thanks for easin' my mind, Joe. You've just given me reason for about twelve months' worth of nightmares."

Curtis fell silent, trying to quell the tingling sensation that grew between his shoulder blades as the patrol car approached a pair of huge black wrought-iron gates. In spite of Sergeant Joe's sage admonition, he imagined that this unwelcome image unfolding before him must surely be just as it is at the gates of hell.

I Recall

I recall the circumstances and the setting in which Curtis Jefferson told his epic tale as clearly as if this happened last week. This sounds cliché, I know, but I believe I owe this curious clarity to a certain transcendence of time which, after all, is the essence of the story and which seems to attach to my conveying of it. You'll see what I mean down the road.

The original and very extraordinary telling of the tale occurred during one of the many quests or schemes that our band of clowns took up on a weekly or daily basis—usually conjured up by our erstwhile ringmaster, David Matthews. This time, he informed us that the biology department of the nearby college was offering a twenty-dollar bounty on rattlesnakes (twenty-five for sidewinders) for use in their desert reptile laboratory. Since many of us still lacked the status symbol of that age and era—a Schwinn Stingray bicycle—we were ripe for any get-rich-quick enterprise. And so it was easy to tempt no fewer than eight of us "jaydees" into a Saturday night visit to the melon fields east of town to capture our share of the venomous vipers.

We conspired to work in twos—one spotting with a flashlight, and one with a catchpole. David decreed that each team was to take a designated acre-sized plot so we could cover the greatest possible area with our number of "hunters" and thus increase our odds of actually snagging one of the coiling critters. When we partnered up, I was quick to request Curtis for my team, not only for his notorious agility, but for his legendary courage as well. Besides, he had the best catchpole, an eight-foot arrangement fashioned from an old cane fishing pole and a length of thin clothesline fed through the eyelets, forming a wide loop at the end. He agreed to team up with me, obviously recognizing my superior flashlight, a six-volt dry cell Rayovac lantern that put out a powerful beam for a good fifty yards or so.

"Sure, I'll go with the Catholic boy," he agreed. "Shoot, with Pope Paul on our side, we're like Saint Patrick. Those serpents don't stand a chance!"

He and I were now a team.

We paired off and struck out eastward on our bikes toward the primary canal that kept the melon beds regularly irrigated. We reached it and the margins of the fields right at sunset. I am still amazed at the clarity with which I can picture the events of that soft spring evening.

"Vince and me, we're gonna ride up this side road a ways until we see a likely spot," Curtis announced at length. "Don't anybody cross over into the field within a hundred yards of where we park our bikes, or else we'll be bustin' some jawbones—get it?"

He was staking out our territory in advance with a concealed grin. David may have been in charge, but he always ceded authority to Curtis when the junior high legend spoke this firmly. The rest of our troop waited behind while Curtis and I got a head start on finding his "likely spot."

The single-lane maintenance road ran out like a dusty ribbon stretched atop a raised earthen berm, not unlike a small levee. Our two-man bicycle procession rattled single file southward, down the darkened gravel path. The swollen canal coursed along on the left of us, and a steep bank fell off to a smaller, swiftly running ditch on the right. Beyond and below this flowing lateral, the shimmer of flooded fields glinted faintly through the deepening shadows. Stately rows of cottonwood and eucalyptus trees formed a windbreak at the fields' margins.

The evening darkness now descended more deeply with each passing moment like a drapery of gloom. The subtle glow of a gray-blue band at the western horizon was fading fast. A waxing crescent moon rode high overhead, casting a feeble light over the land. About a quarter mile up the road from the bridge we stopped and laid down our bikes by the edge of the ditch.

"This is a prime spot—I can tell," Curtis declared as he pointed out into the darkness. "See that gleam of the water? The irrigation is runnin' through the rows, but it's not all the way flooded yet."

I strained to discern what he was looking at but made out only a few fingerlike glimmers in the darkness of the fields that lay at the foot of the slope below us. He apparently had much better night vision than I. Still, what he said made sense, at least from what I could make out. The water running through the furrows would drive any type of critter up onto the raised beds where they'd be restricted to only one avenue of escape.

Curtis fiddled for a while with his catchpole, as he hummed the tune to the Sam Cooke rendition of "Another Saturday Night." He fussed with the size of the noose he'd opened up at the end of the pole like it was a critical detail. Maybe it was. Not to be outdone, I pulled my dry cell lantern from the gunnysack I'd brought along to transport the scaly creatures that we were certain to capture. I polished the lens with the edge of my T-shirt, preparing for the mission.

Curtis eased down the sloping bank to the gurgling ditch and gingerly leaped across. I followed suit. As my colored companion had predicted, a large irrigated melon field stretched out before us in the dark. I switched on my trusty light and panned the area. It was as he'd said—literally hundreds of alternating furrows and raised beds lay in rows before us. The young melon vines were just starting to send out their leafy shoots, offering scant refuge for any fugitive reptile. It was ripe territory for rattlesnake hunting, no question. Fertile ground for spawning fables as well.

"Listen for the rattle," Curtis said. "They'll buzz as soon as they see that bodacious searchlight of yours."

We listened quietly there for some time, waiting for a telltale buzz, but there was nothing but the soothing babble of the coursing ditchwater. The Evening Star was brightening, and the silent stand of San Tan Mountains to the south—always before the prominent sentinel soaring up from the desert floor—cloaked itself now, only a shadowy memory.

A lone coyote raised a plaintive howl in the distance.

"Shit!" Curtis exclaimed.

"What is it?" I asked, confused. "Should I turn off the light?"

"No, it's not that. It's the damn coyotes—they give me the willies."

"That's funny, Curtis. I always heard you weren't scared of *anything.*"

"Well, I'm not exactly *scared* of 'em—but they are pretty damn creepy."

"Some past experience, maybe?" I wondered aloud.

"Somethin' like that."

I waited for the beginning of one of his famous tales, but there was only silence. In time, I pressed him further.

"I didn't know they had coyotes in Louisiana, Curtis."

"No, but they've got plenty of 'em down at that God-forsaken Fort Grant."

Now we'd come to a critical juncture. Curtis had no qualms about admitting he'd spent time down there—we all knew it anyway. Curiously though, he would never get into any detail as to what it was like. But the reform school myth was our parents' ultimate scare tactic, and we were all dying to know. I held my peace for a moment, hoping he'd continue; but again there was only silence, so I pressed him.

"So, what was it like on the inside down there?" I asked with sort of a feigned indifference.

"I don't want to talk about it after dark."

I waited again and pressed further.

"Look, it's been almost a year, and that place is over a hundred miles away. I would think you'd be able to talk about it by now—especially in such a quiet and peaceful place as this."

"Let's just let it lie and hunt snakes," he snapped.

We both fell silent and started to move along a raised bed, me panning the light like a beacon, him at the ready with the catchpole. The clods of damp dirt that broke beneath our canvas tennies filled my head with an earthy fragrance. The stillness was palpable; it pressed like resonating snares against my eardrums. A good five minutes passed before he spoke again when we reached the end of another row.

"It's not so much that I don't want to talk about it. Hell, I've been draggin' this tale around like a goddamn lead weight for months," he said, somewhat out of the blue. "It's more like I don't know *how* to tell it."

"Are we talking about Fort Grant again?" I asked this cautiously, having been soundly rebuked for floating the subject just moments prior.

"Yeah—it's like somethin' I'm needin' to get off my chest that's more than just a story; I just don't have the slightest notion how to start."

"Well, like they say—begin at the beginning." It was a pathetic prod, but it was all I could think of.

"Oh, that's just *brilliant*," he teased. "You must have stayed awake all night dreamin' up that jewel."

"Sorry."

"I'll say it was."

"Okay, Curtis, I guess I just can't believe I'm hearing all this hemming and hawing from the fable master of the Escobedo neighborhood. I mean, everybody knows you're the best yarn-spinner in the East Valley."

The ambient glow from my flashlight revealed a flattered smile that flashed across his features but then melted into a thoughtful frown.

"No, Vince, this ain't no yarn, man. It's like a whole 'nother world, and if I tell it all and tell it truthful, it's liable to take all night, maybe longer. Besides," he continued in a lower voice, "there's parts that are tough to swallow and parts that I'm none too proud to confess. The only reason I'm even toyin' with the notion of tellin' you is 'cause I know you're a good listener."

You're a good listener. I took this to mean he knew that I was able to suspend my sense of disbelief without much difficulty. No kidding— what a laughable understatement. I grew up in a town that was founded on a mirage by a Mormon missionary named Leland Jacobs (thus the absence of an apostrophe in Jacobs Well), I was steeped in a faith that was and is riddled with bizarre religious mysteries, and I was shepherded through my youth by a handful of superstitious threats and unseen consequences. I was ready to hear anything.

"I'm ready to hear anything," I assured my young colored friend.

"Okay, but like I said, this might take all night."

"No sweat," I declared stoically, for I rightly sensed that we were now forfeiting the excitement of a nocturnal snake-hunt.

We sat down cross-legged on the soft earth and I instinctively switched off my light. I was immediately stricken dumb by this privilege, as he started to relate the story in his musical bayou drawl. Still, I was in no way prepared to fathom the profound depths of the tale he was about to plumb. It was as he'd said: parts challenged my willing suspension of disbelief; parts disturbed my youthful sensibilities; parts made me wonder how he'd come by the knowledge of them without having been present at their occurrence, except by clairvoyance. I listened attentively, though, making mental notes, as I somehow sensed that someday I would be moved to relate the tale myself. Now, I hope to re-create it with some semblance of justice in my humble effort to flesh it out in the retrospective telling that follows.

Welcome to Our World

The gravel-drive welcome mat to Fort Grant led to an arched opening—a maw that stood gated by two stark wrought-iron panels. The heavy black double-drive gate swung slowly inward at the approach of the patrol car, as if the visit was expected by some unseen sentinel. Joe eased the black-and-white Galaxie into the archway and exchanged a few pleasantries with the gatekeeper. Curtis peered past the entryway into the inside yard. He caught sight of a fairly tall uniformed man ambling away from the gate. The outfit was the same faded blue that the gate sentry wore, and Curtis, eyeing the strolling figure intently, naturally assumed him to be one of the guards.

Then, with an unexpected suddenness, the guard halted and whirled around in place. He faced the patrol car, and locked on to Curtis's gaze, as if aware that the boy was staring. Curtis was instantly horrified: the face was hideous beyond belief—a mask of decaying flesh that hung dripping from semi-exposed facial cartilage. A toothless cavern that barely resembled a mouth gaped in a frozen leer. At the center of this ghastly visage, twin gashes like small open wounds flared at the bottom of a fleshy knob. Running pustules dotted the pallid cheeks and forehead. A wispy topknot like Spanish moss crested the otherwise hairless pate. A pair of loathsome horizontal slits, situated below the brow where eye sockets would normally be, revealed the lecherous gleam of pale white orbs—two colorless grapes that seemed to penetrate Curtis's dread. The boy sat petrified for a few fleeting seconds, transfixed by the sheer monstrosity of the thing, before finally averting his widened eyes in revulsion and finding his voice.

"Holy shit, Joe—look over there at that!"

The figure now turned his features away and resumed the slow hike toward a cluster of buildings huddled in the distance.

"Look at what?"

"That *thing* over there—he makes the Phantom of the Opera look like Cary Grant."

"You mean him?" Joe asked, gesturing toward the uniformed figure as the car breezed past. "Get used to it, Curtis. None of the guards here are exactly pretty."

"No, Joe, I don't mean ugly like Jack Elam. I mean ugly like Lon Chaney's worst nightmare."

"I already told you—don't start with the fantasies. You're about to piss me off."

"But Joe, you didn't see that face! Oh man, it was like—"

"Curtis, you put a sock in it—now!"

Sensing the futility of continuing, the boy stifled a string of descriptive comments and did his best to suppress the terrifying image of the guard's features. *Poor guy must've gotten his face burned in a fire or something*, he reasoned, *like James Whitmore in* Face of Fire. Pity subdued the boy's revulsion.

Inside the confines of the adobe walls, Joe's squad car proceeded across a huge expanse of crushed granite and mica, the tires throwing up a loud crunching sound. Joe brought the car to a gradual stop at midfield. The faceted gravel bits sparkled like gold and silver sequins in the afternoon sun.

"This is the parade ground," said Joe. "Plenty of room to exercise and keep up your fitness program. I think there's even some equipment. Just don't go telling anybody that you're in training to be the next Cassius Clay. You don't want to attract any would-be challengers, kiddo. And that welcoming set of structures up ahead . . . is home, sweet home for the next twelve months."

The cliché went over like a sumo wrestler at an Olympic high-jump competition.

"Be it ever so humble," Curtis muttered, rolling his eyes.

Fort Grant State Industrial School for Boys appeared just as the sergeant had described it on the long drive down—a hodgepodge scattering of incongruous buildings nestled behind formidable adobe walls at the margins where the parched Sonoran Desert met the foothills of the Pinaleno Mountains. It had once been a military outpost for US cavalrymen during the Apache Indian campaigns of the late 1800s. Some of the surviving structures reflected the antiquated frontier-ranch style of that era. But the actual school building, the "Academic Hall," resembled the common two-story red-brick schoolhouses that were similarly constructed all over the West in the 1930s as part of the depression-era relief acts—similar in every respect, with the possible exception of the steel-mesh panels welded over some of the window openings. Rounding out the architectural smorgasbord, a handful of wood-framed barracks-style buildings seemed to have been more recently tacked on to the random cluster. If there was any consistent architectural theme behind the design scheme, it was well concealed.

Joe eased the car back into motion and brought it to a stop in a dirt lot alongside a lone blue Chevy convertible. It was a sparkling-clean late-model Impala with wire wheels.

"Nice wheels," Curtis muttered as the two exited the cruiser.

Joe escorted a reluctant Curtis along a network of gravel pathways to the largest building in the cluster—a white stucco edifice with a red-tile roof that a stenciled sign identified as the "Administration Building." Sergeant Joe pressed a doorbell button and a muffled buzzer sounded from within. Joe waved at a peephole viewer, and there came a loud click. The cop ushered the trembling boy inside.

A long gray laminate counter loomed just inside the door, and a tall, dark-haired gentleman with steel-blue eyes and a receding hairline greeted the policeman from behind it. Curtis guessed this official-looking man to be somewhere in his middle forties.

"Hello, Joe." He spoke in a serious but pleasant tone. "It's been a long time."

The man was wearing a folded blue paisley scarf across his forehead like an Indian headband. Curtis found this article to be out of place with the man's otherwise conservative attire.

"I'm sure you've heard this before, but you haven't aged at all, Lieu-tenant!" said Joe.

"It may seem so, but I'm pretty sure there must be a portrait of me collecting dust in an attic somewhere that's aging most horribly," the gentleman chuckled.

The two shook hands and the "Lieutenant" turned to Curtis.

"So this is the new inmate?"

"Yes, sir, Lieutenant—this is Curtis Jefferson, and here's his file."

Curtis looked down at the floor in deference, but his eyes went askance to a nameplate on the counter that read *Roy Whitcomb, Headmaster*. He wondered silently where Joe got the *Lieutenant* part.

"Come closer, young man," said the headmaster. "Let's have a good look at you."

Curtis approached the counter timidly, with eyes lowered at first, but gave in to the temptation to glance around at his surroundings. The industrial gray walls lent a drab cast to the office in spite of the generous natural lighting. An ancient ceiling fan squeaked overhead, like a prehistoric bird, with each dizzying revolution. A nondescript desk, littered with loose papers, displayed a vintage Underwood typewriter. Several wooden tables, similarly cluttered, with mismatched chairs, rounded out the picture of disarray beyond the counter.

Inevitably, Curtis's wandering eyes met with the headmaster's, and he was instantly riveted by the way those pools of blue penetrated him— looked *into* him. Neither of them spoke, but Curtis thought he heard a confusing string of words from inside his own racing mind, just as clearly as if they had been given voice, and in the same tone and timbre as if uttered by the man standing in front of him:

By Jove, you just might be the one . . .

When the headmaster turned to Joe again, Curtis studied him more closely. He stood erect with shoulders thrown back like a military man and he spoke with a sense of authority and sophistication. The deep-set eyes accentuated a weathered, deeply lined brow and prominent cheekbones. He sported a pencil-thin mustache just above a taut upper lip, which reminded Curtis of a younger David Niven. The crisp white dress shirt and tan slacks vigorously clashed with the bandana headband, and the unmistakable scent of English Leather aftershave followed his move-ments like an invisible cloud. Curtis sensed a distinct air of nobility about the man—nobility and mystery.

Sergeant Joe studied Curtis's case file with the school's headmaster while Curtis struggled with a "little-lost-boy" feeling in this strange place. Presently, another man appeared from a side room adjoining the office behind the counter and introduced himself as "the Doc" to the newly arrived pair. The headmaster scarcely acknowledged his presence with only a grunt.

The Doc clutched a white handkerchief, habitually clapping it over his nose and mouth, sniffing intermittently. "You'll need to come with me for your physical, young man," he told Curtis in a hoarse voice that was almost a whisper.

The Doc, like the headmaster, was tall and similarly aged, but with a shock of long, unkempt red hair and steel-rimmed glasses that comically magnified his hazel eyes. He was slender, but with a slight paunch at an imagined waist, and he revealed a crooked row of tobacco-stained teeth when he spoke. Curtis noticed that he wore the same white shirt and tan pants as the headmaster.

"You need to go with the Doc, Curtis," said Joe. "He'll bring you back here when he's done with you. We've got a ton of paperwork."

That lingering sense of apprehension whelmed again as the Doc swept Curtis out a side door and onto another gravel path. The grounds were deserted, and the boy wondered about this as the two walked along—wordlessly, at first.

"The other inmates are all in class over at the Academic Building," said the Doc, breaking the silence as if he'd intuited Curtis's unasked question. "The first mission of a reform school is to educate," he added.

The boy marveled at the way this odd-looking man had anticipated his voiceless inquiry. The two walked several hundred feet down the gravel walkway in silence again, except for the Doc's incessant sniffing, past three large clapboard buildings. They appeared similar in design to the Army barracks constructed during the war—the ones Curtis had seen on the newsreels that played at The Palms movie house back in Jacobs Well.

"Those are the dormitories," said the Doc as they passed the drab erections. "You'll be bunking in the middle one."

I wonder why the middle one? Curtis mused to himself, stifling the urge to ask out loud, per Sergeant Joe's directive to keep to himself.

"The dorms are segregated," the Doc stated, once again demonstrating a disquieting affinity for telepathy. "Not by race, but by age," he continued. "Although I think you will find that those inmates of a particular . . . oh, *persuasion*, shall we say . . . tend to gravitate toward their own kind. After all, that's just *natural,* isn't it?"

"I suppose so," Curtis replied.

"Sir—I suppose so, *sir.*"

"I suppose so, *sir*," Curtis parroted.

"In any case," the Doc went on, "you'll be no doubt pleased to find that the colored population here is more than adequately represented. Do you get my drift?"

"Yes*, suh!*" Curtis concealed a grin, hoping that the dripping jive would go unnoticed.

The path finally ended at a modest ranch-style cottage with white shiplap walls and a sun-bleached cedar-shake roof. A wide covered porch with a plank floor welcomed them to the entrance.

"This is the infirmary," the Doc stated proudly as he opened the door. "If you are ever ill or injured, this is the place they'll bring you. Be sure to remove your shoes before entering!"

As they entered, a battery of overhead fluorescent-strip lamps flickered and then shone forth, ballasts humming, as the Doc clicked on the wall switch. The brightness of the large room just inside the door was startling in contrast to the gray administration office. Curtis blinked. The plaster walls, ceilings, and even the polished concrete floor were all painted white. Four white-enameled tube-steel beds with crisp white top sheets were arranged in separate areas in the room, partitioned off by white fabric drapes functioning as room dividers. The antiseptic atmosphere was enhanced by a strong medicinal aroma.

Once inside, the Doc washed his hands in an enamel basin, donned a pristine lab coat, and directed Curtis to disrobe and sit on a cold examination table. There, the boy received the predictable pokes and prods with stethoscopes, tongue depressors, and little rubber mallets, followed by the inevitable penlight probes of all orifices.

Upon completion of this battery of indignities, the physician carefully loaded his pokers and prods back into a steel cabinet that glowed with ultraviolet light, then washed his hands once more, again scrubbing diligently. Curtis noted to himself how pale, almost luminous, the Doc's face looked in this intense artificial light.

"How old did you say you are, young man?" the Doc inquired, as he scribbled in an open folder.

"Just barely turned fifteen, sir."

"Well, you are remarkably well-developed for having just turned fifteen," he observed as he drew some clear fluid from a vial into a large syringe.

"That's because I've been workin' out every day for over a year."

"Working out?"

"Yeah, you know, trainin'—liftin' weights, push-ups, sit-ups—the whole routine."

"Well, whatever it is, you've got the physique of a well-muscled eighteen-year-old."

Curtis grew a bit uneasy with the way the physician was surveying him. He felt poked and prodded all over again, visually.

"Can I get dressed now, sir?"

"Right after I inoculate you. Stand at this window and lean on the sill. This is an intra-muscular shot."

"Huh?"

"I'm going to give it to you in your bottom."

Curtis complied and gazed out the double-hung window over at the expansive parade ground. Outside, a forty-foot flagpole sported the stars and stripes along with the blue-orange-yellow of the Arizona state flag just below, but both had been raised only halfway up the mast. A sharp sting in his right buttock startled him from this momentary distraction.

"All done—you can get dressed now," said the Doc. "Do you have any questions?"

"Yes, I do, sir," Curtis replied, as he retrieved his jeans and T-shirt. "What was the shot for? I had all my shots in school."

"I inoculated you for various infirmities that seem to be peculiar to our inmate population. It's nothing to be concerned about. Anything else?"

"Yeah, why are the flags at half-mast?"

"I couldn't tell you," the Doc replied as he glanced out the window. "Well, they *aren't*, as a matter of fact. Come see for yourself."

Curtis was dumbfounded to see both flags flying at the top of the pole. "That's so weird," he mumbled.

"Well, I'm sure there's a simple explanation," the Doc muttered almost inaudibly. "If I had to guess, I'd say someone started to lower the flags prematurely and was corrected by someone else of authority. After all, it's a good hour until sundown."

"I guess that's possible," Curtis conceded. "But I didn't see nobody anywhere near that flagpole the whole time you were stickin' me with that lawn dart you call a syringe."

"All right," the Doc said in an impatient tone. "We're done here, and I know the Lieutenant will be giving you an orientation lecture. If you have any more questions, you can direct them to him," he concluded, as he hung the white lab coat back on the coat rack.

The Doc shepherded Curtis back toward the sprawling two-story administration building. Curtis noted with interest that it seemed to be the only building that displayed any vegetation at all. In fact, the profusion of trees, hedges, shrubs, and flowers adorning the immediate site that encircled the stucco edifice suggested an oasis, in comparison to the stark absence of growth surrounding the other buildings.

The Doc and Curtis reentered the building through a verdant arbor of overgrown cat's claw and passed back into the office where Joe and the headmaster were still bogged down in paperwork. The physician forced a smile as he dismissed himself, briefly flashing his yellow teeth.

Curtis settled down on an aging vinyl-upholstered chair for what seemed like hours as the tedious red tape continued to unravel. Apprehension slowly gave way to boredom. He pulled the Joe Weider exercise pamphlet that Joe had given him from his duffel bag and began to scan it again, as he had a dozen times already.

Bored and restless, the boy finally rose from the chair and drifted toward an open window that looked out over the old parade ground.

The sun was beginning to settle down into the shadows of the Galiuro Mountains in the distant west, while Curtis surveyed the inside grounds through squinted eyelids.

As the golden globe crept lower, something peculiar, a queer movement at the west side of the parade ground, caught his attention. *Odd*—the silhouetted shapes of three men, *seemingly suspended some ten feet above the ground*, materialized with the backlighting of the solar illumination.

This must be some kind of weird mirage, Curtis thought. *They must be standing on some sort of platform that I can't see . . .*

He shielded his eyes using a downturned palm as a visor to get a better look at this visual anomaly, and the images came into clearer relief. The fine hairs on the back of the boy's neck prickled, and he gasped aloud as the reality of the scene suddenly hit home. Curtis was witnessing the bizarre aftermath of an execution—*it was a hanging!*

The three corpses, heads thrust forward and down as if bowing in deference to the victorious noose, dangled grotesquely from three very stark and very solidly erected post-and-beam gallows. A light sundown breeze blew across the parade ground and stirred the three hanging men, twisting them slightly into a stiff-limbed, macabre sort of dance of cadaverous marionettes.

Curtis retreated back into the confines of the administrator's office and tugged at Sergeant Joe's light-blue sleeve.

"They still *hang* people here, Joe!"

Sergeant Joe shot the headmaster a look of wonderment and shrugged.

The headmaster laughed as he took his place at the center desk.

"Now you're making me long for the good old days, son," he chuckled. "There are definitely times when I wish we still could, but we haven't had a hanging here at Fort Grant since 1882, when three turncoats were executed for desertion."

Curtis regarded the headmaster suspiciously, and pleaded with Joe to see for himself. The officer reluctantly followed his young prisoner to the window and looked out across the open yard.

"Just what am I supposed to be looking for, Curtis?"

Curtis just stared incredulously at the empty parade ground. No scaffold, no gallows, no tethered corpses—only the flags, at topmast, fluttering lazily in the pre-evening breeze.

"They were there, Joe—three of them . . . I *saw* them, twistin' in the wind an' such!" he insisted, pointing across the yard.

"Sunset sometimes plays tricks on your eyes, son," the headmaster called across the room from his desk. "Temperature inversion, no doubt," he added. "Listen, I'd better get this final paperwork done so we can get this boy some grub before the mess hall closes." He fed a carbon form into an old manual typewriter. "Sounds to me like he may be hallucinating from malnourishment. But I think your part's complete, Joe. You're free to go any time."

Sergeant Joe bent a bit to speak in a low voice to Curtis. "You remember what I said about keeping a low profile while you're here?"

"Yes, I do, but—"

"But *nothing*. Just keep your head down and keep your spooky stories to yourself—*comprendes*?"

"Joe, you *can't* leave me here," Curtis blurted in desperation.

"Curtis, we've been through all this."

"I know, but this place is just not right. I mean, isn't there somethin' about cruel and unusual punishment? I've heard there is."

"It's one of articles in the Bill of Rights, I think. What does that have to do with leaving you here, Curtis? We agreed there wouldn't be a scene."

"Yeah, but this place is *very unusual*. And it would be cruel to leave me here."

"That's all bullshit, and you know it. You just need to grow some backbone, Curtis. Maybe a year in the slammer is just what you need to tone down that wild imagination of yours."

"Yes, sir—I guess you're right," the boy muttered, knowing his plea was falling on deaf ears.

"Of course I'm right. Now, have you got that Joe Weider pamphlet I gave you?"

Curtis nodded. "It's in my duffel bag."

"Okay, then hit those barbells tomorrow, and don't quit until you look like Sonny Liston!"

Curtis grinned weakly—a thin disguise for the serious sense of foreboding he felt.

Joe continued as Curtis followed this last familiar face to the door: "Do what I told you and you'll be all right, kid—work hard, study hard, stay busy, and keep to yourself. Twelve months will fly by. You got it?"

"Got it!"

"Good!"

"Hey, Joe, one more thing," said Curtis.

The headmaster was waiting to buzz Joe out through the front security door.

"What is it, Curtis?" Sergeant Joe sighed, impatiently glancing at his watch. "I'm gonna be late getting back as it is."

"How come you know so much about this place?"

The door buzzed and Joe pulled it open. He glanced back before he stepped out.

"Never mind," he snapped. "You just mind your own business."

"That's a cold shot, Joe!"

The door banged shut on Curtis's last connection with the outside world. He was alone with strangers in an unfamiliar, seemingly unfriendly, and "very unusual" place.

Presently, yet another clearly older gentleman entered quietly from the side entrance and stood silent and motionless, as if at attention. He wore a blue uniform, not unlike Sergeant Joe's, only somewhat disheveled. His bushy brown hair was tinged with gray at the temples.

"Over here, young man," the headmaster called to the distracted boy. "Turn and face me when I'm addressing you."

Curtis complied but lowered his eyes as previously directed by Joe. The uniformed man emptied the contents of Curtis's duffel bag onto one of the tables and pawed through the white A-shirts and briefs while the headmaster spoke.

"You should know a few things about our institution so that you can get off on the right foot. We have a very tightly structured daily schedule arranged around a weekly calendar that Marcus here will go over with you."

The old man tipped his head in acknowledgment, as he returned Curtis's belongings to his bag.

"You are expected to learn it very quickly and follow it quite conscientiously," the headmaster continued. "Ours is the best-disciplined regiment in the territory . . ."

Curtis looked up in puzzlement at the choice of words, and the old man in the uniform rolled his eyes.

" . . . And I am going to assume you will help us uphold that reputation to the best of your ability, so I will dispense with the usual description of the consequences, should you stray from the path in that regard. Needless to say, you will hear about them in the yard in any case."

"Yes, sir."

Curtis felt as if he should salute or something, but then thought better of it.

"Now, you are here for a reason—because you have failed, in some manner, to accept your civic responsibility. Our aim is to reindoctrinate you with that sense of responsibility. To that end, you will, on a daily basis, perform a number of chores to sustain yourself and your fellow inmates."

He paused for a moment for emphasis, then continued again.

"You will perform these chores diligently and cheerfully, but this is not a labor camp. We believe here that a reform school's first mission is *to educate.*"

He pointed to a white sign on the industrial gray wall that echoed his words.

The first mission is to educate!

"We strongly believe that a robust education rightly places its recipient in the true context of civil society. It enlightens him as to his place in the universe, so to speak, thus making him an informed and voluntary contributor to the greater good. So I suggest . . . no, I *demand* that you prepare yourself to listen and to learn, young man. Now, you are dismissed!"

With that, the headmaster turned on his heel and disappeared within a maze of hallways and doors that lay beyond the front office.

"Come on, son," the old uniformed man directed with a heavy drawl, beckoning out the side door.

"Where are we goin'?"

"To get educated."

pernicious Origins

Will Farnsworth hated his young client—even wished him dead, and he would gladly do the deed himself if he could come up with a way to pull it off undetected. And because he was compelled to make these bi-weekly pilgrimages to the little lord's hellhole in the desert to "consult" with him, he'd come to similarly loathe his superiors in the law firm, most of his parasitic colleagues, and the opulent family that had spawned the adolescent vermin. He'd even begun to resent Carol for her innocent and unwitting part in his ongoing quandary. Perhaps most of all, he detested Will Farnsworth, Esquire, University of Arizona School of Law class of 1961, Law Review editor for two years running, top scorer on that year's bar exam, second-year practicing attorney. He reviled the bright young lawyer that he scrutinized in the mirror every morning, for allowing himself to be duped into endlessly performing these loathsome duties every first and third Wednesday of the month. Had it really been over a year?

He glanced into the rearview mirror of the jet-black Lincoln and glowered at the rooster tail of desert dust that dogged his northbound progress. The wide, slab-sided luxury car seemed more comic than majestic out here in the boonies: a chrome-and-lacquer "lead-sled" out of place with its whitewall tires chattering along the unpaved wash-board roads that crisscrossed the arid landscape. The dashboard clock nagged at him about a mounting tardiness. It was approaching noon, and the mercury was already creeping beyond the typically uncomfortable heat of a midday in early April. Will flipped a toggle on the walnut dash to activate the reefer unit and released a sigh that came from his very core.

The handsome young attorney's eyes scanned the shimmering image of the bleak Sonoran expanse, then blurred as he gazed back a mere eighteen months. It was a pinnacle period in his life when he supposed himself to be a promising upstart litigator—a respected newcomer to a prestigious Tucson-based firm. He had interned with McBride, Matthews, and Robson during his final year of law school, and his apprenticeship was warmly received by all eight litigating stallions in the firm's highly regarded stable. A fast-track offer toward an associate's position and a long list of promised perks, including a healthy signing bonus, enticed the young Farnsworth into an ironclad agreement with his mentors before he'd even finished acing the Arizona bar exam. He would be number nine.

The refrigerated air blowing from the louvered vents now cooled his hate-fevered brow. He tapped the power-brake pedal of the rolling fortress as he pondered an approaching tee intersection in the roadway ahead. The dearth of road markings and the monotonous landscape out here beyond the citrus groves always vexed him, no matter how often he came this way. Was it first tee left, then second tee right, or the other way around?

Acting on a vague recollection from two weeks before, he opted for the right, and a slight depression of the accelerator brought the 430-cubic-inch Ford Marauder engine back to life. The long black car fishtailed slightly across the sandy surface of the remote back road but promptly returned to an arrow-straight trajectory. The way now seemed somehow familiar, although the desert vegetation out here was sparse and maddeningly repetitive. One-armed saguaros everywhere. Richard Kimball would go nuts on the mirage potential here.

An all-too-brief honeymoon period with the firm had ensued, in which the shower of unanticipated "benefits" seemed inexhaustible—the right car, the right country club, and even a sizeable down payment on the right custom home in the Catalina foothills overlooking the city proper. His newlywed wife, Carol, was every bit as dazzled as he was by the sudden onrush of affluence. It might have been somewhat destabilizing if not for Will's solid belief that such lofty heights were ultimately deserved. After all, these were entitlements due to his hard work and personal sacrifices. It was simply a matter of delayed gratification, and he was now merely collecting on previous effort.

Hard to believe that it was no more than fourteen months ago that things began to creep in a southerly direction, giving way to a stunning headlong fall from grace. He'd been assigned by his superiors to deliver a package to the Fort Grant reform school and to consult with an important client's son who was being detained there. Simple enough, or so it seemed.

A short briefing in the conference room with the colleagues who had mounted the defense in the boy's case brought Will current with the facts. In the throes of what some called an overzealous wrestling hold, the young man had inadvertently throttled a high school teammate during a practice match. The conviction of Harvey Huish on the grounds of negligent homicide seemed inconsistently harsh for the way Will's colleagues described the event: "an unfortunate accident." The circumstances taunted Farnsworth's curiosity and he became eager to study the case file for himself.

———◆———

Another jog to the right brought him into even more familiar territory. A boarded-up citrus-packing plant, recently abandoned for the off-season, loomed a quarter mile off on a side road to the west. The main gravel roadway, as flat as a Sonoran tortilla up to now, began to gradually rise. The polished steel rails of a now-quiet spur glinted in the noonday sunlight and were swallowed up by the northern horizon. San Pedro County fruit was seasonally crated and shipped by rail from here, merged with that of the greater Phoenix area groves at a rail hub in Jacobs Well, then hauled off to points farther north to be consumed where citrus production is unheard of. This plant happened to be a part of the Huish family's immense holdings.

The lawyer smiled, wryly. Fort Grant was only another fifteen minutes away. The crushed granite roadway began to twist very slightly this way and that, as it gently rose and fell. The ebony beast of an auto followed the dancing gravel course as if on tracks.

———•———

A quick review of the kid's case file and trial transcripts satisfied some questions, but raised others. Harvey Huish had originally been charged with voluntary manslaughter, and much of the testimony supported the gravity of the charge. The boy had knowledge that the potentially deadly choke hold was an illegal maneuver, according to amateur wrestling regulations. The choking was prolonged beyond the coach's penalty whistle. Teammates and student onlookers gave chilling testimony that the juvenile defendant was actually whispering in the victim's ear as he choked the life out of him. The defendant had to be physically subdued by his coach and teammates before he would release the fatal hold. And finally, the most potential damage came with a somewhat substantive rumor that defendant and victim were involved in a romantic triangle with a particularly alluring student teacher. The evidence to indicate the mens rea, or mental state of intent, was quite damning from any point of view.

But in a move that defied explanation, the prosecution floated a last-minute offer for a plea to the lesser charge, and a hasty deal was made. The judge responded with a fairly lengthy sentence that would extend beyond the kid's legal adult age, but the first two years would be spent in juvenile detention—easy time—with a chance for early release predicated on good behavior. Farnsworth's runaway imagination leaped forward to the conclusion that someone had pulled some strings to secure what amounted to a hand-slapping for murder.

———◆———

On clearing the summit to a sustained rise, a vast scenic overlook unfolded before Will, allowing a distant glimpse of Fort Grant's ivory-white stucco walls. And there was something else: nestled just off the right shoulder of the road and at the bottom of the long downgrade that fell before him, a derelict pickup truck rested passively at the far side of a dry wash. The young attorney eased his right foot onto the brake pedal to slow the strong downhill momentum that the big Lincoln was gaining. He glanced at the plain nine-by-twelve cardboard box that sat undisturbed on the passenger seat beside him.

———

A little research into the family history cemented young Farnsworth's mounting suspicions. The kid's father was an important client, all right; he was possibly the wealthiest property developer in the entire Southwest. His holdings included two major retirement communities in Tucson and Phoenix, a chain of forty "motor hotels" scattered across the tri-state region, and one of the top four hotel/casino complexes in Las Vegas. This, in addition to a vast citrus-producing empire, controlling interest in two southern Arizona copper mines, and a silent partnership in the Los Angeles Dodgers ball club. The guy was a tycoon in every sense of the word, and if anybody could call in a political favor to get his kid off the hook, it was Sam "Pinky" Huish.

But there was more—much more. The firm's files on the Huish family extended back several generations. In fact, when Will Farnsworth had asked his paralegal, Betty Wood, to pull the Huish files, she laughed and guided him to a locked office comprised of wall-to-wall and floor-to-ceiling steel file cabinets, all exclusively dedicated to housing the one family's legal records.

Spending hours at a time in "the vault," as the Huish room was affectionately dubbed, was apparently poor form, as his forays to the inner sanctum drew whispered remarks about "obsessing" from colleagues and seemed to raise eyebrows from superiors. But the deeper Will's research went, the more convinced he became that the law firm of McBride, Matthews, and Robson owed its very existence to a ponderous backlog generated by the legally questionable activities of the Huish family, and always had. A perusal of the cases dated back to the second half of the nineteenth century and, with a little reading between the lines, translated into an epic tale of graft and corruption that would likely make Mario Puzo blush with envy.

———

Farnsworth idled the big car slowly across a familiar single-lane concrete bridge that spanned one of many dry creek beds, past the debilitated '56 F-100 pickup that rested at the far side. The hood was propped open, and a wisp of steam was escaping from the pressure-release cap at the top of the radiator. The khaki-tan body was festooned with black pinstriping, and a "RENEGADE" monogram plastered in cursive black lettering decorated the rounded front fender. The cab was unoccupied.

Will detected some movement in the shade of a nearby mesquite tree. He crept to a stop, threw the transmission into park, and lowered the charcoal-tinted power window on the passenger side, squinting from the sudden brightness allowed by the absence of the darkened lens. Through the clear desert air he heard the faint whistle from the radiator and he could just make out the shadowy form of a man sitting cross-legged under the deep green of the rugged old tree.

"Hey, chief," the young lawyer called through the window, "you gonna be okay?"

The form rose up stiffly, but rose up tall—six-feet-two, by Will's reckoning—and strode into the sunlight. The old Indian patriarch's face was deeply sun-browned and as rough and rugged as the bark on the big old mesquite he'd been sitting under. Farnsworth noted that he clutched a large pouch that hung from his shoulder by a rope sling. He wore something of a demented-looking grin as he approached the Lincoln, his long, untethered gray hair stirred by a gentle desert breeze. The facial expression, though not outwardly menacing, had a certain canine quality; the old relic projected a vague animality that struck Will as a little more than disquieting.

Will fought down a reflexive urge to pull away from the scene. After all, he was already late for his meeting, and Harvey Huish always needled him for tardiness. He really did not have time for this. But the old man's piercing coal-black eyes now riveted him there. His faded denim jeans hung on his slim waist, secured by a beaded leather belt. He was shirtless, but his bare brown torso, remarkably toned and well-muscled, belied the obvious advanced age that his craggy face indicated.

"I said, are you gonna be okay?" Will repeated. "I mean, are you disabled . . . uh . . . broken down here?" he stammered, wondering if this native codger even spoke English.

"I'm fine, thank you," the old man replied in a gravelly voice as he peered in the open window. "How are you?"

"I can't complain," said Will. "But you seem to be in some distress here, old friend." He beckoned toward the apparently crippled pickup.

"Oh, he's just a little thirsty. I'll just let him rest a bit, then give him a drink."

The old Indian hoisted the canvas water bag aloft to indicate his ample supply. It was the kind that the "last chance" gas stations hawked to novice desert motorists with the theoretical purpose of warding off ill-fated breakdowns, such as this.

"But what about you?" he asked Will. "Are you going to be all right?"

Farnsworth had the uneasy feeling that the old coot seemed to sense how poignant his question was.

"Oh, I'll muddle through, I guess."

The old man nodded and rubbed a leather cheek. "You want some of my water?" he offered with a wide grin, holding the canvas bag up again. "It's blessed by spirits, and I've got plenty."

"Thanks, but no thanks."

The old man had gradually approached the car and was now half-leaning into the open window, preventing the quick exit that Will was contemplating.

"Want to buy some genuine Indian jewelry? Apache craftsmanship, guaranteed. I made it myself."

The old man dangled a large rectangular lime-green gem tethered to a braided silver chain inside the window of the big black car. The necklace and setting were rather ornate, but the gem was striking in its sheer simplicity. The edges of the stone were trimmed in multiple bevels, while the stunning color was that glowing green of early Bermuda grass reflecting the soft light of a rising sun.

"San Carlos peridot," he declared proudly. "Indigenous to the Apache Reservation. Only place in the country."

"I don't carry that much cash," said Will. "Wish I did. It's a fine piece, really."

"You didn't ask how much." The native coot's eyes now fell on the cardboard box that rested on the seat.

"Well, I only have a twenty on me, and I know pretty well that—"

"You may need a San Carlos peridot to help you to 'muddle through,' as you say. The stone brings health and protection."

"Maybe next time I'm out this way, chief."

The old man just stared, leaning at the window for the longest time, his smile frozen.

"All right, then," the wizened "chief" relented at length, the canine quality returning to his face. "Thanks for stopping, young man."

He backed away from the car as the power window went up and the Lincoln lumbered on.

Will was still shaking off the inexplicable weirdness of the encounter as he settled back into his rearview reverie, poring once again over the stacks of files from the Huish "vault."

From his research, Will learned that Stanley Huish, a Welsh immigrant and the first traceable family member, had settled in the Tucson area in the autumn of 1850 after a short-lived participation in the California Gold Rush. Favored with a lucrative claim and an uncanny string of wins at the poker table, Huish abruptly cashed in on both—prematurely, some said. Excusing himself from explaining how his equal partner had mysteriously vanished, the young, thrice-blessed entrepreneur bade farewell to Sacramento, and ventured out to the center of the Sonoran desert "for the healthy climate."

Armed with his sizeable stake (doubled by his partner's apparent demise), he began to speculate as a broker in the commodities needed by the military to maintain their presence in the Southwest. Contractors like Huish were better positioned to buy grain, produce, and livestock directly from small farmers and ranchers, and then convey the amassed goods in voluminous amounts to cavalry quartermasters, helping themselves to a hefty markup in the process. By aggressively exploiting this entrepreneurial approach, Stanley Huish established himself as the most successful merchant in the Arizona Territory by the end of the Civil War, profiting quite handsomely from both sides of that fray.

Through the graces of the territorial governor, Anson Safford, with whom Huish had become quite cozy, the gregarious Welshman "negotiated" the office of Adjutant General, "acquired" vast sections of desert property, and began to "appropriate" water rights from several major drainages—displacing hundreds of native occupants in the process. Before his death in 1912, he'd organized and chaired the regional water users' association and helped to engineer a system of canals that brought life-giving irrigation to his own otherwise-barren properties. Stanley Huish had left behind the sprouting seeds of an empire, and a legacy of ruthless practices that demanded vigorous legal defense. This became the founding purpose behind the old established firm of McBride, Matthews, and Robson.

Taking a page from the old man's catalog of nefarious deeds, Henry Huish, the eldest of Stanley's two boys and the primary heir, parleyed his father's residual political influence into lucrative military contracts for the purchase of long-staple Egyptian cotton, which was a direly needed commodity for the First World War effort, and which, just coincidentally, already happened to grow in abundance on the dozens of the Huish family's irrigated plots.

Henry's brother, Bruce, was cut into the cotton venture in exchange for strong-arming Mexican labor brokers into providing "affordable" wage-slaves for planting, picking, and ginning. A bat-wielding brute with a legion of similarly treacherous cohorts, Bruce became notorious for living up to his well-earned nickname, "Nudge."

As they had anticipated, the cotton demand dried up with the war's end, but the shrewd Huish boys had already sidestepped the market glut and moved on to bigger and better things. They'd plowed the fields

under, planted orange groves, and formed the Southwest Citrus Grow-
ers' Association, the most powerful agricultural cooperative in the
region. The huge, burgeoning membership, which was force-fed by
various methods of coercion, fueled the elections and greased the palms
of "friendly" public officials—political bosses who, in turn, guaranteed
tax relief, a "relaxed" enforcement of labor laws, an uninterrupted flow
of cheap water, and transportation subsidies to build rail spurs to the
packing sheds. A series of sweetheart relationships with independent
trucking chieftains that brother Bruce had cultivated during the cotton
boom formed the third side of an iron triangle, one that put Arizona on
the map as the third-largest citrus-producing state in the nation.

But far and away the most ingenious and ambitious member of the
Huish clan was Henry's firstborn, Sam, never to be confused with his
younger brother, Robert, who seemed bent on perpetuating the fable of
the prodigal son. Sam Huish was born with all the cunning of his
predecessors, but he had a congenital defect: the smallest digit on his
right hand was paralyzed, garnering him the unfortunate nickname
"Pinky." The only possible handicap that imperfection might impose
would be in sipping tea. But more to the point, it earned him an easy,
uncontested deferment from military service during the Second World
War.

As a gift on the young man's twenty-first birthday, Henry conveyed
to his industrious son the deed to a 160-acre citrus grove in Yuma,
giving him wide discretion in the use of its profits, but secretly hoping
that Pinky would use the proceeds to attend law school, which Henry
saw as a stepping-stone to public office and the façade of legitimacy. But
what Pinky did instead made him the marvel of the family.

Following in his father's footsteps, Pinky sought out family allies in
the government and, using the acreage as collateral to finance the
material, contracted with Uncle Sam to build an internment camp on his
newly acquired grove for "the relocation of Japanese Americans," in
accord with FDR's 1942 executive order. Labor and transportation came
from Uncle Bruce, who had kept up his south-of-the-border relationships and even incidentally acquired a border-town brothel to
accommodate some of his darker perversions.

Pinky personally oversaw the project and demonstrated a knack for construction operations management by completing the project under budget and ahead of schedule. But here was the kicker: since the project only called for clearing a small percentage of the orange trees, Pinky kept most of the grove in production and arranged, as part of the contract, that the internees would be utilized, free of charge, to provide the labor to maintain the grove and harvest his crop. In effect, he not only tripled the expected five-year income from his plot in the first year, but he rendered the remainder of the operation *cost free* for the duration of the war, while providing a *patriotic service.*

While most of the family applauded Pinky's prodigious performance, there were some muted suggestions that the entire operation, though deftly managed, was nothing more than a once-in-a-lifetime fluke never to be duplicated again. Unfettered by taunts of "lucky break," and not one to interrupt tradition, Pinky had already sunk the proceeds of his first venture into another grove, this one in the East Valley near Apache Junction, and had sealed the deal on building another internment camp. The repeat performance amazed the family, but they had not yet seen what Pinky Huish was capable of. Not by a long shot.

———◆———

A sudden flash of mottled tan bolted across the road just in front of the lumbering Lincoln, jolting Will from his retrospective musings through the Huish family annals. He jerked the steering wheel hard to the right and swerved, barely missing an unusually large fleeting coyote that skittered along the gravel drive and then vanished into a tamarisk thicket on the left shoulder of the road. Close call.

———◆———

Now, Will Farnsworth was no puritan; in a certain respect, he admired the entrepreneurial rise of the Huish family, and their ascension to glory, powered by the thrust of Arizona's "five Cs": cattle, cotton, citrus, copper, and climate. But Will was particularly impressed by Pinky's ingenuity. Where Stanley was a visionary, and his offspring were organizers and opportunists, Pinky was an empire builder, and the internment camps merely formed the first rung of a ladder of ambition that extended to altitudes beyond imagination.

The Arizona camps housed a staggering number of "evacuees," mostly Japanese Americans from the West Coast. Estimates of 14,000 in the Yuma camp and 18,000 in the Apache Junction camp were not exaggerated. While the conditions were something less than comfortable, they were not inhumane. Nevertheless, shortly after the mass relocation, several civil rights groups rose up in protest to what they termed an unacceptable mortality rate. Most of these groups decried the very act of the internment, but one focused sharply on improving the "intolerable" conditions. Curiously, when "Citizens for Fair Play" (CFP) was formed for this purpose, all resources for litigation and lobbying were provided, pro bono, by none other than McBride, Matthews, and Robson. Reversal of the policy of evacuation and internment turned out to be a lost cause for the other groups, but the CFP's notion of improving conditions for innocent evacuees gained some traction with public officials.

The government-mandated upgrades to facilities were performed by Pinky's contracting firm, and "improvements" were made in the form of expanded utilities—water, sewer, gas, and electrical. Easements that suspiciously resembled those for a residential subdivision were laid out and cut through the groves, providing better lighting, more toilets, and heated dormitories in the winter for the camp residents. Recently developed evaporative coolers were incorporated to make the unbearable summer heat more tolerable. The "unacceptable mortality rate" at the camps plummeted. Pinky had gained another rung on the ladder, laid out the groundwork for the next step up, and was lauded as a humanitarian in the bargain.

The whitewashed walls of Fort Grant now loomed large in the broad windshield. The incongruity of the plastered adobe ramparts rising from the desert floor up against the horizon always conveyed the suggestion of a mirage to Will: a Spanish castle. The image evoked the lyrics to a syrupy Mel Torme tune that he and Carol had adopted as their love theme.

But the sight of the walls also brought home the grim reality of facing Harvey Huish once again, and he winced at the prospect. Every encounter had brought him heartache and humiliation. Every visit had tightened the tether that bound him to his young master, until his love for his wife—the source of his bondage—gradually turned to bitterness and resentment.

But soon, very soon, he would change all of this.

———◆———

Will further discovered that Pinky Huish followed the progress of the war effort very closely, angling for the opportunities that history promised. He lined up investors (including a faithful family following) to buy up and stockpile cheap Mexican cement from the kilns in Sonora. He established two concrete batching plants—each one located near the site of each internment camp, set up a cement-block fabricating operation in Casa Grande, and bought into a gypsum drywall mill in Phoenix. When the war finally ended, Pinky was already in position to meet an anticipated housing demand by transforming his two orange groves into ready-made affordable residential subdivisions. His formula for cheap construction— small lots, cement-block structure, exposed concrete floors, drywall interiors with "popcorn" textured ceilings, and mass-produced swamp coolers that perched nicely on asphalt shingle roofs—became the blueprint for all Southwestern builders of the era; but an early lead, based on insider information and shrewd positioning in the building material industry, put Pinky's burgeoning developments at the front of the pack.

More family groves were transformed into more housing tracts as recently discharged soldiers and sailors poured into Pacific ports and swarmed inland in search of the American Dream. The post-war baby boom, Veteran's Administration loans, and GI Bill benefits fueled the Midas touch of the Huish family, and Pinky scaled the ambition-ladder to the dizzying heights that he was destined for. The vertically integrated empire he developed rested on a diverse complement of industries: housing, commercial development, mining, manufacturing, tourism, and entertainment.

Sam "Pinky" Huish was the master of all he surveyed, and it was all good. All good, that is, with the possible dark exception of his only son, Harvey. And it was that one exception that compelled Will Farnsworth to detest the source of his very own precarious livelihood.

First Dilemma

Sergeant Joe's sage advice for surviving on the inside seemed to be working well for Curtis, at least for the first several weeks—remarkably so for one whose friendly nature rebelled at the whole notion of solitude. Aside from a near-confrontation with a couple of the older inmates, the boy-convict stayed true to his word, kept his head down, and settled into the Fort Grant routine without any serious bumps in the road. But in the long run, Curtis's magnetic presence and his natural attraction to people were forces to be reckoned with, and each day was a struggle to maintain his solitary status. In fact, when it came to remaining a loner for the duration, he really didn't stand a ghost of a chance.

And in spite of first impressions, Marcus the guard turned out to be a kind and helpful old gentleman—almost a mentor, in fact. The disheveled dorm guard put up a stern front, but he spent a good deal of time during Curtis's early days explaining the mandatory policies and procedures of the place to the new kid when he wasn't trying to persuade him of the virtues of country-western music, which constantly blared from a tiny transistor radio that the leathery Texan carried with him.

Once Curtis completed the first week of familiarization, however, and appeared to grasp the routine, Marcus gradually withdrew to a disinterested distance, which Curtis tacitly understood to be for the better.

His parting excuse was classic Marcus: "Hell's bells, surely you can see that I'm busier than a three-legged cat in a sandbox, even without the added bother of new-inmate orientation."

The daily regimen at the Fort was pretty strict and left little time for any wayward activities. There were no television sets. There was early mess at daybreak in the common dining hall, then two hours of chores, followed by several hours of directed study in age-segregated class-rooms, midday meal, more school, dinner, a compulsory study hour taken in the large school library, then lights-out an hour after sundown in each of the three dormitories that were also divided by age group: one for ages ten to twelve; one for ages thirteen to fifteen; one for ages sixteen and seventeen. The daily chores were performed on a rotational basis, including mess hall detail, laundry detail, and facilities mainte-nance. Lighter clerical duties were bestowed on trustees—inmates who cultivated the good graces of administrators and guards.

Fort Grant housed about three hundred juvenile offenders. The ra-cial makeup of the population was more or less evenly split among Indians, Mexicans, and Negroes, with a smaller but significant minority contingent of Anglo inmates. All of the facilities were racially integrated, not from any moral imperative, but only out of economic and practical necessity.

Curtis noted that the Doc had described the environment pretty accurately, with most ethnic members "keeping to their own kind," in a population that was "more than adequately represented" by people of color.

All activities were performed under the close scrutiny of state-employed schoolmasters (who all wore white shirts and tan slacks) and guards (who all wore baggy blue-gray jumpsuits); and it was an assumed consensus among inmates that no nonsense was tolerated. A policy of corporal punishment was vigorously implemented, and it was common knowledge that one trip for a "striping at the woodshed" was quite sufficient to discourage any testy little yardbird from straying much beyond the very strict lines of discipline ever again. All well and good, except for the fact that the inmate-to-staff ratio was about thirty-to-one during the daytime shift; then it fell closer to sixty-to-one from dusk until dawn, when the nonresident guards and teachers would take their leave.

It was during one of those slack periods in oversight that Curtis came closest to violating his self-imposed policy of keeping to himself. Two of the older boys, one bigger than average, the other of even more massive proportions, stepped to the head of the line at early mess one morning, and Curtis, who had dutifully awaited his turn, indulged in an expression of annoyance at the deliberate discourtesy.

"Some of us have to wait in line for our food," he remarked quietly, as if to himself, but loud enough for the queue violators to hear.

"And then there are those of us who don't, *boy!*" the smaller of the two white boys retorted as he grabbed up a full tray of scrambled eggs and potatoes.

Now, Curtis had noted that the mandatory spring and summer uniform that was provided for inmates consisted of a plain white T-shirt and blue jeans. The dress code was compulsory, and every other boy in the mess hall this morning was in perfect compliance; yet this boy wore a pin-striped sport shirt, a pair of Bermuda shorts, and atop a head of shaggy blond hair he sported a blue ball cap. Clearly, this was brazenly flouting the rules that Marcus had meticulously spelled out to Curtis.

The larger boy, who resembled a golden-haired sequoia tree, demanded loudly that a mountain of food be heaped onto his tray and then strode up to Curtis. "Dis food smells delicious, doesn't it, *boy*?" he taunted in a thick Germanic accent. "I bet dat yawr really hongry."

The buzzing line went quiet, and Curtis reined in the nearly irresistible urge to escalate the encounter. Instead, he cast his ebony eyes downward as the two blond boys broke away and sidled past, sneering and chuckling as they departed—one of them with a peculiar falsetto laugh. Curtis grimaced at how much more humiliating the episode had become than if he had just kept still over the infraction. *Almost started a rumble over line cuts?* He could almost hear a stern admonition from Sergeant Joe ringing in his ears, and he silently admitted that this wasn't his smoothest of moves. Fortunately, the tension passed quickly, and a second helping of sausage patties put the incident out of the younger boy's mind.

The only relaxed, semi-structured time periods came during the two physical education periods—thirty-minute sessions, one at nine and one at two—taken by all three hundred on the huge parade ground. There was no coach, only the guards who kept a watchful eye as best they could on the self-organized games of basketball and soccer. A token amount of well-worn exercise equipment was made available, which the older boys generally monopolized.

There was a tacitly acknowledged order of superiority among the three dorm groupings, which was never challenged. Curtis learned that the youngest boys were "the chicks," the middle group, "the hens," while the older boys declared themselves "the roosters." The thinly veiled innuendos implied by the labels of the barnyard caste system were not lost on Curtis, and in keeping with his deliberately low profile, he made a conscious effort to respect the pecking order, in spite of an unusually mature physique that might have qualified him for automatic advancement. Mingling between the age groups during the PE period was discouraged, if not forbidden, and the younger boys were usually relegated to footraces or inane playground games until some of the roosters invariably got bored and gave up a ball, a court, or a field.

Curtis looked forward to these twice-daily breaks, which he used to pursue a solitary discipline of exhaustive physical training. A natural-born pugilist, a day or hour never went by when he lost sight of his dream to box his way to an Olympic gold medal at the 1968 games, as his hero, Cassius Clay, had done at the Rome games in 1960.

There were a number of bodybuilding devices available just outside the equipment storage room—chinning bars, parallel bars, even a sand-filled inner tube for weighted dips and knee bends—but only one set of ancient Healthways barbells, which was usually taken by three or four of the roosters. The young Negro boy would bide his time by doing numerous sets of dips on the parallel bars, push-ups, sit-ups, and agility drills—keeping vigilant, but never meeting the older boys' curious glances, until they would eventually tire of the rusty old weights and surrender them to his waiting hands.

Never wasting a second of his turn at the barbells, he'd run through the lifting regimens that he'd memorized from the Joe Weider pamphlet during study hour. There was no bench, so Curtis pumped up his upper body with a combination of military presses, bent rowing, standing curls, and prone pullovers, increasing the weight with each set until his arms went rubbery with fatigue.

The results of this unwavering devotion to training became apparent in short order. Curtis's upper body, already well-muscled from a natural endowment, gradually began to take on the sculpted appearance of a classic Greek form, as the Doc had darkly observed. Moreover, the development was not limited to definition and appearance. The young Louisiana native was soon lifting more weight, adding more repetitions, and covering more running distance in less time than ever before—a rapid physical evolution fueled, in part, by a ravenous consumption of the surprisingly palatable reform school victuals. Curtis was becoming a food-stoking, stamina-boosting workout machine—a human metabolic engine.

The Joe Weider strategies proved fruitful, and the first tenet of Sergeant Joe's advice seemed to be paying off in spades. With the elimination of the leisure-time activities like television watching normally enjoyed on the outside, self-discipline could be imposed more effectively in the austere environment on the inside, and a focus on personal improvement bore visible results in less time. The trouble with this was easily predictable and equally disturbing: inside of a month, Curtis was drawing some significant and unwanted attention to himself among inmates and staff alike.

Not surprisingly, it was the other Negro boys that first openly approached their colored colleague and tried to recruit him into their ranks. They offered Curtis the security of numbers in exchange for the obvious advantage that his involvement could give them in deterring any racially fueled confrontation that might erupt. He very diplomatically pointed out that, although he already belonged to their brotherhood by virtue of his color, he preferred to keep to himself, much to the clique's chagrin.

"You'll change your mind, and we'll be around," waved a statuesque, ebony-colored boy whom Curtis had recognized from time to time around the confines of the place.

Next, the older white boys who regularly used the barbells proposed a relaxation of protocol by inviting Curtis to take his turn with them. Again he declined, expressing his preference to respect the established order and their claim to privilege, but taking extra pains to convey, with an economy of words, how appreciative he was of their generous offer.

It became readily apparent that Curtis wanted to remain a loner, and all groups were prepared to respect that wish, however reluctantly, with a tacit understanding that the invitation to alliance would remain open for him. Everyone understood and respected, at least for a time, Curtis's preference for isolation—all, that is, with the glaring exception of Randy.

That first uninvited contact with Randy came on the coattails of Curtis's initial encounter with the macabre—an event that occurred around three in the morning on a Monday during the third week in March, when Curtis was awakened by an overwhelming urge to urinate.

A typical dormitory layout at Fort Grant consisted of four one-room sections, each housing an expansive open-plan area cramped with rows of two-tiered Army surplus bunk beds, roughly twenty-five to a room. Each dorm clustered around a central connecting lobby—a wide common corridor that served as a vestibule to the front entry and to the large shower room that also housed the toilet facilities. The entry door was always propped open in the spring and summer to allow the cool night air into the stuffy apartments. A chair and folding card table were strategically placed just ten feet inside to provide support and comfort for a supposedly vigilant, but usually snoozing, dorm guard.

This night, as Curtis made his way quietly down the corridor toward the latrine, he noted that Marcus, the henhouse guard, was absent—presumably making his rounds about the individual dorm rooms. The old man's miniature transistor radio, the size of a cigarette pack, stood on end atop the folding table. A connected earpiece lay beside it, hissing with a barely audible Hank Snow, declaring fabled bragging rights to "I've Been Everywhere," like some tinny, microscopic auctioneer.

The young inmate paused momentarily to gaze outside through the open doorway. A lone mercury vapor lamp that perched atop a tall yellow-pine pole buzzed dully, illuminating the yard just beyond the dormitories. The metallic whir of insect song had died away with the early evening heat, and a cool silence now dominated the arid land outside. He glanced up through the glass transom above the door and pondered the brilliance of the half-moon, perfectly centered in that window.

At the far end of the parade ground, Curtis noticed the barely moving glow of a pair of car headlights. It was a queer fact, however widely known, that the reclusive headmaster never left the confines of the compound. But late at night, once or twice a week, he would take his precious Impala for a spin around the inside grounds. Some said he was accompanied by his close buddy, Jim Beam, but that was nothing more than legendary speculation.

The combined voices of a large pack of coyotes suddenly set up a mournful chorus, baying in unison from some darkened arroyo in the near distance beyond the walls. Curtis shuddered at how human their cries sounded, like some wounded band of victim souls protesting a tortured plight. He ducked into the latrine to relieve himself.

As he emerged from that rank facility, he was stunned to see *the form of a young woman* framed in the center of the open doorway! Stunned, if only by the fact that Curtis had never seen a woman on the campus before, he froze in place. She was more of a silhouette than a figure; she was facing the left doorjamb, apparently oblivious to the boy's presence, and only her left profile was exposed to Curtis's view. Even in the semi-darkness, the boy could see that she was naked to the waist!

"Whoa!"

Curtis was so startled by the sudden appearance of this nocturnal siren in her partial nudity that he let out a poorly stifled yelp, which apparently caught the young maid's attention as she slowly turned her body in his direction. The subdued light from the mercury vapor lamp outside now exposed her ample bare breasts, but also her right facial profile—and what Curtis saw made him cry aloud in sheer terror. *That side of her face was gone!*

Gone, or at least mutilated beyond all recognition. The right lobe of her skull was caved in; the right cheek and lip were torn from her visage, dreadfully exposing a bare, shattered jawbone; the remnants of an eye, now just a gelatinous orb, dangled by a single sinew from a vacant socket. She was clearly a victim-soul—a horror to behold—and she was beckoning now to Curtis with outstretched hands that appeared to be smeared with her own blood.

The terror-stricken boy turned to flee, but ran straight into old Marcus, the errant dorm guard, returning from his rounds within.

"Hold on, young man!" Marcus thundered. "What's all the ruckus?"

He blocked Curtis's desperate exit, and the horrified boy could only point backhandedly toward the doorway with a trembling left hand, his face now buried in the open palm of his right, eyes slammed shut.

"So!" the guard demanded, after peering out the door at length. "I'll ask again—what's all the fuss about?"

Curtis turned reluctantly toward the doorway and blinked in disbelief. The entranceway was devoid of any sign of the terrifying apparition he'd encountered just seconds before!

"I just . . . I just . . . ," he stammered, and then fell silent.

"Son, you'd best be tellin' me what this is all about, or we're going on a trip to the woodshed to loosen up your tongue," the old man growled.

Curtis's mind raced for an excuse.

"I got up to pee, and when I came out, I must've stepped on a damn goathead," he blurted, unable to come up with anything better on the spot.

"Well, now—that explains things much better. Didja get it out?"

"Yeah . . . yeah. I tossed it out the door."

"Well, you ought to slip your shoes on before you come out here from now on. There's scorpions come in here all the time, for God's sake—you'll step on one an' I'll have to take you to the infirmary. Now, that's a place you'll want to steer clear of."

"Thanks . . . thanks, Marcus. I'll remember that."

"Yessir, there was a whole passel of 'em runnin' around in the roosters' shower room just last week," the old man muttered thoughtfully. "Scorpions, I mean—wavin' an' whippin' their nasty poison tails around. Should'a seen them naked boys hoppin' around just to keep from getting' stung. Musta been thirty of 'em—scorpions, I mean. Mighty peculiar," he drawled, rubbing his chin, "there bein' that many at once, I mean. Never seen such a thing. Mighty peculiar, indeed."

Marcus seated himself, still muttering. He picked up the earpiece of his tiny radio, inserted it, and scowled: "That's another thing. Every time I turn around, somebody's changed the damn station on me."

He pulled the earpiece jack out, automatically switching the music to the quarter-sized speaker that blared out a current favorite in top forty fare.

"That's about the saddest excuse for music ever to offend the airwaves."

Curtis was still shaken from his encounter with the apparition of that mortally wounded woman, but he kept his wits about him and bade the old guard good night, returning to a bed that offered no rest for the remainder of the night.

Special Delivery

The dusty black Continental turned left onto what amounted to no more than a cattle path and rolled slowly toward the brilliant white walls of Fort Grant, right on up to an iron double-drive gate. Will Farnsworth stopped the car, tooted the horn lightly, and the panels glided open. He pulled into a designated parking space and waited for the sentry to approach the driver's-side window.

"Afternoon, Mr. Farnsworth," greeted the gate guard. "I've already rung for Jeb to come over and conduct the procedure."

"The procedure" once consisted of a cursory pat down and a "search" of the contents of any packages. Jeb, the chief guard who always performed this charade, had been handpicked by Harvey Huish long before Will became ensnared in this foul web of corruption.

"I understand Mr. Harvey is already waiting for you in the conference room," the old sentry continued.

The young lawyer bristled. He hated the way the staff always referred to his client as "Mr. Harvey," as if he were some kind of little lord. And he hated being reminded of his tardiness. He was sure to get needled for it by the little snot-nosed bastard, and Will was in no mood for it. The earlier reminiscing on what he'd discovered of the Huish family background and the present routine were now dredging up the disturbing memory of his first meeting with Harvey. That was always good for raising his blood pressure.

That initial encounter was fourteen months ago when he'd delivered the first package on the premise that he would be "consulting" with the then-sixteen-year-old inmate. Back then, as now and on every ensuing biweekly visit, the delivery itself was the main event, at least as far as

Harvey was concerned. The "consultations," though a secondary pretense, gained in importance as the date of his hearing loomed ever nearer. Still, it was always the package that was the first order of business, and with each delivery Will mired himself deeper in the swamp of complicity.

That initial package had been placed by his paralegal on his desk a year before on what began as a bright January morning, with the assurance that its contents had been thoroughly verified by his superiors. She'd added the instruction that the brown-paper wrapping was not to be disturbed until a reform school staffer, specifically a guard named Jeb, received it for screening.

"What's in it?" he had inquired, nonchalantly.

The aide, Betty Wood, ran down a list of a variety of magazines, ranging from *Time* and *Look* to *Sports Illustrated* and *Mad Magazine*. The frequency of the visits, it was explained, was to keep the young man "current with developments of the outside world." Will stifled the urge to ask how *Mad Magazine* contributed to that noble endeavor. He was further instructed to let Jeb, the guard, know that there was a picture of Benjamin Franklin on page forty of the *Reader's Digest*, whatever that meant. Regardless, the main thrust of the visit was to get the boy thinking about positioning himself for some good-behavior recommendations from the reform school staff, which would be used to justify a hearing for the early release that the firm was planning to request.

Like today, the wait for Jeb on that first visit was agonizingly long, as he recalled. The head dorm guard had eventually shown up at the gate with greasy food stains on the front of his rumpled blue uniform, and a half-chewed toothpick hanging out of his mouth. He'd greeted Will indifferently in a heavy Southern twang, directing him to a small anteroom adjacent to the sentry post where he'd wrested the plain brown package from the young lawyer and performed a cursory upper-body search, then tore the paper from the package like a child on Christmas morning. He opened the lid on the cardboard box and went right for the *Reader's Digest* without being prompted to do so. The guard flashed a toothy smile as he retrieved a plain, unmarked envelope from between the pages and stashed it in his pocket.

Will filed this troubling behavior away for later deliberation, as the disheveled guard returned the package to his keeping and whisked him away along a gravel path to a large stucco building, down a darkened hall to an old-fashioned raised-panel door with a weathered brass knob. The guard pushed open the door, announced Will's name as if he were addressing royalty, and stepped aside, beckoning the young lawyer to enter. Will mused to himself that the guard might have blown a fanfare if he were able.

The door closed behind the anxious attorney as he entered the small, dimly lit conference room. A fresh-faced teenage boy was seated at the end of an antiquated oval table. *Seated*, however, was a tortured stretch of the term. *Sprawled* would more accurately describe the youth's indifferent pose, sneaker-shod heels propped on the tabletop, metal folding chair tipped back on two legs, hands clasped behind the head to relieve a neck that apparently couldn't be bothered with supporting the weight of a skull. He was vigorously chomping on a wad of gum as he regarded Will with a critical eye. At length, he released the intertwined fingers from behind his head, raised his right hand, and crooked two inwardly turned digits to indicate that Will should approach.

"The package," he demanded.

Will placed the package on the table in front of the boy as if paying tribute to some medieval nobleman. The kid was a bit bigger than average for sixteen. The long blond hair was wetted and greased with gobs of Brylcreem, a pronounced wave in front that fell forward, sides swept back into exaggerated "fenders." The mandatory reform school "burr" haircuts that Will had heard about evidently did not apply to young Mr. Huish, who was apparently still clinging to the James Dean image. In spite of the outdated reflection of social immaturity, the kid appeared somehow older than his years.

"Will Farnsworth," Will announced, as he stretched forward his hand.

The young man made no attempt to break his reclining pose to accept Will's greeting. In fact, he eyed the outstretched hand with the same regard he might pay a dead carp.

"You're late," he observed after a long pause, and finally rocked his chair forward to a four-point stance. Will noted with interest that the kid's head was rather outsized. A large rectangular face and lantern jaw accentuated the effect. It wasn't so pronounced as to call it grotesque, but the cranium was unmistakably one hat size too big. That, Will decided, was one weighty factor in what made him look older.

"Traffic was murder out there on the Pony Express trail," Will joked, trying to dispel the awkwardness of retracting the refused handshake.

Harvey Huish began to paw through the contents of the package as Will unfolded a chair and seated himself.

"I hope there aren't any *Playboys* in there. I wouldn't want to get disbarred for contributing to the delinquency of a minor."

Dead silence. It was another feeble attempt at trying to buddy up with humor, and Will immediately dismissed any further notions of going down that road.

Harvey thumbed distractedly through each of the magazines before speaking.

"So, you're, like, the new hotshot mouthpiece who's supposed to get me sprung from this hellhole—is that it?"

"My name's Will—"

"I heard your name before, so don't waste your breath again," the boy broke in.

"—and I'm here," Will continued, his jaw tightening, "to confer with you about a possible hearing for early release."

"Like, how early? I was hep to lose this scene before I got fingered." The kid spoke with a slight lisp, owing to an exaggerated overbite and two overgrown upper incisors that lent a singular rodent-like quality to his facial appearance.

"We're shooting for six months from now. It all depends on getting some letters of commendation for good behavior from some of the staff." Will was relieved at getting down to business: "I was thinking that . . ."

"You a Dodgers fan, Will-ee?" Harvey interrupted, again.

"That's *Will*, and no, I don't follow sports. See, I've been in a place called law school for the past three years. It's a lot like reform school, in that they cut you off from the outside world for long stretches of time and punish you, mercilessly."

Will caught himself too late trying to be flip again. The kid was staring daggers.

"Let's get a few things straight, daddy-o, so you don't end up like the last shyster they sent down here."

Will suppressed an urge to yank the kid's bad Elvis Presley hairdo off of his oversized scalp.

"First of all, you work for *me*, so I'll call you whatever I choose—and I choose *Will-eeng*, as in *will-ing to do anything* for his client. If I say 'paint a fart,' you say 'what color?' *ya* dig?"

The lawyer pictured all of the perks of his short-lived career vanishing—the car, the house, the Friday-noon tee-times—as he imagined himself standing and planting a right fist in the little punk's smirking puss. He closed his eyes instead, took a breath, and ran the image of a singing Bucky Beaver performing the jingle to the Ipana toothpaste television commercial through his head. This would pass.

"Now," the boy continued, "I don't like to be kept coolin' my heels, so if you expect to keep this job, I'd start coming early if I were you. That way if you run into a cattle drive, or a dust storm, or a band of renegade wagon burners on your way here, you won't keep me hangin' on the line. Can ya dig it?"

Will breathed slowly and deliberately. *Brusha, brusha, brusha—new Ipana toothpaste.* This would pass.

"Yes, clearly," he said through clenched teeth.

"Cool, and so if I were you, Willy-boy, I'd catch up on the Dodgers and start following them like it was your religion."

"I'll be their number one fan." Will found himself tugging nervously at a thin silver chain that draped around his neck. "Anything else?"

"As a matter of fact, yes: Do you always dress *like that* when you meet with your other clients?"

Will cast his eyes downward, as if surveying his own apparel. He'd chosen casual to conform to the location for this meeting—a pair of brown corduroy jeans, a solid light-blue oxford-cloth shirt, and a pair of buckskin Tony Lama boots. It had seemed appropriate for a visit to a reform school in the middle of the desert.

"Why, no—I just thought . . ."

"Well then, try to have the same respect for me. I'm sure they pay you enough to buy a decent suit, don't they?"

Will seethed inside, but maintained a façade of composure, with the exception of the continued tugging at the necklace chain. Bucky Beaver danced through his skull. *Brusha brusha brusha—new Ipana toothpaste.*

"I've got a navy blue and a charcoal gray. Got a preference?"

"Don't get wise, bright-eyes, or you'll be buyin' the rest of your threads at a rummage sale, dad."

The unconscious tugging intensified, and the circular metal disc that dangled from the chain popped out of his shirt. He rubbed the St. Thomas More medal that Carol had given him between his thumb and forefinger as if it were a magic lamp that might make him vanish from this humiliating scene. St. Thomas More, Carol had explained to her agnostic husband, was the patron saint of big families but also the patron saint of lawyers, so she had passed it on to him just before he sat for the bar exams. His phenomenal scores and the wish to humor his new wife convinced him to continue to wear it, but concealed under his shirt to ward off misplaced assumptions and unwelcome comments.

"So now that we, like, have our little understanding," said Harvey, "why don't you go on with that rap you were layin' on me about an early release—hmm?"

Will took a deep breath again, erased Bucky Beaver from his mind, and regathered his thoughts.

"Well, as I was saying, we need to start laying the groundwork for some letters of commendation for good behavior from some of the staff here."

"Laying the groundwork?"

"Sure—just developing some goodwill with key people."

Will secretly wondered if Harvey would grasp the term "goodwill."

"That's a piece of cake. Like, I've already got Doc and Jeb eating out of my hand."

"That's good—especially with the school doctor; he'll be able to write an articulate letter. We can always ghostwrite something for the guard. I've got some reservations about his communication skills already. Would the doctor be willing to be deposed?"

"The Doc will stand on his head and sing 'The Purple People Eater' if I tell him to," Harvey boasted.

Will pulled a legal pad from his briefcase and started to take notes.

"What's the doctor's proper name?"

"Couldn't tell ya, dad."

"That's okay, I'll find out. How about the guard—Jeb, wasn't it—what's his last name?"

Harvey just shrugged.

"I can get that too," Will muttered as he jotted. "Now, what about the headmaster—can we count on a good recommendation from him?"

"That's a pretty tall order," said Harvey.

"Why's that?"

"He's an odd duck—one of those guys who avoids getting involved. Can ya dig it?"

"What's his name?"

"Roy Whitcomb, but everybody calls him *the Lieutenant.*"

"Why?"

Harvey shrugged again. "They just do. Who knows why—who cares?"

"Just curious. And speaking of which, how come you know his name and not the others'?"

"He's got a nameplate on his desk."

"Well, he's the nut we've got to crack," said Will. "If we can get him to sign a commendation letter, we're on the green; without it, we're out in the rough—it's that cut-and-dried."

"Sounds like you've got your work cut out for you, Willy-boy."

"Well, you too. You've got to generate that goodwill with the head-master—maybe work your way up to trustee. That's what I mean about laying the groundwork. That's up to you."

"Hell, the only kind of goodwill I can come up with he doesn't seem to understand."

Will began to feel uneasy about the possible semantic difference he and his client were having with the term *goodwill.*

"Well, listen, why don't I do some background research before we start to move forward on any of this, okay? We've got some time."

The young inmate was nodding mechanically, but he now seemed somehow transfixed. He appeared to be staring vacantly at Will, or rather at Will's chest.

That was it: he was fixated on the religious medal that swung loose below the young lawyer's open collar. Harvey reached out with an admiring smile and touched it lightly.

"What's this?" he inquired in an innocent tone.

"Saint Thomas More—he's the patron saint of lawyers. It was a gift from my wife."

Will grew more uneasy as the boy scrutinized the medallion.

"No kidding. You Catholic, Willy?"

"No, but she is."

Harvey leaned forward, cupped his fingers behind the medal, and pulled it closer toward him, as if to inspect it more critically. "Is it real sterling silver?"

He gripped the tiny charm between thumb and forefinger just as Will reared back to retract it. The delicate chain snapped at the clasp link, as Harvey closed his hand around the token and withdrew it from Will's poorly aimed effort to snatch it back.

"Damn it!" Will shouted as he rose from his chair. "You've broken it now."

"Well, it's pretty flimsy," Harvey chuckled in a strange falsetto, almost puppety sort of cackle, as he rose and backed away.

"Give it back!"

Will lunged forward in an attempt to seize the boy's T-shirt, when a sudden jolt of what felt like a paralyzing electrical shock surged through his upper body.

"Cool it with the temper, Willy. That's not very professional behavior, you know."

Will went to his knees and shuddered as the surge subsided.

"Wha—what just happened?"

"I don't know what you mean, Willy, but you should try to control yourself better. Why don't you sit back down and take a deep breath?"

Will rose to his feet and leaned on the tabletop to steady himself.

"Give it back, you little bastard!" Will was still trembling from the mysterious jolt he'd just received.

"Now, that's no way to talk to your client, Willy—not very friendly at all. Try to be cool. No, I think I'll just hold on to this for safekeeping until your next visit. Call it my insurance that you'll keep our appointment," Harvey taunted as he strode to the door and fingered a button-buzzer. "Who knows?" he continued. "It just might help me to generate some of that crazy *goodwill* you keep beatin' your gums about."

Two uniformed guards appeared at the door presently, Jeb and another.

Harvey exited with the unfamiliar guard, tossing out an abrasive parting shot: "Now you be a good little errand boy next trip down, and don't forget to wear your best threads when you bring my package. Oh, and don't be late, y' hear? You make me cool my heels, and I just might cool your income—dig?"

Jeb waited for Will to collect his composure along with his briefcase before escorting him back to the Lincoln. The lawyer considered telling the guard about the necklace incident, but recalled what Harvey had said about Jeb "eating out of my hand," and thought better of it.

"Drive careful there, counselor," said the guard. "We look forward to your next visit."

Little professor

At daybreak, Curtis resolved to visit the headmaster and tell his tale. He could not fathom how that young woman could possibly have survived those horrific wounds. The inevitable discovery of her tortured body, stripped and beaten, and in close proximity to the Fort, would raise questions throughout the camp as to who was up and about last night.

The new black kid, Curtis thought wryly, *jumpin' around spoutin' off some cock-and-bull story about a goathead.* That's what Marcus might say upon questioning.

Although he was definitely uneasy about it, Curtis built a hope that coming forward and volunteering information would help deflect any suspicion that might come his way. That, or it might be his undoing.

In keeping with his own reclusive image, the Lieutenant took his breakfasts at a private table in the mess hall on weekdays. Curtis strode reluctantly to the mess hall early, found a vacant bench, and scanned the room for the headmaster, who was already seated. The boy would wait for him to finish and rise to leave for his office before confronting him with the news. That's when a particularly skinny young kid with horned-rim glasses and a ferret-like face placed an empty tray on the table in front of Curtis and plopped down opposite him.

"Not hungry this morning?" the kid asked good-naturedly, noting that Curtis had not taken a tray.

Curtis glanced around uneasily to see if anyone noticed the gall of this scrawny kid to break the notorious loner's self-imposed solitude. No one seemed to. With his pasty complexion and bony arms, the kid looked like a juvenile version of Don Knotts. Curtis just stared icily, not blinking until his eyes began to water.

"I don't guess you got too much sleep last night, did you?" the lad inquired further.

Curtis finally broke his silence.

"Looky here, kid—are you writin' a book?"

"No, why?"

"Because you ask a lot of questions."

The younger boy giggled nervously. "Sorry—I just came over to meet you because I heard you were from Jacobs Well . . . like me. My name is Randall Kartchner, but you can just call me Randy."

Curtis glared sourly at the boy's outstretched hand.

"Why don't I just call you lucky—as in lucky-to-still-be-alive after bustin' in on my quiet time."

"You're not terribly sociable, are you, Curtis?"

Curtis scanned the room again to make certain that no one would see him actually talk to the other boy.

"Listen, weasel-neck, if you're the Welcome Wagon, you're a little late," he hissed. "And if you've got some kind of 'Jacobs Well Social Club' you want me to join, you can count me out on that action too—get it?"

Curtis noticed now that the headmaster was getting up to leave.

"Now if you'll excuse me, I have business," he muttered as he rose to follow.

"Suit yourself," Randy said a little coldly as he polished the thick lenses of his glasses with a paper napkin. "Just one parting word of advice, though. If I were you, I would not tell anybody anything about what you saw last night."

"Pardon me?" Curtis stopped dead in his tracks and sat back down, blinking in wonder. "I didn't quite catch that. What was it you said?"

The other boy sat quietly, savoring the sudden turn of attention. He cleared his throat and responded after a lengthy pause.

"Did you notice that *moon* last night, Curtis?" he asked matter-of-factly. "It was the brightest half-moon I think I've ever seen—still slightly gibbous, I'd say, but waning nightly."

"No-no-no!" Curtis blurted in staccato. "Don't you be talkin' about no *moon*, kid."

"It's such an interesting thing, though," Randy continued, undaunted. "Actually, half-moon is a misnomer. It's technically called a last-quarter moon.

And did you know that the boundary between the illuminated hemisphere of a half-moon and the darkened hemisphere is called *the terminator*?"

"You stop foolin' with me, kid, or I'll bust your dorky little head like an overripe cantaloupe. Now, tell me again what you said before." The tone was quiet, but menacing.

"Oh, you mean about what you saw last night?"

"That's what I'm talkin' about and you know it!" Curtis growled. "Now, how would you know that I saw somethin' . . . let's say, *out of the ordinary*, last night, huh?"

"Oh, you'd be amazed at the things I know," Randy replied. "In fact, you'd be wise to stick close to me—you might learn a thing or two."

"Yeah, well if you're such a fuckin' know-it-all, Einstein, then why don't you tell me what it was you think I saw last night?"

"You mean besides the half-moon?"

"Don't mess with me, kid. I've got a temper."

"Again, the name's Randy, and let's just say that nobody else saw her, and nobody is ever going to find where she went, unless they start digging holes. So you would do well, Mr. Jefferson, to just keep it between you and me, or you're going to make yourself a reputation here as something of a lunatic."

Before Curtis could gather his wits and respond, the buzzer that summoned the young inmates to their assigned chores sounded. Randy rose abruptly, raced away, and melted into the crowd of boys discarding their breakfast trays at the checkout station.

———◆———

Two hours pent up in a classroom running over in his mind the past several hours of events was almost more than Curtis could take. At morning PE he started his regimen as usual by running a couple of laps around the perimeter of the parade ground, each lap spanning a distance just short of a half mile. The pleasant exertion eased his apprehension somewhat. He scanned the infield population, hoping to catch a glimpse of his recent acquaintance, but no sign of the pale lad emerged.

Following the first leg of the second lap, Curtis turned southward and caught sight of a movement above the horizon that gave him pause. Dozens, perhaps a hundred hovering vultures, circling slowly counterclockwise had formed a dense gray cloud of dipping and dancing wings—a descending avian vortex that undulated against the bright blue sky and drilled down to the desert floor. Curtis reckoned that the center of this animated funnel cloud fell perhaps a quarter mile to the southwest of the camp.

The boy knew that circling buzzards out here in the desert were a pretty common sight, but never more than a dozen or so. Even more curious, the cone seemed to be thickening, fed by steady streams of more incoming birds.

Curtis turned east as he completed the southbound leg of the course, turning his head to keep watch over the unusual sight. He pondered for a moment the possible cause for this curiosity—what could be attracting such great throngs of the scavenging fowl? Perhaps the body of the girl he'd encountered the night before? He quickly dismissed the thought, surmising that a single human body would never attract or support the appetite of such burgeoning droves of birds.

"Cattle!" he exclaimed aloud between panting breaths. He visualized for an instant a number of strays or free-ranging livestock, cut off from their water source. He put the whole scene out of his mind, completed the course, and fell into his usual routine of floor exercises on the infield, keeping vigil over the quartet of roosters who now held the monopoly over the rusty old Healthways barbells.

"I once read a short story by Daphne du Maurier." A familiar voice startled Curtis. "See, these huge flocks of birds started attacking people."

Curtis looked up from a set of sit-ups into Randy's pallid face, then glanced over at the formation of circling vultures. The rotating funnel cloud was beginning to dissipate.

"Listen up, little fool—you read some strange shit. Are you fixin' to tell me that those buzzards are attackin' people out there in the desert?"

"Of course not," Randy chuckled. "What I am saying is that *those* birds are *feasting on people*—dead people, to be completely accurate. Dozens of them."

"Listen to me, kid . . ."

"Randy's the name," the younger boy reminded.

"Okay, Randy," Curtis conceded as he rose from the grassy infield. "You've been ramblin' on about a lot of weird stuff that's spinnin' my poor head around—but I need to know what you meant by what you said earlier this morning about . . . you know . . . *her*."

"Her?"

"Don't play dumb, now. You're gonna piss me off all over again."

"Oh, you must mean your dusky damsel with the sad face."

Curtis gulped. "So you saw her too?"

"Not last night, but I do see her from time to time," Randy bantered, cheerily. "Not really my type, though. The girl's only got half a brain, you know."

"I don't understand," said a confused Curtis.

"I think you will in due time, my friend. Suffice it to say for now that you seem to have a penchant for seeing things that others don't."

"Penchant?"

"Yes, you know—a gift."

"Or, maybe a curse."

"Perhaps—depends on your point of view," Randy suggested. "The point is no one will believe what you saw last night if you try to make it known, and you'll just buy yourself a lot of unnecessary trouble by doing it."

"But I can't keep somethin' like that to myself. It's way too serious."

"All right, then just wait and see if any mention of her surfaces. If no one else comes forward with a report of a walking dead girl, take my advice and file it away under 'inexplicable visions and events.' That's a file that's going to get pretty fat during your stay here, I guarantee. Meanwhile, I see your bar has freed up."

He pointed to the quartet of weight-lifting roosters who were now beckoning to Curtis. "You don't want to miss your turn. Oh, and by the way," he added in parting, "you don't want to miss any more breakfasts either, or you won't make welterweight by '68."

"Yeah, okay—thanks." Curtis was now completely mystified.

"See you around, Curtis." The younger boy grinned as he padded away.

"Yeah," Curtis muttered under his breath. "I got a real spooky feelin' that I will."

Captured Queen

After that first visit to Fort Grant, Will fumed for the first half of the ninety-minute trip back to his office after the shameful treatment at the hands of "that arrogant little prick," one of several original epithets that he hurled at the walnut dashboard of the stately Lincoln. His arm was still sore from that strange seizure he'd experienced in trying to retrieve his good luck medal, but he dismissed it as a muscle spasm of some sort. Then, as the gravel roads got wider and he started to pass through the orange groves at the edge of town, he simmered down a bit and began to run over the less inflammatory aspects of his visit—aspects that spawned suspicion rather than loathing.

It now occurred to Will that from the moment he'd entered the gate at the reform school, the focal point of interest had always rested with the package he'd carried down, and not the client conference, such as he'd assumed. Jeb had retrieved an envelope from the box. Harvey would not so much as even speak to him about business until he'd taken inventory on its contents. And there was that last stinging reminder— the "errand boy" remark about not forgetting the package. Will quickly connected all of this with the claim that the kid had made—words to the effect that he had the Doc and Jeb eating out of his hand; and the conclusion he drew from the combined evidence was hard to refute: he'd been drawn into a network of petty graft.

Immediately upon arriving back at the office, Will requested that Betty Wood arrange an ad hoc meeting with Stephen Robson, Will's superior and mentor, to report what had happened and to enlist his help in determining who in the firm was at the other end of this gross lapse of ethics. He could read Betty's face on her return from the old man's office that it was no dice.

"Will," Betty said as she allowed his glass office door to close behind her, "Mr. Robson is booked solid this afternoon, but he asked me to explain some things for you to consider."

"Have a seat," Will sighed as he pressed a button on his phone marked "busy."

He poured a tall glass of cold water from a stainless steel pitcher that he kept habitually perched on a glass-topped side cart and collapsed into his plush black leather office chair.

"Any chance I could grab a few minutes with him after hours? It's really urgent."

She shook her head. "I told him so, and that's how he anticipated the issue."

"So he'd probably already figured that the kid would drive me bananas—is that it?"

She nodded demurely. Betty Wood was a good fifteen years Will's elder, but he often detected the vestiges of an allure from a younger year that were downright distracting at times. Their close collaborations on researching precedent cases while he was an intern became the basis of the only true friendship that he could claim within the firm.

"And does he also know that I am on the verge of quitting over this?"

"It would be a huge mistake for you to even say that in front of him," Betty cautioned. "You could lose everything over a few unfortunate remarks made in the heat of anger."

"It wasn't just the way I was treated by the little viper, Betty," Will ranted. "Someone here in this office duped me into participating in a crime. I could be disbarred!"

"Listen to me, Will," Betty said forcefully, "it's not as black-and-white as you make it out to be!"

"Then please enlighten me—I'd like nothing better than to have this all go away."

He took a long pull from the tumbler of water.

"Your predecessor, Phillip, was assigned to Harvey Huish when he was first incarcerated," she explained. "The family made it clear to the firm that the boy was to be provided with any of the comforts that he requested, and so Phil made it a habit of carrying Harvey's 'allowance' down to him every other week when he went—just some spending money, at first. The amounts gradually increased until they became quite significant by anyone else's standards."

"What the hell would he do with 'spending money' in reform school?"

Betty stood, took a glass from the side cart, and poured some water. "You're not going to make this easy, are you?" She tossed her head in an aggravated manner, rustling her auburn hair.

"Sorry, Betty. I don't mean to be rude, but I feel like my career's shutting down before it even gets started—all over some little juvenile delinquent's 'allowance'!"

"It doesn't have to be that way if you'll just try to see things in the right perspective."

"Yeah, right—a crooked perspective."

"Do you even want me to finish?" Betty sighed as she began to pace the floor.

"Yes, please do!"

"After Phil passed away three months ago, I continued to have the packages sent down by courier until replacement counsel could be selected. That replacement turned out to be you, Will."

"Lucky me."

"Becoming personal counsel to a Huish family member is an opportunity that some of your colleagues would kill for. But your appointment had nothing to do with luck. They selected you because you are the brightest and the best."

The flattery appealed to Will's vanity, and it briefly took the edge off his anger.

"In any case," Betty continued, "I saw no reason to interrupt the deliveries, and if you think our little convict is a demon under normal circumstances, try withholding his allowance for two weeks. The tantrum is a terror to behold!"

"So you're the facilitator that's entangled me in this?"

Betty nodded feebly, eyes cast downward.

"And do the partners . . . does Robson know about this?"

"We don't trouble the partners with the details; that would be below their station. But don't be naïve, Will. They've made it pretty clear that our number one mission in life is to service the Huish family to their satisfaction, and if some of our methods offend your innocent sensibilities, well . . . that's something you'll have to resolve with the mirror."

"Betty, I don't want to hurt you or threaten your position here," Will muttered after a pause, "but I just can't be a part of this."

The paralegal's green eyes flashed as she slammed the water glass down on the cart.

"Well, don't look now, Buster, but you already are!"

With that, she stormed out of his office.

Will was aghast. How could this be happening? This was even more inconceivable and unexpected than the earlier events at Fort Grant. Far from assuaging his troubled mind, Betty had confirmed his worst fears: the firm was complicit in a breach of ethics that could bring the whole house of wayward lawyers down around their own ears.

He was at a loss as to what to do next. Should he confront Robson with this and risk losing all? If he took this outside the firm—say, to the Department of Corrections or the American Bar Association—what proof did he have? Was he just overreacting from the leftover soreness he felt over the verbal pummeling he'd taken from his juvenile client? Should he wait and get some objective distance, or would waiting deepen the appearance of his own involvement?

Will pondered all of these notions that danced before him for a while, then picked up the phone and fingered the rotary dial. He would explain the entire situation to Carol and get the perspective of a cooler, more objective head. Would she even believe such an unlikely scenario?

Odd. The phone at home rang interminably. She was usually at the house working on dinner at this hour. He slammed the phone down and swore. The one time he dearly needed her opinion, and she was probably out spending money that may soon vanish.

An hour passed and after several more unsuccessful attempts to call his wife, Will decided to pack it in and head for home. That's when Stephen Robson happened by and stuck his wizened face in Will's door.

"I hear you took a verbal beating from our beloved little savage down at Fort Grant this afternoon," he chuckled, "but I see your scalp is still intact, so it couldn't have been that bad."

"Oh, it was worse than 'that bad,' Stephen," Will choked. "Can you—"

At that instant, the desk phone let out an abrasive ring. Will seized the receiver and slammed it back down in one motion. The elder attorney raised an eyebrow.

"Look, Will, I know you've got something of a tiger by the tail here, but we chose you for this assignment because we knew the little hood would be no match for your wits. Just don't let him get your goat, and you'll get all the details ironed out—you'll see. You know," he added in his best Robert Young tone, "there's a reason why we call this a *firm*, Will. We need to stand like bricks in a wall. That's how we weather these seasonal tempests. You think about that a bit, son."

"You don't understand, sir."

But before Will could find the words, Betty walked up and tapped on the glass to announce herself. The old man, somewhat taken aback, opened the door wide to let her in. Her face was distressed.

"I'm terribly sorry to barge in, but University Hospital is on the line for Will."

The two men gazed at her in puzzlement. Will picked up the phone and his face blanched.

"Yes," he said into the receiver. "She's having what? . . . I'll be right down!"

Will heard himself speaking, but felt detached from his own voice: "Carol's at the emergency room; she's having trouble breathing."

"You best get down there, boy," the old man barked. "We can take this matter up another time."

"Will, are you okay?" Betty asked, sounding sincerely concerned.

Will drifted out of the office and down the hall stunned, in a stupor.

"Keep us posted," the old man called after him.

The young lawyer did not later recall the elevator ride down to the parking garage, nor the fifteen-minute drive across town in rush hour traffic. When he finally came to his senses, he was standing in the emergency room gazing at his unconscious beloved, lying on a gurney.

Carol was barely breathing, when she breathed at all. There was a faint light-blue cast to her cheeks and pronounced dark circles under her eyes. She looked as though she had one foot on the wrong side of the cemetery gate.

A bevy of doctors and nurses peppered him with questions. No, he'd never seen her like this before. No, she did not have a history of asthma or emphysema. Finally, a young intern took him aside and gave him his best explanation. Carol was undergoing some sort of episode of tracheomalacia—a collapsed windpipe. It was closed so tightly, in fact, that the ER team could not force-insert a lubricated plastic tube to open the airway. The doctor told him he thought the only option was a tracheotomy, and that it should be performed without delay.

Will told the doctor to get the consent form, when one of the nurses came up to report that he, Will, had a telephone call at their station desk. Must be Betty, he thought, checking up.

"Will Farnsworth," he greeted. "Who am I speaking with?"

"Hello, Willy. I called as soon as I got the bad news."

A chill went through the young lawyer's body. It was Harvey Huish! "Wuh . . . how . . . ?" Will stammered.

"Oh, I know you must be speechless, dad, but I didn't want my favorite lawyer to be alone in, like, his hour of need." The young convict punctuated the sarcasm with his signature staccato laugh in spine-tingling falsetto.

Will began to sputter incredulously as the despicable voice continued.

"You've gotta be absolutely *terrified* that you're going to lose your lovely wife, but I called to clue you in that *it ain't necessarily so.* That's Gershwin, isn't it?"

Will could not speak due to the rage that was building within his skull.

"Willy, you there?"

"Yes!" Will hissed. "How could you do this?"

"Okay, tune in carefully and all of this sad vibe will go splitsville. Call old man Robson and tell him that your wife is fine now, and that you and I will come to an understanding—you got it? Man, I hate to see old

Robson all bugged out like he is right now. You should be ashamed for gettin' him so bugged out, daddy-o. He's a real gone dust bunny. I mean, he's got a bum ticker, you know."

"You little bastard, when I get a hold of you . . . uh . . . ack!"

Will found his voice suddenly cracking, as though his throat were parched from thirst.

"Shh-shh," Harvey whispered soothingly. "Now you're chokin' just like she is, only just a little. See how it feels? Don't you have any sympathy?"

Will now felt as if some unseen elastic ligature was constricting his throat, closing off the airway. Then, just as panic began to chill his limbs, the sensation vanished as instantly as it had beset him, and he was presently able to draw in a deep breath, much to his relief and astonishment.

"There now," Harvey continued, "just make the call and tell the old man what I said. It's that simple. What have you got to lose? Like, I hear they're gonna start cutting on her any minute, but that won't help. On the other hand, you two lovebirds could be back at the pad holding hands and groovin' to that way-square squawker Mel Torme on the hi-fi in an hour if you'll just cool it with bein' such a fucking drag."

Will placed the receiver down and shut his eyes. How could anyone be so incredibly cruel? It was inconceivable! And yet . . . *how in the hell could he know about Mel Torme?*

He thought about the choking sensation, then the words: *What have you got to lose?*

He turned and looked through the glass portholes on the double doors to the ER. He could see the nurses and interns prepping Carol for the surgery.

Will mechanically picked up the receiver and dialed a nine to get the dial tone for an outside line. Transfixed by the sight of his wife fighting for her life's breath, he dialed the old man's direct number. He went numb as he gazed on his helpless beloved with her ghastly bluish death mask.

What have you got to lose?

"Hello, Stephen. This is Will," he said in a robotic monotone.

Incredibly, he saw Carol's hands move, then grip the rails of the gurney.

"Yeah, it seems like she's gonna be all right," he announced, his voice breaking under the weight of the lie.

Astonishingly, though, his wife now opened her eyes wide.

"Yeah," he continued, "she really gave us a scare."

He was on the verge of sobbing now. He cleared his throat and mustered all the false composure he could.

"By the way, Stephen, I've had some time here to think, and I am confident that I can work with the Huish kid. I certainly do appreciate the case assignment."

The words were forced and hung like bitter ashes in his mouth.

But now, through the glass, he could perceive the unmistakable movement of his beloved's rib cage rising and falling beneath the billowing patient smock. Miraculously, she was, with a stunning suddenness, inhaling and exhaling without restriction.

He dropped the receiver and burst through the spring-loaded doors.

"Carol!" he cried and rushed to her bedside. The bluish graveyard patina had already left her cheeks and she continued to huff and puff as if devouring the very air she'd been deprived of.

He knelt next to the gurney and tenderly kissed her outstretched hand. Tears flowed freely from his downcast eyes.

Tears of joy for her miraculous recovery.

Tears of sadness for the loss of his freedom.

That evening, fourteen months ago, Will Farnsworth finally came to fully understand what it was to become a slave, not just to self-conceit and to material affluence—but quite literally, a slave to another man.

Horsemen from Hell

Curtis remained bemused by Randy's startling comments, and by his precocious manner and preternatural command of the language. The remarks about birds eating people, about the girl with "half a brain," about no one ever finding her—these verbal puzzles were eclipsed only by the wispy boy's pronouncement that Curtis had "a penchant for seeing things that others don't." And so it wasn't just Randy's outsized intelligence that was unnerving; what amazed Curtis was his proclivity for knowing things that should have been out of his realm of experience. The kid had to be clairvoyant.

Taking the younger boy's advice, Curtis suspended a trip to the headmaster's office and kept silent about his encounter with the battered young woman, waiting for possible mention from other sources. True to Randy's prediction, though, no word of a finding or a sighting ever emerged, which only fed Curtis's sense of bewilderment. He looked for the younger boy throughout the day to possibly gain some explanation surrounding the astonishing events he'd recently experienced. But there was no sign of Randy at all that day, and Curtis retired to a fitful sleep immediately following lights-out.

Just after midnight, he awakened with a start, feeling through the pitch blackness of deep sleep the unmistakable touch of a hand on his bare forearm.

"Don't speak!" a voice whispered. "It's just me."

Curtis could barely make out the frail and now-familiar form of Randall Kartchner, as his vision adjusted to the darkness.

"What the hell are you doing in here?" Curtis demanded in an equally muffled voice. "I mean, how did you . . . ?"

"Your guard's sound asleep—snoring like a freight train, and I can always slip past mine. I was a cat burglar by profession, you know. That's why they've got me residing in these exclusive digs."

"Doesn't surprise me a bit," Curtis yawned.

"Well, listen—I came to wake you up because I remembered you were tired from last night's scenario, and I didn't want you to sleep through it," Randy whispered.

"Sleep through what, little fool?" Curtis whispered back. "'Cause right now I could sleep through an air raid—you know, complete with sirens and atomic bombs?"

"Something very critical—you'll be grateful."

"Thanks for thinkin' of me, pal," Curtis murmured, "but in a tug-o'-war between you and Mr. Sandman, right now Mr. Sandman's winnin' hands down."

"You know, a great man once said, 'There will be sleeping enough in the grave.'"

"Some happy-head *he* must've been. Sounds like some jive-ass coffee commercial."

"You don't get it—I don't want you to miss this, Curtis!"

"Miss what?"

"Shhh . . . listen!" Randy admonished under his breath.

The numerous pairs of double-hung windows that dotted the exterior walls of the old clapboard edifice were propped with a slight opening and nailed fast to the wooden jambs. Curtis sat up and strained to hear anything above the whine of an attic fan and the quiet moan of the air movement through the steel security mesh that covered all windows, but he detected no other sound. He shook his head in the dark, as if Randy could see this.

"It's quieter tonight," the younger boy whispered. "The moon's waning; we need to go outside by the wall—we'll hear it better from there."

"You're loony tunes, kid!" Curtis exclaimed, almost out loud. "I'm not goin' anywhere outside of this bed, much less outside the door of this dorm."

"Don't argue," Randy hissed. "You've got to hear this before it goes quiet again. You've got to hear it or none of this other stuff will make any sense to you."

86

"All right, already," Curtis whined as he reluctantly drew the top sheet from across his perspiring torso. "This better be good, kid, or I'm gonna knock your little dick in the dirt."

"The name's Randy."

"Okay, kid," Curtis sighed. "This better be good or I'll kick your *Randy ass* up between your shoulder blades, then. How's that?"

Curtis rose in the darkness, quietly slipped into his canvas-top sneakers, and followed Randy toward the door to the corridor, wearing only a pair of boxer shorts. The hushed discussion had apparently not aroused any of his bunk mates, and the pair padded stealthily past old Marcus, who had long since been lulled to sleep by the transistorized crooning of Gentleman Jim Reeves. A nocturnal breeze met the boys at the bottom of the exiting concrete steps.

"I can't believe we're doin' this!" he exclaimed in a hushed tone, once they were beyond earshot of the dorm building. "Somebody's gonna spot us and turn us in."

"I wouldn't worry too much about that," the younger boy assured. "Nobody ever tries to escape from here; that's why there's no serious night watch. But just the same," he continued, "I'm not one to tempt fate. Let's move over where the light's a bit more subdued."

He gestured toward the darkened south quarter of the parade ground—the farthest from the mercury vapor lamp that buzzed and glared down on their highly visible trek to the wall.

"So, Randy, is it true that the headmaster drives his car around on the parade ground after hours?"

"Yeah, but he won't be indulging in any nocturnal sojourns tonight."

"What makes you so sure?"

"Because I lifted his coil wire."

"You *didn't*!"

"Not to worry," Randy chuckled. "I'll replace it before daylight—he'll never know unless he decides to sally forth, so to speak."

"You sure talk funny, kid," Curtis observed. "Kinda like an egg-head . . . or . . . or, I know—like the professor on *The Dobie Gillis Show*!"

"You mean Professor Pomfritt."

"Yeah . . . Professor Pomfritt—that's it!"

"Well, don't go feeling too special. You're not the first one to accuse me of being precocious—what, with my *mat-tooer* vocabulary and all."

"How the hell did you get so damn smart anyway?"

"First of all, brilliance was always in the genes. My father is a research scientist and my mother is a college French teacher. And then I've always been something of an information hound—but never so much as in the past year."

"What's so special about the last year?"

"Well, since about this time last year, I suddenly developed this voracious appetite for knowledge. I started literally living in the library, soaking up facts, figures, philosophy, and good literature like an info-sponge. You might even say I feed my hunger for understanding the way I've seen you devour a good meal—with much gusto!"

"Geez, kid—who even uses a word like *gusto*?" Curtis chuckled derisively.

"It's the absolute perfect word to describe my delight with the consumption of knowledge."

"All I know is I can't understand what you're sayin' half the time, O Wise One."

"Ah, wisdom—that's another matter entirely. Wisdom and intelligence: never confuse the two."

The frail-looking youngster led the way onto more shadowy ground, and Curtis noticed a certain hobble in Randy's gait.

"You not only talk funny," Curtis teased, "but you *walk funny* too."

Randy stopped and turned around. "What's that you said?"

"You heard what I said, *gimp*," Curtis chuckled. "You got a little stitch in your giddy-up, that's all."

"You'd walk funny too, Curtis, if *you'd* been gang-raped by a dozen *roosters* twice your size!" Randy retorted, coldly.

The smile froze on Curtis's face. An awkward silence ensued.

"I . . . I . . ." he stammered, scrambling for something sympathetic or consoling to say, but Randy cut him short.

"Faked *you* out of your shoes," he giggled playfully.

Curtis scowled. "I swear, kid, if it wasn't for those dorky glasses of yours, I'd dot your eyes, here and now!"

"Shhh!" Randy shut down the banter and stood motionless. "Can you hear it *now*?" he demanded in a suddenly serious tone.

Curtis suspended his own motion, and even stilled his breathing to hear what Randy was hearing. For the first few seconds there was nothing but the beating of his heart. Then, a certain muffled sort of *pinging* echoed softly from a distance, like billiard balls clacking together on felt-covered tables. No, now it sounded more like dozens of dry river stones colliding against each other in the darkness.

"What *is* that?" Curtis wondered aloud.

"*I* know what it is," Randy said, "but I want *you* to identify it yourself."

Curtis continued to listen, but shook his head, still unable to peg the continuing sound.

"Let's go up on top of the wall," Randy finally suggested. "I know where there are some footholds for climbing."

With curiosity trumping his natural misgivings, Curtis silently agreed and the two trotted the remaining distance to the nine-foot-tall adobe barrier. Randy pointed to some deep horizontal cracks in the white-plaster finish coat that allowed the boys to hoist themselves to the wide shelf at the crest. The top plane of the adobe monolith was a good two feet wide—broad enough for a sentry to pace on patrol in more vigilant days past. The two settled atop the wall, sitting cross-legged, and stilled themselves for clearer listening.

"See." Randy pointed to the moon. "You can almost *see* it waning!"

"What does the moon have to do with what we're supposed to be hearin', *brainiac*?"

"Everything!" Randy returned cryptically.

"I don't get it, and I never did understand about all that waxin' and wanin' of the moon. It's confusin' as hell."

"It's easy to tell the difference," said Randy. "When the bright portion is on the right, it's waxing, or growing. When it's on the left, it's waning, or shrinking. When it's under half, it's a crescent. When it's over half, it's a gibbous. Pretty simple."

"*Pretty simple*, huh?"

"Shhh!" Randy cautioned. "Now listen!"

Curiously, the sound was not only more intense but seemed much nearer now, as if it was moving toward the Fort. There were also more background sounds that accompanied the now-amplified pinging of stones—sounds like the squeaking of dry leather and a curious metallic tinkling.

"Horses!" Curtis exclaimed in a subdued voice.

A rattling exhalation and an answering neigh in the distance confirmed Curtis's answer.

"How many?" Randy riddled further.

"A bunch. I don't know . . . a half-dozen—maybe ten," Curtis guessed.

"Try thirty."

Curtis listened more critically and nodded as the depth and breadth of the noise seemed to support Randy's estimate. The occasional *whoop-whoop* of a riding crop and the musical jangle of spurs rounded out the suite of sounds that the riders composed.

"Who are they?" Curtis asked at length.

"Who do you think?"

Curtis took a stab. "Maybe a posse looking for that poor Indian girl—I don't know."

Randy shook his head. "In the middle of the night?" he scoffed. "Doesn't make much sense to search for someone in the dark, does it?"

"I guess not—'specially out here in *Nowhere Central.*"

"Besides, I told you before, she doesn't even exist on this side of the dirt. You need to stop thinking in terms of the present with these events. These horsemen, for instance—you need to start wondering who they *were.*"

"Kid, you're startin' to give me the creeps."

"That's fine—as long as it gets you *thinking.*"

The two sat in silence atop the adobe rampart for a time, listening to the rhythm of dozens of hooves stamping out a tempo across rock shelves in the near-distant desert. Curtis thought he sensed some visual movement of shapeless shadows passing between stationary shadows of mesquite and palo verde, but there was no form that his eyesight could focus on. The sound gradually faded into reverberating echoes and finally disappeared down some faraway canyon.

"Okay, kid," Curtis demanded. "What the hell was that . . . ?"

"Keep still," Randy hissed. "It's not over yet."

Minutes passed and no sound materialized from across the vast desert. Curtis, still fatigued from the previous night's insomnia, closed his eyes and allowed his tired head to roll forward. He was napping intermittently when the wail of the coyotes went up, just like the night before.

"Hear that?" Randy spoke in an excited voice.

"Sure do," Curtis replied. "Heard 'em last night too. That's got to be the biggest and loudest pack of coyotes I've ever heard."

The mournful chorus of yelps and yowls built with every passing moment until it was almost deafening.

"Coyotes, huh? Is that what you hear?"

"And what do *you* hear, professor?"

"Well, why don't you close your eyes and listen—*really listen.* Then maybe you can tell me."

Curtis reluctantly did just that. With eyelids tightly pinched shut, the focused sound became for the boy remarkably less like a mournful chorus, and more like a collage of individual voices—almost *human* voices, not howling, but screaming and crying. Curtis sat and listened, transfixed, for quite some time until the tortured songs of a hundred victim voices at last died away into a dull murmur. With eyes closed, it was easy for him to nod again and slip into a state of half-sleep. That's when the dull murmur dreamily morphed into verbal expressions—emitted in moans rather than spoken, and raised in unfamiliar tongues. In his torpor, Curtis imagined that he could somehow fathom the meaning of the foreign words . . . and they were tormented voices *pleading for mercy, begging for deliverance from some unspeakable horror, interspersed with growling demands for vengeance.*

The subliminal volume and the frequency of these ghastly pleas ascended again rapidly until it became a crescendo of human noise, sending a surging chill through Curtis's bare torso and then his limbs, then collapsing again into a moan on a cool breeze. The voices seemed to be whispering to *him* now, personally.

Follow the path . . . they said. *Come to us . . .* they hissed.

The sudden realization that these voices were now directed at him struck terror at Curtis's core. The tone was menacing. What were they, and were they coming for him?

He raised his head with a jerk and opened his eyes. The voices instantly fell silent, and only the sound of a cool desert breeze passing through the brush and trees remained. Curtis's limbs were cold, and his back ached. His hands trembled and his fingers twitched, inexplicably.

"Jesus Christ—did you hear what I heard?" he asked quietly, voice quivering.

There was no answer. He scanned the darkened top of the wall and then turned around. He was alone! He now paid alarming notice to what he thought was a faint glimmer of gray luminescence in the eastern sky.

Curtis swore, leaped from the wall, and started to trot toward the shadowy cluster of buildings in the distance. It was nearly dawn!

"That goddamn Randy," he muttered aloud. "I'll whup his skinny little ass!"

Interlude (the first)

"So, are you with me so far?"

I guess I hesitated before I answered, but understandably so. "Yeah, I'm with you, Curtis."

Twilight was gone, and the deep purple band in the west had long since faded to black. At this distance, effectively removed from the intrusive effect of the lights glowing back in town, the starlit canopy of the heavens was nothing less than stunning. The nearest layer of the galactic luminarias shone brightly by the hundreds, perhaps thousands. The secondary tier of celestial jewels twinkled behind the brightest stars in dazzling relief, appearing somewhat less brilliant individually than their kindred lights in the forefront, but exponentially more numerous and therefore equally as breathtaking. The most distant backdrop comprised a milky haze of innumerable universal suns arrayed as a white lace mantilla of luminosity against the vacant blackness of utmost space. The combined effect of the tri-layered matrix of stars granted the gazer a seldom-experienced depth of vision that evoked an overwhelming sense of the infinite.

"You don't sound too sure about that, Vince."

I broke my precious slack-jawed communion with infinity to consider my next response, when something else intervened. Floating across a dark and silent distance of furrowed ground came a muffled hooting and hollering, apparently coming from a fortunate cohort of our ragtag band. Flashlight beams waved and danced from a faraway citrus grove; their radiant shafts oscillated like visual laughter.

"Sounds like someone's snagged a rattler," I observed aloud.

It was not a serious distraction from the dialogue, but I thought it might buy me a little more time to collect my thoughts. My inquisitor would not let it be so.

"Man, you are sidesteppin' like a one-eyed fiddler crab," Curtis scoffed.

"No . . . no, not really," I refuted, rather weakly. "I'm just taking time to think about it so I can respond honestly, and I guess if you're talking about buying in to everything you've laid out so far, then I'd have to say that you're not too sure yourself."

"Say, what?"

"That's right," I returned, with a little more confidence. "If you think about it, you've tried to explain away every weird event that's happened in your story so far."

"For instance?"

"For instance, that guard you saw at the gate when you first went in—the one with the disfigured face. You explained that one away by telling yourself he must have been burned in a fire."

"I did say that, didn't I?"

"You did, and you even compared him to James Whitmore in that movie *Face of Fire*."

"Umm-hmm . . . uh-huh, but that's just one 'for instance,' Vince. What else you got?"

"Well, you made a special point of describing the shot that the Doc gave you, so I thought you were suggesting that the flags at half-mast and the three men hanging from the scaffold might be some kind of drug-induced images from something in that syringe."

"Ah man, that's bull!"

"No, really. The thought crossed my mind," I insisted. "And the thousands of buzzards you wrote off to dead cattle."

"And what about the girl?"

"Yeah, what about the girl, Curtis? If you really believed your own eyes, why did you hide what you saw from Marcus, and why did you let Randy sidetrack you so easily from your decision to take it to the headmaster?"

"Because I was scared and confused. I thought nobody would believe me."

"Understandable, but not terribly convincing. Even the voices in the coyotes' howling—you made it sound like you were just having a nightmare."

A long, uncomfortable silence intervened. The jubilant hooting from the adjacent grove had died away. The gentle gurgle of irrigation water from the nearby ditch became the dominant sound for what seemed like several moments. I was certain I'd pissed my friend off with my blunt honesty and I'd nearly given up at that point on hearing any more of Curtis's tale, when a low, familiar chuckling came rolling through the darkness. I could almost see that famous gleaming grin of his.

"I guess I must be tellin' this tale just right," Curtis said, "'cause up to that point, I really didn't know if *I* could even believe my *own* senses."

"Well, of course!" I agreed. "You went through enough strange encounters in a few days to fill up a whole television season of *One Step Beyond*. I think I'd be more than doubting my senses. I think I'd be doubting my own *sanity*!"

"That comes later." It was a hint that he would indeed continue.

"Listen, Curtis," I added, "I'm not skeptical, and I'm not all that naïve either. I just want to try to keep an open mind and enjoy the story. Just one thing . . ."

"What's that?"

"Can I stop you and ask a question once in a while?"

"Okay, just don't make a habit of it."

"Agreed. Now, please continue," I implored as I cast my gaze upward again to that sparkling canopy of infinite starlight. "And don't leave anything out, please."

"Be careful what you wish for."

Location! Location! Location!

The dervish-dancing wind returned with a vengeance, scattering Kenny Armenta's jewelry display, this time actually lifting from the ground the coal-black velour blanket that had provided the staging field for his jewelry arrangement. Silver bracelets and turquoise necklaces rained onto the gravel shoulder in front of the rural bus stop with a sad little tinkling sound that enjoined the roar of the swirling vortex.

"That's twice today," he groaned aloud to no one, as he peered out from the protective shield of his enfolded arms.

Not only twice today, but it was twice every consecutive day since Monday that the dust devils had visited the roadside vendor's prime location on the southbound shoulder of state highway 75. Today was Thursday, the fourth day of the blustery assaults and an otherwise meteorologically passive midday, marking the second week of a mild month of March.

The ancient Pima lapidary cast his focus upward into the sunny canopy and furthered the observation. "Strange weather we're having these days."

Strange indeed, for these were not your garden-variety twenty-foot whirlwind gusts—not by anyone's reckoning. No, these unwelcome windy visitors were those freak skyscraper-sized gyres—mini-cyclones that suck up truckloads of abrasive sand, loose vegetation, chattering newspapers, clothesline flotsam, and any other miscellaneous debris not nailed, glued, or welded down to the desert floor. These particular dust devils seemed to have a curious hunger for Kenny's trinkets, sucking his precious jewelry into their yawning vortices on a regular basis.

Kenny calmly cursed the towering funnel as it whipped and whirled his dusky presentation blanket in a fevered fandango. Oblivious to his profanity-laced protests, the twisting column breathed not the slightest hint of an inclination toward giving up its faux-velvet dance partner. In spite, she twirled higher and higher, kicking and cavorting away across the wide desert sky. The portly old man spit a viscous wad onto the ground to punctuate his spontaneous sonnet of vulgarities. Stricken dumb by his own poetic genius, he stood motionless now, silently watching the outlaw wind carry away on raven wings his high hopes for a lucrative day.

At length, the now-forlorn Pima hawker padded over to salvage what was left of his handiwork. He methodically unbuttoned and removed his denim shirt to use as a makeshift sack for collecting the far-flung diaspora of his treasured children—onyx bolo ties, turquoise rings, copper and silver bracelets, and colorful heishi necklaces—plucking them from the gravel and tenderly placing each piece into the improvised bundle. This was not a banner day.

Kenny was naturally disheartened by the disruption to his business dealing, which he had to admit was already inching to the south side of nil. But the aging artisan stubbornly attributed this trough period in sales to capricious market circumstances. There would be an uptick in activity any day now, he persuaded himself. It could only get better.

Now, however, the plot of his choosing seemed more attractive to the malevolent wind spirits that had plagued his encampments of late than to potential customers. If this kept up, he might have to weigh the benefits of another spot, however reluctant he was to move. This kind of ambivalence was quite foreign to Kenny's nature, and he sighed audibly at his own inner uncertainty.

Upon dolefully gathering up the last of his errant inventory, the old man waddled shirtless back to an adjacent bus stop ramada to check his tin cash box. He breathed a sigh of relief on seeing that he had indeed closed the sheet-metal lid earlier, as he'd recalled. There were only a few bills and coins stashed inside—residuals from a previously profitable season that he now used as primer for making change. He took heart in what scant encouragement came from knowing that the wind spirit had only fleeced him of his blanket and a few trinkets.

Kenny seated himself on the bench under the ramada and began the long wait for his wife, Primrose, who was not scheduled to pick him up for several hours. The warm breath of a soft desert breeze exhaled gently out of the south over an adjacent ridge. Barely perceptible caresses of dry air tickled Kenny's bare chest. The silken sensation on his dewy flesh proved hauntingly familiar, and although it had been several years since he was last so embraced by the seductive touch of the desert spirit, she returned to him now, and the old man was reminded that, under particular conditions, certain sensory events have a transcendent effect—allusions to immortality.

He raised his right hand up before his face, palm away, and gazed at the broad silver strap bracelet that encircled his wrist. A round image shimmered from the center of that wristlet like a watch dial—several rings of descending diameter contained within each other lay etched in the metal. A close examination revealed that those black-enamel-filled concentric circles actually formed a radiated path, culminating at a V-shaped void at the top of the outermost rings—a void containing a tiny human form rendered in primitive stick-figure style. The labyrinthine rings seemed to vibrate with a pinwheel effect that Kenny found intensely hypnotic.

"I'itoi," he whispered from the recesses of a near-fugue state, "the man in the maze."

It was a combined effect of the caresses from the desert spirit and the dazzling image of the geometric talisman that entranced the aging Pima, and he sat transfixed for several moments, barely breathing as his ancient soul swelled from within.

At length, the chill of reality intervened. Without the presentation throw, there could be no display, so any hope of salvaging the business day was dismissed. The next few hours would be given over to a series of solitary reveries and catnaps.

"Oh, well," he said to no one. "What the hell anyway."

He shaded his eyes and squinted at the stark blue sky to follow a beguiling aerial ballet in the circling of a lone red-tail hawk.

But before his neck could seize up from that long skyward gaze, Kenny became distracted by the approaching drone from the north of a straining V-8 engine, down-geared and pinging from a long southbound ascent. He lowered his eyes to focus on a buckskin-colored '56 F-100 pickup gradually cresting the hill. It rolled slowly onto the gravel shoulder at the bus stop, kicking up little eddies of dust in its wake. Kenny could see the lone driver clearly through the wide wraparound windshield, as he leaned across the bench seat to crank down the passenger-side window.

"Hey, old coot!" a similarly aged native called to him, engine still idling. "You need to put your shirt back on before you shock the entire countryside with your jelly rolls and blubber muffins."

Realizing now that in his quest for a suitable sack to stow his treasures, Kenny had removed his shirt, forgetting how grotesquely obese he really was. Even so, it was rather rude for this virtual stranger to make him feel so self-conscious about it, even if it was in good-natured jest.

Nevertheless, he held up his bundle in explanation. "I needed a bag."

"Then you can have my first wife!" the other old Indian roared in reply, then fell into a fit of laughing-coughing-wheezing-choking at his own sitting attempt at standup humor.

"No thanks," Kenny replied in deadpan earnest, "I've already got a good woman."

"A contradiction in terms, if you ask me," quipped the craggy-faced relic from the truck cab, "but then I imagine she must at least be *sturdy*, eh?"

"I suppose that's true," Kenny returned politely, his eyes directly meeting the stranger's. "She is much younger than me, and she is Tohono O'odham. The Papago are sturdy people."

"If you don't mind my saying," the stranger observed, "you look a little long in the tooth to be waiting for the school bus."

"I'm waiting for my wife to pick me up. We have only one car," Kenny explained, "and she needs it to go to the community clinic in Coolidge. She's a nurse there. We live near Sacaton."

"So what's in the bundle, chief?"

Kenny rose from the bench and trudged over to the truck, shirt-sack in hand and cash box under one arm. "Indian curios," he declared proudly, "my lunch sack, and a bottle of water." He briefly apprised the other of his name, his business, and his glum immediate circumstances, ending with the fact that Primrose was not expected for almost four hours.

"Four hours is much too long to wait," said the driver in a gravelly voice. "I could *walk* to Sacaton in three."

"It's over ten miles. I couldn't get that far in a long day, especially with a load."

"I can believe that, Kenny. Still, in the course of four hours one of those goddamn nuisance bears could come along, eat you, take a nap, and poop you out before your Papago squaw would finally come along and find nothing but a steaming pile of grizzly pooh. That would be you."

"All things are possible."

"Well, just for safety's sake, I'm going to give you a lift into Sacaton."

"I'd be much obliged. I could phone Primrose from my house and tell her not to come."

"Okay, but first grab an empty gunnysack from the back of the truck and stow your stuff in there."

"You're very kind," Kenny said as he carefully transferred his items into a burlap pinto-bean sack. He noted with interest the monogram on the front fender flare spelling out the word *RENEGADE* in black cursive lettering.

"Don't mention it," said the driver. "I consider it my civic duty, 'cause you need to get your shirt back on. You're a walking scandal, I swear; you look like a pink water balloon with nipples."

"You know," Kenny said as he twisted the passenger door handle and mounted the running board with a grunt, "I don't think Milton Berle is in any danger of losing his job today."

The coiled-spring suspension groaned in protest as the truck listed slightly starboard.

"Maybe not," the other grinned, as he pulled the column-mounted gearshift lever down, "but somebody could justify putting a bullet in Don Rickles's head any day now. I need to keep in practice."

"All things are possible," chuckled Kenny. "So what is your name, stranger?"

"Ezra, for short," Ezra replied, letting out the clutch and easing the truck back into the southbound lane of the highway.

Ezra was wearing a white cotton shirt and tan khaki pants. The deep lines in his leathern face indicated an age beyond even Kenny's, but his form was lean and surprisingly youthful.

"Ezra *what*?" Kenny pressed.

"Just Ezra," he returned. "My people didn't take Anglo or Mexican names like yours did, *Kenny.*"

After a long silence, Kenny offered an observation. "You're a long way from home, Ezra." He was referring to the now-apparent fact that Ezra was an Apache Indian, not a Pima and probably, therefore, from San Carlos, quite some distance to the north.

"I'm not quite as far from home as you might think."

Kenny pondered the curious remark, noting to himself that very few if any San Carlos Apaches lived outside of the reservation up near Globe.

"So, Kenny, how's business, dust devils aside?" asked Ezra in a genuinely curious tone.

Kenny recited his tale of woe and blamed the dearth of traffic on the calendar. But he had high hopes. Spring weather typically teased out an onslaught of tourists during the final days of March and early April, before Nature turned up the cosmic oven. Elderly winter residents of the Valley of the Sun typically squeezed in their final day-trips to other parts of the state before returning to their native haunts in the Midwest, where the summer heat was more tolerable.

"It's early in the season," he observed.

"Oh, I beg to differ," said Ezra. "I think your bus stop location and this highway offer no commercial potential whatsoever, regardless of the season."

"But I thought about it and planned," said Kenny. "I read that the scenic route from the Valley will attract more tourist-types who are headed for Tucson or Tombstone. I read that many visitors to the East Valley avoid the traffic and the mess of Phoenix altogether. Highway 75 offers a good bypass with many sightseeing opportunities." He spoke as if he was quoting verbatim from his source.

"What sightseeing opportunities are those?"

"Well, just look at all the desert flowers that are already blooming. Aren't they beautiful?"

"Just lovely. What else?"

"How about those magnificent Galiuro Mountains?" said Kenny as he gestured toward the western horizon.

"You're putting me to sleep. Anything else you can name that's supposed to make this cow path a magnet for tourists?"

"Let me see. There's the Tom Mix memorial."

"Oh please, don't make me laugh. Nobody even knows that pile of rocks exists except for the local hotshot vandals who use the stupid metal horse for target practice."

"Tom Mix was a legend," Kenny countered. "He left behind a huge following. Every year, hundreds of his admirers make the pilgrimage to that crossing up the road where he met his fate, just to pay their respects. I read it in the *Sun Valley Tribune*."

"Oh, that's where you've been poisoning your mind. Of course, it *has* to be true, if you read it in the newspapers," Ezra scoffed. "So how many of these hundreds of pilgrims have you counted passing by this way today?"

"There have been five cars in the past three hours," Kenny admitted, "counting yours. But it's early in the year. The paper says the peak visitor period for Tom falls in mid-April. It seems he's still very much admired. Folks will come from all over to pay homage, because he was a hero of the Old West."

"Mangas Coloradas, Cochise, and Geronimo—*they* were the heroes of the Old West," grumbled Ezra. "Listen, Kenny, Tom Mix was a third-rate horseman, the same as any common rodeo clown, and he was already washed up when he drove his gaudy Cord convertible into the ditch twenty years ago. I've ridden with some superbly skilled Apache equestrians in my day that could ride daisy chains around that pony-phony. Not to mention, he looked like a buffoon in that goofy ten-gallon hat of his."

"There was nothing phony about Tom Mix," Kenny retorted. "He did all of his own on-camera stunts. Got himself injured many times in the process."

Ezra quietly shifted down into second, letting the engine slowly brake their southbound momentum. A throaty growl from under the hood arose, then diminished in volume and timbre as he eased into a right turn and pointed the old pickup westward onto a narrow, scarcely paved lane.

"I won't argue that he might have blown out his testicles a couple of times jumping into the saddle like a moron," the Apache smirked. "I just say he was a phony because of all the false boasting he did to promote his career."

"Such as?"

"Where do I start? Old White-Eyes was not a member of Teddy Roosevelt's Rough Riders, as he claimed. He did not fight in the Boer War or the Boxer Rebellion, as he claimed. He was never a cadet at the Virginia Military Academy, as he claimed. In fact, though he did enlist with the Army, he was listed as AWOL for the last half of his stint. He was a deserter! He fabricated all of his rootin' tootin' adventures as a Texas Ranger, a job he only held for a few measly months, and he was never wounded in gun battles with desperadoes." Ezra glanced over at Kenny, whose face was now crestfallen. "Shall I go on?"

Here, the sketchy patchwork of asphalt ran completely out, and the old truck rattled along on a rough gravel stretch.

"If all of this is so," Kenny retorted in dispute, "then how do you explain all of his great success?"

"His success was based on the white man's folly, and it was the death of him," Ezra returned as they motored along the remote road. "Did you know that the object in the car that killed him was a suitcase full of money?" Ezra nodded vigorously to drive the point home. "Yessir, smacked from behind by an aluminum suitcase full of silver dollars. Broke his goddamn neck. How's *that* for a message from above—that is, if you believe in that sort of thing?"

Ezra glowered through another long silence.

"Why do you take such pleasure in tearing the man down, Ezra?" asked Kenny.

The Apache's obsidian eyes flashed. "I only wish to make the point that the white man's heroes are false and short-lived. They are quickly forgotten, and certainly undeserving of an Indian's admiration."

"I harbor no ill feelings for the white man, or his heroes," said Kenny, "but I know that the Apache people are renowned for their undying hatred."

"You have no standing to judge what is in the Apache heart," Ezra snapped. "But even the Pima people have righteous cause for a vendetta against the whites. You are too young to remember the great fertility of the Pima fields in the river bottoms when the Gila ran free. The wealth of crops that your forefathers, the Akimel O'odham, brought forth from the floodplains was plentiful enough to feed all the people of the entire Sonoran region—Indian, Mexican, and Anglo alike. The Gila lowland was the breadbasket of the Southwest, and your people were good stewards of it."

"I have heard the stories of the plentiful harvests," Kenny muttered sheepishly. "I thought they were wildly exaggerated."

"Understated is more likely," growled Ezra. "But that was before the Anglos came with their paper claims and diverted the Gila to their fields upriver. They turned your fertile lands into desert, and your abundance into poverty within a matter of just a few years. You still call yourselves 'The River People.' So where's your river? It's a bad joke!"

"I don't doubt the truth in what you say, Ezra, but that does not cause me to resent Tom Mix," said Kenny. "And for someone who clings to so much hatred for the white man, you have no trouble speaking like one."

"I have walked the face of this earth for many years, Kenny. I am many years your elder, my friend, and I have learned much in those years. One of the most vital things I have learned from the white man is his language and its power. It is with his language that he dominates."

"I don't understand."

"Then let me put it this way. When the Spanish brought horses to our land, did we survive by fighting them on foot?"

"No, I guess not."

"Of course we didn't. We took his flea-bitten nags and bred faster and more agile ponies. We developed riding skills that would have put the Cossacks to shame."

"I have heard that."

"And when the white-eyes came with rifles, did we defend ourselves with bow and arrow?"

"No, I suppose not."

"Not those who survived. We took their weapons and turned those instruments of death against them. Our marksmen were among the best in the world."

Kenny rubbed his temple as if this propaganda was hurting his head. "If the red man was so superior in so many ways, how did we come so low?" he asked.

"A fair question, Kenny," the old Apache sighed, "because there is no doubt that our warriors were peerless fighters. Consider the battle at the Little Bighorn River."

"Yes, the Lakota were a fierce people. I have heard the stories."

"But there were two causes that defeated us," Ezra observed with narrowing eyes. "First, we were overwhelmed by the sheer numbers. There was no possible defense against the flood of white faces from the East. But the other, and perhaps more devastating, cause for our eventual domination was the white man's cunning use of his sophisticated language system. They beat us down with words and papers."

"How is that possible?"

"We were defeated with false promises, lies, and secrets. Consider how they took the Gila River away from your people without so much as a shot fired. They took it with words."

"Then you are saying that the English tongue is superior to the Native American?"

"Not superior—but more devious. They have words for things that our people don't even have thoughts about," Ezra growled. "That is why I have devoted myself to mastering the English language—to arm myself with my enemy's weapon, just as we did with the horse and rifle."

"You do speak very well, Ezra," Kenny conceded. "Did you go to the white man's college?

"For a little while, but I developed most of my skills from reading books and watching television."

"Watching television . . . that is amazing," Kenny murmured. "So was it the television that taught you to hate Tom Mix so much?"

"To some extent, yes. His movies were the forerunners of all the crappy TV westerns, like Hopalong Cassidy and Gene Autry. The myth of the celluloid cowboys only served to perpetuate the white man's disrespect for the native people. When the Anglo whelps play 'cowboys and Indians,' who do you think the bad guys are?"

Kenny affirmed the obvious answer with his silence.

"And where do you suppose that sentiment comes from?" Ezra demanded, rhetorically.

The two rode on in silence for nearly ten minutes. The truck made another right turn and headed north.

"You may be right," Kenny conceded at length. "Perhaps the Pinal Pioneer Parkway is not the best location for an Indian's roadside business."

"We're coming up on Sacaton," said Ezra. "Where's your place?"

"Turn left at the crossroads just ahead."

"Kenny, let me give you two pieces of advice before we part company," offered Ezra. "One, give up on that deserted old byway and move your enterprise over to a roadside rest stop off the new Interstate 10. The new construction was recently completed, and the traffic is heavy. Also, there's the benefit of fewer dust devils, not to mention that plenty of tourists will use it to make better time, and for its historic character."

"What historic character?"

"It's the old Butterfield Stage route, of course—that ridiculous, mule-drawn rattletrap that the Mescalero Apache attacked on a regular basis in a prouder day."

"Ah yes, of course—the Butterfield Stage. I had almost forgotten," Kenny nodded. "Our 'River People' sold food to them, and the Apache raided them. By the way, this is my house up here on the right."

Ezra pulled the truck over and stopped in front of a dilapidated adobe shack. An overfed mongrel approached the weather-beaten picket fence and wagged a stub tail at the sight of Kenny in the truck.

"What is the other piece of advice?" asked Kenny.

"Only to stop believing what you read in the white man's newspapers. Men who write for the press put things down as they *imagine* them to be, not as they really are. But don't stop reading them. They improve your English, and they advertise the best buys on groceries."

Kenny nodded at the simple logic in this. He felt convinced now that he had based the location of his roadside business on a withered myth. He reached into the gunnysack on his lap and produced a plain copper bracelet.

"Please allow me to repay you for your kindness in driving me home."

"No, thank you," Ezra waved him off. "Even though your Pima craftsmanship is inferior to the Apache, that piece has much more value than the cost of my gas."

"Perhaps, but it is what I have to offer."

"Then offer this instead: give me your word that you will take my advice. The simple satisfaction that you will prosper from it will be payment enough."

"I had planned on it anyway," said Kenny as he opened the passenger door and stepped onto the running board and into the roadway. "You make a pretty good argument," he said through the open window.

"Good," said Ezra with satisfied finality. "You won't be sorry. I'm convinced you'll make a killing. By the way, give my best to that Papago wife of yours. I may just drop in on you two someday." He gave the thumbs-up, then looped around and accelerated away.

"All things are possible," Kenny repeated.

———————

Ezra was parked back at the bus stop intersection within a quarter hours' time. He snatched up the black velour throw that he'd purloined just an hour before from behind the seat back and shook it out in the breathless air before spreading it on the gravel clearing in front of the ramada. From a large burlap sack that had ridden in the bed of the truck he produced a profusion of precious items and meticulously placed them in a symmetrical arrangement across the throw—silver conchos laced into belts with tinted black rawhide; finely crafted silver bracelets curved to simulate the horns of mountain sheep; signature Apache tear-drop and delicate loop earrings spangled with onyx gems; peridot rings engraved with primitive animal glyphs; braided silver necklaces tethering flawless centerpieces of turquoise or tiger-eye quartz; and bulky silver belt buckles inlaid with geometrically elaborate matrices of turquoise, obsidian, and coral. Ezra worked until the big throw was filled with what appeared to be a year's worth of work for at least a dozen skilled artisans.

He was just completing the quick-and-dirty assembly of a many-armed wooden stand, a framework evidently designed for the draping display of loom products, when a creeping southbound motorist pulled onto the shoulder and rolled to a dustless stop. It was a two-tone blue 1960 Chevy BelAir with Indiana plates. The passenger-side window cranked down and a pasty-faced elderly lady opened her mouth to speak when her husband shouted loudly from the driver's seat to Ezra, startling his wife from a questioning expression into one of near heart failure.

"Say, chief, can you direct us to the Tom Mix memorial?"

Ezra had experienced many tourists afflicted with the curious notion that sheer volume might be enough to breech a perceived language barrier.

"Of course," Ezra grinned as he approached the car. "It's about five miles further up the road," he said, pointing south. "There's a wash at milepost 115. The memorial stands on the far side of the wash, just off the eastern shoulder of the road."

"What did I tell you?" the woman clucked at the driver. "So, what's a wash?" she asked innocently. "We're from back East," she explained, as if they were interplanetary travelers announcing their celestial visit to a Martian local.

"A gully," Ezra translated. "It's called Tom Mix Wash because that's where he met his untimely death." He gazed upward wistfully and muttered: "A real tragedy for all of us Western folk."

"Well, we're old fans of the Cowboy King, you know," stated the man quite sturdily. "Come to pay our respects."

"Is that so? Well, in that case, I should show you my genuine replica of the belt buckle he wore in *Destry Rides Again*. I'm sure you'll recognize it. What better way to commemorate the Cowboy King, right?"

"Oh, I don't—"

"Look, Don," the old woman interrupted, "the sign says *authentic* Indian jewelry." Then she whispered: "You know that Indians *can't lie*, don't you, Don? It's part of their *code*."

She pointed at the makeshift sign that Ezra had propped in the back of the pickup.

"You're absolutely right, ma'am," Ezra agreed. "All of my merchandise is hand-crafted by local Apache artisans, guaranteed genuine."

"Maybe he has some Indian blankets, Don."

"Well, maybe we could . . ."

"Do you have any Indian blankets?" she begged. "I can't go back home without an Indian blanket or at least a throw rug!"

Ezra smiled. "You're in luck, ma'am. I was just getting my loom goods out for display."

Both doors popped open at once and the two aging tourists began their perusal of Ezra's wares.

"Maybe you can show me which belt buckle was Tom's," said Don.

"Of course," Ezra grinned, as he directed the wary old Hoosier to the buckle department on the throw. "By the way, sir, did you know that Tom Mix was a pallbearer at Wyatt Earp's funeral?"

"The hell, you say?"

"It's a historical fact," Ezra assured, as he noted the slowing approach of another car, this one with Nebraska plates. "Yessir, old Tom was a true hero of the Old West, if there ever was one."

Cock o' the Walk

It wasn't all intuition that told Curtis that the string of uneventful days and nights was too good to last. Truly, it was more common sense than anything that told him this fragile hope for consistency would never hold for long—not at Fort Grant.

Curtis had managed to maintain his regular exercise regimen in spite of a couple of nearly sleepless nights early in the week, and the routine pursuit of an ordered program aided the boy in putting Monday's and Tuesday's mysterious events in a rational perspective. Perhaps the most calming influence was the conspicuous two-day disappearance of Randy in any of his daily activities. The strange boy's absence played the key role in Curtis's regaining a firm grasp on reality. He was back to being a loner, and liking it.

In fact, the only item that deviated from normal in his usual routine was the waiting stage that usually preceded his use of the barbells during the "Physical Education" period. This was because the four roosters to whom he deferred "first turn" were involved instead with some strange sort of gymnastic activity on the infield of the parade ground during the entire PE period, morning and afternoon, every day since Monday.

All week long, Curtis watched with curiosity between his sets of military presses as several standout roosters repeatedly attempted to mount each other, kneeling in succession atop their cohorts in diminishing tiers. The base layer of boys consisted of the same four roosters who usually worked out on the barbells ahead of Curtis, plus one huge blond-haired boy kneeling at center. Then three bigger-than-average boys kneeled upon the lower boys' backs, while two rather wiry boys scrambled to a precarious perch near the top.

The eleventh boy was the top rooster in several respects. Curtis recognized him as the boy who'd cut to the front of the mess hall line several weeks before. He was evidently the leader and the architect of this doubtful attempt at acrobatics. From the way he barked orders at the others and rotated position assignments, it seemed that he wielded some serious measure of authority over the rest of the troop.

Curtis noted with amusement that there appeared to be no logic or method to his constant changing of positions. It was more like random experimentation, and no matter how this rooster-boss arranged the lineup, one tier or another would invariably collapse before he could finish his bound to the top.

At first attempts, this chief cock would cackle loudly in a peculiar falsetto laugh at the jumbled mass of writhing bodies as he bowled them over with his onrushing vaults. But as the week progressed, it became apparent from his tone that his amusement was waning.

"Get your candy-asses off the ground and try again," he'd shout. "You worthless slugs really bug me. You're enough to fuck up a wet dream. Can you tell I'm gettin' real bent outta shape?"

Today, after a last attempt that netted a particularly early collapse, the others complained that they were tired and thirsty.

"All right, ladies," he groused, "take five for the drinking fountain, and get your sorry asses back out here pronto; the clock's ticking and the PE period is almost shot."

Curtis studied this rooster-boss with some interest. He was around six feet tall and broad-shouldered with a slightly sunburned glow, apparently owing to his light complexion. A seriously pronounced overbite forced his upper front teeth to rest more or less permanently on his lower lip. Curtis imagined him to be the eldest of the roosters—a heavy shadow around the chin, cheeks, and upper lip indicated a maturity that other boys were just approaching. He wore a Los Angeles Dodgers baseball cap, and a valance of shaggy blond, near-white hair spilled out from around the bottom rim. The other boys parted as he passed, and the last thirsty rooster to suck the stream of water from the fountain instantly yielded the bubbler to the approaching leader. The air of authority that surrounded this man-boy was almost palpable.

Curtis caught himself staring and averted his eyes when he noticed that the other boys were glancing his way, but too late. He thought he heard his name muttered among the chatter at the fountain, and in a moment the leader was standing before him, sizing him up as he finished a set of military presses.

"That's quite the pile of iron you're pumping there, dad," he smiled as Curtis completed a tenth repetition and planted the bar back on the ground. The fabricated grin exposed the overbite further, giving the boy's face an awful rodent-like appearance.

"I add weight on the last set," said Curtis, breathing hard. "Tears the muscle down."

"The buzz from over there tells me you're pretty damn strong for a young cat. That so?"

Curtis simply shrugged his shoulders, modestly.

"Yeah, they also tell me you're quite the loner."

"I keep pretty much to myself. Seems like the best way to stay out of trouble around here."

"Yeah, that's cool, up to now; but I think it's high time you got down with our crazy acrobatics team, man. We could use a bit more muscle on the third tier of our pyramid."

"Thanks, but I don't think so," Curtis said. "I need to keep after my trainin'—gymnastics is not my thing."

"Well this *is* training of the best sort, dad."

"My arms are pretty rubbery right now from liftin'—I don't think I'd do you much good. Besides, the PE period ends in a minute or two."

"True enough. You should join us, then, at the start of the afternoon period; you'll be fresh."

"I don't know . . ."

"Listen, kid," the older boy snarled now, clearly losing the polite façade, "this is not an invitation, dig? It's a fucking *order*!"

Curtis spat a stream onto the ground in front of him. "Funniest damn thing," he growled low, as he wiped the dribble from his bottom lip, "but I gave up on takin' orders the day my daddy died."

The older boy stared icily for a moment, and Curtis returned the glare in kind.

The white boy broke the silence first: "You don't know me, kid, so maybe you should ask around before you take a wrong turn down the road of no return. So listen up, boy, I'm going to give you another chance. Three o'clock . . . parade ground. Be there, or be square." Then he turned his back to walk away.

"Don't hold your breath," Curtis called out.

"I won't," the other boy called over his shoulder, "but I may hold yours!"

Someone just behind Curtis whistled low and spoke in sotto voce.

"Oh man, that last comment was pure poison."

Curtis knew it was Randall Kartchner even before he turned around.

"Mine or his?"

"Both."

"What does that mean?"

"Well," Randy explained, "you would have to know a lot more about your newfound enemy's background, but most particularly what his crime was."

"Okay, so who is he, and what is he in here for?"

"His name is Harvey Huish," Randy replied, "and he was tried and convicted two years ago for squeezing the life out of one on his wrestling teammates. Throttled the kid with his bare hands for putting the moves on his girlfriend, they say."

"Yeah, *right*," Curtis scoffed. "Give me a break. This place is for small-time troublemakers, not killers."

"That's another thing you wouldn't know about Harvey. He comes from a very old and very wealthy family in Tucson. His father managed to get his charge reduced to accidental homicide so he wouldn't have to do hard time."

"Nobody has connections like that," countered Curtis.

"Pinky Huish does," said Randy. "He's a big-time developer all over the Southwest. You've probably read about him and all of his shady dealings in the newspaper."

"Yeah, like I spend my days with my nose buried in the *Sun Valley Tribune*." Curtis rolled his eyes skeptically. "So how is it that you know so much about this Harvey guy? And while we're at it, tell me how it is that you disappear for so long and then pop up whenever and wherever you please. What's goin' on with that?"

"Simple answer to both questions: I'm a trustee. I work as a clerk in the headmaster's office, so I'm not required to attend classes or participate in the rest of the routine either. I mean, the stuff they teach here is way below my intellectual level anyway. It would be a waste of everyone's time."

Curtis just blinked and kicked at the parade-ground gravel.

"Explains a lot, doesn't it?" Randy continued. "I have access to all the inmates' files and I spend a lot of my free time in the archives at the library. As I said before, you'd be surprised at what I know—even what I know about you!"

"And just what is it you think you know about me?"

"I know that you're in here for burglary and attempted arson." The boy hesitated before he continued. "I believe the burglary part, maybe, but you're no firebug. If I had to guess, I'd say you were framed, isn't that right?"

Curtis mumbled something indiscernible. Then in a louder tone: "So what you say about this Harvey Huish is true—he's a killer?"

"Yeah, and there's more."

"I thought there might be."

"You wanna hear?"

Curtis gulped and nodded, but at that second, the buzzer signaling the end of the morning PE period sounded.

"I'll meet you at midday meal, Curtis. There's a lot more that you need to know."

Curtis started to trudge dejectedly toward the classroom building.

"By the way," he called back, "thanks, kid."

"For what?"

"For cluin' me in."

"Don't mention it. You can thank me by calling me by my proper name."

"What is it?"

"The name's Randy, damn it!"

"Randy Dammit? Now that's a helluva strange name, Mr. Dammit."

115

chewing the fat

" **C**an I interrupt you for a moment, Will? I have some news that I suspect will be welcome, and I want to deliver it in person."

It was Betty Wood on the intercom. Curiously, the tone was even a tad more ebullient than her usual cheery professional voice.

"Sure thing, Betty," Will Farnsworth replied. "I could use a break from all this goddamn drudgery. Come on over."

It had been more than a year since the young attorney's first encounter with Harvey Huish, and the ensuing bitter exchange between him and the very astute paralegal had long since been smoothed over by a series of close collaborations that seemed to net consistently positive results for the two of them. Betty proved to be a valuable ally and confidante in his dark dealings with his sole client, the teenage terror of Fort Grant, and Will had eventually come to realize how fortunate he was to have this highly proficient friend after all.

She appeared presently at his glass door attired in her usual professional best—a form-fitting gray cashmere sweater that emphasized an ample bosom, snug black calf-length skirt, and classic black three-inch heels. The somber neutral colors only served to accentuate the stunning radiance of her auburn hair. Will always figured that the firm must have done a nationwide search to find such a combination of intelligence and allure. She mischievously concealed something with one hand behind her back as she tapped the glass with the claw-like fingernail of the other. Will rolled his eyes at the exaggerated tease and gestured for her to come in.

"This may be a mixed blessing," she proposed. She produced a manila file folder and fluttered it against her breasts as if fanning her throat before placing it on Will's desk. "But I think you'll agree that the pros far outweigh the cons."

"Oh my God—somebody murdered Harvey!" Will mock-guessed.

"When are you finally going to come to the realization that Harvey Huish is our meal ticket, Will?" she sighed as she sat with her legs crossed on the sofa opposite him.

"I guess when Little Lucifer stops tormenting me, Betty. But hey, let's not get off on a tangent. What's in the file?"

"Nothing quite as earthshaking as Harvey's untimely demise, I'm afraid—but something fairly salacious, nevertheless. Of course, you may prefer to read it yourself direct from the file."

"Stop teasing, Betty. You know I want you to sum it up for me. What's going on?"

"Just a little break from the monotony—a criminal defense case that Stephen wants you to cover for him." Her green eyes flashed and she spoke excitedly. "And yes, it *is* a homicide."

"Oh my, that does sound promising. So please, dear lady, give me the juicy details."

"Okay," she started, barely concealing the delight in her role as the narrator, "the murder took place on the Gila River reservation, so, as you know, it falls under the jurisdiction of the federal district court."

"Hold it right there, Betty. First, who is the defendant, and what is he charged with?"

"He's a Pima Indian—somewhat low on the totem pole, if you'll excuse the witticism—one who allegedly murdered his wife in their little hovel on the rez."

"Hmm—sounds exceptionally unexceptional. Tell me, just what is Stephen's interest in this alleged homicide—is it simply a pro bono case?"

"Not exactly. You see, about a year ago Stephen put the bug in Pinky Huish's ear that there is a legal loophole in the sovereign status of Indian land that might someday allow for legal gaming—casinos—on Indian reservations. Since then Pinky has very cunningly developed relationships with the chairmen of various tribes. One of those chiefs, Peter Mendoza of the Akimel O'odham tribe, has grown particularly close to

Pinky through a number of construction projects on the Gila rez that they have collaborated on over the past several years."

"Wow, I gotta hand it to Pinky. He's got his little finger in every pie—even pies that don't exist yet."

"Oh my, you have no idea yet how involved and how powerful the Huish family is, Will. It's positively staggering."

"Okay, I take your word for it. But why did the old man single me out for this? I thought I was supposed to focus my sole attention on the junior prince of darkness."

"As I said, this case falls under the federal jurisdiction. Stephen thinks that your background in criminal law and procedure makes you best suited for this particular one. Besides," she added, "I think he wants to see how you handle yourself in a courtroom setting before you present Harvey's case."

"All right, enough on venue. Just give me the facts, ma'am," Will demanded in his best Joe Friday voice.

"Okay, it seems that this very lowly member of the Pima community allegedly murdered his much younger Papago wife in a very grisly manner."

"What do you mean by that?"

"I mean, she was thirty-three to his fifty-five, and from a different but somewhat allied tribe."

"Okay, I know what you're doing and it's wearing thin. Stop teasing."

"I want you to digest the appetizer before I get to the meat. You know I love to tease."

"Cut to the chase, Betty. What do you mean by 'a very grisly manner,' huh?"

"Let me ask you first—what did you have for breakfast?"

"Huevos rancheros. What the hell does that have to do with anything?"

"Well, hold on to your huevos, mister, because this gets pretty nauseating."

"Jesus, what do you want, a goddamn drum roll, Betty? C'mon—spit it out!"

"Okay, okay—I'm getting there. Keep your shirt on." She lowered her voice now, like a big sister easing into a ghost story for the younger kids.

"Apparently this Pima guy is really a depraved character. The coroner said she bled to death from a gaping throat wound."

Will remained in silent expectation for a moment. "That's it? He cut her throat? I mean, that's pretty ghastly, but really not exactly—"

"No, that's not all." Betty opened the file, pulled one eight-by-ten glossy black-and-white photograph from the folder, and placed it carefully on the desk so that the image was vertically correct from Will's perspective. He grimaced, took in a sharp breath, and nearly recoiled.

"My god, Betty! What the hell is that?"

"That's the coroner's photo of a middle-aged Papago woman with about a pound of flesh missing from her throat—her esophagus, her trachea, and both carotid arteries, torn from the gullet like a slaughtered animal."

Will shuddered but could not avert his eyes from the decidedly grisly photo. "How the hell . . . ?" he managed to gasp.

"Oh, it gets worse. Take a look at this." She laid another photo down on the desktop in front of him. Again, he shuddered as he imagined the obvious connection to the first photo. It depicted a shirtless, rather portly Indian man, expressionless, with what was obviously fresh blood running from his mouth and dripping from his chin. A pair of distantly focused eyes signaled a vacancy sign—no soul in the house.

"Sonofabitch!"

"The tribal cops went to their house when she failed to show up for work yesterday morning. They found them both on the kitchen floor in this bizarre sort of embrace, his mouth against her throat, her blood smeared all over his face. As shocking as it is, the tribal police came to the obvious conclusion—he chewed her throat out, Will! Can you believe it? He ate her goddamn throat out!"

"Ah, Christ, Betty—that *is* pretty nauseating. Hard to imagine that any human could sink that low. Strange, though, I haven't seen anything in the papers about it—have you?"

"And that's the whole reason behind our participation in this gruesome little episode. Pinky Huish and Peter Mendoza want to keep a lid on this incident, if at all possible. If the newsboys get wind of this story, they're bound to give it the front-page treatment. Scandal sells papers, but it's bad

PR for the tribe. Mr. and Mrs. Arizona out in Sun City will surely resurrect the notion that those primitive people out there on the rez are all just bloodthirsty cannibals, after all. It'll be a serious setback to the kind of community relations that Pinky is trying to develop with the Indians."

"So, what are we supposed to do?"

"Well, this guy's obviously a real nutjob in the first place. We just need to convince the district court judge that he's not fit to stand trial."

"Insanity defense? That's a pretty tall order."

"Not when the fix is already in with the prosecutor."

"Pinky bought off a federal prosecutor?"

"Went to law school on a Huish Foundation scholarship," Betty smiled slyly.

"Jesus, is there anything Pinky can't do?"

"Couldn't keep his kid out of reform school."

"A stint in a country-club reform school is a pretty sweet outcome from a DA's wet-dream of a murder case," Will retorted. "And don't forget, he's about to skate away from that confinement shortly."

"You've got something up your sleeve, don't you? I don't know why you won't share it."

"Let's just get back to the matter at hand. So, I'm not expected to give our native carnivore the best defense possible—am I getting this right?"

"Pretty much, Will. At the arraignment, you will ask to approach the bench and in a low voice request that your client be detained in the maximum security ward of the state hospital until he can be found fit to contribute to his defense. The prosecutor, having been apprised of the evidence to support your request, will concur. The judge will have no other recourse than to concede, and your loony tunes Indian will be quietly carted off to the funny farm. End of story."

"Pretty slick, I must admit. So, Betty, where is my 'loony tunes' client being held right now?"

"Pima County Max—in solitary. The tribal police held him in their tank initially, but he was transferred pretty quickly when the jurisdiction issue arose."

"Who did the initial questioning?" Will mumbled as he leafed through some pages in the file.

"The tribal cops did an interrogation, if you could call it that."

"Meaning?"

"Meaning the monster apparently lost his voice. The state corrections shrink says he's been in a 'vegetative state' since the incident," said Betty. "Pretty convenient, if you ask me," she grumbled, "but it does help you make your case."

"Went into shock at the realization of what he did, I suppose," Will mused.

"Not hardly. You see, the tribal cops found a half-empty bottle of something on the kitchen table at the scene."

"White-man's fire water?"

"Even more potent. State analysis says it was some kind of elixir—extract of datura, mescal, and an essence of morning glory seed suspended in an unidentified liquor base."

"So, you're saying he went on some sort of drug-induced rampage?"

"That, and what I'm saying is that you can cite some physical evidence to show why the guy has suddenly become mentally incapacitated."

"From what you've told me so far, that shouldn't be too tough after all," Will asserted. "Sounds like he's definitely checked out of the reality hotel," he added as he continued to delve into the file. "Hey, Betty, it says in this forensics report that no teeth marks were found on the victim's throat. Isn't that odd?"

"They theorize that the tissue was torn, rather than chewed off."

"And it also says that none of her missing tissue was discovered at the scene. What do they 'theorize' on that?"

"The obvious and disgusting conclusion is that he ingested it."

"Did they bother to . . . ?"

"Yes, Will, they did pump his stomach," Betty answered in a slightly annoyed tone. "And no, there was no evidence of her tissue. The digestive process apparently took care of that."

"Any tissue caught in his teeth?"

"None that was immediately evident."

"So you're telling me that the contention that my client actually committed the homicide is completely based on circumstance."

"Listen, Will," Betty snapped, "don't you go Boy Scout on us. This is an open-and-shut case, and confinement in the state hospital up in Phoenix is the best possible result this creep could ever hope for. Culpability or lack thereof has nothing to do with our objective."

"Calm down, Betty. Don't you think I need to poke around a bit, even if just for appearance's sake? People really ought to see that I am doing due diligence for my client."

"I suppose so—just as long as you don't attract too much attention in the process. Remember, the main goal is to make this happen quickly and quietly."

"Don't you worry about that, my dear. I know who signs my checks. By the way, what name does our carnivorous client go by?"

Betty dug through the file, eyes landing on the criminal complaint.

"Kenny Armenta."

Cock-o'-Two

Curtis was admittedly troubled by this new dilemma of the roosters' attempts to draft him into the human pyramid plot. And he was particularly haunted by Harvey Huish's thinly veiled threat, given his newfound enemy's apparent proclivity for choking his adversaries to death. The dual predicaments—this, and the unresolved mystery of the bludgeoned girl—left the boy in a quandary, and his mind raced over all manner of possible scenarios during the class periods between morning PE and lunch.

When the buzzer sounded for midday meal, Curtis's head was spinning. He raced for the mess hall double-time to look for Randy. There was no sign of the boy, but he spotted a now-familiar Dodgers ball cap across the room. He cautiously took a tray of food and retired to a quiet corner, keeping his distance. He had nearly consumed his plate of pinto beans and tortilla when his pale comrade finally placed an empty tray across the table from him and sat down.

"Hey, Randy."

"Hey, Curtis."

"I thought maybe you ditched me again, man."

"Oh, so you finally figured out that playing the loner may not always see you through, huh?"

"Maybe I need a little backup on this one," Curtis admitted. "Anyway, you made it sound like there's a lot more to this whole story—is that right?"

"Yeah, Curtis, it comes down to this: you don't want to be any part of that human pyramid, no matter what else Harvey threatens you with."

"Why's that? Not that I want to anyway, but you make it sound so, I don't know, *criminal*."

"Because the human pyramid is part of a pretty stupid escape plot, and when it falls apart, you'll end up taking the fall for it. It's Harvey's moronic way of trying to get over the wall."

"Oh, isn't that great?" Curtis scoffed. "And I suppose I shouldn't ask how you know, but I'm sure *that* isn't written down in somebody's file."

"Not exactly, but sort of."

"What do you mean by *that*?"

"Well," Randy began, "I know from his file that Harvey's eighteenth birthday falls on the last Monday of April—April thirtieth, to be exact."

"So?"

"Don't interrupt—you'll disturb my train of thought."

Curtis rolled his eyes upward, but gestured with his hand for Randy to continue.

"In addition to that, the Huish family lawyer has extended his usually brief visits to over an hour lately."

Curtis just made a "hmmph" sound and shook his head.

"I also learned, from lots of eavesdropping in the administration office, that Harvey Huish has a court appearance scheduled the very day after his birthday. Are you following where this leads?"

"I'm not sure. Can you give me a hint?"

"No, I'm just going to tell you. I know it's a conclusion, but it's not a stretch. Harvey's dad's lawyers were putting together a special hearing for an early release. As a plan B, they're trying to put together a case to keep Harvey here in reform school for the remainder of his sentence rather than transfer him to state prison in Florence—hard time. Harvey isn't so sure they can win, because he knows—and I know—that either way, the headmaster won't commit to giving him a good behavior recommendation on his review."

"I get it now—Harvey's riggin' himself a backup plan to escape if the lawyers don't get him some kind of a deal!" Curtis exclaimed.

"Well, you got part of it," said Randy, "but you still lack a good deal of the information, and I don't know if there is time to get you to understand all of this completely."

"Well, start talkin', Randy, 'cause the lunch-hour period is almost over. I'm gonna have to face that bastard in a few hours, and I'm gonna need the whole story to know how to deal with him."

"Okay, Curtis, first of all, the escape isn't exactly a backup plan."

"No?"

"No, if Harvey trusts his daddy's lawyers and they don't come through, he goes straight to prison from there—no second chances to escape from a minimum-security facility like this. The escape plan is a choice that he has to make beforehand, and it sure looks like he's leaning in favor of a quick breakout."

"I thought you told me no one ever tries to escape from here because it's in the middle of nowhere," Curtis groaned.

"Of course these are exceptional circumstances, Curtis," Randy reminded him. "Harvey is the only convicted killer that was ever incarcerated here and, well . . ."

"Well what?"

"It's partly speculation on my part, but I have no doubt that he has outside help lined up. After all, no Fort Grant inmate before him ever had the resources that he does. My guess is that he has somebody on the outside who is going to meet him with a jeep in Bonita Springs in the wee hours of the morning on Monday, the first."

"Bonita Springs?"

"It's just a gas station and a café, about seven or eight miles south of here," said Randy, "but there's a network of mining and forest service roads just beyond there that a jeep could take clear to California without hitting a single paved highway anywhere."

"Good riddance," Curtis grinned. "I've only got to duck him for a few weeks, and I'm home free."

"No," Randy corrected. "That's not right."

"What do you mean?" Curtis demanded. "It seems pretty simple to me."

"I mean that Harvey Huish must never leave here—never."

"That's crazy talk, Randy. I swear, if I keep hangin' around with you, they're gonna cart me off to the loony bin! What makes you say he should never leave this place?"

"First, because he's a murderer. People who get away with murder tend to murder again. Do you want that on your conscience, Curtis?"

Curtis shrugged. "I suppose not," he muttered, "but what the hell has that got to do with *me*?"

"Just be quiet and listen! Now, second, and most importantly, it's because he is directly related to all of these strange hallucinations that you've had here recently."

"What do you mean by that, Randy? That's more loony tunes stuff. Oh shit, you got my head spinnin' again!"

The buzzer sounded to dismiss the midday meal, and Randy rose to leave.

"You sit your skinny ass back down here and do some more explainin'!" Curtis demanded.

"I can't, Curtis. I've got to go. Tell you what. I'll meet you back here in the mess hall at dinner. That's the best I can do under the circumstances. It's a good place to learn things beyond what's on the menu."

"Fine—and in the meantime, next PE period, I've got to deal with the Tucson strangler in a Dodgers ball cap who wants me to help him get over the wall. It's a stupid plan in the first place. He might just as well *pole vault* over the wall with his ego-dick. His odds would be better and he wouldn't need me or any of those other clowns to do it. Maybe I'll suggest it."

"Don't underestimate him just because of one stupid tactic," Randy advised. "He's pretty bright, really. Some people are just such egomaniacs they don't think they are capable of having a stupid idea."

"Oh that's just *great*!" Curtis whined. "So he's bigger *and* brighter than me. What am I supposed to do—hide for three weeks?"

"Just don't let him bait you into a confrontation—at least, not right now. Use your wits, you'll be fine." With that, Randy disappeared into the exiting crowd as before.

"Guess there's no time like the present," Curtis mused aloud to himself, "to try something different."

ᴍan in the ᴍaze

"**D**oesn't add up."

The three-word statement came across clearly and startlingly blunt. The young Pima officer made the unsolicited declaration in stark contrast to the mumbled *yes* and *no* responses to Will Farnsworth's prior questions regarding his assigned client's homicide case. Until now, Will had been more conscious of a certain item among Kenny Armenta's personal effects that were arrayed on the table before him—a curious bracelet with a set of concentric circles etched into its surface—than of the tribal cop's perfunctory replies. Will abruptly raised his eyes from the miniature notepad upon which he'd been scribbling random thoughts and sketching images evoked by the bracelet. He had been assuming from initial impressions that this interview would net him zip. Now he was riveted.

"What do you mean by that, officer?" Will studied the face of the native policeman sitting opposite him at a cedar picnic table in the outdoor lunch-break area of the Gila River Tribal Justice Center. It was as if he was seeing him for the first time; the brown visage was as stony as the young man's tone, but the narrowed coal-black eyes projected a flame suitable for cutting steel plate.

"You heard me."

Will had learned that Officer Eduardo Cruz had been the first tribal policeman to arrive at the scene of the murder, making the grisly discovery and, as the arresting officer, he was high on the lawyer's list of potential witnesses. He looked to be about Will's own age, but that is where the resemblance began and ended; and nowhere was the contrast more distinct than in the use of language. While the young attorney used words in purposed profusion, the Indian policeman offered them with the miserly reluctance of an etymological Scrooge McDuck. Yet the frank three-word statement of doubt spoke volumes, revealing more to Will than any of the long-winded dissertations he'd received from the various "experts" he'd interviewed previously.

"Sure, I heard you," Will conceded, trying a more good-natured tone. "And I know that's a phrase you cops always use when the facts don't support the conclusion. I've heard it dozens of times. But would you mind telling me, please, why or how it 'doesn't add up'? Because, I gotta tell you, man, I'm all ears."

A warm breeze teased the young Indian's long ebony hair as he glanced at Will's right ear and then his left, as if trying to determine whether the lawyer's ears were indeed outsized. Will found himself feeling the awkward sense of one who isn't quite certain if he is being mocked or not.

"Which?"

"Which what?"

"Why or how?" the officer growled impatiently.

"I'm not sure . . ."

"*Why* or *how* it doesn't add up. You asked to know why or how. Which do you want to hear?"

"Oh, um, either one—your choice, chief." Will cringed over letting the demeaning moniker slip, but it was too late to take it back.

"Okay, Perry Mason—first *how*," Officer Cruz grunted. Will winced at the well-aimed verbal payback. "Forensics guys said there were no human teeth marks on Primrose's throat. That's true. They say that's because he allegedly ripped her flesh with his teeth and swallowed the evidence."

"That's what they're telling me," Will muttered.

"What they're not telling you is that Kenny Armenta was a flabby-armed old jewelry-maker who wore dentures and ate very little meat as a custom."

"You mean he was a vegetarian?" Will began jotting again in his notebook.

"No, I mean what I just said. He ate very little meat, which was mostly because he said it gave him heartburn. He just didn't have the stomach for it, so he was pretty much a beans-and-frybread guy. That's how he got all roly-poly. But why do you focus on such small details that take away the attention from the point?"

"Which is?"

"Okay, I'll repeat it. Kenny Armenta was a weak old roly-poly guy who wore dentures and avoided eating meat. Does that sound to you like a man who could wrestle his younger, more agile loved one to the floor, rip her throat out with his teeth, and swallow a pound of human flesh?"

"No, I suppose not," Will admitted sheepishly. He was tempted to add "hard to swallow," but rightly judged that the facetious double entendre would be wasted or ill received. "I get your point. But listen, Ed—can I call you Ed? You sound like you know my client pretty well. Is that right?"

"That is right, but now we're getting into *why* when we're still talking about *how*. And no, you can call me Officer Cruz."

"Okay, sorry. Can you just keep going on *how*, please, officer?"

"Yes, if you're finished interrupting."

Will made a zipping of the lips gesture. Eduardo Cruz rolled his eyes and continued.

"There was that half-empty bottle of liquor sitting on Kenny's kitchen table when I arrived. That didn't add up either. Kenny and Primrose, neither one was a drinker. Sure, Kenny would drink a beer with you if you twisted his arm, and Primrose was known to have a glass of wine on special occasions, but the Armentas never kept alcohol in the house as a general rule."

"May I insert just one question, please?" Will begged as he continued to furiously scribble in the notepad.

"If you have to," Cruz allowed, begrudgingly.

"The state lab says that the liquor you cited was really some kind of narcotic elixir. Could that have possibly been some kind of native ceremonial sacrament they were taking?"

"*Pfff!* That's going to fit nicely into the *official* story, isn't it?"

"And is there a reason why it shouldn't?"

Cruz spat on the ground. It was the first fervent demonstration of his disdain for his inquisitor. "You fucking white-eyes and your ignorant notions about native people—you will never learn."

131

Will was taken aback by this unexpected flair of emotion. "I apologize if I somehow offended you, and I admit my ignorance," he conceded, mustering his best tone of contrition. "Please enlighten me so that I can give my client the best possible defense."

"Is that what you call it?"

"What do you mean by that?"

"Kenny and Primrose were both cradle Catholics," Cruz continued, ignoring Will's question. "That's how they met. Many of our people persist in the faith of the early missionaries. The Pima people have no shaman. These herbal drugs you speak of are of no use to us. The Navajo and Yaquis and some Apache may use them in some secret ceremonies, but the Gila River people have no interest in such things. Still, I'm sure the official story will play well with the wise men of the federal court. But it was the presence of that bottle and its contents that first led me to doubt that the Armentas were the only ones in that house at the time of the murder."

After a long silence, Will was the first to speak.

"Is that all there is to the *how*?" he asked, deliberately avoiding any development of Cruz's apparent theory.

"No. I haven't mentioned the dog. Kenny had a dog he named Bingo."

"That's original," Will sniggered. "What kind was it?"

"Heinz fifty-seven, as if that matters," Cruz sighed. "What does matter is that Bingo never strayed beyond the limits of Kenny's yard. He played and ate and slept in that yard for years. He was whelped there and as far as that dog was concerned, no world even existed outside the Armentas' picket fence. Kenny used to leave the gate open as a joke to show them both what a big pussy Bingo was. But when I got there, Bingo was gone. No mutt at the gate, wagging his stump tail as always. It was the first sign that something was very wrong."

"Okay, if that's all there is to *how*," Will ventured after another silence, "then can you get into *why*—that is, why it 'doesn't add up,' as you say."

"Sure—simple as this: what happened in that kitchen is unthinkable to everything that Kenny Armenta was."

"Can you expand on that a bit?"

"I suppose so. As I'm sure you gathered, I knew Kenny Armenta very well. He was my father's cousin. But more than that, he was a good friend to me. He taught me how to polish gemstones when I was a kid so I could trade them for spending money."

"I'm sure you had a very special relationship."

"Not really," the policeman countered.

"Sure sounds to me like—"

"What I'm saying is that for Kenny, that was not special. He was a friend to everyone who knew him—kind to everyone who met him. Maybe that was his undoing."

"What do you mean by that?"

"I mean that he was too trusting. He would let the devil himself into his house rather than doubt his sincerity."

"Do you believe that someone else committed the murder of his wife?"

"Someone or some *thing*—I don't know. What I do know is that he loved that woman more than he loved himself. And Kenny Armenta wouldn't swat a horsefly if it bit him, much less snuff out the light of his life. No, it is impossible to believe that he could commit this monstrosity."

"It's pretty hard to make a case for his innocence when he was found alive with the victim."

"Well, there's another obvious explanation that you, Mr. Mason, are ignoring—I think deliberately."

"And that is?"

"That the perpetrator had no interest in killing Kenny—that Primrose was his target victim. Perhaps Kenny witnessed the whole scene. Perhaps that is what took his mind away."

Will retrieved a visual memory of the photograph of the victim that Betty Wood had revealed to him. He shuddered physically as he recalled the image of butchery and imagined the brutal sort of evil that could perform such a horror. His deductive mind latched on to the fact that Primrose was a Papago living in a Pima household—that was the only quality that made her a standout from any other soul on the rez. But the Papago and the Pima were cousin tribes. A tribal vendetta made no sense. Moreover, a third-party theory without any evidence of such was quite a stretch.

"Forgive me for saying so, Officer Cruz, but those are a lot of *perhapses*."

"Perhaps so," Cruz sneered, "but then, you never met the man."

"Okay, so you say the man was a candidate for sainthood, and of course I take your word for it, sir, but the court will want a little something more than that to go on. Your testimony to his character will be helpful, but the earlier stuff will definitely shed some doubt on his guilt."

"That's a leap."

"Excuse me?"

"That's a leap—that you think I will testify to any of this in court."

"Well, of course I believe you'll testify. Don't you want to defend Kenny from prosecution?"

"Have you tried to question him yet?"

"No, but I have it scheduled for tomorrow."

"Don't even waste your time. You'd do better talking to an adobe brick. Kenny doesn't live there anymore. Whatever happened that night took him out of himself."

"That's what I've heard. So what's your point?"

"Just that it really doesn't much matter what they do with his shell; that's not Kenny anyway. And the tribal council is right to want to hide such an outrage from the general public. Better that the old guy goes quietly to the funny farm on Van Buren Street than to start an investigation and possibly leak everything to the scandal-hungry press. They'd be happy to paint us all as bloodthirsty savages and turn the clock back a century on the progress our community has gained."

"Then what about defending his integrity . . . his memory—do you want him to be remembered as the perpetrator of such unspeakable evil?"

Eduardo Cruz smiled wryly. "Like I said, Kenny had a gentle spirit; he was kind to everyone he met. There's not a single soul living on this reservation who believes Kenny did this horrible thing to his wife. We arrested him simply as a matter of procedure."

"Okay, if you have no intention of testifying to any of this, why are you disclosing it to me now, officer?" Will blurted, trying hard to conceal his growing frustration.

The long silence that ensued was not owing to the lack of an answer, but an opportunity for Will to ponder the question. At length, the young tribal officer revived the dying conversation with another avenue.

"I see that the man in the maze has caught your attention." Eduardo pointed to the sketch Will had rendered of the pattern on Kenny Armenta's bracelet.

"Oh, I was just doodling earlier," Will replied, seizing the opportunity to continue. "The image is interesting."

"I thought maybe you saw it on the door of my police car, or on the monument sign in front of the Justice Center."

"Now that you mention it, I thought there was a vague familiarity about it, but I couldn't quite put my finger on it."

"The man in the maze is our tribal emblem, but I'm sure it applies to all of humanity."

"The bewilderment, confusion, and disorientation of man," Will sighed. "Yes, the symbolism is quite transparent and the message is certainly universal."

"That is a pessimist's point of view," Cruz grunted rather indignantly. "We see it as a test, not a condemnation—an ordeal representing the journey through life and the choices we make along the way. Of course, the walls of the maze are the limitations and obstacles we encounter, but if we persist and make the right choices, we make our way out to the promise of the higher life."

"No offense, but that's a fairy tale scenario that is quite consistent with my own people's myths," Will burst out, agitated again. "Officer Cruz, I asked you a minute ago why you fed me all of that information but won't testify to it in court. I ask you again—why would you do that? Why would you give me information that I can't use in court?"

"To trouble you."

"Trouble me?"

"Yeah, to trouble you with the truth, Perry." Cruz flashed something vaguely resembling a smile. "Or maybe give you some direction. It's up to you what you do with it. Truth's a funny thing. Could be a favor—could be a curse."

"Well, thanks a helluvalot, chief."

"Hey, don't mention it. And say hello for me to Della Street."

135

Interlude (the second)

"Okay, Curtis—hold it right there!" I uttered without thinking. Curtis, along with the rest of the night, went dead silent. I had startled even myself with the bluntness of my outcry, but the exclamation was reflexive and irretrievable. Nevertheless, Curtis took my command at face value.

"Okay, do you want to tell me why in the hell you're stoppin' me here? You know, there's a certain momentum that goes along with story tellin', and right now you're like some little flea-bitten prairie dog holdin' up an outward-bound freight train."

"I'm truly sorry, Curtis. I didn't mean to make it sound so demanding. It really sort of jumped out of me. I just couldn't hold it back."

"You're not answerin' the question, Vince." The low, growling tone of voice signaled a certain pent-up anger. It had a threatening sort of James Cagney quality to it.

"W-well it's just that it feels like you're sort of . . . I don't know . . . maybe, um, *drifting*, just a little," I stammered.

"Drifting?"

I marveled that he could express such a full measure of resentment and incredulity with the inflection of a single word.

"Yeah, drifting," I continued, like a babbling moron. "You know, like you're getting away from the main story and going off into left field with all these other people who don't seem to have much to do with Fort Grant at all."

"You know, Vince," Curtis sighed, "I think maybe I pegged you wrong."

"How so?"

"Well, at first thought I had you figured for somebody who could take in all this twistin' and turnin' with an open mind for listenin' and not try to steer it onto a straight road. Was I wrong?"

"No, I don't think so. I just find it hard to follow who these strange characters are—Ezra and Kenny and Primrose—and what they have to do with the story. And just incidentally, I wonder how you could know their thoughts and conversations from miles away in the slammer." I blurted it all out, now feeling cornered but wishing I had never broached the issue to begin with.

"Isn't it pretty plain to you by now that this story is *so* much bigger than me?" The tone had now become somewhat patronizing.

"Yes, which brings up another problem: How in the hell are you ever going to finish over the next few hours?"

"Look, Vince, if you want me to continue, you're gonna have to let go a little more. Let the story go where it wants. Give up the straight pavement, the hard curbs, the in- and out-of-bound lines and the time zones. In other words, get your train off the rails. And speakin' of time," he continued, "what does your watch say?"

I looked at my Timex with the luminous dial. The hands read 11:15, but the ticking second hand seemed to be stuck at the thirty-second mark. The slender needle would sort of pulsate, but never advance.

"I don't know. My watch seems to have stopped."

"Okay, Vince, what do you say we go on with the story—do you think you can just let it flow? It's got a life all its own, you know."

I nodded dumbly. He must have seen the affirmative motion, even in the deep darkness.

"Good!" he exclaimed. "Because I really *need* to continue, for sure. And by the way," he added, "there's nothin' wrong with your watch. We just have all the time in the world now."

At that time in my life, I'd never encountered the literary term *the willing suspension of disbelief.* Nonetheless, that night Curtis taught me the meaning behind that concept. I resigned myself to listen with a more malleable mind, and the story flowed on as Curtis had so aptly described: "with a life of its own." Now I was more fully taken into the current of its profound enchantment.

An Epiphany

"Okay, *spook*, I get the picture," Harvey Huish declared. Curtis raised the bar, pressed it to his tightly pursed lips, then let it fall to the ground with a rattling clang. It was only a word, but it served the bully's purpose. Curtis now fought to stifle a rage that bubbled up from his belly like molten lava. He stepped toe-to-toe with his adversary now, staring upward into his steely-blue eyes.

"I told you to be out on the parade ground," Harvey snarled. "Are you dense, or what?"

"I chose not to." The simple statement had the ring of finality to it.

"Well, then it was a very unhip choice. Just ask any of these other roosters how cool it is to be in my gang. They got it made in the shade. Besides which," he continued, "who said there was a choice?"

"I chose not to," Curtis repeated.

"Well, this just goes to show how far wrong things have gone. I'm sure that you must've listened to your hero, *Martin Lucifer Coon*, on the tune box one time too many," Harvey taunted. "So many times, in fact, you're starting to believe that you and your kind actually are *free* to choose."

Harvey's loitering roosters were starting to gather around. The huge blond kid, who apparently was the top cock's second, wore a face of loathing that was particularly menacing. Curtis quelled the building anger at the racist insults, knowing that they were just part of a ploy to get him to throw the first blow. Harvey Huish was nearly a head taller and maybe twenty pounds heavier than Curtis. But Harvey lacked the chiseled definition of a trained athlete that Curtis had developed. In fact, Harvey had grown rather soft since his wrestling days back in high school—a by-product of the easy life he'd cultivated in the stir.

"But just look around you," Harvey continued to rant, "and those walls tell quite a different story. You're about as free as a caged animal—just a monkey in the zoo!"

"Oh, make no mistake; I *am* free," Curtis declared quietly, but coolly.

"What's that you said, boy?"

"I think you heard me right," Curtis shot back. "I'm about as free as I need to be. I make my choices and I pay the price, if need be. That's freedom, by my reckonin'."

"You are just about a mouthy young nigger," Harvey growled, "and your smart-ass tongue just cost you your last chance to join my ultra-cool gymnastics club."

"And as for that wall," Curtis continued as if he hadn't heard Harvey's epithet and his thinly veiled threat, "I go over it whenever I please." The seed of an idea had sprouted and Curtis was laying the groundwork for it in his own mind.

"That so? Well, you better start climbin' there, Sambo, 'cause the tigers are comin' to eat your hell-bound hotcakes alive!"

Curtis's skull felt like a pressure cooker on a high flame, but he kept his voice firm and even in his response.

"Maybe we ought t' see what you got without your candy-ass tigers. You got the stones to meet me somewhere—somewhere alone, that is, *Bucky*?"

A couple of the background roosters chuckled for a second until Harvey shot them a chilling glance.

"That can be arranged, spook," Harvey grinned. "But be careful what you wish for. If I ever get a grip on that black stovepipe throat of yours, we might be able to arrange a far-out visit to your real-gone dead daddy."

"You best be able to make it stick," Curtis returned, "or I might be payin' a visit to *yo mama!*"

With that, Harvey sent a left hook at Curtis's right temple. A strong brown hand shot up like a Nike missile, snapped onto the white wrist like a vise, and diverted the blow just short of contact. The enormous strength in the younger boy's grip surprised the enraged Huish boy.

"Southpaw, eh," Curtis bantered, "like that limp-wristed rubber-arm, Sandy Koufax. Hey, is that the best you got?"

The reflexive assault that followed from Harvey's right hand was expected and likewise intercepted by Curtis's left.

"Temper, temper," Curtis admonished, condescendingly. "Don't lose your cool over your crummy Dodgers."

He exhaled through his mouth, blowing little droplets of sweat that had gathered on his upper lip into the bigger boy's reddening face.

"I'll have your nappy fucking head for this!" Harvey fairly screamed.

"What's this all about?" old Marcus thundered as he stormed forward. "There will be no fighting here on my watch!" He brandished a leather sap. "You older boys head on out to the field and go about your business, or I'll knock some sense into y'all."

Curtis released the bigger boy's wrists with a slight push-off. Harvey grinned maniacally as he rubbed them and backed away.

"Watch us practice, Sambo," he sneered. "Every time that pyramid collapses, I'll be thinking of you!"

"And every time it does, I'll be laughin' my ass off at you!" Curtis returned.

"You just think you're playing with fire," the fair-haired boy hissed through clenched teeth, "but you're really flirting with death."

"Not too bright, Harvey," old Marcus called as the white boy and his cohorts retreated, "to be kickin' up dust around that house of cards you've built yourself."

"Thanks, Marcus," Curtis offered when the others had departed. "Thanks a lot."

"Don't mention it, son," the old dorm guard returned. "You just watch your back. That Harvey's more dangerous than a blind dog in a meat house, and he's had his hackles up lately. You need to know that I can't always be around."

The boy simply nodded a grateful confirmation as Marcus walked away, slapping his sap into his left palm.

Curtis completed his weight-training regimen, noting with a few glances yardward that the human pyramid did indeed continue to collapse with each of Harvey's attempts to mount it.

"Why does he go about it like that?" Curtis wondered aloud as he racked the weights in the equipment room. "Why doesn't he just—"

But his musings were interrupted by the rumbling approach of ten running boys. Were they coming for him, or was this just the usual stampede for a drink at the fountain? Curtis did not wait for the answer. It was time for his wind sprints in any case, and he bolted like a thoroughbred out of the gate on Derby Day for the distant wall. As he'd feared, the herd of running boys abruptly changed direction and made a beeline toward him. Curtis broke into a lightning sprint.

"Run, Sambo, run!" Harvey called from the back of the pack. "These tigers don't turn to butter!"

Curtis had a fairly long lead, and he was more fleet of foot than his pursuers. More to the point, he knew exactly where he was going as he directed his flight to the blind south quarter of the parade ground.

"There's nowhere to run to, Brillo-head," Harvey taunted. "You're trapped like a little black rat!"

Curtis approached a now-familiar section of the wall, and sprang upward to gain a foothold. He clambered up through the footholds and hoisted himself to the top of the wall. Standing up tall on the wide crest of the adobe parapet, he turned to face down his pursuers.

"C'mon boys," he grinned. "One at a time—and I'll stomp your stupid honky heads one at a time too!" He did a little dance up there and pointed at Harvey Huish, taunting him. "Especially you there, *Bucky*. Yeah, you. C'mon up; I'll bust your fuckin' hamster head!"

One of the boys started to reach for a handhold, but Harvey stopped him cold.

"Get away from that wall—get clear away, all of you!" he commanded. "Go back," he continued. "Go get a drink. I'll handle this from here."

"You're not quite as dumb as I thought, gerbil-jaws," Curtis gloated from his lofty perch. "But you're still as white and ugly as a toad's belly."

"Curtis, get down from there before somebody sees you," Harvey pleaded. "I'll leave you alone. Just get down—the guards will see you!"

"Gladly. It's just like I said—I go over this wall anytime I please. Now, keep a cool tool, suckah-fool!" Curtis sang out as he leaped to the ground *outside the wall.*

Harvey cursed and retreated from the rampart in a trot.

Now I'm really screwed! was Curtis's first thought as he recovered from his jump down. *What the hell was I thinking?*

He looked out on the vast desert that fell away from the low rise upon which the Fort was situated. The thickets of creosote brush, the patchy clusters of yucca, and the occasional stand of mesquite looked anything but welcoming when viewed through the shimmering waves of heated air.

Curtis could not help but notice the stark contrast in the desert from the last time he'd seen it almost two months ago. The color of the landscape had completely withered away in the premature heat. Running away from the Fort and from his trouble was a tempting prospect, but the oppressive heat of the day diminished that option. He would have to search more than a mile of adobe wall to see if he could find a good climbing place to get back over the daunting barrier.

"No reason to worry," a voice called from behind him.

Curtis whirled around and found himself face-to-face with Randy.

"Stop sneakin' up on me like that," Curtis shouted.

Randy grinned and continued. "It's easier to break back in. The plaster on the outside is full of cracks—no need to patch it, I guess."

"Makes sense," Curtis muttered. "But *hey*—what the hell are *you* doin' out here anyway?"

"Oh, I come out here a lot just to think. Speaking of which, that was some pretty fast thinking you just did back there!"

"Huh?"

"Yeah, in fact it was a small stroke of genius the way you showed that blue-eyed goon a way over the wall without his stupid pyramid. You must have had an *epiphany.* Now he'll probably leave you alone and concentrate on his new plan."

"Yeah, but now I gave him a sure way out—he'll escape unless I rat him out," said Curtis with some remorse.

"Trust me; it's much better this way."

"How's that?"

"Well, he won't need his *minions* anymore, for one thing—so you'll only have to steer clear of him," Randy concluded.

"And . . . ?"

"And this way we'll know exactly *where* he'll be coming over the wall on the night of his escape."

"I still don't have the whole score on all of this . . ."

"It's probably better that you don't have the complete picture. It'll all dawn on you some day. Right now, you just have to know your part."

"Right now, I just need to get back inside the wall before I'm missed."

"No hurry, Curtis," Randy assured. "First we need to take a little side journey."

"No fuckin' way," Curtis asserted. "I want to go back inside—now!"

"Why, because it's *fish Friday*?"

"No, because just the thought of a side trip with you scares me even more than the idea of a rumble with Harvey," Curtis retorted. "You're *spooky* as hell, Randy!"

"Listen, Curtis—I've done nothing but help you deal with a few strange events that are not any of my doing. There's nothing to fear with this little hike I'm proposing, and it will take less time than it would for you to find a way back over the wall without my help."

"You tell me where the footholds are right now, or I'll flatten your beak!"

"Right this way, Curtis," Randy chuckled at the empty threat. "It's only about a quarter mile southeast of here."

Curtis turned and reluctantly allowed Randy to lead him away from the wall, down a gravel path that wove its way in and out of the thorny brush.

"Take notice of your surroundings," Randy directed. "You'll need to find this way again from memory."

"Why?"

"All in good time."

At length, the path dropped into a sand and gravel wash where the going was slowed by the slippage in their strides. The beads of sweat collecting on Curtis's forehead started to trickle down his brow.

"I thought you said we were only going a quarter mile, you little Twinkie."

"Maybe a little farther than that," said Randy. "The desert is quite striking in the late springtime, don't you think?"

"Oh yeah—striking."

"No, I mean it—you should appreciate the flora and fauna that are indigenous to your surroundings," Randy admonished. "For instance, just look at that great saguaro off to the side there. Doesn't it look like a soldier saluting? Just look at the way the one arm is raised across the brow, while the other hangs down. It's uncanny!"

"Uncanny."

"And up ahead," Randy went on, "that century plant spire looks just like a great jousting lance."

"Uh-huh, right," grunted Curtis.

They continued up the sandy arroyo, and Randy commented again.

"Look, Curtis, the pads on this prickly pear are arranged so they look like just like a four-leaf clover, don't you think?"

"No!" Curtis snapped. "I think it looks like a goddamn cactus, that's what I think!"

"Try to use your imagination, Curtis, and note these landmarks well. They'll help you find your way later. Now, here's one that should get your attention," he noted, following another brief jaunt through the sand. "Does this look like a 'goddamn cactus' to you?" He pointed to a tall cluster of spiny branches.

"I don't know—why?" Curtis glowered.

"Because it's a *crucifixion thorn*, and I'd advise you to etch this one in your memory without fail."

"Okay, okay. I follow your drift!"

After several minutes' march through the wash, Randy climbed up the left bank and broke through a thick clump of tamarisk. A path rose before them and grew wider as they progressed until it dropped down into a curious clearing—a flat depression in the landscape about 150 yards in diameter—a tiny basin, devoid of any sort of indigenous brush or cactus.

"Can you remember how we got here, Curtis?" Randy inquired. "It's really important."

"I don't know—maybe. What the hell *is* this place, anyhow, Randy—and what are all of these stones?"

Curtis was referring to the dozens of small mounds surrounding them, each made up of a dozen or so smooth, round, softball-sized river rocks, possibly culled from the wash the pair had just departed. Each mound seemed to be equally spaced—about six feet in every direction—which created a certain stark, symmetrical grid effect. The barrenness of the very ground gave the individual mounds a visual emphasis that was almost surreal.

"It looks like some kind of rock garden," Curtis mused.

"Not hardly," Randy muttered. "It's a *cemetery*, Curtis!"

"What the hell do you mean, a cemetery?"

"Just that—a primitive graveyard . . . a place where they bury the dead."

Curtis glanced around himself. What Randy said seemed to fit the place. He began to swat what seemed to be an inordinate number of fat house flies that were now buzzing about his face.

"There . . . there must be over a hundred mounds here . . ."

"A hundred and forty-four to be exact," Randy interjected. "And there's a body—or at least a smattering of bones—under each and every mound, guaranteed."

"You counted them?" he wondered aloud as he waved the tiny winged harpies away from his nose.

"Nope—read about them in a history book," said Randy, who, curiously, did not seem to be bothered by the buzzing tormentors. "The mass burial took place in just a few hours—the cavalrymen worked frantically to keep ahead of the vultures." He outstretched his hands as if he were presenting the place to Curtis. "Don't you find it absolutely fascinating that nothing seems to grow here?"

Curtis shuddered. "*Fascinatin'* is not the word I was lookin' for."

"The soldiers originally dug the clay out of this site to make their adobe bricks when they were building the Fort. That's why it's hollowed out," Randy explained. "There's a natural drainage swale over at the south end, so it never holds water, even during the monsoon season. It became a perfect campsite for hundreds of Aravaipa and Pinal Apaches when they congregated here back in the 1870s . . . then," he went on, "it became a convenient gravesite after the incident."

Randy had been speaking with his back to Curtis, surveying the desolate bowl, but now he turned and addressed his friend with an

PATH OF THE HALF MOON

uncharacteristic gravity. The pale tone of his facial skin took on a ghastly gray in the direct sunlight.

"Does this place seem somehow *familiar*, Curtis?"

"How could it? I've never been here before."

"Oh, I don't know—sometimes first-time things seem familiar, you know?"

"What I know is that this place gives me the creeps, Randy," he breathed. "Can we just go now?"

"Sure, just keep track of landmarks as we retrace our steps. You'll need to figure out the way back here soon."

"I don't think so," Curtis stated flatly. "No way."

"Just pay attention to your surroundings right now," Randy directed. "You'll soon change your tune. And by the way," he added, as he made his way back up the path toward the sandy arroyo, "can you guess how long it will take you to get from this gravesite to the wall on a dead run? No pun intended, of course."

"What a comedian."

"Also, Curtis, do you know what the one good thing about being inside the walls of the Fort is?"

"Can't imagine."

"It's that the things out here on the outside can't get to you."

"Hard to believe that there's any goin's-on more wicked than the shit that goes on back there."

"Believe it, my friend. There is."

Best-Laid Plans

"Willy!"

Will broke from his reverie with a start. It was Jeb, the redneck guard, complete with his leering grin and annoying Southern drawl, who disturbed the lawyer's retrospective mental tour of fourteen months prior.

"Took you long enough to get out here," Will groused at the guard as he unfolded himself from the driver's seat of the jet-black Lincoln.

"Well, you're the one who's runnin' late, mister," Jeb returned.

"Yeah, well I stopped to help somebody who was broken down out there on the road," Will explained, as they marched to the anteroom for the "procedure."

After months as nothing more than a charade, "the procedure" had devolved into just a brazen tearing open of the package and seizing of the payoff behind the scant cover of the half-closed anteroom door. No pretenses of a pat down or a precautionary search were necessary anymore. Will was complicit, and a tacit understanding of confidence prevailed.

"You know, Jeb," Will mused aloud as the guard led him to the conference room, "I've wondered for quite some time now why you find it necessary to flaunt your impropriety."

"Huh?"

"You know, the way you openly collect your greasy little perk without taking any pains to conceal it from me. Are you proud of your part in this shameful arrangement?"

"Oh my! Don't we have the bold tongue today?" Jeb cackled.

Will did feel a certain self-righteousness that he'd been careful to restrain during these agonizing visits. He now felt some small bit of relief from the oppressive power of Harvey's grip, just in knowing that he now had a bargaining chip. But he cautioned himself about overplaying his hand just yet.

"No, I'm just sort of curious why you don't at least make some token effort to hide the transfer itself. I mean, you don't have to be so blatant about the very act."

"Well, now that you mention it," Jeb sniffed," I have been pretty sloppy. To tell the truth, I guess I just like seein' you squirm, Willy. I like the way it sticks you when you're completely powerless to do anything about it."

"But why do you hold me in such contempt? I haven't done anything to deserve it, and you don't even know me."

"Oh, but I know your *type*, all right. You young brainy ones with your big words and your fancy titles, all runnin' around in your fine clothes, thinkin' you're better than anyone else. Well, you're no better than me. Your money's as dirty as mine—there's just maybe more of it."

"Is that what you think—that I'm doing this for the money?"

"Why else? That and the fact that you're already in it up to your ears," Jeb chuckled.

It surprised Will at first blush that Jeb was apparently unaware of the supernatural grip Harvey had upon him and, more specifically, on his wife, Carol. But then, Jeb was just a bumpkin pawn in Harvey's insidious network of schemes. Will's false assumption that all of the boy's minions shared an otherworldly awareness was dissolving.

Of course! Why would this drooling moron know of the anguish that had tortured the young lawyer's every waking hour since that first meeting over a year ago? How desperately helpless he'd felt following these bi-weekly "conferences," at which—if he'd so much as allowed a note of disapproval of his young charge's plans to pass his lips or even a raised eyebrow—the consequences instantly adhered. The hollow expression that haunted his beloved's features upon his arrival at home, the terrified look that, once again, signaled her labored breathing, would inevitably manifest. None of these suffocating spells ever equaled the brush with death Carol had endured that evening last year at the emergency room. Even so, the lesser but frequent attacks drove the message home quite sufficiently. Under the influence of these constant reminders, suspension of disbelief came quickly, and it didn't take long to establish a causal connection, nor for the Pavlovian conditioning to become second nature. The young upstart lawyer soon became as obedient as a well-trained lapdog.

But this time would be different.

"Let me get this straight, Jeb—your sole motivation for facilitating the young prince's fountain of graft is strictly monetary?"

"Huh?"

"You're in this for the measly hundred bucks every two weeks?"

"You'd be amazed at what kind of entertainment the flash of a Franklin will buy a hound like me down in Nogales these days," Jeb said with a suggestive wink.

"*Nauseated* would be more the word, I think," Will muttered, half to himself. "But there's no other persuasion . . . no other *force* that holds sway over you?"

"Nope. I mean, what else would there be?"

"Nothing, I suppose, except maybe fear of discovery."

"I don't think discovery is very likely, given the circumstances."

Will fell silent at that, convinced of Jeb's ignorance about Harvey's paranormal powers. The two entered the familiar stucco building and quickly traversed the dimly lit corridor to the raised panel door where Will's sinister client waited as usual. This time would be different, though. He turned the brass knob and entered as Jeb continued on and disappeared at the end of the hall.

Harvey was sprawled across a chair, as always. His look, however, had evolved in those fourteen months. Back in August, he'd traded the greasy "duck's ass" hairstyle, à la Elvis, for the dry, flyaway surfer look that was currently sweeping up and down the West Coast. More recently, he had added a Los Angeles Dodgers ball cap as a topper. And while the blond bangs lent some camouflage for the Frankenstein forehead, the image transformation did little to blunt the continuing need for a major orthodontic undertaking.

"You're, like, late, daddy-o."

Unfortunately, the Edd "Kookie" Byrnes linguistic style hadn't gone the way of the DA yet.

"You're right, but before you go into a conniption fit, I want to share some good news with you," Will announced as he placed the expected package before Harvey in the usual way, like tribute to royalty.

"Share away, Willy-boy . . . and this better be real good vibes. You know how I hate to be kept coolin' my heels. *Carol hates it too*," he added with a wink.

Will opened his briefcase, removed a letter-sized envelope, and pushed it across the table toward the lounging juvenile. Harvey's curiosity overcame his sloth. He sat forward, seized the unsealed envelope, and removed the enclosed letter.

"It's a commendation letter of good behavior signed by the man himself!" the boy exclaimed in astonishment.

"Well, sort of," Will corrected. "Read the whole thing."

Scanning down the page, Harvey's eyes widened.

"It says there's a tape recorded deposition that he made here this past Monday." Now his eyes narrowed. "But what's with all these 'copy' stamps all over this letter? I don't get it—clue me in."

"That's because it's just a prototype—a model—of the genuine item," Will replied.

"So, like, where is the *genuine item* . . . and where is the tape?"

"Let me explain from the beginning," Will returned, seating himself at the table opposite his client. "As you know, Headmaster Whitcomb has, over my many visits to his office, expressed an obstinate reluctance to either appear or write on your behalf to the parole board. While he stubbornly insists that he is completely neutral on the matter, I suspect that he does not share in the affection that some of the other staffers here seem to have for you."

"His loss," the boy muttered. "So why the sudden change of heart?"

"More sleight of hand than change of heart, I'm afraid," the lawyer replied.

"What's that supposed to mean?"

"It means that I took it upon myself to enlist Jeb's aid in purloining an old requisition form with Whitcomb's signature. He also procured a few blank sheets of Fort Grant letterhead for my questionable purpose."

"Go on, Willy-boy. I'm startin' to dig it."

"Well, needless to say, it took me several weeks, a gallon of midnight oil, and a ream of onion-skin paper to get all of the eccentric flourishes right, but owing to my indefatigable effort, I now possess the dubious distinction of holding the first runner-up title in the competition for proficient execution of the good Lieutenant's rather singular signature—the man himself holding the top slot, of course."

A leering grin began to expose the protruding front teeth as Harvey faked some corny hand gestures that suggested a mockery of worship and idolatry.

"Man, I could listen to you beat your gums like that all day, daddy. Please continue, O multi-syllabled one."

"You'll notice there's a paragraph referring to a medical condition that will prevent him from giving a deposition in person when the board meets in Phoenix next month, and I got the Doc to sign off as a witness."

"It's even notarized and stamped," Harvey observed, admiringly, as he caressed the raised letters of the state seal on the paper.

"My paralegal, Betty," said Will. "She's a jewel."

"She sure is," the boy concurred. "Now, what's the skinny on this tape recording, Will?"

"That took even more creativity and effort on my part."

The young lawyer reached further into the depths of his brown leather briefcase and produced a miniature reel-to-reel tape recorder. Harvey could see that the take-up reel already bore a quarter of the tape. Will pressed the play button and the young inmate instantly recognized the voice of the Lieutenant, tinny as it was, issuing from a speaker the size of a fifty-cent piece. The commentary was apparently lifted from a line of questioning already in progress.

Oh, I would indeed say that Mr. Huish has comported himself quite admirably during his incarceration. In fact, he has been functioning as a trustee with us for the better part of this past year.

The audio then cut to static rather abruptly, and Will hit the stop button.

"It's just an excerpt from the original," he explained. "But what did you think?"

153

"I wonder how you got the old stick-up-his-butt to lie like a dog."

"Like I said, sleight of hand, not change of heart," said Will. "I surreptitiously recorded my conversations with the headmaster on several occasions to get a good sampling of the Lieutenant's typical intonations and verbal nuances. He has a rather unique way of speaking, you know—almost antiquated, I'd say."

"Yeah, I know what you mean. The square cobwebs really bug me. Get to the point."

"Don't be impatient—it's very relevant to the issue. You see, the more distinct a person's speech and verbal mannerisms, the easier they are to impersonate. I inquired into some of your father's Las Vegas contacts, and found a certain very famous entertainer, a voice impressionist, who was only too happy to accommodate a close personal friend of Pinky Huish—up to and including making a tape that was obviously of questionable purpose."

Harvey's lower jaw was now going slack in awe.

"And," Will continued, "let's give credit where it's due: I personally composed all of the questions and answers to the phony deposition, taking great care that our impersonator friend included all of the unique phrasing that the Lieutenant typically uses. You have to hear the whole tape to appreciate it. We went through a couple dozen takes before it was perfect. Whitcomb's own mother would swear that every word came out of her sweet boy's mouth, no question."

"I gotta hand it to ya, Willy—it's got the smell of brilliance to it," Harvey chuckled. "I always knew you were a hip cat from that first day you darkened my door. We just had to tease it out. Now, where's the tape and the original letter?"

"Nestled away for safe keeping," said Will. "You see, they're just the foundation of the scheme. They have to be submitted as part of a routine—a standard procedure—and at just the right juncture, so there's little time for scrutiny or follow-up. Timing is everything."

"Yeah, but this stuff is so convincing, why would they bother to even question it?"

"Well, that's the heart of the plan. We give them a solid submission up front, and we time it perfectly so the board doesn't have any reason to verify, or the time to do it, if they were so inclined. I think it will be a couple of weeks before I see my window of opportunity."

"That's good, 'cause I want to groove to the whole tape before you ship it off to the man," said Harvey.

"I think I've captured some of the best excerpts on this copy to keep you entertained."

"You're not diggin' what I'm layin' down for you, Willy. I want to hear the whole tape, the original tape."

The tone was taking a sour turn.

"Better that you didn't. You should appear genuinely surprised to hear it for the first time at the hearing."

"I'm a good actor. Now where is the tape?"

"I don't know."

"Don't be cute."

"No, I am in earnest. I've had it put away where even I don't have access to it."

Harvey scowled. "This is really uncool, Willy. Your chick's not gonna be jumpin' with joy for you when you get home tonight, and that's a fact, Jack."

This was the first time in fourteen months that Harvey had more than furtively alluded to the supernatural grip he held over the Farnsworth couple. He was obviously very pissed.

Will raised his hand in a cease-and-desist gesture. "Don't do anything until you've heard me out."

"Like I said before, this better be good."

Will stood and began to pace the floor before speaking.

"Professionally speaking, Harvey, I am charged with providing you with the best representation that the law allows. Given the circumstances, I think you'll admit that, with this plan, I have gone way beyond that professional obligation in my efforts to win you an early release."

"Given the whole scene," Harvey interjected, "you didn't have much choice."

"I'd hoped that you wouldn't see it that way, but I anticipated that you would, so I took some rather elaborate precautions to keep the keys to your freedom out of reach until we've modified our 'understanding.'"

"I don't like where this is going, Willy. Don't bring me down, man."

"I hired an outside law firm to retain the services of a private investigator who was instructed to stow the tape in a safety deposit box in any randomly selected city anywhere in the West. His generous final payment and that of the attorney is contingent on their following my explicit instructions down to the last detail."

"Which are?"

"The attorney is not to reveal to me who his detective is, but when a certain amount of time elapses, he will disclose a telephone number where I can reach him. Upon my calling the private eye, he will direct me to the location of the tape and surrender it to me. But there's a hitch."

The boy inmate shrugged his shoulders and raised his palms, indicating *what's the hitch?* in pantomime.

"The hitch is that if I try to contact him prematurely, or if I fail to contact him within a certain time frame, he is instructed to erase the tape and destroy the evidence. The payments for my clandestine agreements are held in trust and are to be released under the various conditions of completion. The best part of this is that McBride, Matthews, and Robson don't have the vaguest notion about this plan. It's all down to me."

"Not bad, dad, but I'm sure there's a flaw or a weak link in it somewhere . . ."

"Maybe, but I repeated the whole scheme using other parties for the letter. The letter refers to the tape, and the tape refers to the letter. Neither is valid without the other. The likelihood of circumventing the precautions with both sets of players is nearly nil."

Harvey Huish sat quietly for a time, wondering whether he detested or admired the cunning young lawyer. At length, he whistled low in approval.

"Very cool, Will," he conceded, tipping his Dodgers cap. "Now, not that I'll admit, at least not yet, that you're in any position to negotiate; let's just pretend for the moment that you are. Then, the big question pops: What is it you want from me, more bread?"

"No, and I don't want much. Just a little trinket that rightfully belongs to me anyway."

Harvey faked a bewildered expression, so Will made it clear.

"I want the Saint Thomas More medal back."

All the Way Home

Will Farnsworth was still pacing the floor, nervously.

He watched Harvey closely to gauge his reaction to the request. It seemed like wild speculation that the key to Harvey's brutal enchantment over Carol resided with the Saint Thomas More medallion. But regardless, there was no denying that the spell was all too real. The little fiend actually could reach out at will from this distant fortress right into their home seventy miles away and throttle her at any time, day or night. And once the irrefutable evidence of this forced Will to suspend his disbelief in the dark dilemma, it wasn't long before his mind reached beyond science and reason toward other realities in order to somehow grasp the supernatural principles that held him and his lovely wife hostage to this juvenile hoodlum from hell.

"Man," Harvey responded after a long silence, "I just can't figure out what the big deal is about this square little necklace. Must be somethin' really outta sight, eh dad?"

"Well, if it's no big deal to you," Will returned coyly, "then why don't you just return it as a token of your gratitude for my extraordinary effort?"

"Listen, Will, I'm sure a lot of what's been going on with me and you has been tough to swallow—no pun intended." The predictably unnerving falsetto laugh ensued.

Will stifled an urge to rail at the boy's trivialization of his misery.

"But you should trust me that my . . . um, *weirdness*, has more to do with this place than with your wife's little trinket."

"This *place*?" Will was interested, but guardedly so.

"Yeah, it's crazy, man, crazy. Like it's been spookin' me since I landed here. I mean, this place is like some kind of crossroads between our world and the twilight zone," the toothy fiend mused. "You know, when other players asked Babe Ruth how he hit the long ball, he just said, 'I don't know, man. I just hit it.' That's me. I don't know *how* it works; I just kind of go with the flow, can you dig it?"

"No, I can't," Will declared bluntly. "I don't know anything about spirits and spells and witchcraft and voodoo and portals to the nether-world. I just believe in what I see, and what I see is that you've seized some kind of metaphysical stranglehold over my wife, and it started when you snatched away her medallion. Now, as far-fetched as it sounds, it's the only connection you have with Carol, and I think it's the source of your power over her, so I want it back!"

The declaration was just short of an outburst, and Will wished he'd restrained himself better.

"Suppose I really bring you down and just say no?" Harvey sneered.

"Like I said before," Will reminded him, "if I so much as try to contact my attorneys before the designated time, they are instructed to have the document and the tape destroyed. That would be a shame."

Harvey rubbed an adolescent beard shadow thoughtfully. Will studied his features, trying to discern where this was taking him.

"You know, Willy, I hate it when somebody tries to put the squeeze on me."

"Sorry. I tried to keep it friendly."

"You have no idea how badly I want to get out of this place and get on with the rest of my life."

"And the last thing I want to do right now is sabotage your chances . . . but I will, if I have to. Please don't make me do that."

There was the slightest hint of a whine in Will's last phrase that made Harvey grin. "Wouldn't you think I'd retaliate and just finish her off? Or, better yet, maybe just keep bumpin' up the pressure until you complete the job?" The boy held up his right hand and slowly clenched it to illustrate his point. "Her throat is very tender, Willy—how would you say—*compliant*. It yields to the slightest pressure, a sort of *sweet surrender*. Hell, I think she's actually beginning to enjoy our little events, in a twisted sort of way. I know *I* am."

Beads of moisture broke out on Will's upper lip, but he kept his temper in check.

"Of course I thought about that," he sighed. "I've thought about it *a lot.*"

After several months of harboring the guilt of somehow unwittingly contributing to Carol's misery, of constantly carrying a chilling tightness around in his chest, something inside him shifted. The change was subtle at first, almost subconscious. He was growing weary of the helplessness that dogged him day and night. Intellectually, he knew that the source of all his pain resided with Harvey—that was clear. But the subliminal truth was that Carol was the boy's instrument. After all, it was Will who was the object of this ungodly persuasion dynamic, the suspended sword—*he* was the ultimate victim here, not she. It was *he* who was the slave and who suffered the suffocation in spirit each time she fell prey to the unseen grasp. In fact, after countless floggings, Will was beginning to blur the distinction between the teenage tormentor and the lovely scourge that the little bastard wielded.

From the moment of that subtle shift in roles from her to *him* as the primary victim, the descent of their relationship, at least for Will, was an easy downhill path—a gradual slope, soft under foot. Without the grand rites of romance to ward them off, the everyday slings and arrows known to every marriage began to take their toll. Each petty disagreement, each accusing glance, each cross remark, each tiny criticism—all slowly but certainly chipping away at the foundation of harmony, until one day Will gazed upon his former beloved and felt only resentment and betrayal. Carol would be the undoing of all he had worked for, unless he moved to extricate himself from this wicked snare.

Will stopped pacing, turned to face Harvey, and steeled himself.

"I'm going to stand my ground on this, Harvey." His words were mechanical. "You do whatever you're going to, but if you force my hand, believe me, I won't hesitate to vaporize your ticket out of here with a simple phone call."

Harvey gaped.

Will did not so much as blink. The conviction was unmistakable. Knowing that Harvey could spot a bluff blindfolded from the next county, the young lawyer had mentally prepared himself for this moment over the course of months. He was truly willing to sacrifice Carol, if need be, to emancipate himself. He had to be.

Harvey now leaned forward and peered into Will's eyes, trying to penetrate his level of intent.

"Wow, dad, let me get this straight," the boy-convict wondered aloud. "You're putting your beloved Carol's life on the line for a religious trinket?"

"It's something more than a trinket, we both know that," Will retorted. "And yes, I am now willing to risk all on the chance of regaining our freedom."

His response had all the feel of a noble declaration, but it belied something much lower. The skillfully crafted words of the able attorney really meant *I refuse to live with this indignity any longer, and I will go to any lengths to cast off these fetters, which includes offering up my wife's life in forfeit, if it comes to that.*

And Will knew, as did Harvey, that it was only Carol who was really at risk in this gambit. His research into the matter had unearthed what was said to be a strong, though antithetical, parallel between Catholicism and voodoo. Carol's belief in the power behind the Saint Thomas More medal paradoxically fueled her vulnerability to one who wielded it for ill purposes. Harvey's first and only attempt to assault Will directly with it had been weak and short-lived. He'd always suspected that there was a fine line between faith and superstition, and it was the supreme irony that his agnosticism was now his shield and saving grace.

True as well, Will's hard-won career was on the table along with his wife. But that short-lived triumph had transformed into a pyrrhic victory of the worst kind. The lawyer was resolute in this as well. He was young and bright and resilient. There was time for him to relaunch, if need be.

The long silence that ensued was finally broken by Harvey.

"If I gave up my *nudge*, how can I be sure you'll follow through with your plan to spring me? I know how much it bugs you to stoop to my level of dealing with things."

"First," Will stated solidly, "I will because I want more than anything to continue to reap the considerable rewards associated with representing the heir apparent to the most lucrative empire in the Great Southwest."

"Second?" Harvey probed. He pressed his fingertips together and mustered a thespian frown to disguise his delight in the flattery.

"Second, because it's apparent through my recent activities that I was the willing author of this latest subterfuge, and thereby, as Jeb so aptly put it just now, I'm already in this up to my ears."

Harvey nodded silently.

"Finally," Will continued, "knowing what I know about you, I'd be quite the fool to make myself the object of your retribution, wouldn't I?"

Apparently convinced, Harvey rose and stretched out his hand.

"Gimme some skin, Will; lord knows I love a gambler!"

Wondering which *lord* he referenced, and recalling with some trepidation the jolt he'd taken on a previous attempt to touch the little prince, Will nevertheless gripped Harvey's right paw and, to his astonishment, held the medal in his own hand upon withdrawing it from the unholy clasp of feigned camaraderie.

He stared into his palm and studied the medallion. It was a simple sterling silver disc, about an inch in diameter, a crude likeness of the scholarly saint engraved in relief within a center field, enclosed by a thin, raised rim. Stamped into the rim were the words *Saint Thomas More pray for us*. A tiny silver eyelet was soldered at the top for suspending the medal from a necklace chain. There was nothing particularly strange or unique that Will could discern to indicate any latent power within. It neither glowed, nor gleamed, nor radiated heat. From all outward appearances, it was quite innocuous and quite inanimate.

"I don't know how it works either," Harvey admitted. "I just kind of wing it."

"You *wing it*?"

"Sort of. Like I told you before, it's more this place, the Fort, than anything. I just get empowered by being here, dad. Charms like this just help to direct it. Like it's really wild, man."

"How long have you been here, again?"

"Just over two years."

"Well, life in a cage is almost over for you, so get hip to this," Will grinned as he pocketed the amulet. "If you're going to make it on the outside, you better start losing the Maynard G. Krebs routine."

"Huh?"

"You've been in the slammer too long, pal. Nobody cool talks like that anymore."

"You *jivin'* me, dad?"

"No jive, but here's a tip: just substitute *dude* for *dad* and you're already halfway there."

Moments later, as he walked to the car, Will inhaled the almost overpowering fragrance of citrus blossoms that permeated the air here. He noted that he had not registered any pleasant odors in months. He took it as an incidental pleasure to the lifting of his spirit on this momentous occasion of his emancipation. As he sped away in the long black Continental, he pondered the significance of the medal some more. Carol had explained that saints were formerly mortal spirits who could intercede in earthly matters by the power of grace. Medals helped to focus prayers of invocation to particular saints who "specialized" in certain types of matters. Harvey had mentioned that the Fort was a *place like some kind of crossroads between our world and the twilight zone.* Surely by removing the emblem of a spirit who had a foot in both worlds from a hinge-point place where those worlds collided, he had disempowered the curse that enslaved him.

Or rather, the curse that had enslaved *Carol.* And wouldn't Carol be ecstatic when he, her conquering hero, would burst through the front door and announce their ultimate liberation from the clutches of the little buck-toothed monster. It would be time for celebration. Roses, wine, music, dancing, and the bawdy bedroom wrestling that those romantic preliminaries heralded. She would never know that he had steeled himself from experiencing these feelings and had reduced her life to nothing more than the offering stake in a dark crapshoot with an adolescent demon. He astonished himself at how quickly he was able to dismiss that cold and calculated attitude he'd fabricated from necessity and was now able to rekindle the frolic and fire that she'd always inspired in him.

The entire world suddenly brightened for Will, and he laughed out loud as he tromped on the accelerator upon ascending a steep, familiar hill. As he climbed, tires slipping on the gravel lane, he thrilled at the brilliant colors of the fervent desert landscape falling away to his right. Multitudes of tiny yellow palo verde flowers formed a continuous arboreal canopy that stretched for miles with a lemon glow that his eyes drank in like liquid light. Patches of ruby red ocotillo blooms flashed like laser beams.

Oddly, a fleeting thought of Kenny Armenta passed through his mind. Now that the matter with Harvey was resolved, he might be able turn some of his efforts toward defending the mute and defenseless old Pima jeweler. Maybe Robson would allow him some latitude in that matter now that he'd validated himself as a valiant knight in the esquire's court.

But such issues would be addressed in their due time. Right now, romance eclipsed any far-flung notions of justice. Thirsty for a taste of what surely awaited him at home, he rummaged blindly through the console and pulled out a four-track tape cartridge, plugged it into the newly innovated Muntz stereo system, switched tracks to play "My Romance," and adjusted the seat back to a semi-reclining position—the better to enjoy the sweet romantic lyrics that only Mel Torme could intone.

He glanced in the rearview mirror at his dusty wake as the bulky car crested the hill, fishtailing slightly at breakneck speed, and caught a fleeting glimpse of the blinding white stucco walls of the Fort receding in the distance. The red-tile roof of the administration building and the windswept colors of the state and national banners at the top of the mast peeking over the ivory monolith reminded him, once again, of the romantic vision of storied castle ramparts.

Hurtling downhill, Will refrained from tapping the brakes and instead allowed the inertia of the big car to carry him more quickly down the lane toward the side of his beloved. He searched in his pants pocket for the Saint Thomas amulet—the prize he would present to her—and looked away to the right again for one more visual dance with the floral symphony that the desert afforded at this height. The black Lincoln dropped rapidly toward the foot of the hill, and the colors lost their dimensional radiance as they reduced to a thin, yellow line against the horizon.

Having lingered a few seconds too long with Nature's springtime canvas and Steve's softly conjured images, the lawyer's straying eyes snapped forward to the road ahead, just as the flashing image of a beige pickup truck leaped up before him—dead ahead in his path. Stupid old fogey was pulling onto the one-lane bridge that spanned the arroyo here, offering its broad side as a sure flirtation with a T-bone collision. Happening in the blink of an eye, and with no other options, Will stood on the power brake pedal, which did nothing to slow the downhill momentum of the careening mass of steel and glass. The tires chattered over the yielding gravel as the bulky Continental went into an uncontrolled skid. A series of black cursive letters spelling out the word *RENEGADE* flickered before Will's eyes, then disappeared as the old Ford truck completed its turn onto the bridge.

The broad, shiny chrome front bumper of the Lincoln impacted the concrete bridge abutment dead center at fifty miles-per-hour. Even the inertia behind the 4,927-pound vehicle traveling at that speed lacked the energy to so much as budge the massive support column. In the next instant, the dual side-by-side headlamps shot out of their sockets like pop-gun corks, as the delicate floating rectangular grille folded into the hood like an accordion. Rending steel and shattering glass shrieked to the highest heavens as the long slab-side body continued to thrust forward, folding inward on itself, embracing the stalwart concrete pier.

The 430-cubic-inch Mercury Marauder engine, stopped dead by the immovable piling, sheared its motor mounts and came crashing through the flimsy firewall into the cab like a thousand-pound battering ram. Will's legs were immediately pulverized by the rearward travel of the engine block at the same instant that the walnut steering wheel collapsed in his hands and the forward momentum of his torso crushed his chest against the exposed steering column. Head and shoulders continued to lunge forward through the shattered windshield, and the forward-vaulting motion of the death coach snapped his neck, just as the sawtoothed fragments of glass remaining in the frame completed the decapitation. The head continued to rocket through the open void that had, a fraction of a second before, been a wall of safety glass.

The continuing forward thrust from the rear drivetrain of the vehicle sought an upward arc, and the sleek luxury car rose erect for an instant, like some huge mechanical gymnast launching into a handstand. The hurtling wreck exhausted the remainder of its unspent energy tumbling forward, catapulting Will's severed head onto the roadway of the narrow bridge in the process, like an aggressive service in a tennis match. The disembodied noggin skittered to a stop mid-lane, as the once-proud car, like an overweight comedian performing a bone-jarring pratfall, came crashing down with a twisted-metal groan onto its flawless jet-black roof. The rear-hinged "suicide doors" burst open in a final gesture of physical tribute to the absurd.

———

The antique pickup truck rolled along to the far end of the bridge and sputtered to a stop on a narrow shoulder above the arroyo. With the engine still idling, the shirtless old chief with the decidedly canine facial features dismounted and slowly trudged back toward the demolished Lincoln. He stopped several yards short of the wreck to study Will Farnsworth's jettisoned cranium, the central plant for the neurological manufacture of devious plots to release a teen demon upon an unsuspecting populace, all for his own selfish purposes. It lay faceup in the roadway, flesh abraded from the brief sleigh ride across the rough pavement with hair blood-sodden from the crimson shower that had erupted from the stump of his neck upon separation. Tiny shards of safety glass encrusted the cheeks and forehead like sparkling gems in the bright afternoon sunlight. The upper lip was peeled back and dangling by a sinewy thread like a quartered tomato, grotesquely exposing numerous shattered incisors and cuspids. Eyelids pasted wide with horror, the corneal coverings were already clouding a milky white from the dry air. The hideous death mask bore scant resemblance to the formerly handsome visage it had been just seconds before. A shiny disc glinted in the sun from the surface of the concrete next to the severed head. The words *Saint Thomas More pray for us* flashed up at the leering Indian chief, a message dripping with grim irony.

"Saint Thomas More had a similar problem, young man," the Apache fossil admonished loudly at the head, as if the increased volume could bridge the chasm between worlds. "Similar problem, similar outcome," he snarled more than spoke.

Seemingly satisfied with this furtive declaration, the old native relic returned to his F-100, shifted into low, and slowly let out the clutch, creeping away from the scene.

"Just like you," he muttered, "he failed to choose his friends wisely."

Weeds

As promised, Randy directed Curtis to a place along the outside of the fortress wall that was riddled with pocks and cracks in the outer coat of plaster, making for convenient hand- and footholds. Reentering the Fort would indeed be as effortless as leaving it had been.

"You go first," Randy told Curtis, "and be careful that nobody sees you."

The young colored boy scrambled up the side and crouched at the top of the parapet, scouting first for yard sentries or unfriendly inmates. As anticipated, Curtis spotted a blue uniform positioned on the parade ground not forty feet from his vantage point. Fortunately, the guard's back was turned toward the wall, and the distance was enough to mute the scuffling sounds and the nervous panting that Curtis now fought to subdue. He turned his head to warn Randy and, true to form, his skinny sidekick had vanished without a trace.

Heart-pounding panic seized Curtis at the prospect of this guard spotting him atop the wall, so, taking his chances, he immediately rose up and stepped off the crest of the rampart, free-falling the eight-foot distance to the surface of the inside yard. He landed in a rare patch of withering weeds with a loud thud. The guard, apparently startled by the noise, turned his way—it was Marcus!

"Well, well—if it isn't my little brown buddy again," he chuckled. "You just pop up everywhere like a gopher in a truck patch, don't you?" He beckoned toward a pile of brown burlap on the ground next to him. "Well, don't just stand there teeterin' on your heels—grab a gunnysack!"

Curtis was still regaining his footing from the leap back to imprisonment, but his mind raced to grasp his circumstances.

"Sure, Marcus," he said, flashing a forced grin as he snagged one of the empty old potato sacks from the pile. "Now what am I supposed to do with it?"

"What—didn't they send you over here for weed detail? I was expecting one more inmate."

Curtis glanced around and noticed two other boys off in the distance crouched in the weeds.

"Yes, sir . . . uh . . . weed detail, yeah," he stammered, still looking for direction. "But they didn't say exactly what that meant. I mean, they didn't give me any outright instructions, so to speak."

"*Instructions*?" Marcus hooted. "This doesn't take a college education, son. Just start pulling the obnoxious little sprouts out of the ground until you fill the gunnysack or the hour runs out—whichever comes first," he directed, as he seated himself on the white plastic lid of a five-gallon Igloo water can.

"By hand?" Curtis wondered aloud.

"No, by this five-horsepower rototiller I've got in my back pocket," Marcus growled. "*Of course by hand*, boy. *Work* detail is supposed to include *work*."

With that, Curtis knelt and threw himself without further question into plucking strands of goathead runners and rattlesnake weed, tufts of desert thistle, foxtail, and an occasional infant tumbleweed, stuffing all of the little misfits of nature into his sack, which seemed to enlarge as he worked.

He was still wearing his gym shorts from his earlier workout, and before long the crushed granite was wearing painful abrasions on his knees. Pulling the spiny weeds bare-handed was no picnic either. They snapped off in the dry dirt and made his knuckles bleed.

A solid half hour passed. The sun was glaring like a heat lamp. Salty sweat from Curtis's brow ran into his eyes, making them blur and sting. Gnats buzzed about his face and, at one point, the boy unwittingly knelt in a bed of black ants.

"*Piss-ants*—sonofabitch!" he shouted as he jumped up and swatted the tiny clinging stingers from his bare knees and shins.

At length, Marcus called all three of the boys in for a quick water break. He pulled the lid off the top of the orange water can and the three took turns with a metal dipper they plunged into the cold water. They drank some and ran some of the cool liquid over their heads that were already wet with sweat.

Refreshed, the other two returned to their nearly completed task of filling the bags with miscreant vegetation. Curtis, however, tarried to further quiz the old guard.

"Marcus, don't you have any hand tools to dig with? These weeds are just breakin' off," he complained as he picked stuck-on bits of gravel from his knees, "and the roots are just gonna sprout again."

"No matter," Marcus returned. "The Lieutenant just doesn't want to see the weeds. He doesn't really care much about the roots. Besides," the old man grinned mischievously, "if we pulled 'em out by the roots, we wouldn't have any more material for weed detail next month."

Curtis just gaped, incredulously.

"By the same token," Marcus continued, "we can't have a bunch of inmate hoodlums running around stabbing each other with weeders and assaulting the staff with garden claws, now can we?"

"Aw, c'mon, Marcus," Curtis countered, "The boys in here are pretty tame. You talk like we're all wild-eyed axe murderers."

"I'd go along with that," Marcus concurred. "Leastways most of 'em are just a nuisance—sort of like these weeds." He rubbed the white stubble around his drooping jowls a bit and added: "But some are more like serpents, hiding among the weeds."

The thinly veiled analogy was not lost on Curtis.

"You mean Harvey, don't you?"

Marcus was silent for a moment, then spoke low, as if the walls had ears: "You best watch your back there, son. You picked the wrong hombre to tangle with."

"It wasn't my choosin'," said Curtis.

"Never mind that part, then. You just need to know this: I've seen a lot of bad boys come and go in my years here, and that Huish kid is the worst of the bunch. He is bad to the bone; he's got lots of friends inside and outside; he's big and strong and, oh . . . did I mention that he doesn't have much use for colored folks?"

"Yeah, I picked up on that," Curtis sighed, then took another long draw from the dipper. "Marcus, what is it that makes a boy like that so . . . so . . . damned *evil*?"

The old man replaced the lid on the water can, sat back down, and rubbed the jowls again, as if he were milking wisdom from his weary head.

"Ignorance—that's how I'd sum it up."

"Ignorance?"

"Yeah—if somebody doesn't have any sense of the difference between good and evil, I'd call that ignorance of the worst kind."

"But I always figured that people just had a sort of *inborn* notion of right and wrong—that we just don't always *choose* to do right. Isn't that so?"

"Yes-siree-Bob, I believe that's right with most folks. But as they say, *nothin' good can grow from a bad seed*, and every now and then some two-legged viper comes along that don't know bad from good. They've got no guilt or remorse for any of the wicked things that they do."

"A fish never feels wet," muttered Curtis.

"What's that?"

"My mama used to say 'a fish never feels wet.' She said a truly bad man don't know he's bad because he's steeped in badness—that it takes a good man to know the badness *inside* of himself."

The old man pulled a small brown bar of tobacco from his shirt pocket, bit off a chunk, and tucked it back away.

"Well, your mama sounds like a wise lady. Too bad you didn't listen better. Maybe you wouldn't have got thrown into this snake pit."

"Shoulda, coulda, woulda," Curtis muttered grimly. "But Marcus," he continued, "how come this 'bad-to-the-bone' Harvey seems to have so many friends? Seems like people would steer clear of such an evil guy."

"Did I say *friends*? There must be a better word for it." He stroked the stubble again. "Let's just say that *scavengers* and *parasites*—they tend to follow predators around. It's in their nature."

Curtis just shrugged, unsatisfied with the truncated answer.

"Look, kid, did you ever wonder why the food in this reform school is better by a damn sight than Army chow?"

"Yeah, well, I don't know about *Army* chow, but I have wondered about that. It's not as good as my mama's cookin', but it's the next best thing—better than the cafeteria food at school, that's for sure."

"Okay, and have you noticed that the rooster's dorm has a great big air-conditioning unit installed in the back?"

"Can't say as I have."

"And you might not care, but our schoolmasters here earn better salaries than any public school teacher in the state of Arizona. Not only that, we get all new textbooks every year!"

The old man paused to spit a brown stream of viscous saliva onto the ground. He eyed Curtis to see if the puzzlement in the boy's eyes had vanished, but it truly had been magnified by Marcus's comments, if anything.

"Listen," he continued, "you'd have to have been here two years ago to notice that all of these improvements just mysteriously happened shortly after the young Mr. Huish appeared in our midst. Coincidence? I have my doubts, Curtis."

"So do you believe that his daddy has all that much money and power?"

"More wealth, from what I hear, than you or I could even imagine. And he didn't exactly come by it honestly—nor did *his* daddy, or his daddy before *him*."

"Well, none of that cuts no ice with me," said Curtis. "And that Harvey Huish—he don't scare me. I'll whup his ass, if I ever get him alone."

"You know, my pappy used to say somethin' somewhat similar to what your mama told you. He said *a man can't know what courage is until he's known fear first*. But hell," he continued, "he was talkin' about men, not boys. Seems like boys just naturally tend to think they're bulletproof."

"Sounds like your daddy was 'bout as wise as my mama."

Marcus spat into the dust again, then rose to conclude the conversation: "You best get back to work, now. Those weeds won't pull themselves out of the ground, and the Lieutenant doesn't like to see foxtails and tumbleweeds when he makes his rounds."

"Okay, Marcus, but one more thing. Why do they call the headmaster *Lieutenant*?

"Just always have, that's all. Now quit jawin' and get to it!"

Curtis started to trudge over to where he'd left his gunnysack lying in the weeds.

"Oh, and by the way, Curtis," the old guard called, mock-stern, "the next time you take a notion to go over that wall, think again. I might not be so inclined to turn my back."

Curtis blanched, but he answered quickly, just the same: "Yes, sir—that's a trip I never plan to make again."

"See that? You're getting that education we talked about already."

Strange Encounters

But Curtis failed to keep his vow to himself never to return to the cemetery site. In fact, he returned several times before lights-out that night. It wasn't for lack of resistance, and it was true that he managed to keep himself from actually scaling the wall to the outside again, so he was able to keep his promise to Marcus, at least in the physical sense.

But in fact, the image of the path to the primitive cemetery was developing a certain magnetism in his mind. Randy's powerful suggestion that the memory of "the way back" suddenly became critically important to him. His scrawny comrade's ethereal voice conjured a repeating visual playback in the young colored boy's mind with an intensity that was approaching irresistible. It was as if an eight-millimeter home movie was constantly playing, rewinding, and playing again at the edge of his awareness. Any unguarded slip into a dormant mental state brought the moving pictures—of the serpentine path through the brush, the sandy arroyo, the succulent landmarks, the tamarisk thicket, and the barren basin with the mounds of stones—bubbling to the surface of thought with a startling vividness.

Perhaps even more curious to Curtis was the coinciding recurrence of a dream that had fallen onto the subconscious wayside for several years, but came back this night in perfect replication—not just in detail, but in sensory impression and in the same deep emotional context as before. It was, as it always had been, as if he were meeting his father for the first time; however the feeling was comforting and familiar as if they'd been lifelong pals. Comforting, that is, until he considered the last spoken phrase that his long-deceased father offered in the dream.

But this first recurrence followed a couple of aberrant incidents that could not be ignored.

It was indeed "fish Friday" at the mess hall, and in spite of the dizzying events of the day—or perhaps because of them—Curtis was ravenous, and he attacked his double helping of finny food and fried potatoes like a starving refugee.

"Man, you're wolfin' down the groceries like you haven't eaten in a week!"

Curtis barely glanced up to acknowledge Randy's now-routine appearance at the table across from him. He continued to shovel heaping forkfuls of chow from the metal tray into his snapping jaws with great gusto, and tersely nodded at his frail companion, who parked himself on the bench without a tray of food.

"Take your time," said Randy. "I'm not going anywhere."

Curtis gulped down a huge mouthful and simultaneously forked a final oil-soaked morsel. His attention returned to a book that Randy had propped open on the table with the cover facing Curtis. He scanned the content of that cover with some curiosity. The daunting image of a young white man wearing dated sparring togs posed in fighting stance adorned the cover in reddish brown sepia tones. *Boxing*, read the simple title in bold block letters.

"So what's up with the book, toothpick—are you gonna take up fightin' so the roosters can't kick your bony little chicken-butt?"

"Actually," said Randy, "I find the art of pugilism quite fascinating."

"That so? You know, judgin' by your puny little pipe-cleaner arms, I don't reckon you could punch your way out of a wet paper bag if your miserable life depended on it. You'd do better to take up runnin'—better yet, *prayin'* might be your best hope."

"Oh, how original—you're *so* terribly clever," Randy retorted. "You really should have your own stand-up routine."

"So I've been told," Curtis grinned. "But you're not really thinkin' about takin' up boxin', are you?"

"No, I'm not interested in damaging my hands on some moron's wooden head," Randy answered, "but I do think I would make an excellent manager-trainer."

"How do you figure? What the hell do you know about boxin'?"

"Well, it's pretty clear to me that I already know enough about training to teach you a thing or two."

"Tell me about it, professor—for instance?"

"For instance I can see that you're way too fixated on bodybuilding, and if you don't modify your routine pretty soon, you're going to wind up a walking pot roast."

"You don't know shit from Shinola about my program, Einstein. It just so happens that my long-term goal is to bulk up so I'll be boxin' AAU welterweight division by the summer of '66. I need to bulk up so as to establish myself as contender for the gold before the '68 games. Besides, with the strength I'm building on the weights, I'll be packin' a punch like a mule kickin' downhill way before then." Curtis held up a clenched right fist and flexed a sinewy forearm.

Randy would not be dismissed so easily. "I'm sorry, Curtis, but you've got at least three more years of rapid natural growth going for you, and a stand-in-place slugger is just not your style; I'll concede that strength is a critical element, but it's only one of four in a winning combination."

"And in your book, what are the other three?"

"I'm not going to give away all of my strategies. Besides, I refuse to waste my training expertise on a scoffer." Randy's eyes flashed. "Maybe Gerd Brinkerhoff could use a good manager." He was referring to Harvey Huish's hulking henchman.

"Don't even think about it, you little dork. If that knuckle-draggin' Nazi just learned to lift his lead feet, he'd be dangerous."

"Then maybe he'd appreciate my advice."

Curtis sighed. "Okay, mister manager, you win. I'm listenin'."

"All right, Curtis, the weightlifting is fine to a point. But if I were your trainer, I'd shift a good deal of the emphasis from bodybuilding, and supplement it with lots of agility and endurance drills. Keep up the muscle development by all means, but not at the expense of your speed. All that Charles Atlas stuff is all show and no go. You keep bulking up at the rate you're going, you'll look great on the back page of a comic book, but forget about boxing."

175

"I don't do Charles Atlas," Curtis corrected. "I'm on the Joe Weider program!"

"As if he's any different," Randy countered. "Weider's just another muscle-mag hawker who wants to turn you into a meat mountain. That kind of muscle-bound physique is for gawking at, not for serious fighting."

Curtis shook his head in wonder. "Is all that stuff in that book?"

"Not exactly—you can get a lot of valuable facts from reading books, but it's all in what you do with those facts. It's common sense that really matters."

Curtis's attention span was interrupted by recurring hunger pangs. He looked down at his empty tray, then turned to look with some dismay at the length of the chow line. Second helpings would not be offered until all of the first-comers were served.

"Hey, Randy," Curtis piped, "if you're not gonna eat, why don't you go get a tray full of food for me? I can't talk on an empty stomach."

Randy's eyes bugged. Curtis had just put away more food than the younger boy had ever eaten in a week. "Okay, I'll do it if you return a favor."

"And just what might that be?"

"Think about the path we took today—the way down and the way back—while I'm standing in line for you."

"Is that all?"

"Yeah, for now. Just think about it. Can you do that? Visualize, if you will, each one of the landmarks we saw—it's important."

Curtis shrugged. "Whatever you say, twig-man. Just be sure to get a heapin' helpin' of fish."

"Okay, watch my book, I'll be right back."

Randy rose and queued up for chow while Curtis "watched" his book. His secondary motive for sending Randy off was to open an opportunity to browse through this pugilist's manual and perhaps glean some pointers from it. The subtitle read: *Naval Aviation Physical Training Manual.*

Curiously, as he began to leaf through the pages, his mind abruptly drifted to an image of the saluting saguaro, that being the first landmark along the path down to the crude cemetery. Curtis shook his head as if to dismiss the unbidden mental picture, and the image blurred, only to morph into another visual manifestation: the stark upward thrust of the century plant shaft, the next landmark they'd encountered on the path.

"What the hell?" He tried hard to focus on the various illustrations in the book, but the images that dotted "the way down" continued to materialize in succession before his eyes—the odd clump of prickly pear, the crucifixion thorn, and the thicket of tamarisk saplings.

The boy remained mesmerized by repeated runs of these visions—an internal cinema—until Randy at last returned with a platter of steaming victuals, at which time the involuntary reverie vanished as if by unspoken command.

"Hey, you little weasel-neck, have you been messin' with my head somehow?" Curtis growled as Randy placed the plate before him.

"Well, that's gratitude for you. I camp out in that agonizingly slow line for you for the better part of ten minutes, and my thanks is that you stick me with yet another degrading name."

"Don't play innocent with me, bone-man. Somehow *you* made me recall all those stupid cactuses . . ."

"*Cacti*," Randy corrected. "And technically only two are actually cacti at all."

"Who gives a flyin' fuck what you call 'em anyway?" Curtis shouted, drawing some unwanted attention to himself. "I just want you to tell me how you put those weirdo pictures in my head. Did you hypnotize me or somethin'?"

"Calm yourself down and eat some food before it gets cold," Randy cautioned.

Curtis muttered something that involved Randy performing an oft-invoked but biologically improbable act with cactus, and began to shovel great spoonfuls of nourishment into his mouth, muffling the tirade with the highly effective word-muting qualities of a viscous fish-potato mash.

"Stffufknkaktsupyrrskneeass!" he exclaimed, projecting flecks of food across the table.

"Look, Curtis," Randy retorted, "it's not fair for you to try to hold me accountable for every psychic event that you encounter here. Remember, more than anything, it's just the nature of this place—that and your apparent predisposition to experiencing it all."

The pure enjoyment of eating now engaged Curtis so completely that all resentment was instantly eclipsed. He merely nodded.

"On the other hand," Randy continued, "you should never underestimate the power of suggestion, my friend, especially when it is dictated by such a superior mind."

"Gfkkyrslf!" was the unintelligible response.

"You shouldn't try to speak with your mouth full," said Randy. "My grandfather used to say, 'If you're going to talk, talk. If you're going to eat, eat.' Now, you eat while I talk."

Curtis glared, but complied.

"All right," Randy continued, "I've got a proposition for you."

Curtis widened his dark eyes and shot him a look that said, *I'm listening, already!*

"You take me on as your manager, and I'll not only share my new-found gems of training wisdom, but I'll provide a concealed facility where you can work out in private—out of sight from Harvey and his boys. It'll be sort of a training sanctuary. How's that sound?"

Curtis gulped. "How can you manage that?"

"It's what a manager does—*manages* things. I happen to know of an area that's off-limits to the general population, and I have access to it. Now, given your recent run-ins with the 'cock-of-the-walk,' I'd say now's the time to make yourself kinda scarce, wouldn't you say?"

"Maybe so, but what's *your* angle, beanpole?"

"It's purely an altruistic gesture on my part, I assure you."

"An *ultra-who . . . what*?"

"A token of my friendship, and I have a certain aversion to seeing you getting pummeled by a gang of thugs. Anyway, meet me tomorrow morning at the side door of the academic building right after the buzzer sounds for first break, and bring a pair of gym shorts. I'll have everything ready."

"Whatever you say, slim." Curtis polished off the remnants of food on his tray and looked up toward the serving area. "Hey, all the first-comers are served; I'm gonna go get seconds," he declared.

"That would be *thirds*," Randy reminded.

"Who's keeping score? Besides, I've got the metabolism of a hummingbird, so I gotta keep eatin' to keep my wings beatin'!"

"You better hope so, my friend," said Randy, as he got up to leave, "because when we get started tomorrow, you're not going to want to be carrying an ounce of surplus ballast."

Curtis rose to queue up for seconds when he spotted a now-familiar blue Dodgers cap across the hall. Harvey Huish was just leaving the line. Driven by an insatiable hunger, he dismissed his cautionary inklings, sidled up to the food line, and loaded up his tray. As he turned to make his way back to his bench seat, he caught sight of Harvey sitting several tables away, but facing him. The older boy's piercing blue eyes locked on to Curtis's and, for a moment, he seemed to hold the younger boy captive with an unnerving gaze. Even more alarming, as Harvey stared, *Curtis could actually hear his voice as if it were coming from inside his own head.* The lips were definitely not moving. Nevertheless, the voice was Harvey's. It was as if the blond boy were a ventriloquist and Curtis his dummy.

I'm gonna throttle you 'til your little black heart stops, spook!

Curtis closed his eyes and shook his head vigorously, in an effort to shake away this voice and this hypnotic glare. When he looked back up, Harvey's attention was fixed down at his tray, intent on the meal before him. Fear trumped hunger. Curtis turned quickly away, dumped the contents of his metal serving tray into an industrial-sized Rubbermaid trash can, discarded it at the washing station, all the while keeping a weather eye on his nemesis.

Curtis stepped warily out of the mess hall and into the warm evening. He turned and paced toward the camp library to attend the mandatory after-dinner study hour, still shaken over the psychic disturbance from moments before.

The wink of the sun was disappearing behind the peaks of the Galiuro Mountains, and the shadows of dusk were stealing across the dirt walkways between buildings. The path to the library passed by the decrepit administration building where Randy worked. A window was opened adjacent to the walkway, and a wave of cooler-chilled air coursed through the opening, carrying the melody of a song that was playing on the radio just inside. Curtis recognized the lyrics, and a memory made him linger to listen and to bathe in the slipstream of refreshing air.

It was an aging rendition of a show tune that his mother used to play repeatedly on an antiquated portable record player. That was years ago—he couldn't have been any more than six or seven. He closed his eyes and saw the old 78-rpm disc whirling in that old turntable well, as Peggy Lee wove her vocal magic to Rodgers and Hart's "Where or When."

"Move along, kid!" a sharp voice demanded. "There'll be no loitering here by the Lieutenant's window." It was one of the meaner camp guards, and the very mention of the Lieutenant made the boy's breath go shallow.

"Yes, sir . . . sorry, sir!" Curtis answered, resuming his trek to the library.

As he approached the doorway, he noticed several other young inmates waiting outside on the stoop. They were early and the door was still locked. Curtis kept his distance and waited in the shadows just off of the path. The familiar melody was still playing in the distance, but it was muffled now and distorted by the intervening space.

He closed his eyes and tried to recapture the visual memory of his mother's bedroom where she kept her old phonograph, and where the black-and-white photograph of his pilot-father, clad in his dress uniform and bedecked with medals, sat perched on a dresser.

But that image now faded. It was abruptly eclipsed by the vivid moving picture of the path to the gravesite, this time in subdued light, and Curtis now visualized himself running down the sandy arroyo, noting with an even sharper recognition each desert landmark as it whizzed past.

"I thought I told you to move along, kid!"

The same guard startled Curtis once again. The accent was straight out of Dogpatch.

"Sorry!" Curtis snapped to. "The . . . uh, the door is still locked."

The guard glanced toward the entrance to the library where the door was now propped wide open, and the yellow light from inside was spilling onto the stoop.

"Well, it *was* locked," Curtis stammered. "I guess I was daydreaming,"

To his shock, the guard cuffed the boy sharply with an open palm across the left ear.

"Then wake your nappy head up before I run you off to the woodshed!"

An orange flame of pain leaped up the entire left side of Curtis's face, and the boy's eyes teared up briefly as he hurried to the entrance and ducked inside. His ear was still ringing as he stepped up to the checkout desk and requested his Joe Weider clipboard, which the English schoolteacher, who doubled as the camp librarian, kept tucked away for him on a shelf behind the counter. Curtis was surprised but not amazed that Randy's *Naval Aviation Physical Training Manual* peeked out from behind the pamphlet as he removed it from the clipboard.

"Weasely little beanpole pops up everywhere," Curtis muttered to himself.

As he settled down into an old dilapidated desk at a secluded corner of the room, a wave of fatigue gradually stole across his usually animated spirit. While it was mandatory to attend, this was not a structured or an enforced study hour; it was designed more to settle the inmates before lights-out; and, true to form, Curtis began to nod before very long.

The campfire was roaring and the flames leaped up much taller than a six-year-old child. The snap and crack of the sugar pine logs sent sparks leaping high into the summer night air, and the boy's dark eyes shone with enchantment as he stared into the blaze. The breathy sigh of a warm breeze fanned the miniature inferno, and with the random arrangement of the wood created a fiery vortex that, to the child, resembled some sort of flaming dervish dancer.

It was the close of a perfect day. Curtis and his father had caught more catfish than they could possibly eat. The meal, taken under the stars that shone over the bayou, surpassed any gourmet

181

feast imaginable; and the two were now enjoying a balmy Louisi-ana evening together, naming the constellations that were arrayed across the southern sky like the lights of a celestial city.

Curtis's father had allowed the boy to gradually overbuild the campfire, much to the child's delight. The roar of the flames drowned out the deafening whir of a million insects singing out of tune, and the radiant heat from the blaze bathed the boy's face with warm caresses, drawing him closer to the heat and motion of the hypnotic dance.

"You're getting way too close, son," his father softly admonished in his deep baritone. "Better get back before you get burned."

Curtis awoke with a start and sat up straight at his sequestered desk. He was back in reform school in the middle of the Arizona desert, and his father was long since dead—had been since before Curtis could walk or speak. He'd been a Navy pilot, killed in the Korean War—shot down over the Chosin Reservoir. Curtis had only known him by the picture that his mother kept by her bed and by the medals she kept in her jewelry box. Nevertheless, the boy somehow managed to fabricate the memory of a man he'd never known and treasured a recurring dream that conjured all the sensory details of a "real" event that he'd never truly experienced.

This time, however, the focus was on the warning, and his father's only words—a portent of sorts—stirred in Curtis a sense of foreboding. All the aberrations—the hanging men, the voracious birds, the girl with the mutilated face, the horsemen, the gravesite—all came rushing in at once, and the confusion and the revulsion were more than he could bear. The stinging in the front of the face came just seconds before the welling up of water to the eyes. The boy sobbed as tears spattered his Joe Weider pamphlet on the desk in front of him.

"Daddy, I just don't know what the hell to do," he choked in a whisper.

He fought hard to regain his composure, wiping the salty water from his chestnut cheeks and brushing the starburst spatters from his treasured exercise guide. That's when he noticed the small staple-bound stack of dog-eared pages with a typewritten cover page.

Fort Grant: A History

Curtis glanced around to see if he was alone. He was. He did not recall that any material had been left on his desk when he first sat down. There was a blank library card stuck between the pages at about half the thickness of the bundle, and he opened the manuscript to the marker. He scanned down the page, as was his habit. He keyed in on familiar words and phrases, while glossing over those foreign to his understanding. His darting eyes first landed on a sub-heading that seized his attention:

Fort Grant Massacre

The first couple of sentences read:

> It was January of the year 1871 that Lt. Roy Whitcomb took command of Fort Grant, a remote outpost named for the famed Union Army General. The modest cloister of crude adobe buildings lay nestled among the sun-baked mesas of the Aravaipa Valley, along the San Pedro River.

The next line that caught his attention read:

> Pinal and Aravaipa Apaches who had long since surrendered to the US military established a campsite, settling just a stone's throw from the security of the Fort, and under the protective wing of the friendly lieutenant.

Skipping down the page, he read:

> Upwards of 150 Anglos, Mexicans, and Papago Indians made the fifty-mile trek from Tucson to Fort Grant, arriving under the cover of darkness on the night of April 29.

Scanning down some more, he riveted on the word *slaughter*, just as the lights began to flicker off and on. It was the signal to shelve all the reading material and make for the dormitories. Curtis picked up the manuscript, fastened it to his clipboard, and rose to make his way to the checkout desk.

"That manuscript needs to stay in this library, young man."

Catching a faint whiff of English Leather, Curtis turned to see who was addressing him and found himself standing toe-to-toe with the Lieutenant! The boy had not spoken with the man since that first day during the intake process. In fact, as far as Curtis knew, this fabled figure had never been seen straying after dark so far from the administration building as the little stone-paver patio adjacent to his apartment, where he was known to down copious amounts of bourbon after hours and suck down five-dollar Cuban cigars. Word had it that a trip to the woodshed was guaranteed if a boy so much as held his mouth wrong while answering this legend. Speaking to him was less an honor and more a trial.

"I . . . I know, sir," Curtis gulped. "I'm just taking it up to the desk now, sir."

"Well, see that you do."

The Lieutenant wore navy blue slacks and a bright blue Hawaiian-style shirt. As before, he wore a blue bandana across his forehead. And just as before, it was conspicuously inconsistent with the rest of his outfit. Except for a quick glance at the impeccable attire, Curtis kept his eyes fixed downward at the black wingtip-style shoes.

"Yes, sir," he responded.

Curtis turned quickly on his heel and started briskly toward the desk, hoping that the brief encounter had come to a close, when the Lieutenant's deep baritone stopped him cold.

"Son?"

"Yes, sir." Curtis reluctantly turned halfway toward the Lieutenant and looked again down at the elegant shoes.

"Look at me when I speak, boy!"

The sign of deference had been misconstrued, and Curtis looked full into the face of the myth-of-a-man in panic. The features were stony, and the pencil-thin mustache emphasized the tight upper lip. The eyes, however, were a bright blue-green, almost teal, and they conveyed a certain light from within.

"Yes, sir . . . sorry, sir."

"I only wanted to ask you," he continued in a softer tone, "if you actually read any of that material."

"Some of it, sir. Some of the words are kind of hard for me, though."

"Do you understand the word *massacre*?"

"Yes, sir—I do."

"That's good; it might help you to understand some of this nonsense that seems to happen around here."

"Help me sir? Help me how?"

The older man smiled knowingly.

"Let's just say that it might help keep you from losing your grip!"

"Yes, sir, I'll keep that in mind, sir . . . um, when I feel myself losing my grip, that is."

"See that you do," the Lieutenant repeated, mock-sternly.

"May I be excused now, sir?" the boy half croaked.

The towering figure now half-heartedly raised a right hand toward his forehead. "Dismissed."

Curtis's first instinct was to whirl and run, but he restrained himself, pacing quite vigorously instead to the desk, checking his clipboard in. Without hesitation, he then exited the library under an accelerated stride, daring not to look back.

Mr. Sandman

"Okay, *string bean*, what is this place supposed to be?" Curtis wondered aloud. "And where are all the camels and the pyramids?"

He and Randy were both peering through the mesh of a chain-link gate that barred entry to a walled yard that looked to be a bit smaller than an acre square. Curtis beheld a miniature sandscape, tucked out of sight behind a long, six-foot-tall adobe wall that sequestered an isolated lot. It was an austere site, devoid of any flora save for an ancient-looking gnarled mesquite that thrust starkly upward from the center of what resembled the most barren, God-forsaken patch of Death Valley imaginable. It was barely mid-morning, but the pollen-laden springtime air of the desert already seemed to shimmer with the heat. A dozen or so tubular steel "T" posts dotted the sandlot, and under closer scrutiny, it was apparent that they were clothesline poles, or once had been.

"What does it look like to *you*, brilliance?" Randy taunted.

"It looks like some scene out of *Captain Gallant of the Foreign Legion*," Curtis quipped.

"*Captain Gallant*?"

"You know, Buster Crabbe and his gang of dune-trotters in those funny soldier hats with the white hankies all hangin' off in back."

"Oh please, spare me your vulgar description of the renowned French *kepi*," Randy sighed as he grasped a combination lock that held the gate latch fast.

"Well, you little brainiac. You really think you know it all, don't you?"

"I know something about a lot of things, and a lot about some things. And to answer your question, this used to be the laundry annex, once upon a time." Randy beckoned with a jerk of his chin toward a small ramada that housed a row of empty trough-style basins and an old iron water pump. "But now it's your own new personal gymnasium!"

He whirled the dial on the lock left and right until the shackle popped open and he pulled it from the hasp. They stepped inside the gate and surveyed the desolate yard.

"Well, what do you think?"

Curtis *harrumphed* and spat onto the gritty surface of his "gym" floor; the viscous wad of spittle clotted up into a dry, granulated marble immediately upon contacting the sandy ground. "I think it's a little lean in the equipment department, bone-man."

"You're not using your imagination," Randy retorted. "Besides, I intend to develop things as we go. I envision an *evolving* facility, along with the development of its sole client. Meanwhile, we've got everything we need right now to get a good start."

"What the hell're you talkin' about, pencil-boy? There's nothin' out there but *sand*, man!"

"And that's exactly what the doctor—I mean, the trainer—ordered: *sand*."

"You got to be puttin' me on, boy!" Curtis hooted. "I think maybe you've got some sand in your skull there, mister trainer."

Randy glared. "Just let me know when you're finished with your sad attempt at comedy and you're ready to get serious."

Curtis summoned a facial expression of contrition that was too exaggerated to be genuine. "Oh, please forgive my clownin' 'round. Sometimes I just can't help myself. But hey, I'm all ears now, *sir*."

"You apparently have no appreciation for what a lucky find this was. A sandlot is the best possible environment for our training, and this one is hidden away from watchful eyes. You ought to be grateful for a place to get away from Harvey and his henchmen during the in-between hours," Randy scolded. "But the sand is a bonus. It's a vital training device that's better than any equipment."

Curtis glanced around again. The trunk of the tree and bases of the clothesline posts were partly submerged in the fine buckskin-colored powder. "Where did all of this sand come from anyway?"

"Decades of accumulation, my friend. The configuration of the walls creates a windbreak whenever the wind blows out of the south. Every time there's a dust storm, it deposits another layer of sand right here. It just falls to the ground. It's a natural phenomenon that's a . . . a literal windfall."

"How do you figure—sand, *a windfall*?"

"You remember yesterday I said there are four critical elements to a winning combination in boxing?"

"Yeah, and?"

"Well, the sand provides a condition that will help you develop two of those qualities in short order: speed and endurance—but mostly endurance."

"Sand, Rand? You got to be puttin' me on, man."

"Look, Curtis, you just have to trust me on this. It's not an experiment; plenty of world-class athletes train in the sand and get remarkable results. But we're wasting workout time and breath on worthless chatter. Why don't we just get started—okay?"

Curtis spat again in expression of his unwavering skepticism.

Randy suddenly brightened. "Oh, I get it!" he exclaimed. "You're *afraid*, Curtis."

"What the hell you talkin' about, fool? There's nothin' to fear here—just a bunch of worthless dust is all."

"No, you're afraid that it might slow you down, scared it might hurt your precious ego to run the slowest quarter mile of your life, aren't you?"

Curtis glowered, but Randy would not let up.

"I can't believe you're actually this *gutless*. The pride of Jacobs Well Junior High, daunted by the dunes—intimidated by a little grit!"

"You button your lip before I nail it to your teeth, you little weasel."

"Well, show me it's not true, then."

Still doubtful, but more averse to the slightest perception of cowardice, Curtis finally relented. "All right, Mohammed, just show me to the oasis."

Randy excitedly pulled a familiar-looking metal whistle tethered to a familiar-looking blue lanyard from his pants pocket and draped it around his neck.

"Hey, isn't that Marcus's whistle?"

Randy just grinned and produced a fancy stopwatch from his other pocket.

Curtis whistled low. "Man, you are some kind of klepto, kid."

"I prefer to be thought of more as a master prankster than a petty thief. But either way, these things will be put to a nobler purpose for a while, and they'll be returned before they're missed. Now, let's get started, shall we?"

"Fine, but if this doesn't do me a world of wonder in less than a week, stick-man, I'm gonna pound a fuckin' sand castle up your ass, I swear."

———————

The initial sandlot session lasted more than an hour, and it was brutal. Being Saturday, outdoor exercise time was extended. That suited Randy just fine, but it had Curtis secretly praying for a reprieve long before the period was up. Randy had Curtis run the perimeter of the yard clockwise for timed intervals of two minutes. The boy-coach signaled the close of each period with a little toot on the whistle—just a toot, no loud blasts that might call unwanted attention. He fastidiously marked each point of completion in the sand, and even drew with his finger a little numeral beside the mark to indicate the point in sequence of effort.

"A lap around the yard is about four hundred yards," Randy had told Curtis at the outset. "We'll track your total distance for each drill, and strive for improvement on distance with each period's effort."

The running drills were performed in three two-minute "rounds" to mimic the duration and number of rounds of an amateur boxing match—two sets at the beginning and one at the end of the workout session. The sand giving way under each tread made any headway a tiring challenge, and hope for any semblance of speed seemed impossible. Curtis's lungs burned with a yearning for more air, and his calves and thighs turned to rubber after the second drill of the first set. His arms likewise leadened and gradually fell lower to his sides, an ungainly deviation from his usual proud striding style.

"Arms up!" Randy shouted. "I want to see your hands in the guarding position while you run." Curtis was amazed at how quickly his arms became too weary to comply. "Keep them up on guard!" the boy-coach insisted, ignoring Curtis's apparent exhaustion. "You're leaving yourself wide open for a haymaker."

It was all Curtis could do to plod along and occasionally raise a hand to brush the streaming perspiration from his eyes.

At the end of the first set Randy beckoned Curtis over to the ramada for a quick water break. He was twisting a cork into the mouth of an old wine bottle as the weary colored lad approached the welcoming shade of the bleached-wood canopy. A large tin dipper dangled by a thin wire from the dripping spout of the old iron pump. Randy raised the ancient pump-handle and thrust downward to summon the gurgling rush of clear, cool well water that gushed forth from the spout. Curtis strode up and caught the tapering end of the liquid burst to fill the dipper to its brim. He brought the tin rim to his lips and took in a long, life-giving draught. The relief the boy felt at this thirst-quenching intake went to his very core. Randy pumped on the handle some more, bringing up successive bursts of cool refreshment, as Curtis poured more water at his mouth than he could swallow, allowing the surplus liquid to dribble down his bare chest and belly.

"Go ahead and cool off your head too," Randy said, as he pumped some more. Curtis did just that, the water beading up and rolling off of his coarse black hair. He sputtered and spit from the cool soaking.

"Man," he finally spoke, still struggling to regain his wind, "this little watering hole really *is* an oasis." He teetered slightly as he stepped back from the pump. "I figured that my legs would go to rubber runnin' in the sand like that, but not my arms too. I can barely lift them, and they're all shaky."

"The oxygen debt you build up is in your blood. It affects all your muscles as it circulates," Randy informed him with an air of authority.

"What do you know about that stuff?" Curtis challenged, still panting.

"Plenty, it's just human physiology—simple chemistry, really, but rather fascinating in practice."

"You don't say! Man, just who do you think you are, Sir Isaac Newton?"

"Nice compliment. I told you before, I know something about a lot of things and a lot about some things. And by the way, your five-minute break is past up. Time to pound sand again."

Randy instructed Curtis as he reluctantly returned to the field. "Try to pace yourself this time. Don't try to go all out all the way. And keep your hands up during the drill. We don't want you so fatigued that you go sloppy on the last round."

"Okay, coach," Curtis replied, half in earnest.

As the aspiring young pugilist resumed cantering around the perimeter of the yard, he took his friend's advice and held some of his effort in check. Nevertheless, his calves began to burn halfway through the second drill, and his lungs ached for more air by the third. He finished the set more winded and having covered less ground than during the opening session, but he'd kept his arms held up in guarded position for the duration, drawing an unexpected compliment from Randy as they headed once again for the pump.

"I think you'll have to admit now that this whole sand scene is a gift," said Randy. "By now you should know that you'll never build any serious stamina without it."

"How do you figure?" Curtis wheezed, still short of breath.

"Because, Curtis, you're a *natural*—that's part of the problem."

"You'll have to excuse me . . . but I don't follow your drift. Bein' a *natural* has done me . . . nothin' but a world of good . . . up to now. How could it be a problem?"

"Stop talking and take some deep breaths; you'll recover quicker. Let me do the talking."

Curtis rolled his eyes, but took those deep breaths just the same.

"You know," Randy continued, "if your only goal is a quick run up the ranks of amateurs, then super-endurance is not as critical as it would be to someone who aspires to a professional career in the ring. Amateur matches only go three two-minute rounds. Strength, for that matter, isn't all that important in the amateurs either. They score on clean blows landed, not knockdowns. But I suspect that you are looking beyond the '68 Olympics toward something even bigger than the gold medal."

Randy cranked the handle on the pump and Curtis cupped his hands, taking in the refreshment of the cool stream once again. "You got that right," he gasped between gulps. "I'm gonna be the heavyweight champion of the world!"

"Well, now you're talking, sport. But if you're gonna go ten rounds with some slugger like Sonny Liston, you need to start working on your stamina now, because in a war of attrition, the win will go to the fighter with the best endurance. And this is the time, my friend, while your respiratory and circulatory systems are still in development, that you can build on your natural endurance, take that developmental window and make yourself into a super-athlete who can go the distance."

"Oh, I know what it's like to go the distance, and then some."

"Huh?"

"That's right, coach—see, I've been fighting in a league where there aren't any bells or rounds or one-minute recoveries. Been doin' it since I was around eight years old too. How's that for a *developmental window*, eh?"

"You're talking about back-alley brawls and such, aren't you?"

Curtis nodded with a wry grin. "That's where I learned to fight and learned it well. Took a few sorry-ass whuppins before I figured out how to dance, but after that—well, let's put it this way: I haven't heard the word *nigger* or *coon* for the better part of these past seven years. Haven't, that is, until I wound up in this hellhole."

"Yeah, well, get used to it, because I'm sorry to say that that's the vocabulary around here, at least among most of the white roosters."

Hell, it don't matter. I just turn a deaf ear to it now. I'm supposed to keep my head down while I'm in here 'til my time is up—at least, that's the plan."

"Curtis, in spite of all your good intentions and efforts, I think you have to admit that *that* strategy is going by the boards fast. And speaking of plans, what do you think of my training regimen so far?"

"Seems a little *out there*, if you ask me," Curtis quipped. "But if you think you can improve on perfection, I'll be your *sandman*—for a while, at least."

"Good!" Randy exclaimed with renewed enthusiasm. "Then c'mon over here and check out this next drill."

Curtis followed Randy to the section of the infield where he'd marked out a series of lines in the sand that formed a square approximately sixteen feet to a side.

"This 'ring' is roughly the size used in amateur matches—Golden Glove regulation," Randy instructed. "I want you to get comfortable with the limitations it poses. It ought to feel downright claustrophobic at first to an open-field brawler such as yourself."

Curtis noted a diagonal line stricken at each corner roughly two feet inward from the right-angle intersection. "How come you closed off the corners like that?"

"The corners are death traps as far as you're concerned," Randy cautioned.

"Death traps . . . hmm."

"Yeah, if a real slugger ever corners you, you might as well say your prayers, 'cause you're goin' down for certain—no two ways about it."

"Goin' down, huh?" Curtis mumbled. "So what's your answer to this certain death, coach?"

"Backpedaling."

"Backpedaling?"

"Stop repeating everything I say," Randy grumbled. "It's annoying and redundant."

"Redundant?"

"Please try to be serious for once. Now, step inside the ring and do as I say."

Curtis bent, grinning, and mimed a boxer's cocky entrance into a roped ring, springing up and down like a pogo stick upon clearing the imaginary tethers.

"Awwllll right!" Randy directed. "I want you to jog the perimeter of the ring without stepping on or across any of the lines that close off the corners."

"No sweat."

"Backwards."

"Backwards?"

"You're doing it again."

"Backwards?"

"Stop it! Yes, backwards. You need to develop a reflexive memory for backpedaling within the confines of a regulation ring while deftly avoiding those corners like the plague. I want you to make a circle in a square and live in it until you can trace it stone blind, like you had curb feelers—backwards and forwards, but mostly backwards."

"*Deftly*—like this?" Curtis began to trot in reverse along the edge of the ring but failed to turn at the first corner, almost stumbling as he tried to correct.

"No, not like that," Randy chided. "Try just walking backwards for a couple of laps until you sort of feel the borders. Assume that your fighting world, Mr. Jefferson, just got significantly smaller. Now, *adapt!*"

Curtis complied with a couple of cautious walking turns around the ring, then resumed his little backward jog-dance for a few clockwise laps.

"That's pretty good," Randy shouted. "Now, reverse direction."

Curtis performed the same half-speed astern jog, counterclockwise now. Randy had him continue this drill for about five minutes, reversing direction every minute. Upon completion, the young trainee was not nearly as winded as from the distance drill, since he had paced himself.

"That seemed sort of pointless," he grumbled as they made for the pump. "I didn't even break a sweat."

"On the contrary," Randy retorted, "This agility drill is probably the most instructive thing you'll do today—or maybe all month."

"How do you figure?"

"All those evasive moves you taught yourself in street fights will now have to conform to the limits of the ring. It's quite different from an alley. You can run, but you've only got two hundred and fifty-six square feet to hide in—considerably less than that if you stay out of the corners."

"Still seems like a waste of time to me. The ropes will tell me where my limits are."

"The limited size of your venue needs to be second-nature," Randy insisted stubbornly, as he pumped the old iron handle again. "When you are ready, you'll know that sixteen-foot diameter like the edges of your bunk bed."

195

Curtis finished the session with the perimeter run-walk, and he had to drag himself to the life-giving pump at the close of the final drill. He was even more fatigued than on the previous two efforts. The water, as always, was like a liquid transfusion from heaven.

"Take a bath in it," Randy chuckled. "You've earned it."

Curtis grinned and splashed some more water onto his heated face. He sputtered joyfully from the cooling effect, then came up with a thoughtful question. "You've done an awful lot here, and I do appreciate it. But I can't help wonderin' just what *you're* gettin' out of all this work."

"What, do I have to have some ulterior motive? I can't just be a 'Good Samaritan' here?"

"Good Samaritan?"

"No, really," Randy insisted, "it's just like the Good Samaritan story, only with a twist."

"What do you mean?"

"Curtis, you know the parable, don't you?"

"Refresh my memory."

"Well, the story's about a traveler who gets the shit beat out of him by some robbers who take his money and leave him by the side of the road for dead."

"Didn't he know about traveler's checks? The commercials say you should never carry cash on a trip," Curtis interjected innocently.

"Don't be ridiculous. This is a biblical story—they didn't have traveler's checks back then, bonehead."

Curtis shrugged. "They should have. Maybe the Samaritan wouldn't have got his ass whupped."

"No, it wasn't the Samaritan who *got his ass whupped*, as you say."

Curtis stared blankly. "Who did then?"

"It was the traveler," Randy explained. "Now let me finish my goddamn story, Curtis!"

"Okay, okay. You don't have to get all pissy about it."

"All right, then," Randy continued, still perturbed. "So, lots of people walked past the traveler, lying there in the ditch, but nobody helped him until the Samaritan came along."

"What's a Samaritan?"

"Someone from Samaria—can I please finish?" Randy shouted. Curtis pretended to cower as the younger boy continued. "The Samaritan patched up the traveler's wounds and put him up in a nearby hotel until he could recover."

"Nice guy—so what's this got to do with you and me?"

"Don't you get it, Curtis? I'm the Good Samaritan!"

"I guess, but there's just one big problem with this story."

"What's that?"

"Ain't nobody gonna whup my ass and leave me in a ditch."

"And that's the twist!" Randy exclaimed. "I'm going to help you *before* you get your ass beat, not after."

"There's still one other hitch with all of this," Curtis mused.

"And what's that?"

"Anybody starts some shit with me—*they're* the ones gonna need the help, not me."

"Curtis," Randy sighed, "you're incorrigible."

"Thank you," Curtis grinned, taking a bow as if he'd been paid the highest compliment, "whatever the fuck *that* is."

Darkness in the Heir

"Jeezus, shit!"

Harvey Huish was genuinely startled to have stumbled across the familiar rendering in the reform school library. In fact, the ghosts evoked by that stark image literally drained the blood from his already pale face. The appearance of the artwork at this time was too coincidental not to be some kind of portent.

Old Mr. Osgood, faculty director, resident history hack, and renowned facilitator of classroom catnaps, had assigned the "senior students" to write a theme on the early Renaissance. It was in the performance of that assignment that the young miscreant was diligently perusing an art history book on that period. That's when the haunting Brueghel drawing *Big Fish Eat Little Fish* flash-teleported from four centuries and half a world away to jump off the page at him.

"Jesus, *shit!*" he yelped again, recoiling from the page as if bitten by some pit viper.

Marcus, the henhouse dorm guard and erstwhile librarian, shot Harvey a passing look of consternation over this profane outburst that had broken the silence of the reading room from his place at the circulation desk. Harvey, meanwhile, regained his composure and returned a look that vaguely resembled contrition, acknowledging his breach of library etiquette. His wide eyes returned to the morbid conglomeration of images that lay glaring on the table before him: a depiction of dozens of the finny creatures of all assorted sizes, from minnows to whales, devouring and/or being devoured in a grisly sort of feeding frenzy that plainly signified the senselessness in the whole notion of survival of the fittest.

It was the same print that he'd first beheld hanging in the alcove of his father's home office at their palatial Tucson villa. He had a vague recollection of its esteemed place as the only piece of artwork to adorn dear old Pinky's otherwise minimalist lair from the time Harvey was a toddler, but he was twelve before he began gazing in earnest on the spectacle and wondering about the overt meaning behind the vaguely disturbing imagery.

Harvey had always been an intelligent and inquisitive sort of kid, but somehow the artist's intended message had missed its mark with him. Of course, his father's take on the piece didn't help matters much, as the boy had long been nurtured on Pinky's Machiavellian view of the grand scheme. At twelve, the patriarch's influence guided the boy into a gross misinterpretation of the drawing. The overbearing tycoon went so far as to sum it up for his son one sunny afternoon as he found Harvey standing transfixed before the hanging print.

"*That*, son, is a great reminder of why you always want to be the biggest fish," he thundered in his typically boorish manner.

Ironic indeed that the fictional father depicted in the lower portion of the rendering is apparently explaining the true proverbial theme of the spectacle to his own young son, as indicated by the caption at the bottom of the sketch. But neither Pinky nor Harvey could read the Flemish inscription that paraphrased a Latin proverb about justice, and so they were left to devise their own misguided interpretation.

"Always, the biggest fish" aptly described the Huish line's guiding philosophy of ambition up to that point, and it resonated quite well with the lad's natural bent. Now Harvey, like his father before him, was a unique character in many respects, not the least of which was their shared obsession with grand notions of conquest.

Even as a youngster, the contradiction to the conventional wisdom about trust-fund kids that Harvey embodied was startling. One widely held belief is that children born into the lap of luxury tend toward sloth. Not so with Harvey. For him, the wealth was always incidental to the hunger for power that coursed through his dynamic bloodline. Harvey stood out as the one who was always driven by an overwhelming sense of the corrupted kind of pride that demands winning at all costs. He established his assumption of the Huish legacy of outsized one-upmanship at a tender age, as demonstrated by his canny manipulation of the rules in schoolyard contests, but culminating in a certain extraordinary episode. It was a pivotal event in the boy's life that began, coincidentally, as he was pondering the multiple images in the Brueghel sketch outside his father's office, as he frequently did.

He liked to loiter near the door and pick up bits of the one-sided phone conversations that drifted out of Pinky's open office door. Harvey regarded his father as quite the operator, and the old man's skillful exploitation of clients, colleagues, and subordinates never ceased to stimulate the boy's admiration. The voice, though coarse and gravelly, was always confident and superior, which made the youngster beam with pride for his dad's unbroken string of business triumphs. That is why an uncharacteristically plaintive tone of frustration that emitted through the half-open door on this particular occasion caught Harvey's attention. Incredibly, it was almost a *whine*.

"Yes, Stephen—as sure as the pope's Italian, it was him payin' those overnight visits to her room. Those pictures your detective gave me were pretty clear, and I didn't need any porno shots to get the message. Man, to think I even stood the bill for their rendezvous. Put her up in my presidential suite at the Red Rocks Resort for what was supposed to be a shopping trip. What a chump I was!"

Harvey rightly reckoned that "Stephen" at the other end of the line was Stephen Robson, the old man's lawyer and frequent confidant. Who "him" and "her" were was not so certain.

"No, of course I'm not going to confront them; that would be stupid. They can never know that I'm onto their shoddy little tryst, or I'll have the guilty finger pointing at me when one or the other of them meets with an unexpected misfortune. That's right, I said *when*, not *if*. Oh yes, and don't get all sanctimonious with me either, mister. For what I pay you, I'll stretch our attorney-client privilege beyond your worst nightmares. You made your deal with the devil a long time ago; now you can live with it!"

The boy pondered the gravity of the words during the inaudible response by the lawyer.

"Well, that's the hell of it," Pinky continued, "you're absolutely right—if it even has the slightest whiff of foul play, I'll be the number one suspect as the betrayed husband. And even if they can't make anything stick, which they won't, just the accusation would be enough to queer things with some of my clients. Hell, you know I can't afford a scandal right now. I'm really stuck here, Stephen. I don't know whether to shit or go blind. I just know I can't let this go on. It's just too goddamn humiliating—understand?"

Then, the entire weight of the situation came crashing in on the boy with the next round of dialogue.

"Yeah, I should have seen through it, but he's always been just part of the family. He sleeps here in the casita about half the time. At least they had the decency to take it out from under my roof—or at least I think so. I've never seen any evidence of it around here. Gotten even chummier lately, though. He's been taking Harvey out on his fishing boat down in Rocky Point recently. Going again this weekend, I think. You know, Stephen, the hell of it is, I love the guy. I'd been willing to share almost anything I've got with my brother, just not my fucking wife!"

Harvey had heard enough—more than any twelve-year-old could be expected to bear. He withdrew quickly and quietly to the inner sanctum of his upstairs bedroom to dwell on the unwanted information he had gained in his silent surveillance and the imminent impact it would have on his young life.

———

It was three o'clock on Saturday morning when Robert Huish woke his nephew to make the four-hour drive to Rocky Point. The streets of Tucson were eerily abandoned as Robert's fire-engine red '56 Chevy Cameo pickup rolled through the early AM darkness down the Catalina foothills. Streetlights twinkled like miniature novas off the polished chrome grille. The lavishly customized truck turned south on the Nogales Highway, then west on Valencia Road as it gave way to State Highway 86. The way had become familiar and tedious to Harvey, who curled up on the wide tuck-and-roll bench seat with an overstuffed down pillow he'd brought from his bed and pretended to sleep.

Robert stopped for gas and a coffee-to-go in Lukeville before crossing the border into Sonoyta. Harvey sat up, stretching and wiping false sleepiness from wide-awake eyes, but refrained from speaking for over half of the one-hour stretch of Sonoran highway from the border to the beach. The first traces of predawn light bathed the road and the desert shoulders in a faintly glowing gray cast. The very atmosphere was colorless and surreal, like a grainy black-and-white movie.

It was Robert who finally broke the silence by switching on the dash-mounted AM radio. A static-laden signal, owing to the remoteness of their location, conveyed a distorted version of Buddy Holly's latest chart-topper. The famous bespectacled Texas boy's voice crackled over the airwaves.

Harvey folded the pillow around his head, improvising a giant pair of earmuffs and contorted his face into a sour expression that clearly indicated his displeasure with the fuzzy cacophony. Robert, in a ham-handed attempt at being playful, turned up the volume.

Harvey, responding in kind, turned the knob to "off" with a loud click that sounded like an audible exclamation point.

"Hey man, I know you're still sleepy, Bucky, but you could at least say 'good morning,' okay?"

"Good morning," Harvey chanted in a forced monotone. Robert's playful nickname for him, once accepted as a term of endearment, now rang only as ridicule of the boy's exaggerated overbite. He hated the moniker only slightly less than the proposition of dental braces.

They rode on for another ten minutes in absolute silence, the droning of the 265-cubic-inch V-8 providing the solitary sound as the rolling highway rose and fell through a series of arroyos and ridges. Dawn was breaking on a momentous occasion, and "Bucky" could feel his own personal significance rising with the ascension of the sun.

Robert reached over and retrieved his Ray-Bans from the glove box. The sunglasses complemented the windswept blond hair for a movie star look that made him resemble an aging James Dean.

"Okay, what's it gonna take for you to wake up and be human, kid?"

Harvey suddenly realized that he was behaving out of character for the situation, which might start Robert wondering. He mustered a more conversational tone.

"Sorry, Unk, I guess I'm just tired, and a little bored."

"Bored? Hell, you were stoked on fishing our last time out. How many triggerfish did you catch last month, twelve?"

"Yeah, it was cool and all, but my pal Anthony's dad takes him *deep-sea fishing*, whenever they go out. That sounds like *real* fun. Fishing the shallows is starting to be a drag."

To be sure, Robert had always kept the excursions close to shore where he knew smaller fish would be plentiful so Harvey would have fun catching pan fish and would never get skunked.

"I told you before, Buck, that you don't have enough weight or muscle yet to reel in a big fish."

"Oh, I know, but I thought maybe I could just watch how *you* do it, so I'll know what to do when I am ready."

"Well . . ."

"I mean, I want to go for dorado someday, like you do. So why shouldn't I want to learn from the best, huh?"

"Flattery will get you everywhere, kid. Okay, the weather should hold—no *chubascos* in the forecast—so we'll go out to the blue water today. But don't tell your mother. I promised her I'd keep you close to shore."

The fractured asphalt roller coaster that had, for the past fifty miles, twisted and pitched through creosote and mesquite vistas now suddenly aimed due west across an even, sandy expanse that resembled the austere floor of Death Valley. Gulls soared overhead, cavorting in the thermals newly rising from the desert floor as Harvey straightened up and blinked. There was always a glimmer of anticipation, of prescience, just before the first sighting of the sea, that eerie sense of an infinite vacancy just over the next ridge: land's end. The cresting of a gradual but familiar rise in the road immediately gave way to a panoramic scope of the sun-dappled Sea of Cortez. It fell away before them, an azure body of water that stretched to the horizon and past to the north, south, and west like a vast blue portal to the Great Beyond.

Harvey cranked down the window to get a whiff of the pungent sea atmosphere. The iodine essence of decaying kelp, sun-baked shellfish cadavers, and desiccated minnows wafted from the beach into the cab on a draft of already warm morning air. The odor always exhilarated with its primeval putrescence. This day, that olfactory exhilaration enhanced a mounting thrill that some point of no return was imminent. Land's end, indeed.

When they finally pulled up to the marina at the coast, a three-man crew of dockhands had already prepared Robert's thirty-foot Chris Craft vessel, *The Wayward Wind*, for the half-day trip—tethered it to the floating dock, gassed it up, stocked it with bait, water, ice, a dozen twelve-ounce bottles of Carta Blanca beer, six bottles of Coke for Harvey, six Hershey bars, an economy-sized bag of Clover Club potato chips, and six red-chili burritos.

Robert peeled off five twenty-dollar bills to cover the gas, supplies, and a generous tip. "Hope you remembered the church-key, Miguel," he chuckled as he paid the only English-speaking dockhand of the three. "I'd be one sorry sonofabitch if I had to subsist on food and water for a half-day."

"Just yesterday we mounted a bottle-opener on the bridge console next to the helm for you, Capitan," Miguel returned, "just to be certain."

"You're a jewel as always, Miguel," Robert grinned, revealing a pair of prematurely prominent crow's feet. With the prowess of a cat, he playfully sprang from the low pontoon platform, vaulted over the gunwale, and strode aft to check the baitwell. Harvey clambered on board behind him.

"Hey, Miguel—we're gonna need a whole lot more fish heads than this today. We're headed out to the blue water this time, and we'll be doin' some chumming, I imagine."

Miguel rattled off some indistinguishable rapid-fire phrases in Spanish and one of the other dockhands vanished and reappeared with two five-gallon slop buckets filled with the remnants from the previous day's fish cleaning. Robert flashed a thumbs-up toward Miguel as he stepped up to the helm and fired up the twin Evinrude outboards, while Harvey stowed the smelly chum buckets astern next to the bait well.

"Get your life jacket on, Bucky," Robert called above the rumbling of the warming motors.

Harvey complied but complained as part of the routine. "How come you don't wear a life jacket and I have to?"

"Because, when you generate as much hot air as me, you can float from here to China, kid," he answered, shouting now over the low roar of the 200-horse Evinrudes. "Avast now, and cast off, you sorry-ass landlubber!"

Harvey rolled his eyes as always at his uncle's bad pirate impression, but he obediently slipped the looped mooring tethers from two polished chrome cleats bolted to the port side gunwale while Miguel's two peons pushed the vessel away from the dock with blunted gaffing poles.

"Hasta la vista en seis horas!" Robert sang out as the big V-hulled craft lumbered underway. Harvey always noted that his uncle's pronunciation was flawless, and he was conversant enough that the locals knew not to try using the language gap to put anything over on the rich gringo, at least not in his presence.

Robert held the vessel at trolling speed across the harbor, aiming the bow of *The Wayward Wind* toward open water. Harvey stepped up close to the helm to be heard above the low thunder of the twin motors.

"Why do you always overpay those worthless Mexicans, Unk?"

Robert wrinkled his brow. "I grease their palms to keep 'em happy so they don't spit in my burritos or piss in my coffee."

"Well, how do you know they don't anyway?"

"I guess you just gotta have some trust," Robert replied. "Don't you trust your fellow man, Bucky?"

"Not much, and definitely not those stinking spics back there—especially not that suck-ass Miguel."

"Jeez, Buck—where's the love?"

Harvey recognized that it was a rhetorical question and let it lie. But it did conjure up the recollection of Pinky's grating voice booming out of his inner office in one of those one-sided phone conversations with one of his most-repeated aphorisms: *"Always better to be feared than to be loved."* Those words of debatable wisdom now congealed in the boy's mind as he stared across the green-and-gold sunlit water. A slight onshore breeze held a smattering of circling gulls aloft and stirred ten thousand shattered bits of solar reflection on the bay's surface with its warm breath. The sparkling sun-gems appeared to the youngster like shards from a glass explosion floating in silent slow motion.

Better to be feared . . .

Generally speaking, the Sea of Cortez is a mild-mannered body of water—something of a gigantic inlet a hundred miles across and seven hundred miles long, sheltered from the greater Pacific by the long Baja peninsula at its western limit. Its calm waters, year-round warm weather, and abundant schools of dorado and yellowtail made it a sport fisherman's paradise and had for years been one of Robert's favorite playgrounds.

Although *The Wayward Wind* was a stranger to the western shore—the Baja coast—Robert had made himself comfortably familiar with the Sonoran side by exploring all the shelves, trenches, and estuaries within a fifty-mile radius of Rocky Point. This morning he told Harvey they were setting out for the edge of a deepwater trench, about thirteen miles offshore, where he knew the yellowtail were always plentiful.

The instant that the stately craft churned past the buoys marking the harbor limit, Robert called to Harvey. "Steady yourself!" With that, he gradually eased the throttle forward to three-quarters full, unleashing the pent-up fury and roar of the powerful outboards.

Harvey clutched the leaning post behind the helm as the vessel sprang forward. It occurred to him that had he not stabilized himself, or if the acceleration had been more pronounced or abrupt, he would surely have lost his footing.

For a moment he faced the bow and enjoyed the bracing wind and the saltwater spray as the deep hull rose and fell rhythmically. At length, he turned his focus astern to gaze eastward at the foaming white ribbon that trailed in the boat's wake. The risen sun illuminated the pristine froth, amplifying its brightness and creating a glowing image like a long stretch of brilliant winter highway covered in new-fallen snow.

"This is my notion of paradise!" Robert shouted above the wind and the deafening drone of the engines. The breathtaking seaward sprint made Harvey's dark heart race.

The shoreline was already diminishing. In five minutes it was barely discernible. In ten it was a mere memory. Nothing but water now in every direction. The color of the sea went from green to teal, then to deep blue as they motored outward. The scent of the beach gradually dissipated, as did the presence of gulls from the sky. The youngster glanced momentarily toward the northern horizon and found it difficult to determine where the sea ended and the cloudless sky began, they were both such an indistinguishably deep azure.

After fifteen minutes and more than ten miles of travel, Robert cut the throttle to half, then a quarter open. The rolling pitch of the bow and the roar of the motors fell off.

"Do you want to take the helm?" he offered to Harvey. The boy nodded and took the wheel. "Watch the compass and keep the bow pointed to the west," Robert ordered sternly. "And don't even think about touching that throttle!"

"Aye, aye, Cap'n," the boy returned.

It had become routine for Robert to turn over the steerage the moment he hankered for a morning beer. This morning, Harvey counted on that routine. His uncle fished through the box of ice and produced the customary Carta Blanca bottle. He pried off the cap on his newly installed bottle opener and raised the brown glass flagon in a mock toast.

"Here's to a hearty breakfast, matey, and the first of many a dead soldier!" he squawked in his best swashbuckler imitation. He drained the bottle in an uninterrupted series of audible gulps and tossed the empty container into the sea with a flourish.

"Breakfast of champions, sir," said Harvey.

"I hope that's not a note of sarcasm I detect," the elder Huish interjected. "Surely you don't doubt the nutritional value in a bottle of Mexican beer—do you, lad?"

"Of course not, sir."

"Because if I thought you did, I'd have to translate these ingredients listed herein and inform you that this delicious amber brew consists of a healthful combination of barley, hops, rice, and a number of other nutritious grains—not to mention the positive medicinal and laxative properties captured in the fermentation process. Better breakfast than a bowl of soggy Kellogg's Corn Flakes any day!"

"Of course, sir," Harvey agreed, as always. "And if you don't mind my saying, if one bottle is a good breakfast, two must make for an absolutely *great* one, wouldn't you say?"

"Yes, indeed I would say," Robert bellowed. "And since I always do what I say, I will take your advice and have another." And so another empty Carta Blanca bottle went airborne, then seaborne. "Man, this warm sea air is making me thirsty," Robert said and belched. "I could use a beer," he mused, pretending to forget about the first two. "How about you, Bucky?"

This was something new, not part of the routine. Harvey was momentarily thrown. He wanted to continue with the façade of camaraderie, but he needed to keep a clear head. "Sure, why not?" he responded after hesitating.

The light-headed uncle retrieved two more bottles, pried off the caps, handing one to his underwhelmed and underage nephew, and clinked glass flagons in a real toast. "Welcome to your first beer, Bucky. I'm honored to be the one to make the introduction!"

Harvey hoisted the bottle and took a small swig. "Thanks, Unk," he coughed, grimacing from the unsavory flavor of the sour brew.

"Remember, kid, don't ever say a word about what happened out here."

"Oh, you don't need to worry about *that*," Harvey replied.

Robert now reached around the boy and eased back on the throttle to bring the big craft down to trolling speed. The rapid deceleration and then the ensuing lurch forward from the wake-swell ramming up against the transom made the boat pitch unexpectedly, causing them both to stumble clumsily for better footing. Recovering quickly, Robert made his way over to the starboard gunwale and peered into the depths. He detected traces of some shadowy movement gliding several fathoms below the hull. Meanwhile, Harvey seized upon the opportunity to empty most of the contents of his beer bottle over the other side undetected.

"Bring her about and bear due south, Bucky," Robert ordered.

The boy understood and complied immediately.

"I think we're at the edge of a trench," the elder Huish announced. "I'm gonna start chumming. You keep her heading south and don't touch that throttle."

Harvey watched as his uncle waddled astern, lifted the chum bucket, and approached the transom to jettison the stinking fish parts. The boy turned back forward, eyes falling on the throttle, a short metal shaft rising from the operator's console capped with a horizontal red-and-white plastic handgrip. It glinted, winking in the morning sun. With a stony expression stealing across his face, "Bucky" gripped the lever and deliberately shoved it forward. The twin Evinrudes sent up a roar, *The Wayward Wind* lurched forward, and Uncle Robert, the Huish family prodigal, went flailing over the transom into the vast, sky-blue waters of the Sea of Cortez.

performance

Clearly it was the surprise appearance of the Brueghel sketch on the library table that aroused some sleeping memory enough so as to provoke that sudden profane outburst from Harvey (*Jeezus, shit!*). But it was not the recollection of that fateful instance in his past—the murderous motion of an adolescent hand pitching a kinsman into the unforgiving sea—that stirred the unfamiliar surge of fear and loathing from the young man's soulless core. It was neither that nor the ensuing memory that the drawing teased out of that ponderous forty minutes it took for his helpless uncle to finally succumb to that vast watery grave. Oddly enough, it was the central image in the picture, one that had somehow evaded his attention in past viewings: a knightly figure wielding the sword that pierced the biggest fish. It was that sword in the picture, the sword of justice, that harkened a flash vision of the old Indian judge's wrinkled brown face and piercing ebony eyes. It was the sudden and ominous reappearance of that foreboding visage that caused the young reprobate to cry out as if physically injured.

Of course, his uncle's mystery-shrouded demise was inescapably connected to the unforgettable audience with that withered Native American sage and his portentous words; Harvey found it impossible to revisit one part of the memory without pulling up the rest along with it. In fact, the young criminal still savored the fruits of his own premeditated performance on that momentous fishing trip. Not only did he enjoy the elevated regard and unending gratitude of his father and the curious sense of having removed the stain of infidelity from his mother; but just the briefest recollection of those forty minutes in which he held the power of life and death over another human being gave him a thrill that was almost erotic. Still, that narcissistic remembrance inevitably brought with it one infinitely less pleasurable: that old Indian judge.

———◆———

When Robert Huish's head broke the surface about thirty yards astern of *The Wayward Wind*, his face conveyed the expected shock and anger of a man tossed overboard, but his first take on the situation was that his nephew had accidently bumped the throttle which had sent him tumbling for a very sobering dunk into the chilly water. His boat now drifted, motors idling, within an easy swim, his nephew looking on from the transom with what he took to be an expression of sheer panic.

"Shut 'er down, Bucky!" Robert sputtered.

The boy did not move from his petrified pose.

Assuming that he hadn't been heard over the rumbling motors, Robert slipped out of his deck shoes, committing them to the deep, and broke into a lively breaststroke that slowly but surely began to close the gap between captain and ship. The sodden denim jeans and heavy cotton shirt encumbered his movements and he quickly became winded, but he was already halfway there when Harvey called out something that made his emotions instantly shift from shock and anger to horror and despair.

"Hey, Unk, where's all that hot air that was gonna float you to China?"

With that, the boy strode purposefully to the bridge and took the helm. The motors roared to life and churned away, putting another fifty yards between swimmer and vessel before the props fell idle again. Harvey appeared at the transom and grinned. Obviously this was some kind of twisted joke.

Faced with a decidedly longer swim, Robert quickly unbuttoned the fly on his jeans and slipped out of the leaden pants, as he likewise tore his shirt open and jettisoned it as well. Less laden, he set out afresh toward the boat with a thrashing freestyle stroke that brought him back within earshot inside of a minute.

"Stop this crazy shit and throw me a life-ring, Bucky!" he shouted breathlessly, now treading water. "You're gonna kill me!"

"That's the plan, Unk," Harvey called back. "You don't know it quite yet, but you're about to be fish food—you know, *chum*, old chum!" The boy pulled a bottle of beer out of the icebox and pitched it toward Robert. It plunked into the water a few yards in front of him and sank like a stone. "Let me introduce you to your *last* beer, Unk. I'm honored, no, *excited* to be the one to do it. Now go down and get it!"

"You *motherfucker!*" Robert screamed.

"Not me, Unk," Harvey retorted. "*You're* the motherfucker—but not anymore. *Never again!*"

The words clung to Robert like a millstone about his neck as the brazen nephew actually proffered a sardonic fingers-to-forehead salute to his helpless uncle before returning to the controls of the boat. *The Wayward Wind* thundered away for nearly a quarter of a mile and then came about ninety degrees starboard at trolling speed. For a fleeting moment, the curious maneuver caused Robert to hold out just the faintest hope that Harvey had reconsidered following through on this heinous act. That hope died a swift death when the vessel assumed a circling pattern, holding a consistent quarter-mile distance from the condemned swimmer.

The water temperature of the Sea of Cortez hovered at sixty degrees in April—not exactly the North Atlantic, but sufficiently cold to sap a swimmer's strength in short order. Robert was a good pool paddler but no endurance swimmer. Nevertheless, with a grim determination he began to sidestroke due east toward the Sonoran shore, even knowing that he could never by any stretch cover the eleven-mile distance—not in this lifetime. Yet, in spite of the hopelessness of that objective, life, as it often does, refused to submit to certain condemnation, even unto the end.

Harvey circled in the boat like a motor-driven vulture watching his uncle's bobbing head from afar. He mused to himself that the elder Huish looked like a ridiculous blond marker buoy winking yellow flashes from his towhead topknot that followed the cadence of his futile sidestrokes. The boy kept watch over that morbid spectacle of desperation for thirty-five minutes, which seemed like thirty-five hours. His pulse quickened with every sweep of the second hand on his fine Omega watch. His breath grew heavy and labored. A shiver of excitement rattled his adolescent frame. He watched as he imagined that the rhythm of his uncle's hopeless swimming strokes was falling off—that he was witnessing Robert's will to live growing ever dimmer, just as his own power seemed to grow ever stronger.

Suddenly, at least a half-dozen hypothetical what ifs swooped down from out of nowhere, descending upon the juvenile assassin like the mythical harpies of old, accosting his smug self-confidence. What if another fishing boat or shrimp trawler happened along just now? Could happen. What if a small plane crossing the narrow gulf passed low overhead and spotted that bobbing blond head winking from the surface like a floating yellow popcorn kernel? Not beyond the realm of possibility. Or what if that pain-in-the-ass Miguel was to radio *The Wayward Wind* to verify her location and was met with silence? What if Robert actually could swim the eleven miles to the Sonoran shore? Short of that, the longer Robert endured, the more likely the occurrence of one or more of the first three hypothetical scenarios.

In the thralls of this unexpected wave of apprehension, Harvey toyed with the idea of barreling over the helpless swimmer with his own boat, and the twisted sort of justice offered by this new contingency brought a pernicious smile to the boy's lips. But the whole ensuing fabrication of the facts and the presumption of his innocence hinged on the absence of any evidence to the contrary. If a body was to be found, there must be no marks of violence so that even the faintest glimmer of suspicion would be doused from the outset.

"Keep your nerve, Harvey," he spoke aloud to himself. "He won't last much longer."

The sun had risen high above the eastern horizon and it now glared down on the sea like an angry red eye. The blinding brightness of that solar orb reflecting on the water made Harvey dizzy to the point of nausea. He spotted Robert's Ray-Bans lying on the deck where he'd lost them in the fall. The boy scooped them up and proudly donned the dark shades. Eyes now shielded, he scanned the shimmering surface where he'd last seen the doomed mariner. Robert was gone.

While the boy had turned his gaze to retrieve the ill-gotten shades, a leg cramp pulled the dogged swimmer below the surface where he reflexively gulped then sucked in the cold brine until it filled his lungs. His arms and legs convulsed briefly as he went into cardiac arrest, then quieted. Robert Huish's lifeless body glided silently down into the dark gaping maw of the vast tectonic rift that had formed this oceanic gulf, eons ago.

Harvey shook his head at the grim irony. He had watched dutifully, keeping an unbroken vigil for over half an hour, and then during the brief distraction of snatching up the glasses, the son of a bitch slipped under and cheated him out of the final pleasure of watching him go down. Even so, the conjured image of his uncle's final and fatal submersion released a thrill within his core that rivaled any drug-induced rush. Inexplicably, he began to laugh in a high, puppety kind of cackle. He'd never heard himself laugh that way before. It was almost as if someone else, someone even more evil than his depraved self, *were laughing through him.*

———◆———

Harvey looked up from the reproduction of the Brueghel print and glanced around the library, as if perhaps the other occupants might have read his guilty thoughts. Satisfied that no fellow inmate in the immediate confines of that reading room seemed to be practicing mental telepathy, he returned his gaze to the sketch and focused again on the image of the helmeted man with the knife slitting the biggest fish open at the belly. While the furtive figure's face was obscured from view, Harvey visually attributed the visage of the old half-breed municipal court judge to that subject. The face was *his!* Harvey shuddered.

The first and only live, in-person appearance of that ancient relic of an Indian adjudicator and his wooden face happened two days immediately following that momentous morning and was unalterably attached to the memory of Harvey's first homicide. It was to come on the heels of a series of cunning performances that would never allow anyone to suspect that the poor prepubescent lad had any hand in his beloved uncle's unfortunate demise. Well, almost anyone.

———◆———

Harvey drifted with *The Wayward Wind* for the better part of an hour, sipping ice water, opening more bottles of Carta Blanca, dumping their contents into the sea, and watching for the corpse to surface. When it didn't, he tuned the vessel's wireless to Emergency Channel 16 as his uncle had once taught him to do in such an instance. Relief from the unnerving what ifs that came with his uncle's final passing brought back the clarity that the precocious assassin needed to conclude his treacherous act. He depressed the talk button on the microphone, and mustered his best tone of distress.

"Mayday! Mayday! This is *The Wayward Wind*. We have a man overboard! I repeat—*man overboard*! Does anybody hear me?"

Harvey released the talk button and listened to empty static for a long while. After a second similar distress transmission, a voice finally crackled back.

"*Wayward Wind, dónde está?*"

Harvey's Spanish was not on par with his uncle's but he understood a few basic phrases. "I'm not sure where," he whined. "I'm just a kid, a *niño*," he sniveled. "I'm *lost* without my uncle, my *tío*!" he wailed. He actually brought himself to tears, imagining how an innocent twelve-year-old might feel under similar circumstances—if the fall *had* been an accident, that is. Harvey knew instinctively that the jump from *how it might have been* to *how it was* never demanded a huge leap. For him, it was nearly effortless.

For several minutes the channel was jammed with multiple static dialogues, several different voices, dozens of rapid-fire, staccato fragment phrases in Spanish that were beyond Harvey's simple discernment, with the exception of the reference to *The Wayward Wind* being repeated in English several times.

Then, a familiar voice in English, but with the heavy Mexican accent that Harvey always thought affected. It was Miguel, the dock foreman.

"Harvey, what happened? Where are you?"

"Oh, Miguel! I'm so glad it's you!" Harvey blurted, as if he was truly relieved. "Uncle Robert fell overboard. I . . . I don't know what happened. He'd been drinking, like always—"

"Never mind that right now, Harvey," Miguel interrupted. "Where are you? Roberto said you were headed for open water."

"We headed west, Miguel. I think about ten miles or so, but I don't know. All I know is that I can't see land in any direction, and I'm *scared*, Miguel. Uncle Robert never came up. Oh, my God, *he never came up!*"

The despair coming through those contrived inflections resonated perfectly. The boy sounded afraid, disoriented, and confused. Everyone listening in on Channel 16 adopted the pathetic *pobrecito gringo* as their cause for the day. He needed rescue, no question, and rescue was on the way.

A shrimp trawler was the first vessel to appear. It blinked into sight within ten minutes of the last transmission, a dot on the southern horizon that grew into a birdlike shape—its netted booms stretched out on either side like great pinioned wings.

Harvey fired a signal flare into the azure sky to confirm his location. The smoke trail could be seen for miles. He tore the Wayfarer sunglasses from his face and tossed them back to the deck in anticipation of the oncoming scrutiny of the scene and of him. They might have been some use in concealing his dry, remorseless eyes, but he opted to avoid the residual "Mr. Cool" image that might be negatively construed from sporting the stylish specs. The neophyte murderer strode to the stern, leaned over the transom that was his uncle's gateway to doom, and splashed cupped handfuls of seawater into his eyes. The brine stung the corneal tissue, already tender from the ravages of a brilliant sun, but the boy continued until he could barely blink back the pain. Manufacturing dramatic tears from within would have to wait for only the most needed moments, as they came at a premium; but a pair of bloodshot whites would do nicely in the interim.

The trawler's captain hailed the drifting *Wayward Wind* in Spanish as the vessel drew slowly within earshot. *"Qué pasó al capitán?"* the weathered mariner bellowed. The boy lifted his hands as if to indicate a distraught failure to register. *"Dónde está el tío?"* the captain persisted in a clear shout.

Young Harvey nodded his understanding this time and beckoned to the open water behind him as he heaved a shuddering sigh. The ship immediately broke away and began a systematic sweep of the water within a half-mile radius of *The Wayward Wind*, all four of its deckhands scanning the surface with binoculars—to no avail—leaving Harvey to search the horizon for the next rescue vessel.

Another sportfishing craft, much like *The Wayward Wind*, came rocketing out of the eastern vista inside of another ten-minute interval, pushed along by a three-foot rooster-tail of white water. It was common knowledge among gulf boaters that the Mexican Navy, which assumed the same responsibilities as their US Coast Guard counterparts in these waters, was notorious for their lackluster attitude and snail's pace reaction time in such matters. It followed that there was a tacit understanding among mariners in the Sea of Cortez that response to distress calls fell upon willing seafaring peers. And so it came as no surprise when the familiar bow of *The First Draw*, a privately owned vessel that shared a dock at the Rocky Point marina with *The Wayward Wind*, presently pulled alongside the Huish family's craft.

Marvin Tate, a commercial construction contractor from Phoenix and sometime cantina hopper with the dearly departed, appeared at the gunwale and tethered the two fishing boats together. Harvey glanced over to see that Miguel was at the helm as the rather rotund Mr. Tate boarded. The man's eyes were welling as he spoke.

"How did it happen, son?" he inquired gently, placing a limp hand on Harvey's shoulder.

"I really don't know, sir," Harvey choked. "I just heard a splash and I looked up. He was gone, just like that."

Robert's friend stared up into the sky and let out a sigh. "Something just doesn't add up," he remarked wistfully. "Robert was a strong swimmer."

"I know," Harvey agreed. "All I can think is that he must've hit his head on the transom or one of the motors when he fell."

"He fell off the stern?" the man wondered aloud.

Harvey nodded. "He was tossing some chum over the transom."

"I know this is tough, son, but I gotta ask." He hesitated before continuing. "Did a body ever come to the surface?"

Harvey shook his head and buried his face in his hands in silent anguish.

Tate glanced around at the empty beer bottles and came to the conclusion that Harvey had led him to. "Let's get rid of this trash before we head you back to port, son."

"Whatever you say, sir, . . . but . . ."

"But what?"

"Well, what if the police want to see . . . I mean, won't they want to see the boat as it was? I mean, for their investigation."

"Police? Investigation? Hell, I doubt if that sorry excuse for a constable in Rocky Point will ever get off his fat ass and even get around to filing a report before the end of the year," the beer-bloated contractor scoffed. "There won't be any investigation into this, son. Why would there be?" he asked rhetorically. "In fact, according to Miguel here, your family's lawyer, Mr. Robson, is flying down here in that V-tailed plane of his as we speak. Miguel will pilot your boat in with you while I stay out here and join the recovery effort. Robson will pick you up at the marina and fly you back home. Now, let's pitch these beer bottles, son, so there's no god-awful whispering campaign goin' on at the funeral. It's the least I can do for my buddy at this point." He muttered, then, as he tossed the Carta Blanca bottles into the ancient waters, he said, "Investigation into what—a drunken American sportsman falls into the sea and drowns? Happens all the time. You've been watching too much TV, kid. After all," he added, "this *is* Mexico!"

Harvey could barely mask his mirth upon hearing this. Of course, what was there to investigate? An inebriated gringo fisherman falls in the ocean and drowns, leaving his poor grieving nephew—a mere child—adrift and traumatized upon the hostile sea that had just swallowed up his beloved uncle. What would it serve to further upset the boy with a lot of pointless questions?

Harvey looked backward on his fateful performances of the day and took pride. No corpse. No known motive. No third-party witness. No trace or even the faintest suspicion of foul play—only an unfortunate lad who'd been scarred for life, no doubt, by this tragic accident.

But at the tender age of twelve, Harvey Huish had made his bones long before sprouting facial hair, put his house in order, eliminated a useless drain on the family estate, and one-upped his old man by pulling off the perfect murder. He was well on his way to becoming the proverbial *biggest fish.*

The rest of the day's events unfolded just as Tate had predicted. The boy barely waited an hour at the marina before Stephen Robson showed up wearing his most somber face, greased the eager palms of some nosy local *policía*, and spirited the boy off toward Tucson on the wings of his Beechcraft Bonanza before the *federales* ever got wind of any incident at all. The hum of the 260-hp Continental engine nearly lulled him to sleep on the flight back, satisfied by the knowledge that everyone bought his performance. No one would ever suspect what really happened out there that day. No one, that is, except for that goddamn old Indian judge.

Justice Delayed

And that smug and self-assured attitude may well have closed accounts had it not been for some obscure municipal statute requiring that a post-mortem hearing be held when any Tucson resident was involved in a fatality, accidental or otherwise, and regardless of where it occurred. Stephen Robson had informed Harvey of this minor procedural snag during the otherwise silent return trip from Rocky Point, and so the lawyer's Monday morning call came as no surprise. Pinky was currently away on business, and the stained Huish matriarch was still in secret mourning for her lost lover; so the family attorney was the next in line to drive the boy to the court of the Catalina Justice of the Peace late in the afternoon.

Harvey had slept the morning away and was still a bit fuzzy when they arrived at the modest facility. The Catalina JP Courthouse was an aging single-story white stucco building with a red-tile roof—the same Spanish Colonial style as all of the municipal buildings in Catalina. It shared a patch of asphalt with the local police station for parking. The precious few windows that each building displayed were cross-hatched with black wrought-iron bars. This lowest of the lower courts was reserved for the processing of traffic offenders, vagrants, shoplifters, and the like. Harvey donned the Ray-Bans he had salvaged from the boat.

"Nothing to worry about here, Junior," Robson advised on the walk from the car. "It's like I said, just a stupid formality." The lawyer always referred to him as Junior. Harvey didn't know why people couldn't just call him by his given name. "The municipal court judge here is a senile old coot named Natchez Mendoza—Mexican-Indian mix, I'd say. Must be in his nineties. He'll ask you to tell your story, and then he'll nod off while you're telling it. Just keep it short and sweet, and we'll be out of here in no time—less fuss than a parking ticket. Oh, by the way, your father cut his trip short to be here. He should arrive any time."

The two entered a small reception area where an attractive young Mexican woman waved them into the hearing room, an austere, windowless chamber no bigger than the size of a typical schoolroom, devoid of any identifiable décor. Upon entry, the boy and his lawyer found themselves at the rear terminus of a central aisle, which ran between two banks of well-worn wooden benches staring at Marvin Tate, who stood at the other end of the aisle in front of an elevated desk that formed the court bench. Tate, the avowed companion and friend to the deceased, turned his drained face to survey the newcomers. It reflected a ghastly greenish cast from the fluorescent strip-lights buzzing overhead. A matronly stenographer, seated in a tiny desk next to the rail, was finishing up her notes in shorthand.

"Come in and come forward," a gravelly voice boomed from the opposite end of the room. "We're just finishing up with Mr. Tate."

Harvey turned a glaring pair of eyes on his lawyer. "Less fuss than a parking ticket, huh?" he muttered.

"You are excused, Mr. Tate, and thank you for your cooperation."

The sandpapered voice that might have emitted from a Mexican Andy Devine actually came from the occupant of the bench. The Honorable Natchez Mendoza presented himself an almost comic figure—a vaudevillian version of judges of a more elevated stature. A pair of broad shoulders enshrouded in tattered black crepe peeked above the desktop. They supported an outlandishly large, neckless head that simulated a wrinkled leather soccer ball with a diminishing top thatch of wispy white hair. His eyes were narrow with an oriental cast that is curious to most Indian tribes, and a slight Mexican accent hinted that he might be of Yaqui descent. But the darkness of those eyes, those bottomless pools of black, seemed to reflect a deeper, more profound wisdom than his outward appearance conveyed. They penetrated to Harvey's empty core, even from across that long room.

Tate shuffled past the boy and his lawyer, eyes downcast as he made for the door.

"My apologies, your honor," Robson piped up as the two approached, "but I'm afraid we did not come prepared for a formal hearing. After all, it's only been a little over forty-eight hours since the incident, and I'm afraid we're all still suffering from the shock."

"Nothing formal about my court, Stephen," the judge scoffed, "you know that. Young man, you may approach the bench, and, Stephen, you can take a seat after you've directed your client to remove the sunglasses."

Robson crooked his finger at Harvey and the boy surrendered the eyeshades. "Sorry, your honor—too proud to show the red eyes, I suppose," the lawyer explained.

"They're all I have left of my uncle," Harvey added.

From this nearer vantage point, Harvey imagined that the talking head resembled a Halloween pumpkin—a jack-o'-lantern. But still, *those piercing eyes . . .*

"Well, I offer you my condolences, my boy," said Mendoza. "It so happens, I was fairly well-acquainted with your uncle. You see, he was a regular visitor to my traffic court—quite the lead foot on the accelerator pedal, I'm afraid. Seemed a good-hearted sort, though—just a bit reckless. And coincidentally, he accompanied Mr. Tate in here on a couple of occasions, and so I went to the extra trouble of looking his friend up to get his observations. So you see, I am being a little bit more thorough than I usually am with these accidental death inquests—although I'm not wholly certain as to why—but far from formal, I hope."

"We're here to cooperate in any way we can, your honor," said Robson as he sat down on the closest bench to the rail.

"Yes, I'm sure you are, Stephen," Mendoza sighed. "And now, young man, as difficult as this may be for you, I want you to remain standing and recount the events surrounding the unfortunate loss, giving all the details you can recall leading up to, during, and after the incident—anything that seems relevant."

Harvey complied, emphasizing the beer guzzling, and even offered the head-injury theory in the telling, but it was just as Stephen Robson had predicted. Less than a minute into the tale, Mendoza's massive head rolled forward, and his eyelids slammed shut. Harvey thought he detected a buzzing in the old man's shallow breathing, but he kept on with his story right down to the takeoff from the gravel landing strip outside Rocky Point, with the court stenographer scribbling furiously.

Judge Mendoza jerked when a long silence indicated the boy's conclusion. "Is that all you have to say at this time?" he croaked, as if he hadn't missed a word.

"Yes, your honor," Harvey gasped, pretending he was about to cry.

"Would you like me to read the deposition back to you, your honor?" the stenographer inquired.

"No, that won't be necessary. I am ready to rule on the matter," the judge returned, in an annoyed tone. "Given the facts made known today before all, this court rules that the death of Robert Huish was an accidental drowning brought about by his own unfortunate carelessness." The words hung in the air as Harvey relished the legal stamp of approval on his version of the events.

A long pause ensued, as if something had been left unsaid. The lawyer broke the awkward silence.

"Your honor, will that be all?"

"I'm pondering, Stephen. Can't you see that? The nature of my station these days doesn't require much pondering, so I'm a little slow at it. I'm out of practice."

"Forgive me, your honor, I . . ."

"I would like to see your client in my chambers—alone," the old man interjected.

Robson gaped, momentarily. "Your honor, that would be highly irregular, given the circumstances. The boy has just been through a traumatic experience."

"I believe you declared earlier that you were here to cooperate in any way. Indulge me in this, Stephen, as a courtesy to my court. Just a moment or two of counsel, and then I will be silent on the matter for the rest of my days." It was carefully worded, but it carried the implied sense of an ultimatum.

Robson nodded reluctantly to Harvey. "We submit to your request, of course, your honor."

The boy followed the waddling pumpkin head to a tiny office at the rear of the courtroom. Mendoza seated himself behind a small desk and beckoned Harvey toward a folding chair directly in front of it.

"No thanks, I'd rather stand," he responded coolly, apparently irked by the added inconvenience of this private audience and itching for a hasty retreat.

"Well, your arrogance and disrespect don't surprise me at all." Mendoza's voice was little more than a raspy whisper now, soft as an afternoon shadow, yet clearly audible somehow. The man was a walking enigma. He looked the boy up and down with those all-knowing eyes. "How old do you think I am, young man?"

"I dunno. *Really* old, I guess," Harvey answered.

"I am ninety-six years old, by my best reckoning. How does that make you feel?"

"I dunno."

"Well, it should make you feel *really* small. Small indeed and insignificant by comparison to my long life, but you don't feel anything of the sort because you have just recently killed a man and you are so full of yourself, you feel nothing but the intoxicating pleasure of that conquest."

"How can you say that?" Harvey gasped in surprise. "It was an accident. You just said so yourself in court!"

"Please don't insult my intelligence, son. I know the truth." The ancient muni-court judge rose from his chair; despite his diminutive stature and bent form, his pose was somehow intimidating. "What I said was that the court ruled the death an accident based on the facts given. But I saw the truth behind your words as you spoke them, and your face—not a reflection of guilt, but of smugness—told a very different story."

"You don't have any evidence. You're just a crazy old coot!" Harvey wanted to flee, but the old man's magnetic eyes held him fast."

"Crazy, am I? Well, let me tell you what I saw as you were relating your fabricated chain of events. I saw your hand push the throttle of the boat forward. I saw you pitch a bottle at your struggling uncle, instead of a life preserver. I saw you piloting the boat in a wide circle around that poor, doomed swimmer who was desperately clinging to his pathetic life. I saw you waiting for the sea to swallow him up. I saw you emptying beer bottles and scattering them about the boat to support your story. You told me what you really did, but not with your lying words. Shall I go on?"

Harvey began to tremble. "What are you? You must think you have ESP or something, but you don't know. You can't really know."

"I am a seer of truth. It was a gift passed on to me, although there are times like this when it seems more of a curse than a gift."

"Wh-wh-what are you going to do?" the boy stammered.

"Do? There's very little I can do. Our justice system demands a high evidential burden—proof beyond a reasonable doubt—in criminal cases, and rightfully so. I rue the day that my clairvoyant gift would rise to that standard and convince anyone in their right mind that—according on my visions—a twelve-year-old boy murdered his innocent uncle in cold blood. And if I were even to make that suggestion, you wouldn't be the only one calling me a crazy old coot. I'm sure this is beyond your understanding, and it took me years to understand it myself, but the closest we humans can come to true justice must include a presumption of innocence and a measure of mercy, even at the cost of excusing a few monsters like yourself. All I can really do is what I told your lawyer—counsel, and then keep my peace."

"Well, I don't have to—"

"Now! Sit!" the old justice thundered and Harvey yielded to a heavy invisible hand bearing down on his shoulders. He complied and sat without further protest.

"So you see I *know*, without question, that you killed your uncle," the old man continued. "At your age, that makes you a precocious little demon of the worst kind—a *killer* prodigy. You are a living, breathing abomination. Son, you think you've performed some kind of twisted initiation into manhood, but you've really just traded the lion's share of your spirit for a fleeting orgasmic power binge."

"Why are you—"

"Just you shut up and listen!"

The boy was stricken dumb by the very words.

"I too at your age became all too well-acquainted with murder, but on the other side of the equation." Mendoza rolled his head back and revealed that he did indeed have a neck, and that it retained a very prominent and ugly scar across the throat. "And I too experienced a legal proceeding that seemed to mock justice, only from the other way around. Eighty-five years ago, fifty murderers stood trial in a courtroom in downtown Tucson, such as it was, and they were acquitted because ignorance prevailed at that time. From that profound day of infamy, I swore that I would somehow become an enemy of all injustice. Upon being orphaned, I was taken in by a prosperous and well-educated Mexican couple who bestowed upon me every opportunity and advantage that a developing human being could ask for—freedom from want, a loving home, and a superior parochial education were all mine. In time, I forsook all the hatred that I once embraced, and I worked all my life to repay their love and kindness and to gain a level of influence from which I could make a difference for good. I graduated law school and eventually rose to the level of state supreme court justice. From there I made certain that no such travesty of justice would ever occur in my jurisdiction."

"I'm sorry, but I don't know why you're telling me all of this," Harvey whined.

"Because I believe our paths were destined to cross today for a reason," the old man explained. "You see, in spite of an impeccable record on the bench, my superiors relegated me to this lower station because of my advanced age, but I now believe that there was a higher purpose to my demotion, and that purpose is this encounter, so that I can present to you an opportunity and a warning."

"An opportunity and a warning? That sounds scary."

"It should. You just committed a murder at the age of twelve. You've made a Faustian bargain, son, though I'm sure you don't know what that is."

"Sure don't," Harvey shrugged.

"It means you've sold your soul, and rather cheaply, I might add. Any time a human takes another's life for some gain, he's made a deal with the devil. You murdered your uncle to establish a place in your family's hierarchy of ruthlessness, and at such a tender age! Don't expect to ever find any refuge in the innocence of adolescence. You've spent that coin, or rather thrown it away."

"You're scaring me, old man," Harvey whined. "Can I go now?"

"Not yet. I'm not finished. I've only given you the warning, and frankly, everything at this point should sound frightening to you, but

I'm just getting to the opportunity part. The opportunity I speak of is repentance."

"Repentance?" Harvey gasped, as if it was some kind of obscenity.

"Yes, son, repentance. Divine justice is the last and best arbiter of justice and mercy there is, and in your case, I'd say the only avenue of justice left open to you. God's loving justice provided the Perfect Penitent for all the sins of mankind, so that you and I are granted, by grace, a redemption purchased by Christ's blood. All of God's children are granted a chance for redemption, even a lost boy like you. All you have to do is confess your crime—not to a court of law, but a confession to our Lord. Repent and reverse your unholy path, and you will be forgiven."

An uncomfortable silence fell over the tiny room until it was broken by the boy.

"You know, I don't go in much for the God stuff. I really just don't get it."

"And perhaps you never will," Mendoza sighed. "But since you have chosen to embrace the ultimate evil, I feel you should at least be presented with a choice for the ultimate good, however inadequate the venue, and however briefly stated by this lowly witness to His grace. I'm no priest, but God seeks to give grace to those who most need it. I witness to you only because I am the only mortal who knows how dire your need is for that grace."

Harvey simply shrugged again, in hopes that the sermon was over.

"In any case," the old man continued, "I can say with great certainty that if you choose not to reverse this path you have started down, then I see that it ends in a place I know all too well, a place where spirits are restless. There you will become involved with a dark power that will eventually consume you. If you choose wrongly, you will never leave that place." The old shaman began to shudder, as if he were cold. "But remember that until you enter that place, the path back to the mercy of God is always open to you."

Harvey looked deeply into the old man's eyes. Seeing his own reflection there, he asked the inevitable question. "So . . . which way do you see me going?"

"I see only possible paths and possible destinations. Free will obscures the outcomes. There is no predestination in the world that God created.

I cannot predict what you will do, nor am I particularly eager to know." The raspy voice was becoming faint. "And speaking of free will, you are free to go now, young man. I grow weary, and I have said my peace."

Harvey made for the door, but didn't make that portal before the final benediction.

"I pray, young man, that you will choose rightly," the justice croaked wearily. The door closed behind the boy. "But I fear you won't," Natchez Mendoza said to no one. "How could I ever expect you to understand—and yet, how could I ever have kept myself from trying to explain?"

Harvey was met in the hearing room by his lawyer and his father, who had just arrived during the boy's short absence.

"How've you been, son?" Pinky inquired in a tone tinged with forced sympathy. "I am truly sorry I couldn't get here sooner."

"I feel like I've been through hell, Dad. *You* can't even imagine," Harvey replied in an almost condescending air. "Stephen," he said, turning to the lawyer, "you're wrong about that old man. He's not senile. He's completely loony tunes. Nutty as a fruitcake. Talked about Jesus and visions of the devil and stuff. He even said he thought I killed Uncle Robert! Can you believe it? They ought to keep lunatics like that locked in a rubber closet. Instead, they let 'em run a justice court. What a circus! Man, I've been through the wringer lately."

"Well, how about I take us out to an early dinner," Pinky offered. "You can get your mind off of these things. I'll tell you all about that baseball team that I'm getting ready to buy. How's that sound?"

"Great!" Harvey exclaimed. "I'm starved."

"What do you feel like eating, son?"

"Whaddya think?"

Pinky and Robson exchanged a puzzled glance.

"Fish, of course!" the boy chuckled. "Fresh sea bass—a couple filets."

"Son, you know Tucson isn't exactly famous for—"

"Who said anything about Tucson? I wanna fly over to San Diego—Seaport Village, maybe. Can you swing that, Stephen?"

"Well, I suppose . . . that is, if your dad—"

"Why not?" Pinky broke in. "I think I owe my boy a little attention

229

after all he's been through. What about it, Stephen—you up for a late lunch in San Diego?"

"Whatever you say, Sam."

"Oh, and by the way, I'd like to drop in to Rocky Point on the way back to check on my new boat. I wanna talk to Miguel about making a few changes to it," Harvey added. "After that, I want to—"

"Now see here, son," Pinky boomed. "You—"

"No, now *you* see here, Dad," Harvey chuckled maniacally. "You two have a huge favor to repay."

"What are you talking about, Junior?" Stephen demanded.

"You can start by dropping the 'Junior' from now on, Stephen," the boy returned. "And do you really want me to spell it out for you?"

The lawyer's jaw went slack with awe, but Pinky pursed his lips, grimly.

"What changes, pray tell, would you want to make to *The Wayward Wind*?" Pinky asked, with reluctant deference.

"Change the name," Harvey replied.

"To what?"

"*The Biggest Fish.*"

Wrestling with the Darkness

After spending the entire evening in the library studying the boxing book Randy had lent him, Curtis was puzzled when he reached the steps to his "henhouse" dorm building. Rather than finding other inmates waiting for Marcus to arrive and unlock the door, the steps were empty and the door was propped open. On all other nights, the door would still be locked by now while Marcus, the dorm guard who doubled as a cook, finished closing up the mess hall.

Upon entering the wide vestibule-corridor, Curtis immediately identified the source of the break with routine. The hateful redneck guard that had cuffed him on the ear several nights prior was sitting in for Marcus, literally sitting in his chair.

Curtis now faced the odious chore of checking in with the man who had just days ago physically humiliated him without cause. He sidled up behind a couple of other hens and waited his turn to add his name and bunk number to the sign-in sheet, which he did while the new guard eyed him with obvious disdain.

"Wait right there, boy," he grumbled in his backwoods drawl as he picked up the sheet from the wobbly old card table that served as his desk.

"What's the problem . . ." Curtis caught himself almost leaving off the mandatory, respectful address when speaking with staff, "uh . . . sir?"

"The problem, boy, is that I can't make heads nor tails of this hen scratch of yern."

He struck a multiple line through Curtis's name and bunk number with the ballpoint pen that the boy had just handed back to him. He spun the upturned paper on the table so that it faced Curtis again, and returned the pen.

"Try again, boy—and this time you best print, if you can. I don't have all night and better folks are waitin' on you."

There was indeed a short queue starting to form behind him.

"Sorry for the trouble, sir," Curtis offered as he reprinted his name and bunk number.

"Yer days are fuckin' numbered, anyways," the disheveled cracker mumbled.

"Excuse me, sir?" Curtis inquired. "What was that you said?"

"I said, *Don't forget your bunk number*, plain as day. Are you deaf *and* illiterate?"

"No, sir, I'm neither," Curtis retorted, sturdily. "I guess I just misunderstood you."

"You watch yer tone with me, boy," the guard returned. "Woodshed stays open all night, you know."

"Yes, sir—I'll remember that, sir."

The guard's eyes followed Curtis as he dismissed himself with a patronizing little bow and made for the main sleeping chamber.

The air was hot and stifling in the dorm room, as Curtis undressed to his boxers and hung his clothes in the steel locker standing at the foot of the double-bunk. He settled into the lower bunk, pulling the olive-drab military-issue blanket back and lying atop the sheet with only a top sheet for cover, as was his practice. He'd been assigned to the upper bunk on his first day, but the lower had been, and still was, vacant, so the boy had always opted for the cooler bed closer to the floor.

It was also routine that the guard would double-check the completed roster against the physical presence of each inmate at his corresponding bunk number before lights-out, and before the attic fan was turned on. The conditional procedure lent much incentive for every inmate to settle in quickly with no horseplay, and woe be unto the poor fool who delayed the start of the cool night air being circulated.

True to the routine, the hayseed guard strolled into the dorm room and started up and down the rows, checking the sign-in sheet with each bunk occupant. He stopped strolling when he reached Curtis's bunk.

"Says here ye're in the top bunk, boy."

"Yeah . . . I mean, yes, sir—but the lower has always been empty, and—"

"Are you arguin' with me, boy? I say you belong in that top bunk and you best get yer black ass up there, 'cause you're diggin' yourself a pretty deep hole with that tongue of yours."

"Yes, sir," Curtis conceded. "My mistake."

Curtis scrambled to the top bunk and pulled back the cover.

"Well, now—looks like you've gone and soiled two sets of bedding, now," the surly guard smirked, "and it says here that you've got a bunk mate, after all."

"But . . . but all this time—"

"Don't argue boy! You've got one foot in the woodshed already!"

The guard was raising his voice now and Curtis was trying to avoid a disturbance, mostly for the sake of his dorm mates, who were waiting for the air to start moving.

"Sorry, then, sir," he chanted, glassy-eyed.

"Yes, siree," the guard continued with a half-chuckle, "says right here that the lower bunk is assigned to none other than *Mr. Harvey Huish*— imagine that!"

Curtis sat straight up.

"What?"

The guard chuckled demonically.

"Oh, I wouldn't worry," he jeered. "I'm pretty sure Mr. Huish won't want to lie down in bedding soiled by some sweaty little spear-chucker, now would he?" the guard continued as he now moved on down the row. "Of course, you never know!" he turned back and winked at Curtis. "You just never know . . ." and his voice trailed off as he moved away down the line of beds.

The lights went out about as scheduled—just shy of nine—but Curtis lay with his eyes wide open in the dark, wondering about the extraordinary string of events that had unfolded during the past few days. To keep his head from reeling, he mentally imposed some structure on the perplexities, working from the most recent phenomenon backward, tallying a list.

What was he to make of this repugnant guard that had suddenly inserted himself into Curtis's teetering world? And what of his previous encounter with the Lieutenant—and how did *he* know that Curtis was indeed "losing his grip"? Then too, what did that strange typewritten *History of Fort Grant* have to do with the harrowing psychic phenomena that the young Negro boy was experiencing, and how could it "help him"? And how was it that his long-forgotten but nevertheless cherished boyhood dream of his father suddenly resurfaced at this ominous point in time? They were all troubling questions, all demanding logical explanations, no matter how illogical the context.

Curtis pondered the guard question first, and it was the easiest to figure out. He recalled that Harvey had previously alluded to paying his minions rather handsomely. Randy had mentioned and Marcus confirmed that Harvey's father was a Tucson fat cat, and it wouldn't take much to buy off one or two of these underpaid and unscrupulous reform school guards, especially one whose formative years were apparently spent living in a shotgun shack in Tornado Alley. So Curtis could reasonably conclude from this that whatever the guard did might well be at Harvey's direction. He quietly hoped that Marcus's absence had not been part of the plot to harass him tonight, then immediately dismissed the misdirected suspicion.

The encounter with the Lieutenant was not so easy to explain away. He seemed to be somewhat sympathetic with Curtis's plight, yet he left a certain sinister impression that the boy could not dismiss. Then too, there was the strangely extravagant way he dressed, and the rumors of excessive habits. His standard of living—the car, the clothes, the storied indulgences—seemed to exceed what Curtis imagined the income of a mid-level state bureaucrat would support. Perhaps the Lieutenant was on the take as well. The questions regarding this mysterious character would have to wait until Randy, who was best positioned to comment on such matters, could elaborate.

In the meantime, there was the matter of the manuscript. Curtis had merely skimmed the contents very superficially, and could piece together only the background of some inauspicious scenario that had played itself out at this God-forsaken outpost almost one hundred years ago. Curtis thought about the words *massacre* and *slaughter* used in the paper to describe some momentous event that he had not yet unraveled in this tangled yarn. Both words, when taken in the context of sports contests, denoted overwhelming defeat or victory.

Given the circumstance, a hundred or so rabble-rousers, tired from a long trek, versus four- or five hundred sleeping warriors, one might venture only a guess as to who prevailed. Perhaps the slumbering Apaches awoke and absolutely "slaughtered" the visiting team. How the hell was he expected to know simply from skimming a long-winded history lesson what the underlying message was supposed to be? It was another matter to be taken up with the all-knowing Randy on his next appearance.

The only comforting exception in this string of harrowing visions resided with the dream of his long-lost father. Curtis closed his eyes for a moment and tried to conjure the consolation of the pleasant Louisiana evening. It was working! He could feel the warmth of the fire, smell the remnants of the catfish dinner, and hear the overpowering cacophony of the cricket song. And underscoring it all was the security he felt in the presence of his father. Even the portentous warning was consoling as it gently steered the boy away from harm.

You're getting way too close, son. Better get back before you get burned.

Curtis stepped back and turned to his father, looking deep into his dark eyes.

Better get back.

The repetition of the phrase was out of place. And something else: the clothes his father wore now were equally incongruous. He was dressed in a floral-pattern silk Hawaiian shirt, navy blue trousers, and a pair of Florsheim wingtips, hardly the outfit for camping in—and the garb itself was hauntingly familiar.

Get back!

The voice now was not his father's, and it was harsh in tone and juvenile in timbre. The campfire scene now bled over into the vision of

235

a more recent incident. Curtis had entered an unlocked door to the high school gymnasium back in Jacobs Well and was helping himself to a couple of football jerseys—game jerseys with the players' numbers all adorned in the school colors. It was Sunday, and the school was abandoned, or so he thought. He'd been riding past on his bike, noticed the door ajar, and took the singular opportunity to slip inside. The ill-gotten booty was in a laundry pile near the locker room door, and Curtis anticipated an easy snatch-and-dash when a movement inside one of the coach's cubicles caught his attention. An older boy, one whom he recognized from around town, was flicking a Zippo cigarette lighter, igniting a pile of loosely crumpled papers stacked up on a wooden desk top. Curtis blinked in disbelief. *The older boy was setting fire to the gym.*

As the combustion built to campfire size, the boy turned and caught sight of Curtis.

Get back! is what the boy shouted as he ran out the door.

Curtis stared into the heart of the fire for a few seconds and guessed that it was too far gone for him to put out. He started to retreat as well, but suddenly recalled that there was a fire alarm located on a wall above the laundry pile, so he dashed over to the little red box and pulled the handle down. The wailing alarm filled the air and echoed all over the deserted campus. Curtis was almost to the door when the school custodian burst in, armed with a fire extinguisher.

Get back! is what the custodian shouted too, as he charged toward the burning cubicle.

"Psst—Curtis!"

Curtis sat up in his bunk and listened. He scanned the sleeping room for Randy and caught some shadowy movement over by the doorway. He balked at getting out of the bunk for fear of disturbing the irritable old hillbilly guard, but his need for the explanations that his friend could give for his multiplying questions was greater than his wariness. His mind was overflowing with confusing dreams and visions, and he was beginning to think he was going quite mad. The younger boy always seemed able to provide another piece to the puzzle at least, and Curtis badly needed more clues to make some sense of it all.

He quietly climbed down from his top bunk, stealthily padded to the doorway, and peered into the semi-darkness. Off to the right and across the hall, the guard's chair sat empty. He scanned left but detected no movement.

"Randy?" he breathed in a forced whisper.

In an instant, a thickly muscled forearm flashed across his face and drew back tightly across his windpipe. The chest and shoulders of a larger man pressed against his back. He'd been taken from behind, and the rapid closure of his trachea at the instant of exhalation rendered him mute. He could no more cry out for help than he could piss over the moon. The other forearm now pressed hard against the back of his head. The pincer-like stranglehold not only cut off his breathing, but cut the return circulation of the blood from his head as well. His face and forehead swelled dramatically at that instant, and Curtis found himself starting to lose all sense of perception.

His assailant now kicked Curtis's feet out from under him, grappling him to the wooden floor with a loud body slam. Curtis was pinned facedown with his attacker's full body pressing against his back. In his fleeting seconds of consciousness, a hushed voice hissed like a serpent in his ringing ears.

"Don't struggle . . . give it up and you won't suffer!"

Curtis flailed with his last ounce of strength.

"I told you I'd throttle you, Sambo," the sinister voiced hissed again.

A wave of nausea came over Curtis as he felt his assailant's hips rocking rhythmically against his nearly bare buttocks.

"Now you're gonna be my little houseboy. How's that for a final memory in this life, huh? How d'ya like that, you wise-mouthed little coon? You won't even be able to face your daddy on the other side after I'm through with you. I'm gonna bone you so hard, your mama's gonna feel it all the way up in Jacobs Well. Then it's lights-out for keeps."

Curtis's desperate grip on consciousness was waning fast. His vision was nearly blacked out, and the last thing he heard over the throbbing ringtone in his head was that inimitable laugh of Harvey's—a staccato burst of sinister mirth in eerie falsetto.

Then, with the same suddenness as it had begun, the choke hold went slack, and his attacker rolled off the younger boy's back and onto the floor beside him. Curtis fought to pull in enough air to open his trachea. As he recollected his consciousness, he began to cough and spit up bile. He glanced sideways and saw Harvey Huish writhing on his back next to him with his hands over his ears. His mouth was wide open; it was as if he was screaming, but he emitted only a weak issuance of escaping air. The ringing in Curtis's own ears subsided, and he heard the now-familiar and unmistakable chorus of coyotes singing outside the encampment walls, as they had for many nights. Was this the source of Harvey's apparent agony? It seemed unlikely, and yet it also seemed to be so.

No matter—Curtis summoned what strength he could marshal, scrambled to his feet, and very deliberately approached his enemy. Whatever the cause, Harvey was apparently quite debilitated, and Curtis was determined to press his advantage. As he'd seen it done on professional wrestling, he sprang into the air, hovering above Harvey's reeling head with folded legs for a split second, and uncoiled like a great spring, heels pointed downward as he planted the full weight of his falling body onto the forehead of his assailant.

But something happened. His bare heels never connected with their intended target. Instead, they landed with a loud thud on the wooden floor.

"What the hell is going on here?" The hallway light flashed on and the cracker guard approached. Curtis looked down to see how he had possibly missed his mark and was astonished to see . . . nothing! No Harvey and no sign of the life-and-death struggle that had just taken place.

"Oh, it's you again. I should have figured." The guard reached out and grabbed a hank of Curtis's thick hair. "Three strikes and ye're out!" he declared and tugged the boy in the direction of the door.

"But I just got up to pee!" Curtis protested hoarsely as he pulled away from the guard's weak grip.

"Then why were you stomping all over in the hall like that? Is that some kind of new Watusi dance you people do?"

"No, sir, I just thought I saw a scorpion on the floor."

"A likely story," he scoffed as he pushed Curtis toward the door. "Hell, you've been beggin' for a good whippin' all night, boy. You've just used up my patience."

Curtis had little strength to resist, verbally or otherwise. The guard clambered down the concrete step and onto the gravel walkway with Curtis in tow, headed toward the utility room otherwise known as the woodshed. The coyotes continued their mournful chorus away in the distance as the boy marched obediently down the walkway. The gravel hurt his bare feet, and he hobbled along slowly. Before long, they reached the louvered door of a small metal building attached to the administration offices. The guard rattled a handful of keys, unlocked the metal door, and pushed Curtis inside, into total darkness.

"Hey, can you at least turn on a light?" the boy groaned.

"Watch yer tone with me, boy—you're still adding lashes."

A third voice now called out in the darkness behind the guard.

"What's all the disturbance?" it boomed. "Jeb, is that you?"

It was the Lieutenant.

An Officer and a Gentleman

It was pitch black inside the utility building, famously known as the woodshed, but that only made it easier to see what was happening under the subdued moonlight outside the door. The Lieutenant was shuffling up to the guard rather clumsily and was speaking in an unusually loud tone of voice. It was all that could be heard over the overwhelming hum of an electric motor coming from within. Curtis could see the Lieutenant's silk sport shirt was open, revealing a white undershirt that seemed to glow in the moonlight. He was shod in bedroom slippers, and even from a distance of several feet the boy could smell the mixed aromas of burnt tobacco and expensive bourbon.

"What's all the commotion, Jeb? It's after midnight, you know!"

"Yes, sir—I know, sir." The guard was clearly rattled from the unanticipated encounter with his superior. "Just carryin' out a discipline, sir."

"At this hour? It couldn't have waited until sunrise?"

"Well, as the code says, sir—discipline should be administered without delay so as to hitch the punishment to the act."

"I know, I know what the code says, man," the Lieutenant waved the justification aside. "I *wrote* the damn disciplinary code for this place—I ought to know what's in it!"

"Exactly, sir!" Jeb returned. "So I was just followin' yer orders, so to speak."

"Ah, then, all well and good, Jeb," the stately gentleman exhaled, somewhat exasperated with the tiresome word-volley. "Tell me, who is the offender, and what is the offense?"

"*Offenses*, sir," Jeb returned, rather pleased with himself.

"*Offenses*, then," the Lieutenant breathed, fighting a losing battle with impatience.

"First," Jeb announced proudly, "there was loiterin' just outside yer window after mess a few days ago."

"Hmm . . . not exactly an eyebrow-raiser, is it?"

"No? Well then, how about falsifyin' a dormitory sign-in sheet and then assignin' himself to a different bunk?" the guard offered, trying to hide a toothy grin.

"A bit more egregious, I must confess," the Lieutenant sighed. "Is that all, Jeb?"

"Uh, no, sir. Then there was causin' a disturbance in the main dormitory hall, just a few minutes ago."

"Disturbance—after lights-out?"

"Yes, sir. He was leapin' about in the dark, sir. I saw it plain as day."

"Well," said the Lieutenant, clearing his throat, "now I'm curious to see who this heinous fiend is." He stepped forward, flicked a wall toggle, and illuminated the room.

Curtis glanced about the small room as his eyes adjusted to the sudden light. It was jam-packed with tanks and pipes and ducts and motors of every sort. Reluctantly, he turned and met the stern gaze of the Lieutenant.

"Ah, yes," the man remarked to the guard, "I've dealt with this one before."

"That so?" the guard croaked. "Then you see what I mean—a real troublemaker, that one."

"Well, trouble does seem to follow him, at least," the Lieutenant sighed. "Jeb, why don't you let me take it from here?"

"But, sir . . ."

"No, I insist!" the headmaster declared, raising his voice again. "I haven't had the pleasure of delivering a good scourging in quite some time."

"Well, if you don't mind my sayin' so, sir, you don't seem to be in any cond—"

"Let me stop you right there, Jeb," the Lieutenant growled in a grave tone of voice, "before you say something in front of this inmate that I'll make you wish you hadn't!"

The guard stood silent for a moment, seeming to weigh the consequences of pursuing this line of persuasion any further.

"Do you catch my drift, *Corporal*?" the Lieutenant demanded now, quite loudly.

"Whatever you say, sir, of course," the guard muttered glumly.

"That's better . . . and, oh yes, by the way, why are you watching the hen house, instead of Marcus?"

"It's that time of year, sir—*on retreat* is what he calls it. I believe he's holed up in the chapel."

"You don't say. Hmm. Well, all the more reason for you to return to your watch without delay, Jeb—what with double duty and all. Better check on those roosters—they're the livelier bunch."

"Yes, sir. I'll do that, sir. Good night, sir."

"Good night, Jeb."

The Lieutenant closed the louvered door but hovered there for a moment, listening as the old guard's shuffling footsteps faded up the path.

"Poor old Jeb," he muttered. "I'm afraid he's starting to enjoy this sort of thing a bit too much."

Curtis surveyed his surroundings again. He was standing in a sloped concrete walkway bordered on one side by several sections of tubular-steel stock fence that were serving as a sort of makeshift safety barrier. Slung over the top rail, dead center of one of these portable barriers, was a thick, ominous-looking leather strap—the kind Curtis had seen a barber use to sharpen a straight razor. The Lieutenant made straight for it and took it up by its integrated leather handle. It was about three feet in length and the free end was frayed, as if it had been deliberately cut and often used.

"So, Mr. Jefferson," the Lieutenant intoned as he dangled the strap menacingly. "Do you have anything to say in your defense?"

"No, sir—I guess not."

"Come, now—you mean to tell me it was just as Jeb told it?"

"Pretty near, but not exactly, sir."

"Then why don't you state your side of the story? That's the way we do it in America. Don't you think you ought to act like an American, boy?"

"Well, sir—since you put it that way . . ."

"Go ahead, son—say your piece."

"Well, I guess I *did* loiter too long by your window after mess. I was enjoyin' the music and the cool air. I guess I just started daydreamin' and forgot to move along."

"Enough. What about falsifying the dorm roster?"

"Plain and simple, sir. I was assigned the upper bunk when I first came here, but I've always slept in the one below because it wasn't bein' used and it's cooler down closer to the floor. Marcus never objected, and it caught me off guard when Jeb came on watch—but he's right. I broke the rule—can't argue that."

"All too true, I'm afraid," the Lieutenant muttered, stroking his chin. "Now what's behind all of this leaping about after hours in the main hall?"

Curtis cleared his throat.

"Well, sir—it's like this: I got up 'cause I had to pee—"

"Urinate."

"Yes, sir—urinate. Uh . . . well then, on my way to the latrine," Curtis continued, hesitantly, "I saw some movement on the floor—it's real dark in that hall, you know."

The Lieutenant nodded in agreement.

"Well," he went on, "I jumped back 'cause I thought it might be a scorpion or something, and I must've thumped the floor real hard, 'cause ol' Jeb came a-runnin' right away."

"Hmm—and then he brought you directly here, did he?"

"Yes, sir—right away."

"Not a moment's hesitation?"

"None that I remember, sir."

"And yet you don't seem to be in any state of urgency now."

"Uh . . . no, sir—I guess not."

"I see. Well, son, I must direct you to face away from me, grab the top rail of that stock fence there, and steel yourself for punishment!"

Curtis turned his back to the Lieutenant, gripped the rail as directed, and fixed his eyes on a bright, oversized incandescent bulb that lit the room. The hum from the huge swamp cooler that fed the administration building seemed to intensify.

"This," the Lieutenant proclaimed loudly, "is for loitering!"

A loud crack resounded above the din of the cooler motor, and Curtis retained his position, standing still as a post, untouched.

"What, not even a flinch? I'd better lay it on with a bit more vigor!" the Lieutenant exclaimed. "And this," he proclaimed even louder, "is for changing your bunk assignment!"

Curtis continued to stare up at the bright bulb high above all the machinery. There was another loud crack, and this time Curtis caught sight of the razor strop striking the top rail of the fence right next to his right hand. Was the Lieutenant that drunk—or was he missing the mark deliberately?

"Still no reaction?"

Curtis was just beginning to think he was playing a straight role in some kind of weird comic farce, when the crack resounded unannounced and a sudden burst of overpowering pain erupted at his lower back and radiated instantly to all organs and extremities. The boy shut his eyes and flashes of blue light gave way to a familiar vision of a path winding through a gravel wash under faint starlight. He dropped to one knee, reflexively, and struggled to retain control of his excretory functions.

"That," the Lieutenant declared, "is for lying to me." The tone was grave, but controlled. "I despise dishonesty," he continued, "and now you will never forget how stupid it was for you to lie."

Curtis drew himself back up tall, water welling in his eyes.

"That's the spirit! Stand proud—you've paid your debt."

"But . . . I don't get it," Curtis sputtered, turning around, "why would you punish me for something so . . . so *innocent*, and not those other things?"

"You're right about one thing—*you don't get it*. I'm not surprised," the Lieutenant sighed. "Once people fabricate a story, many start to believe it themselves."

"Is that true?" Curtis sniffed.

"Of course it is. It's quite typical, so don't think it makes you special, nor does it negate the sin."

"But . . ."

"Go on, spit it out, son. There's not much left of this night, and I'm growing weary."

"Sir, I don't know if I *can* remember what happened there, other than that story I just told you."

"Hmm . . ." The Lieutenant had to ponder this for a moment. "Mind you," he exclaimed at length, "don't think that this excuses you for lying to a superior, but I'm strangely inclined to believe you. Considering all the confusing hallucinations that I imagine you've had of late, I shouldn't be surprised that your sense of what is real is getting a bit taxed."

"But how would you *know* that?" Curtis blurted, without thinking. "I mean . . . how do you know, sir, about all my crazy visions and dreams and such?"

"I *don't* know what you've seen or heard specifically, but I knew that you were one of the *sentient* ones from the first day I enrolled you here," said the Lieutenant. "Come along. We're finished here. I'll escort you back to the dormitory, and we'll talk along the way."

He switched off the light and pulled the door closed as Curtis exited.

"Sir," Curtis implored, "can I ask you what *sentient* means?"

"Sentient means perceptive or, more to the point, *alive to your surroundings*," the Lieutenant muttered, somewhat embarrassed at having to explain. "For God's sake, son, haven't you noticed yet that you see and hear things that others don't?"

"Only since I came here. I thought it had more to do with this place than with me."

"Well, it *does* have a lot to do with this place. Profound events have occurred here that have created something of a *disturbance* in the normal course of the way things operate."

"I'm not exactly sure what that means, sir," Curtis returned in his most deferential tone.

"And I don't know if I can express it in any better way that you can understand. Suffice it to say that, given the circumstances, you should not doubt your senses, and you should certainly not doubt your sanity."

The Lieutenant's tone was now comforting, and Curtis began to feel as if he might indeed have an ally aside from Randy. But the reassurance diminished as the pair neared the dorm, and Curtis paused at the foot of the steps.

"Oh, don't worry about Jeb," said the Lieutenant. "He may deal out a swat or two, but he'll never do you any serious harm. Trust me—I've known the man for a hundred years."

"A hundred years?" Curtis echoed, incredulously.

"Well, maybe only ninety-two," the man chuckled. "It just seems like a hundred. Besides, he's probably doing rounds at the rooster pen."

Curtis hid a relieved smile and mounted the stairs. Once inside, he noted with pleasure that Jeb was indeed absent from the henhouse watch. But the darkened hall filled the boy with a sense of foreboding, and tiny flickers of that imagined attack of the previous hour troubled his thoughts.

He approached his bunk cautiously and out of habit lay down in the lower bunk. A cold sensation on his lower back caused him to freeze and hold deadly still. The sheets were soaking wet, and the acrid smell of urine filled his nostrils!

He rolled out of the befouled bedding and dutifully climbed to the top bunk. As he lay there, his ebony eyes welling in the darkness, he faintly heard the consoling sound of his father's voice.

Just soldier on, son . . . soldier on.

Revelations

Morning came, borne on streaming shafts of light that passed through the oversized windows of the old dorm building. The new dawning brought several revelations to Curtis, and the boy was undergoing another change in his state of mind as a result—an awakening of another sort.

Perhaps the least of these revelations, he discovered that there was no defiling urine in the lower bunk. The sheets were clean and crisp and there was no acrid after-scent on his now-dry boxers. In fact, there was no physical sign whatsoever that might indicate that any such obscene gesture of contempt had ever taken place at all. Nevertheless, the disgust that he felt from that vile message retrieved the memory of Harvey Huish's foiled attempt to murder him—real or imagined—from the night before.

As he dressed himself, he became aware of the others around him who were rising from their bunks. He wondered about how much of the previous night's disturbances they were aware of.

"Hey, brother, that's a nasty-lookin' welt raisin' up on your back," a voice called out from the next bunk over.

It was one of the other Negro boys who'd earlier tried to recruit Curtis into their clique. The boy was on the tall side, decidedly darker than Curtis, and appeared to be a bit older than the henhouse cutoff age of fifteen. Smiling sympathetically, the boy's comment now assured Curtis that at least his encounter with the Lieutenant had not been imagined. The stinging from the razor strap had long since given way to a mere sensation of heat radiating from his lower back.

"I've had worse," Curtis returned, forcing a grin.

"Listen," the boy continued, approaching Curtis, "some of us noticed that old Jeb seems to have it in for you."

"Guess that's pretty plain to see," Curtis conceded.

"Just want to let you know that the offer stands open—if you need some help in settlin' a score, I mean. You're not the first black boy that's drawn that asshole's attention, and by my reckonin' he's past due for a comeuppance, no lie."

"Well, brother," Curtis said, shaking the other boy's hand, "I appreciate it—and I just might take you up on that, if it comes right down to it. Seems I've made some enemies on accident—without even tryin', that is."

The other boy grinned and pumped Curtis's arm with an even warmer handshake.

"We'll be around," he called over his shoulder as he turned to exit the dorm. "Just call for Leon Hawkins—I'll come a-runnin' and with plenty o' backup!"

Now, in spite of all the confusion over real and imagined events, Curtis was beginning to focus on three objective conditions—hard realities that were clear and clearly paramount in his mind. First, Harvey Huish was intent on making good his promise to "throttle you 'til your little black heart stops." Second, Curtis was determined to prevent that from happening by any means available. Third, he was coming to the realization that he had *allies* in this. In spite of Sergeant Joe's earlier intuitive warning, playing the loner was apparently not the best approach to this predicament—not anymore.

Gradually at first, but more recently in great leaps, Curtis's sentiment toward Randy had come full circle. He recognized the habitual need to seek out the younger boy's heretofore questionable counsel, and now some internal urgency was prodding him to do so once again before another sunset. The mysteries peculiar to this place were quickly becoming an obsession, and his newly acquired friend always seemed to have the answers—answers that might well become key to Curtis's survival.

He and Randy had failed to make a firm commitment to meeting at the sandlot this day, and so Curtis ventured over to the mess hall a bit before the regular Sunday breakfast serving time to watch for the pale-faced kid. But as the queue began to lengthen and the tables began to fill, no sign of the precocious boy presented itself. Curtis decided to skip breakfast based on this development.

Somewhat discouraged in his search for his friend and unsure if another sandlot routine was planned, Curtis instead made his way back to the dorm, changed into a pair of cut-off jeans and his treasured pair of Chuck Taylor indoor track shoes, and started off on a Sunday morning long-distance run. He began jogging at the foot of the concrete steps, and plotted a new route for his run that would avoid any of Harvey's regular haunts—and would definitely steer clear of the breach in the wall. This took him wide around the parade ground, where inmates were already taking advantage of weekend free time and early-morning temperature. He picked up the telltale trail of the Lieutenant's Impala in the dusty gravel, and fell into a rhythmic trot.

The month of April was looming, and the mercury was already beginning to peak in the nineties in mid-afternoon. Even at eight in the morning, the desert air was rapidly warming, and streams of sweat appeared on Curtis's brown cheeks. As his breathing became labored, he slipped into internal thought, and it wasn't long before he visualized himself running down that familiar wash, noting all the redundant landmarks that directed him to that curious basin with the rock monuments.

He semi-consciously passed the point where he would usually cut across the infield to the equipment room. Instead, he hung close to the perimeter and ducked behind the dorms to make the third leg of his lap.

A palpable sense of foreboding overtook him as he moved past the rear of the rooster dorm. He picked up the pace until he reached the familiar edifice that was the henhouse dorm, and he slowed again to a brisk jog. He was actually rounding the rear of the chicken coop dorm, when a voice stopped him dead in his tracks.

"Hey—Curtis!"

It was Randy, and he was calling through an open transom window, apparently standing on a top bunk to do so.

"Hey, Randy," Curtis called back. "I've been looking for you."

"Well, there's a switch," Randy quipped. "C'mon around front—the door's open."

Curtis did so with some misgivings. The dorms were strictly age-segregated and supposedly locked when not in use, and the discipline he'd received the previous night had left a lasting impression. He glanced around anxiously. His need for some direction trumped caution though, and he stepped warily up the front steps and into the sleeping room where he'd seen his friend. There he found Randy alone in the room, still standing on a top bunk and looking considerably paler than ever. In fact, Curtis thought there was a sort of radiant translucence about him. He was wearing a pair of white Levi's with no belt, and a plain white T-shirt, no shoes.

"Wow, Randy," Curtis remarked. "You're as white as a sheet. You look like Casper the fuckin' ghost or somethin'!"

"Yeah, and you look like a melting Fudgsicle," Randy returned. "So what's your point?"

"None, I guess," Curtis shrugged. "I just need to talk about all this stuff that's been happenin' to me lately, and maybe get your take on what it means."

"What stuff are you talking about—is there other stuff?"

Curtis began to relate the events of the past couple of nights, starting with the unspoken threat at fish-Friday dinner. Randy listened with great interest in his reference to the manuscript in the library and the curious way the Lieutenant had confronted him about it.

"Did you read the whole entry about the massacre?"

"I just skimmed it real quick because study hour was almost over."

"It's just as well," Randy muttered. "You don't need to trouble yourself with details."

"Details like what? And while we're talkin' about details, how come you're still standin' on that bunk?"

Randy looked down at his bare feet, and a look of embarrassment came across his face.

"Confinement," he answered with a word.

"What do you mean *confinement*? I thought you said you come and go as you please."

"Well, most of the time I do," Randy returned sheepishly. "But I've gotten myself stuck with this ongoing penalty, and the dues for it require confinement to quarters for a certain time period each month—every last-quarter moon."

"Sounds about like the women's curse. Are you getting cramps?" Curtis teased.

"I fail to see the humor in your comment."

"Okay, sorry. Well, who is it anyway that makes you pay this lame-ass penalty?"

"A higher authority."

"The Lieutenant?"

"A higher authority than him, I'm afraid. Anyway, we're off on a tangent, aren't we? So, what other strange and wonder-filled events befell you last night?"

Curtis recounted the conflicts with Jeb, and Randy waved them aside as trivial.

"He's a henchman—small potatoes," Randy said as he studied Curtis's troubled expression. "But there's something else . . . I think?" he pressed.

Curtis cleared his throat and started to describe Harvey Huish's vicious attack on him in the dark of the sleeping dorm, but balked in mid-sentence, and actually began to physically choke on the words.

"No need to continue," Randy interjected. "Let me say it for you: he slipped a stranglehold on you from behind and started to choke the life out of you. And even now, you can feel the disgusting weight of his rank body pushing you to the floor—a fatal fall, or so it seemed."

"How do you know all of this," Curtis gasped, "without even bein' there?"

"And how many times are you going to ask that redundant question?"

"Fair enough, friend. Then let me take that one back and shoot you this one instead: Was that missed shot at . . . at killin' me . . . was it real or was it just my imagination? I mean, the way he just vanished and all, I just don't know how—"

"O-ho! Now we're getting into some tall weeds!" Randy shouted, with much enthusiasm. "Let me answer your question with a question: Is the past real?"

"Well, yes and no," Curtis responded without hesitation.

"The perfect answer!" Randy exclaimed. "At least, I think you mean the past, or past events, have already happened, and they're 'real' in our minds—in our memories. So, the past is real compared to the future, which is unreal, as it has yet to be determined. Is that what you're saying?"

Curtis nodded, but with a look of uncertainty.

"But what's come and gone—it's only real *in your mind*, don't you see? Whatever you're thinking about in the past doesn't really exist anymore except in your mind—your memory." Randy panted excitedly. "And that memory that you believe in is always passing through your own interpretation. I mean, it's your own version of what *was* real, right? So it's *twice* removed from reality, not to mention it's frozen."

"Well," Curtis responded hesitantly. "I guess so, but—"

"Look," Randy interrupted, "the only real, hard, unquestionable reality is the immediate present—what is happening at this split second. Does that help?"

"Oh, I get it, all right. I'm not dense," Curtis declared.

"Well, then, I guess you already know what you need to know about the chronology shift that occurs around here," Randy smirked.

"Listen, I don't know chronology from Crayolas," Curtis countered indignantly. "What I do know is what my mama would say about all this mixed-up time shit."

"Which is?"

"That it was God who ordered things and put us in the right-here and right-now—what you call 'the present.' That's what He did when He divided the day from the night. He created time, and He put us there—into a here-and-now that's always moving forward. He gave our minds the gift of rememberin', of lookin' back, and lookin' forward—guessin' the future. He even gave some of us the gift of glimpses into what might be, but He wants us to pay most of our attention on the present, 'cause that's where we live—in each passin' second; that's where life's lived."

"Holy shit!"

"Oh, it's holy all right, but it's no shit. Whatever my mama says is gospel truth."

"No, I just mean—"

"And I'll tell you what else she'd say."

"Now I'm all ears."

"She'd say that all this fiddlin' 'round with the natural order of things—with the past bleedin' over into the present and the future and all—well, she'd say it has nothin' to do with the hand of God, but more likely it's got the fingerprints of the other guy all over it."

"Curtis, I'd say your mama is some kind of a theological genius. And incidentally, we don't want to mention that other guy's name around here if we can help it. He seems to hold some serious influence over this place already, and we don't ever want to give him any undue encouragement."

"That's all well and good. There's just one problem."

"What's that?"

"It's just that none of this seems to have a whole lot to do with my question about my near-miss with murder."

"Well, it really does, in a roundabout way. This was all just sort of like stretching exercises for the brain so we can get you into a Fort Grant state of mind."

Randy began to bounce slightly and rhythmically on the bunk.

"Uh-huh—a Fort Grant state of mind," Curtis grumbled. "Just what I need."

"Well, you asked the question and said you'd make the effort," Randy shrugged. "We don't have to do this. I've said plenty of times that you really don't have to underst—"

"No, no, no. I want to know if that assault on me last night was real or was my imagination. I'll try to be serious."

"Fair enough. Now, ask the question differently, because the answer lies with an extreme lapse in the ordering of events as we know them—something that happens quite frequently around here."

"All right, then," Curtis backtracked, "what was—or is—the *nitty-gritty* of that whole spooky scene that *I thought* happened last night?"

"By 'nitty-gritty,' I assume you mean the *nature* of your vision, right?"

"Sure 'nuff."

"Excellent, my friend. Now you're getting a basic understanding of the disorder of events that occur around here. Fact is," he went on, "your experience might be a memory of something that actually happened, a memory of something that never *really* happened—given the limitation of the word *real*—a premonition of things yet to come, or a merging of any or all of the above."

"My, my. That sure narrows it down," said Curtis. "Now we've added in the future to muddy things up just a little more."

"Well, actually it could also be none of the above, but that's unlikely."

Curtis shot Randy a look that would reduce an ice block to a steaming pool. The pale boy backpedaled slightly: "Okay, maybe we should return to earth for a while, just to keep things in perspective."

Curtis noted to himself that Randy was repeatedly raising his arms slightly from his sides, then slapping them back down again in an agitated manner, and now he was completely distracted from his train of thought.

"Okay," said Curtis, now gently directing the discussion, "can you just answer the question in a simpler way?"

"Yes, I can. I can tell you that there is no way in the physical sense that Harvey Huish could possibly have been in the henhouse last night, or even in the dining hall at mess yesterday, because he has been at the infirmary huffing and scheming with Doc since four o'clock yesterday afternoon, and I know he never left."

"Huffin' and schemin'," Curtis exclaimed. "*Now* what the hell are you talkin' about, little bro?"

"Yeah, well, he and the Doc are cooking some kind of plan, and they like to enhance their brainstorming with clouds of ether. The point is, he is going to great lengths to create some ruse—and as much as he wants to snuff your flame out, I don't think he's going to do anything that might disrupt his grand plan right now."

"From what you told me before, I thought his stupid 'grand plan' was to escape before his court appearance date—isn't that right? Isn't that what all that dumb human pyramid stuff was all about?"

"Yes, that's the new plan—but don't mistake Harvey for a dummy just because you hate him. He's clever—clever enough to get away with murder if you let him. Maybe *your* murder, so maybe you ought to turn your attention to the heart of the matter before it's too late."

Now Randy was bouncing and slapping his sides rather frenetically.

"Hey, Randy—you got to pee or somethin'?"

"No, I just get a little nervous on my day of reckoning, okay?"

"Day of reckoning? Is this another mystery?"

"Never mind—just listen. Harvey came up with an idea to help his plan succeed, I'm sure of it. One of his new lawyers stopped by for a conference today, and they gave him a big fat envelope—beaucoup bucks, no doubt."

"To buy off staff, right?"

"That'd be my guess, and to travel on too. See, something happened to one of his other lawyers a few weeks back, and ever since then, his scheming about going over the wall has gone from a backup plan to 'plan A.' He's obviously lost his faith in the ability of his lawyers to get him off."

Curtis was becoming aware that the pitch in Randy's voice was rising gradually with every sentence.

"Not to change the subject," Curtis interjected, changing the subject, "but since you always know so much, can you tell me what happened to Marcus? He seems to have disappeared."

"Sure. Once a year about this time, Marcus takes a couple of days' leave and does a retreat."

"What do you mean, *a retreat*?"

"Just what I said, a retreat. He goes over to the chapel, shuts himself in, and doesn't come out for two or three days."

Randy's head was now cocked to one side and his voice was high and rasping.

"I don't get it," Curtis muttered, cocking his head unconsciously to meet Randy's blank expression. "Is everybody around here this weird?"

"Oh, brother—you haven't even begun to see weird yet."

"If that's true, I don't think I want to stick around here much longer."

"Me neither," Randy croaked. "Listen, you're going to have to excuse me for a minute or two—I'm losing my voice."

With that, Randy's face twisted into a contorted mask of pain and anguish. His right cheek pressed to his shoulder in an ungainly way, and the arm-flapping doubled in both frequency and intensity.

"Hey, Randy! You havin' a *seizure* or something?"

There was no reply, but the spring-and-chain suspension assembly beneath the mattress was singing out under the intense bouncing from the boy above.

"Hey, Randy—that ain't no trampoline. Hey, you're gonna get hurt doing that!"

At that next instant, Curtis was shocked to see Randy's hopping cease as the boy seemed to levitate in the air—*suspended several inches above the mattress.*

"What the hell, man. Cut it out!"

As if on command, Randy plummeted onto the mattress, only to have the spring undergirding give way, as he shot through to the bottom bunk where he came to rest on hands and knees. Curtis sat beside the breathless boy and put a hand on his shoulder.

"Hey, man—you all right? You want me to take you to the infirmary or somethin'?"

Randy shook his head.

"It'll pass," he panted. "And we . . . especially you . . . need to stay . . . away . . . from the . . . infirmary!"

"So what's the problem?" Curtis probed, "You got epilepsy or somethin'?"

"Something like that," Randy puffed. "It happens periodically. It'll pass."

The boy's breathing began to stabilize at length, and he turned to sit on the edge of the lower bunk next to Curtis.

"Okay, where were we?"

"Man, you had me scared shitless for a second there."

"Yeah, well at least that's over with for another month."

"Are you kidding me?" Curtis gaped. "This happens to you every month?"

"Every twenty-eight days, give or take. Whenever the moon's right," Randy murmured, almost to himself. "But hey, let me finish about Harvey, because it's crucial that we know what we're up against."

Curtis cast a skeptical look, but allowed the boy to continue uninterrupted.

"You see, another reason he set himself up with Jeb and Doc is so he won't be missed during any headcounts after he's gone. Between the two of them, they'll cook up some lame excuse about how he fell through the cracks. My guess is they'll claim he's cooped up in the infirmary with some fake illness while he's making tracks westward."

"He's clever, all right," Curtis remarked. "He'll have a long lead on the law, and he's gonna get away without a trace. I just wish he'd hurry up and do it, so I'm rid of him."

"Oh, isn't that typical. When we inject a little fear into the mix—it's hooray for me and fuck everybody else!"

"What do you mean?"

"You know exactly what I mean, or you've got a real short memory. Harvey Huish must be stopped from escaping. He's a killer and you know it—and you know he'll kill again. You want some innocent stranger's death on your conscience?"

"Better that than to be dead myself!"

"Man, I guess I really overestimated you," Randy sneered. "Okay, if guilt doesn't do it for you, try this: Harvey Huish could be four hundred miles away—let's say San Diego, or LA—and he can still be here with you, closing off your windpipe night after night. That's the nature of this place—it's quirky, and Harvey's been here awhile. He's figured out how to navigate those quirks pretty well."

"What *is it* about this place anyway, man? It's like a bad dream with no end."

"It's what you might call an *aberration*—a place where the lines drawn between the order of events and encounters have been blurred by a drastic disturbance."

"But it seems like it's only with me, and especially in the past few days, that all of these strange things have happened."

"Some people are more receptive of these paranormal episodes."

"*Sentient,* the Lieutenant called it."

"Your vocabulary, at least, is growing by leaps and bounds here," Randy chuckled. "Yes, sentient is about the best word I can think of to describe it. And you're right about another thing. Disjointed events and mysterious encounters here are more frequent and more intense during a certain lunar phase—the waning third-quarter moon, to be exact."

"Well, if that don't beat all. I mean, whatever happened to the notion of the *full moon* bein' the bad omen?"

"Jesus, you believe in that full moon stuff?" Randy scoffed. "Hell, man, you know—that's just *superstition!*"

"Now, let me get this straight," said Curtis, "Harvey is gonna check into the infirmary with a phony case of some kind of Creepin' Death, and Doc's gonna give him a head start before he blows the whistle that his patient has flown the coop—is that it?"

"That's his plan—to be long gone before the San Pedro County Sheriff can get a posse together."

"Then why don't you just rat out the whole plan to the Lieutenant and put an end to it before it starts?" Curtis wondered aloud. "Wouldn't you think an attempted escape would buy old Harvey a one-way ticket to hard time?"

"You'd think so. Trouble is, the Lieutenant doesn't listen to a word I say these days. It's almost as if I don't exist. Besides, a lot of my take is based on ill-gotten info—the rest on pure speculation. And in case you haven't noticed, the Lieutenant can be quite the fence-sitter."

"Imagine that. Well, do you ever wonder if the Lieutenant isn't on the wrong side of this whole plot too? I mean, he's a real oddball, isn't he? And why does everybody call him the Lieutenant anyway?"

"He must have been in the Army or something a long time ago, and maybe he is kind of odd," Randy said, after deliberating briefly, "but I doubt if he's implicated. Remember, he's revoking Harvey's lease on these cushy digs. I think he's just indecisive, not dishonorable. Kind of like Hamlet . . . hmmm?" He turned to meet Curtis's gaze. "Or kind of like you."

"Me—why me?"

"Because you haven't gotten on board with the plan yet. You're waffling."

"Maybe I am—maybe I'm not," Curtis grinned.

"Very funny," Randy smirked, "but unfortunately this is serious stuff, and you need to get off the fence and make a decision."

"My mama says that right and wrong decisions are what makes us who we are. Last time I made a bad one, I wound up here. I'm not about to go off half-cocked again."

"Curtis, did you ever hear it said that sometimes a bad decision is better than no decision at all?"

"No, but whoever said that surely never had to pay no dues for a bad one."

"You're impossible!" Randy snapped.

"Well, maybe I'm not on board with this thing," said Curtis, "but who's to blame for that? Fact is, I'm still in the dark about what your plan is. All you ever do is throw out strange hints or crazy comments, and then you sort of whip up some weird visions, all the time mutterin' about some grand scheme. But after all that bullshit, I still don't know what the hell you're talkin' about."

After a long silence, Randy sighed and spoke out in a grave tone.

"The plan is to put an end to Harvey Huish's dirty deeds, once and for all."

"That sounds pretty damn final," Curtis responded.

"And trying to kill you wasn't?" Randy returned. "Desperate times call for drastic measures."

"Good point. So, tell me, how do I figure into this grand plan of yours?"

"All you have to do is divert him from his getaway for a little while until he trips himself up."

"Huh?"

"Just provide a little distraction until he falls into a pickle, that's all. How many ways do you want me to say it?"

"See, that's what I mean, Randy. You talk in riddles and it's all still pretty hazy."

"I'll give up more details when you commit," Randy insisted. "So, what do you say? Are you in?"

"I . . . I gotta think about it. I mean, there's still so much missing from the picture. It's like trying to play *Name That Tune* with two or three notes."

"Fair enough. I'll answer one question in exchange for your commitment."

"Okay, for instance, what does all this mess with Harvey have to do with the ghost riders, and the massacre, and the moon, and all the other strange doings around here?"

"Who says it does?"

"You've said so, that's who—and that's not an answer!"

"And neither is that a question—it's more like a fishing expedition," Randy retorted. "I just don't think you need to worry all the details to death. I want you focused on the mission. Anyway," Randy yawned, "I'm getting tired of trying to get you to commit to something that's designed to save *your* ass in the long run. Why do I care?"

"There!" Curtis shouted. "That's another good question. Go ahead and answer that one—why do you care?"

"What do you mean?"

"Just what I said," Curtis pressed. "What's your angle—what do you get out of this?"

"Plain and simple," Randy returned, "I'll get the great satisfaction of knowing that justice is done."

"That's it? You just want to satisfy your strange sense of justice?"

"It's more than enough for me," the pale boy suddenly choked. "It's about all I've got left in this world, but it's more than enough." He cleared his throat to regain his voice, and continued. "But you can't understand the power of the yearning I have for justice. It's more like hunger."

"Funny, I never heard anybody try to compare a yen for justice to hunger. I think I'd use another word for how you're tellin' it: *vengeance*—that's what you're peddlin' here, mister."

"Curtis, you're the smartest stupid kid I ever met," Randy spat, "and this discussion is over!"

With that, Randy rose and stomped out of the room without making a sound.

"Aw, then fuck off, you little toothpick!" Curtis directed at deaf ears.

He sat wondering what to think for a moment, but was distracted by approaching boot steps in the main hallway. The dorm guard was coming!

Curtis climbed to the top bunk, grasped the lower chord of an exposed roof truss, and swung himself gracefully through the open transom, alighting cat-like on the path at the rear of the building.

Johnny Weissmuller would have been envious.

He rose from the feline crouch and looked all around. No one seemed to have noticed his maneuvers. He continued his morning jog as if it had never been interrupted at all by this unanticipated meeting with his bizarre friend.

Historical Friction

Curtis had hoped that a dialogue with Randy would have cleared things up and eased his troubled mind. But the dilemma continued to plague him long after he finished his late-morning run. His irresistible daydreams swung like a pendulum between the path down to the cemetery and his father's grave warning to "get back, son."

After a cheerless lunch of pinto beans and plain white bread, Curtis made his way to the library. He checked out his clipboard from an unfamiliar staffer and strode over to his isolated carrel—his zone of solace—to contemplate. The Joe Weider pamphlet, which he'd pored over religiously so many times before, now served as a mere front for some serious soul-searching. But as he approached his customary cubicle, he noticed that a bound stack of papers had been left on the desktop. He sat down and at once recognized the dog-eared cover page and the familiar title.

A History of Fort Grant

Fascinated by its inexplicable reemergence, the young man aggressively leafed through the pages until he came to the subtitle he was searching for.

The Fort Grant Massacre

He panned with electric excitement down the page, looking for passages that might fill in the gaps between the fragments that he'd read previously. There was a heading that read only "Aftermath," and he perused the paragraph, but found only a short passage that supported something Randy had mentioned earlier:

> It is interesting to note, though obviously unrelated, that a very few months following the massacre, a seismic event occurred south of the site that caused the San Pedro River to change its course, and the free-flowing waterway that had run for countless centuries past the site where the Fort now stands dried up completely. It literally disappeared within a matter of weeks.

It was odd, but not particularly enlightening. Then, he backtracked through the entries and came to another heading that read "Background." This sounded more promising.

The passage read as follows:

> It is widely believed that a temporary respite in the skirmishes between Apaches and white settlers ensued in early 1871, and that it was perceived by some to be a threat to the livelihood of certain wealthy Tucson merchants who had come to benefit from government welfare programs aimed at placating the native population. Merchants like Stanley Huish had become the middle-men between federally funded campaigns such as the "blankets for peace" program, and the native recipients. A real lasting peace was the last thing that these vendors wanted. And so a number of "raids" occurred in the spring of 1871—performances to maintain the appearance of a full-blown Indian uprising, many of which were alleged to have been planned, manned, and financed by wealthy Tucson merchant Stanley Huish. Some of these "raids" were made against settlers by mercenaries masquerading as Apaches. Some were waged against the Apaches themselves, to provoke retaliations. Such was the raid on Fort Grant.

"Wait a minute!" Curtis exclaimed out loud. "Stanley *Huish*? That sure can't be a coincidence."

He skipped down further and read the following to himself:

In a predawn attack on the camp, the Papago contingent of the raiding party silently clubbed and impaled their sleeping victims. Those few who managed to escape from the initial mayhem were picked off in mid-flight by Anglo sharpshooters who were lying in wait for them. In little more than an hour's time, 144 Pinal and Aravaipa Apaches— virtually all women and children—were murdered mercilessly and without provocation. Many were tortured merely for some demented sense of sport and deliberately mutilated in indescribably horrible ways.

Curtis skipped even further down to a heading that read:

The Response

The outrage over such a cold-blooded mass murder of innocent wards of the government gave rise to protests that were heard all the way back in Washington, D.C., and a decree soon came down from President Grant (ironically, the Fort was named for him) that those responsible should be brought to justice for their monstrous deeds.

A handful of the major participants and masterminds of the crime were indeed brought to trial some eight months following the brutal event. The hearing, which was deemed by many to be a mockery of justice, lasted only a few hours, culminating in the acquittal of all of the accused. Conspicuously absent from the proceedings was Stanley Huish, prominent Tucson merchant and former adjutant general for the territory. While there is no concrete evidence to bear this out, it is widely believed that Huish funded the legal defense for the accused as well.

"Well, well, well," Curtis muttered. "Sounds like the sins of the father have been passed on to the sons, after all."

"I'd say that's quite a leap."

It was Randy again, and the suddenness of his reappearance was startling.

"Maybe you ought to arrange for a flash of light and the stink of sulfur, little friend."

"That's nothing to joke about," Randy retorted. "Besides, I see no reason to announce my entrance."

"Well, you left so pissed, I didn't expect to see you again at all."

"Make no mistake, Curtis, I'm bound and determined to get you on board, and I won't let up until I have your commitment to stop Harvey Huish dead in his tracks, no pun intended. Moreover, I don't hold with any myths about guilt-through-relation. For me, Harvey Huish's own misdeeds are egregious enough without dragging his great-grandfather into it. The point is that we are totally responsible for our own lives, but *only* responsible for our own lives."

This hung in the air for a moment, then Randy concluded in a different tone. "Anyway, this is just another distraction."

"From what?"

"From the hard fact that Harvey Huish has got it in for you, Curtis, and this isn't just some bully waiting after school to pound on you. This guy, for whatever reason, is determined to switch your lights off, permanently. Look, you defied him in front of his henchmen; you made some poorly considered remark about his mother; then, to make matters worse, you humiliated him by deflecting his best shot at you. Oh, and just incidentally, there's the indisputable fact that black is not Mr. Huish's favorite color. Now, he may be temporarily distracted from his vendetta by his escape plans, but hoping that this will all just go away when he escapes is a huge mistake—maybe a fatal one."

"What makes you so certain that his arm *is* that long that he can choke me off all the way from California? What makes you so cocksure that he won't get his head turned by his freedom or by some LA surfer chick that he won't just forget about his stupid grudge and go his own way?"

"Curtis, haven't you learned *anything* about the Fort? Unresolved things like vendettas seem to thrive here, and Harvey's not limited by the normal rules about time and space—not as long as you are here, behind these walls. He can reach out for you at any time—or all the time, for that matter."

"You keep hintin' at that. What the hell do you mean?"

"Well, I've got a pretty good idea what you went through the other night in the dorm, even though you're having a tough time even describing it."

"So what about it?"

"So how would you like to replay that scene over and over again—night after night? I'm sure he'd love to relive that disgusting thrill he gets on a more regular basis, and away from the intervention of wailing coyotes. How would you like to be the nightly victim? Because that's what this place does for him, Curtis. Wanna be a homicidal maniac's houseboy for eternity? The coyote spirits won't always be there to disable him, you know."

Curtis considered the repulsive thought for a moment and shuddered. "Okay, so tell me again what you want me to do."

"First, keep the road signs for the way down to the burial ground mapped out fresh in your mind."

"That's not too tough. In fact, I couldn't get 'em out of my mind if I tried."

"That's good. Then, when the moon is right, meet up with your new-found boyfriend when he goes over the wall, and get him to follow you down there."

"That should be a piece o' cake. He already has this thing about stalkin' me. Then what?"

"The rest doesn't concern you. You just come back to the Fort and go to bed."

"I don't know, Randy. I gotta have more to go on before I can say nay or okay."

"Well, my friend, you know what they say about time and tide, don't you?"

Curtis shook his head.

"They wait for no man. I suppose that applies to boys as well."

The young Negro boy gasped at the gravity of his circumstances.

"Hey, kid, are you reading that?" a third voice called from behind a set of empty shelves.

Curtis turned to see who it might be and was confronted by an unfamiliar guard, apparently the erstwhile librarian.

"Yes, sir," Curtis responded. "It was just sittin' here on this desk, but I did start to page through it."

"Well, browse all you like, but make sure it gets back to the circulation desk when you get done. I've been searching high and low for it all morning. The Lieutenant would have my head on a pike if it ever went missing."

"Why is that, uh, sir . . . if you don't mind my askin'?"

"Because the Lieutenant is the author, of course."

"Well, I'll be damned—did you hear that, Randy?"

Curtis turned back but his friend had disappeared again as suddenly as he had appeared earlier.

"Who are you talking to, kid?"

"My friend, who was just here. Didn't you see him?"

"Nope, can't say as I have."

"It doesn't matter, I guess. But listen—I hate to be full of stupid questions . . ."

"I'm the librarian—you're supposed to be able to ask me questions. That's what I'm here for."

"Sure, well, here's what's been puzzlin' me: Why does everybody call the headmaster *the Lieutenant*? And don't say *they just do*, 'cause that's not an answer."

"I guess because before he was headmaster, he was a commanding officer in the Army," the guard replied thoughtfully.

"Commanding officer?"

"Yep, camp commander for this very fort a number of years ago—last of the cavalry divisions, they say. The Lieutenant has run this place for as long as anyone can remember."

"Kinda weird, isn't it—that he doesn't seem all that old?"

"How do you mean?"

"Uh, nuh—nothing," Curtis stuttered. "I was just thinkin' out loud."

"Well then, don't forget to return that manuscript when you're finished with it."

"Will do—and thanks."

Curtis rose and scanned up and down the nearby aisles to see if Randy was still lurking about.

"Scrawny little weasel tells me nothing," he muttered, "and then I learn more from some old yard-bull in two minutes than I do from him in a week."

He returned to the sanctity of his little carrel and sat back down gloomily. He thumbed absent-mindedly through the pages again until he happened across another interesting heading.

Indecision Leads to Tragedy

The passages that Curtis now fixed upon told an age-old and sorrowful tale:

> The Indians that had congregated at Fort Grant were apparently battle weary and dispirited with being driven by war and weather from one end of the territory to the other. And so they came to settle on the banks of the San Pedro River, which they claimed was their traditional homeland. They set about cutting hay for some of the local ranchers, and gathered mescal, the heart of an indigenous *agave* cactus plant, and their primary source of sustenance.

His eyes started to narrow, and his chin began to lower to his chest, but he shook it off.

"Okay, Curtis," he admonished himself, "you wanted details—now don't get bored with the details—keep reading!"

Pressing on, he happened on a more poignant passage:

> Technically, the members of the encampment were prisoners of war, and, as wards of the federal government, were entitled to the care and protection of the appropriate agency—that agency, in this case, being United States Army.
>
> The officer in charge, a young lieutenant who had previously served and endured a painful Civil War experience, treated his charges with decency and compassion. But, given the aggravated hostilities brewing between the resident Apaches and nearby Tucson-area settlers, he harbored grave concerns for the safety and well-being of those native people under his stewardship.

Curtis looked up and scouted the immediate area for any sign of Randy again, but there was no telltale movement in the adjacent stacks that he could discern, so he returned to the narrative.

> The lieutenant became quite anxious and urged—but did not de-mand—that the encampment chiefs lead their people further to the north to Fort Apache, where they would be removed from the local animosities and would enjoy the protection of a larger contingent of soldiers. When the Apache leaders refused, the lieutenant followed protocol, refrained from any further action, and simply awaited orders from a higher level of authority. Sadly, his reluctance to take it upon himself to roust the squatters from their camp and herd them on a forced march to the safety of the larger, more established fort became his life's failure and the backdrop for the upcoming atrocity.

Curtis panned back up the page and reread the subtitle to the passage:

Indecision Leads to Tragedy

He looked up again, trying to catch a fleeting glimpse of his elusive tempter, whom he was certain had somehow arranged this reading and must be lurking nearby, confirming that the lesson was indeed taking hold.

"Slimy little white snake," he muttered. "He must be behind this, but *how does he do this stuff?*"

Now Curtis leafed through to the last page of the "Massacre" section. Curiously, there was a subtitle in the middle of the page, but no continu-ing text. The heading read:

A Curse and a Prophecy

"Hey, kid—the library is closing in five minutes. Why don't you let me take that manuscript back now for return? I don't want to lose track of it, or it'll be my ass."

Curtis glanced around to get his bearings and to check himself that he hadn't lost track of the time again. "Since when does the library shut down before lights-out?" he asked, somewhat puzzled.

"Since I pulled library and KP duty on the same day, son," the librarian replied. "We're short-handed without Marcus. And since we're 'since-whenning,' since when does an inmate question what a staff member dictates?"

"Sorry, it's just that I was right in the middle of tryin' to—"

"Yeah, well, you can just pick it up from where you left off another time. Right now, your arguing is makin' me late for kitchen prep. You want me to announce who's responsible for a late mess?"

"No need to get touchy about it, sir. Here you go."

Curtis offered up the manuscript to eager hands, and made a quick exit, noting that the hands of the clock on the wall had not quite reached the right angle of three. He'd become aware enough of the rather rigid school schedules to know that kitchen prep never commenced before four.

Now, at the foot of the steps, he paused to take notice of more incongruity. The sky was strangely overcast, although it was only slightly mottled with scattered afternoon clouding, and a swelling breeze stirred the afternoon air. An intuitive sense of foreboding filled the boy several seconds before the throng of roosters appeared from his left, around the corner of the administration building. Curtis recognized the faces. It was Harvey's troop of ten roosters, led by his principle enforcer, Gerd Brinkerhoff.

"*Ged him!*" he heard the huge German boy bellow.

The terrifying command was all that Curtis needed to send his feet into flight, aiming in the opposite direction, toward the Lieutenant's verdant glade—the way that Doc had once designated as the path of no return.

273

Several Steps Beyond

With his escape blocked at either end of the walkway, Curtis's eyes darted about desperately for an alternative flight path. The only way clear was an opening between the citrus trees in the Lieutenant's forbidden grove. There was no time for even a second's hesitation; Harvey's band of toadies were almost upon him.

He hopped the low wall that separated the administration building yard from the inmate walkway and sprinted into the shadowy embrace of the trees, hoping that the unseen far end of the tiny orchard offered no dead ends. The rapid cadence of his footfalls changed to tiny splashes as dry ground gave way to a shallow skimming of flood irrigation. Even in his terrified state of mind, Curtis wondered about the source of this volume of water. Nowhere beyond the distant town of Picacho had Curtis seen any canals or ditches on his ride over with Sergeant Joe many weeks before. It was nothing but desert for miles on end, arid and unbroken by any remote oasis—*Nowhere Central*, as Curtis had put it. But given the dire situation, the water was fast losing its place as a serious forethought.

Dodging thorny lemon branches and fragrant orange boughs, the boy bounded through the grove like an elusive broken-field ball carrier speeding for the end zone in sudden death overtime. His breathing became labored as his legs and arms pumped like pistons to widen the gap between himself and his pursuers. Fight or flight? Not much choice in this case.

The ground in front of the harried young runner now rose slightly, and his feet fell once again on dry ground. The squish-squish sound that his wet canvas shoes made would have been comic under other circumstances.

Curtis anticipated an imminent break out of the trees and into the main yard—a break that never came. Instead, a serpentine path began to take shape as he pressed on, his sustained sprint now falling to the tempo of a quick canter. He listened to the rhythm of his heaving respiration and set his relentless pace in accord with its steady ebb and flow.

Odd.

Judging by the distance he had covered over the last sixty seconds or so, the boy had surely covered a quarter mile of ground and should have not only broken into the inside yard by now, but he would certainly have been met by one of the Fort's formidable adobe ramparts. Yet the way ahead signaled no indication of a clearing or a wall. To the contrary, the foliage seemed to grow thicker, wilder—the path now twisting through a cavernous arbor of dense vegetation.

Grateful for the inexplicable escape route, Curtis could not help but wonder how and why he'd stumbled on this leafy passageway to deliverance from his enemies. Amazing grace, perhaps.

Feeling nearly spent, the harried boy presently dared to slow his pace, and he listened intently for sounds of his pursuers. Heartened that no foreign sound save the winded bellows in his own chest reached his ears, he turned, backpedaled, and peered down the path behind him. Strangely, there was no sign of his usually tenacious tormentor or any of his drooling minions.

Confident, but at a loss as to why he had not been followed, apparently not even as far as the entrance to the Lieutenant's little grove, Curtis nevertheless resumed a jog that would put an even greater distance between himself and Harvey Huish's gang. At this slower pace, he was now able to take in the wonder of his peculiar surroundings.

He emerged from a tunnel of overgrown desert willow and Russian olive branches that seemed to grapple overhead for dominance, and padded noiselessly into the dappled westering sunlight that played about the wooded floor in glowing fragments like the luminous beads of some agitated kaleidoscope. The radiance from that frenzied solar dance virtually animated the entire scene.

His gaze strayed upward, following the gnarled old trunks of an amassed battalion of titanic cottonwood trees that vaulted skyward some eighty feet into the air where they exploded from clawing boughs into dense, verdant crowns of shimmering spade-shaped leaves. A clamoring susurration rose and fell intermittently through the treetops, resonating with a gusting west wind that had rather suddenly kicked up since he'd left the breathless confines of the Fort.

"I don't believe we're in Kansas anymore, Toto," he mused to himself, as he reined in his forward motion to a robotic walk.

A blizzard of downy cottonwood catkins played across his vision like seed-bearing snowflakes through the overhead vista, its deep, solid azure patches peeking through effervescent blasts of jade. The boy was bedazzled by the sensory bombardment raining down from the animated sylvan canopy like a deluge of emerald.

Reluctantly, he forced his gaze back downward as his stumbling footsteps strayed from the curving trail and onto the bosque floor outside the path. The terrain underfoot here was carpeted with a solid bed of desiccated cottonwood leaves in all stages of decay. Curiously, the blustering wind seemed unable to disturb or rattle more than a few loose members. The rest of the dead leaves seemed to comprise an integrated blanket of sorts, pasted into a leathery layer by time and weather over the revolving seasons. The only movement came from feathery balls of tufted catkins, the cotton-clad seedlings clinging together as they rolled silently over top of the leafy mat like restless dust-bunnies.

Curtis redirected his trek back onto the sandy path, noting by many signs that it was frequently traveled. Not a single sprout survived on this wayward trail in its winding course. Human footprints and depressions of horses' hooves, shod and otherwise, populated the entire length and breadth of it. Clustered nuggets of grainy horse manure, some still greenish and shining with moisture, festooned the trail here and there. Yet even this evidence of an otherly presence failed to disquiet the boy.

Passing through intervals of shadow and sunlight and whispers of gentle winds worked their peaceful magic like subtle caresses on Curtis's mind. A curious enchantment eclipsed a creeping undercurrent of anxiety. Such overwhelming disorientation should have sent a warning.

He now broke into a routine of trotting along the sun-drenched stretches and walking the shady ones—a run-walk that covered odd intervals of fifty to a hundred yards, thereby minimizing exposure to the energy-sapping effect of the westering solar sphere.

Presently, his forward progress encountered a fork on the path, and he halted his dumbstruck march. The right fork angled a westerly forty-five degrees from due south toward sunlight, while the left cut to an abrupt right-angle turn and made a beeline to the east, disappearing into a deeper green through a cluster of tamarisk shrubs. A whiff of mystery scented that path. Curtis silenced his heavy breathing and strained to hear what his intuition was telling him. Between the intermittent sighs of the wind in the boughs above, a faint gurgling sound declared its part in the harmony: somewhere nearby water flowed.

But something else, now: a sound more distant and distinct than the babble of the water or the susurration of the wind drew ever nearer, and menacingly so. A low, building cadence of heavy footfalls was approaching from behind—low, but swelling rapidly toward dominance like a tympani roll in the airborne musical score. Harvey's company had finally caught up!

Without glancing back down the path, Curtis made a panic-stricken dash to a clump of pampas grass and fell prostrate behind the concealment of its leafy tendrils. He abated his breathing again as well as he could and strained to discern the sound above his own hammering heartbeat. There was an odd rhythmic repetition in the beating of the footfalls—a signature sound:

Pump-pump . . . pump-pump . . . pump-pump . . .

Hoofbeats! It was a horse, and not Harvey's henchmen after all. Relief and elation nearly spurred the boy to spring up from his leafy refuge and hail the equestrian stranger.

But no. A hard-learned caution intervened to prevent such a rash outburst; he kept to his prone position and his vigilance over the forked trail. There was no other way to be certain who this rider might be, if indeed the horse was even mounted, and what his purpose might be—friendly or otherwise.

Seconds ticked by, a minute at most, before a glimpse of motion and color presented itself at the path's division. From his limited supine position, Curtis could view only the forelegs of the chestnut steed as it halted at the fork, but he could see that it was shod and therefore likely to be carrying an unexposed rider. The boy indulged an irresistible curiosity and raised his torso slightly, straining to see what he could of the mare's human freight.

She nickered at length and tossed her huge head impatiently, jingling the loosened tack. With a whine of straining leather, the rider dismounted. A pair of dusty tan boots hit the pathway floor with a dull, thudding flam, and Curtis retracted deeper into the pampas like a startled box turtle. There was something vaguely foreboding in the approach of this stranger, and the boy's shallow breathing caught in his throat as he tensed for bolting into the thick of the woods where a horse's thundering pursuit would be hampered by tangling brambles.

Curtis readied to spring from the starting blocks, but just as the adrenalin level built to a hair-raising peak, the mare neighed loudly and began a rebellious trot down the left fork in the trail. The sinister rider's boots now turned heel 180 degrees, toes pointed away from Curtis and toward the horse's willful escape route.

"Whoa there, girl," the stranger called in a booming baritone. He caught up a dragging rein as she passed. "I swear, you're worse than a magnet in a smithy shop when you smell water!"

With his heart in his throat, Curtis used this diversion to inch backward like a sand crab, keeping the thick pampas between himself and the spectral pair of retreating boots. The sudden stirring of the mare combined with a welcome gust from the west wind provided some audio cover for the boy's shuffling through the mat of dead leaves.

He listened intently to the hoofbeats fading down the path toward the sound of flowing water. Relying on his assumption that the rider had either remounted or was following along, the boy raised up just in time to catch a fleeting glimpse of the mare's chestnut rump, as it vanished behind a thick copse of tamarisk.

Curtis cautiously emerged from the cover of the foliage. The brief presence of the rider had provoked an instinctive sense of fear and loathing, the source of which he could not discern or even imagine. He cautiously approached the fork again where the choices were once more narrowed to two: he could go back the way he came—back up the path to the confinement of the Fort. Along with this choice came the risk that Harvey and company had lagged behind, but were still following, or lying in wait for his eventual return. The alternative was to press forward on the westward-angling fork. In so doing, he would be plunging ever deeper into unknown territory, ever farther away from the anchoring presence of the Fort, such as it was.

And now, with the imminent return of the sinister rider looming, there was no time for hesitation. He stepped immediately in a southwesterly direction.

Surveillance

C urtis stepped toward his chosen direction, pressing deeper into the
mysterious woods. But in fact, it wasn't so much the lingering
threat of Harvey's minions perhaps waiting to waylay him on the
way back that gave him pause. Nor was it the imminent possibility that the
dreaded rider that had just passed this way might just as likely as not
backtrack the way he had come after watering his steed at the river's edge,
though that too was a potential encounter that he'd just as soon avoid.

Truth be known, it was more a burning curiosity as to his immediate
whereabouts that spurred his heel. A litany of questions danced before
him, teasing out a craving for answers. How had he passed beyond the
walls of the Fort and into this unlikely oasis? How had the existence of
an adjacent river and its fertile flood plain escaped his knowledge? He'd
been outside the walls before, however briefly, with Randy and detected
no trace of this verdant bosque. How had he missed it, and why had no
one ever spoken of it? To the contrary, all talk that he'd ever heard
supported the contention that the Fort was a landlocked outpost in the
center of a vast desert wasteland.

The path threaded its winding way through ever-higher arches of
Sonoran scrub oak and clump river birch, meandering in something of a
southwesterly progression. Eventually, it broke free from the spell of the
trees and rimmed the foot of a steep gravel embankment, devoid of any
vegetation, save a few thorny green tumbleweed sprouts scattered across
the slope.

The boy stopped and surveyed the course that lay before him. The
path skirted the bank for as far as half a mile or so. From what he could
discern, the dusty ribbon of travel was the stark demarcation line

between two worlds. To the left were arrayed the dense woods of the alluvial plain. To the right, beyond the top rim of the embankment, lay the boundless desolation of the sun-baked Sonoran. There was a smattering of knolls beyond the bank about two hundred yards to the west. An old-growth mesquite stood proudly planted at the peak of one of these mounds, its deep jade plumage beckoning on the hot afternoon breeze. Curtis surmised that he might scope the lay of the land from that vantage point and hopefully get his bearings.

Weariness dismissed, he clambered up the steep embankment, dislodging surface stones under slipping treads. The troubling disorientation and uncertainty had to be reckoned with, risk of being spied notwithstanding.

It was nearly five minutes of uphill plodding against a stiff breeze before Curtis reached the peak of the rise where the old tree offered concealment—both from the beating rays of the late afternoon sun and the potential of prying eyes.

The west wind up on this promontory blew even more vigorously than it did in the bosque below, but here it carried the fierce, newly released solar heat that was stored in the rocks and sand of the desert, and it felt like the backdraft from a blast furnace. He collapsed onto a bed of the tiny serrated leaves that the old tree had shed there over many seasons, now mummified yellow versions of their formerly lush selves. Curtis now scrambled for the windward side of the mesquite's broad trunk and the ample cover that it offered, then peeked around the leeward exposure. After a moment's cautious hesitation, he stepped out and widened the scope of his surveillance.

The desert knoll upon which he was placed claimed the uncontested high ground for miles in all directions—a panoramic advantage that likewise rendered him vulnerable to exposure. After all, he was, at least technically, a fugitive. A quick scan assured him that nothing but the familiar barrenness of the Great Sonoran hemmed him in from the north, west, and south—nothing but mica and granite gravel, silicate dust, and broken sandstone, dotted here and there with an occasional clump of cactus and creosote brush for as far as the eye could see. *Nowhere Central, indeed.*

Now his eyes fixed eastward, downward to the emerald treetops of the bosque. The belt of green, which Curtis judged to span a width of a quarter mile at its narrowest and more than a mile where it was not pinched in by sandstone bluffs, stretched from the northern to the southern horizons, and presumably for miles beyond. The sculpted carpet of cottonwood florets was parted at its center by a winding ribbon of shimmering motion—a river, a spirit-coursing artery of liquid life.

Curtis noted that the stream's movement was to the north, the only river he'd ever seen flowing so oddly in that direction. This had to be some sort of dream, one that went a long way toward explaining the existence of an alluvial bosque in the middle of the desert.

To the north lay a void in the greenery—a pocket that housed a stoic fortress. It was the Fort. Curtis recognized the stark white walls, the Spanish colonial design of the administration building, the towering mast flying the stars and stripes. Ironically, the Fort, a symbol of his penitence, provided an orientation anchor for him in all of this wondrous confusion—actually a source of some comfort.

Yet even in its familiarity, something about the layout of the buildings was amiss. The cluster of erections was sparser than he recalled. There seemed to be no classroom building visible and no mess hall that he could perceive. The barracks impressed him as smaller and more rustic. He blinked. Perhaps it was just the angle of his perception, and the administration building was blocking his full view.

To the south, another vacant patch in the carpet of green presented a curious cluster of tiny pyramidal shapes arranged in symmetrical rows. Continued focus finally teased loose a sudden epiphany: it was an encampment of some sort—a bivouac of tents.

And there was more—a buzz of activity. From this distance, it seemed like the frenetic movement of an army of ants, but there was an unmistakably human quality about the bustle. Curtis continued to watch and wonder. It occurred to him that this surveillance of his, although intended to provide some point of reference, posed more questions than it presented answers. If anything, the confusing picture was decidedly *dis*orienting. Here was forest where there had been only desert. Here was a river where it did not belong, running in the wrong direction. Here was a populated campsite where there had been none. Here was the Fort, but even the layout of it was somehow wrong. There was something wrong with all of it.

Having lost a healthy concern for being spotted from below, the weary boy seated himself on the warm ground with his back resting against the shady downhill side of the broad mesquite trunk. Curtis now cast his tired eyes downward, skimming across the tops of the cottonwoods, fascinated by the curious phenomenon that random clusters of the waving florets displayed a bright emerald glow, while the rest of the sculptured canopy remained in relief—a deeper jade color. Even more interesting was the way this peculiar spectacle of luminosity shifted from tree to tree as the wind stirred their lush tresses. Eastward, past the bosque, stretched another expanse of straw-brown plain—a barren, shimmering wasteland that ran out flat for a dozen or more miles before rising gradually to meet the startling upthrust of the Pinaleno Range.

Only these, the Pinalenos, remained steadfast in their appearance, and this vista of the mountains at this time of day, in this light, was nothing less than captivating. Like a crouching caravan of travel-weary camels at rest—some nose-to-tail, some head-to-head, some rump-to-rump—the series of peaks sprawled across the entire stretch of the eastern horizon. The deep orange hue of the declining sun cast their bestial features into three-dimensional relief, and each stony animal virtually crawled with a barely perceptible movement of solar highlights and shadows. Only the Pinalenos, he thought, remained the same, and even they were *moving*.

Curtis's seated position felt more and more comfortable. The mesquite's sturdy trunk began to feel like part of his spine. Its rough, fissured bark made for a great back-scratcher, and he rubbed his shoulder blades against the abrasive skin in a circular motion. He relished this moment's rest.

Tired from the unrelenting scans of the countryside, Curtis's eyes fell shut for only a few second's respite from the strain as he pondered his position in all of this strange dissonance. He blinked several times when he opened them again to regain the clarity of his vision.

In spite of the heat, a wave of trembling passed through the boy's muscular body, much the same way a horse shudders when it senses unseen peril or vulnerability. An uncanny sense that these surroundings were even more alien to him now kindled a dread that overshadowed the wonder and curiosity that had heretofore held him spellbound.

And yet even as he pondered this unshakable sense of alienation, the lengthening of the shadows cast by this cluster of knolls slipped past him unnoticed. They marched downward like darkening phantom shades, skimming the treetops below. Beyond his notice as well, the camelback bluffs of the Pinalenos morphed in hue from orange to wine-red to deep purple.

The tireless rise and fall of the hot desert wind gradually stilled to a warm murmuring breeze.

Curtis rested his eyes again, but this time, the nervous tension in the cords of his neck slackened until his chin rested on his chest.

No poppies needed.

Twilight Time

It was the sudden stillness more than anything that aroused Curtis from the narcotic catnap. The air was now purged of all its infernal agitation and had slowly quieted with the gradual onset of evening shadows.

The silence was deafening, and the creeping lack of movement was palpable, almost suffocating. The boy's sinewy limbs snapped taut in an instant as he shot up to his feet with a start. A sense of anxious dread coiled through his inner core like the steely constriction of a serpent's cold-blooded embrace. Ebony eyes darted about wildly as his situation unfolded before him. The unconscious hope that this world might somehow prove something less than corporeal was dashed upon waking from a dream that had promised more substance than shadow.

The sun was a golden glowing memory of its earlier fiery reign, already tucked behind the Galiuros peaks to the west. The tops of the cottonwoods below had lost their emerald highlights and now melted together into a drab charcoal blanket. The Pinalenos diminished into obscure mounds of ashes to the east. Several stars came prematurely stealing onto the celestial stage above, twinkling bashfully at first above the eastern horizon, but shining forth more boldly by the minute. A faint luminescence emitted from the windows of various buildings behind the graying walls of the Fort, and a lambent flickering of several campfires began to dance about the curious bivouac of the tent city to the south.

Night's curtain was falling, and falling fast.

Stripped of all the sensory bedazzlement that daylight had offered—the depth of the visual field, the explosions of color from bluff and bosque, the whisper of the wind—the sense of alienation that these things had held in abeyance now came crashing in with full effect. He had neither fallen into a rabbit hole, nor passed through the back of a wardrobe. And the closest the boy had ever come to even seeing a tornado, let alone being transported by one, were the desert dust devils that barely had the strength to lift sand and loose rubbish aloft, much less a house. Nevertheless, the rude awakening to reality, or more accurately *un*reality, was right out of the pages of Messrs. Carroll, Lewis, and Baum. Dread quickly morphed into the terror of knowing that he was a stranger in a strange land, and might never see the inside of the bungalow in Jacobs Well again, nor enjoy the big embrace of his warm-hearted mom.

The Fort, as ironic as it might seem, was the nearest thing to an anchor of familiarity that Curtis could fathom, and he longed to huddle behind the refuge of its walls.

Do you know what the one good thing is about being inside the walls of the Fort?
It's that the things out here on the outside can't get to you.

Pools of black emptiness grew around him, vacuous phantoms creeping ever eastward, fed and driven by the waning glow behind the Galiuros range. He could not shake the overwhelming sense that something momentously evil was approaching from beyond time and space, and that he would be snatched up in its sinister manifestation if caught outside those adobe walls after dark. Raw panic seized him, and he bolted down the face of the knoll like a flushed bunny.

In spite of the boy's powerful stride, this terrain would have been difficult to negotiate in broad daylight. But in this subdued light, Curtis was like a blind steeplechaser on a downhill course, and the obstacles he was forced to hurdle at a dead run seemed to reach up from the shrouded ground to trip him up. Creosote clumps, sandstone shards, and tumbleweed remnants assaulted his precarious footing as the downward stumbling sprint gained dangerous momentum.

Somehow, the boy reached the bottom of the grade without falling, and the flat platform of a shelf that his feet suddenly found warned

Curtis that the steep embankment hemming the bosque lay just ahead. Trying hard to rein in the inertia that the downhill run had garnered, he failed to negotiate the crest of the drop-off, and the pumping stride of his right foot found air instead of solid ground. Blind equilibrium told him that his headlong tumble paired with the steepness of the fall line would carry him for a full frontal flip, so he tucked his legs up and waited for impact. His shoulder blades made first contact with the loose dirt, and the radical slope absorbed much of the shock of impact. He instinctively unfolded his legs, and the splayed limbs provided the needed drag to bring a downward slide to a halt.

Curtis scrambled to his feet and took stock of his condition. Lucky break—no fractures, and the peaking levels of adrenaline that coursed through his body masked the pain of the scrapes and bruises he'd incurred. Although the burning sensation radiating from his lower back signaled more serious abrasions where his T-shirt had ridden up on the downhill slide, he sloughed it off with a few buoyant in-place springs into the air and a victorious raising of clenched fists toward the sky in true pugilist spirit.

Reorienting, he found himself planted on the path that rimmed the foot of the darkened declivity. It gleamed before him in defiance of the gathering gloom, subtly lit by the fading luminosity of a slate-gray sky. The winding ribbon of sandy earth spooled out clearly for fifty yards or so, then vanished into the gaping yaw of an arboreal tunnel. Vigorously dusting himself off from his spill, Curtis started northward back up the path that led to the Fort, although somewhat daunted by the foreboding foliage of the bosque.

Despite the ominous course that lay before him, the adrenaline-assisted boy broke into a determined canter that he judged would traverse the distance back in less than ten minutes—just moments ahead of full darkfall. Curtis strode powerfully, making his way in spite of the loose river-bottom soil. The soles of his Chuck Taylor running shoes sensed the uneven, chopped surface of the path. Deep depressions of horses' hooves dotted the trail. Nevertheless, the boy maintained his determined stride while stepping gingerly to guard against turning an ankle in one of the miniature potholes. He plunged boldly through the leafy portal into the inner sanctum of the dusky arboretum.

Passing that sinister threshold, the boy entered a netherworld he had not reckoned on. Precious little light from the lambent canopy above pierced the tightly knitted, leafy mantilla that unfurled from the cottonwood branches—barely enough glow to make out the twisting trail before him for more than twenty yards ahead. Verdant copses of salt cedar now appeared as midnight-blue funereal shrouds, and the cavernous arbors of Russian olive and clump river birch yawned like beckoning doorways to ancient sepulchers.

Absent the afternoon's freshening breezes, the pungent smell of composting leaves from the matted floor of the woods hung oppressively in the motionless air. Then too, the silence that had ruled the evening above and beyond the bosque's reaches now gave way to a cacophony of bleating crickets, coveys of nightjars calling tunelessly from the ground, and the metallic wailing of bullfrogs in the throes of their slimy courtships at the river's edge. Retiring squirrels scolded the boy's intrusion on their sleepy realm, trilling in heart-stopping bursts of chatter from the safety of their perches in the higher boughs.

But now, for no apparent reason, an abrupt hush fell over the woods. No more ringing crickets, croaking bullfrogs or keening nightjars. It was a vacuous silence as if orchestrated by a stilling command from the hand of Death himself. The instant quiet was more than disquieting. Though no alien sound reached his ears, a warning wave of intuition told him that something other than his own intrusion had prompted the sudden silence. He lingered for a moment, but detected no audible disturbance.

Trepidation notwithstanding, the boy recognized that any further delay would likely plunge him into full darkfall before reaching the Fort. Fear of the woods in total blackness trumped his inkling of immediate peril. He reluctantly pressed on into the murk, as whatever miserly bit of ambient light that had managed to permeate the overhead foliage was now rapidly dwindling. The soft, rhythmic padding of his Chuck Taylor ultralight soles and his own labored breathing were the only sounds that registered on his eardrums. Predictably, the absence of more external noise exaggerated the body-driven sounds. Fear was becoming familiar.

Trotting slowly, Curtis's head panned from side to side, scanning the edges of the trail like an oscillating beacon. He could not shake an overwhelming but thus far unfounded sense that some concealed peril lay just ahead. He picked up the pace now, driven by the urgency of the nightfall deadline, as he peered ahead to make out the dim extents of the serpentine trail. Straying from within its shadowy margins, he might meet with some hazard that would cause him to stumble and fall. That, and the rustling of his feet in the mat of leaves might give his exact position away to the listening ears of the unseen, ill-intended phantom of his imagination.

The path ahead approached the murky mouth of another of the many leafy tunnels through which the worn treadway passed at frequent intervals. Curtis fixed his gaze upon the sandy strip that stretched before him as he entered the darkened maw of the arbor at a quickened canter. Russian olive tendrils draping from the overhead arch of the sylvan cavern lightly brushed the nape of his neck like the cold caress of a cadaver's bony fingertips. Shivers shot up his spine and, eyes still focused downward, he sprinted for the subdued afterglow at the arbor's exit terminus.

Breaking into the clear, he raised his field of vision and instantly reined back his headlong dash with a little yelp of fright. Straddling the path just a dozen feet ahead loomed a darkened form, human in proportion, but slightly smaller in stature than Curtis. The diminutive but nonetheless terrifying specter stood likewise motionless with a raised right arm that the mortal boy interpreted as a menacing gesture of some sort. The apparition was planted dead center of a narrow bottleneck where the trail threaded its way between thickets— impossible to pass without an encounter. In the subdued twilight, the outline of the form was nebulous, otherworldly.

Curtis stood frozen in his tracks, daring not even to breathe, not even to blink, lest he stir this diminutive darkling from its paralytic pose. But then, a high-pitched *puppety* sort of sound emitted from the form before him—spoken phrases in a guttural tongue whose origins Curtis imagined to be none other than the lower regions of the nether-world.

"Ndeen' diyih!" the voice cried out like an invocation from some demonic priest.

Curtis's knees bent reflexively like a panic-stricken animal preparing to flee, but the thick foliage on either side of the path barred any avenue of escape, and turning back with nightfall looming was now unthinkable.

"Ndeen' diyih!" the thing exclaimed again, the bizarre voice lilting upward at the end of the incantation, almost as if to question the terror-gripped boy.

"Now you step aside, little bogeyman," Curtis barked with all the false bravado he could muster, "or I'll run you over like a runaway freight train!"

"Nachise', Sika, Ndeen'—*yiyaa*," the voice exhorted in reply, the form now raising the uplifted arm even higher in a vaguely threatening gesture like some pygmy warrior. "Yiyaa . . . yiyaa!"

"Yeah-yeah yourself," Curtis retorted. "Now move out the way before I kick your *yeah-yeah* up between your *yo-hos*!"

Undaunted, in fact, seeming to be only provoked by Curtis's posturing, the dark figure loomed closer, repeating the same eerie phrase: "Yiyaa . . . yiyaa!"

The menacing shape rushed right up to the frightened boy, who raised a right fist in defense. But now a face flashed before him—shining dark eyes and a toothy, disarming grin—that made Curtis hesitate from unloading with the wound-up blow.

In that instant of hesitation, Curtis was stricken full in the face with a sodden mass of cold ectoplasm—wet and cold and slimy, like being smacked in the kisser by a giant ball of wriggling, mucous-laden earthworms. He'd heard before that apparitions like this often *slimed* their victims in the process of frightening them into cardiac arrest. Temporarily blinded by the disgusting residue, the boy stumbled past his attacker and tried to make his way down the path. The gooey pus ran from his forehead into his eyes and nose and mouth. He wretched and stumbled along the path for a ways beyond the thickets, blindly, his tormentor close at his heels, chanting maniacally.

"Yiyaa . . . yiyaa . . . *yiyaa*!"

The fish oil stench of the goo was overwhelming, and Curtis now hacked up some bitter stomach bile, as his wavering stride left the path and pressed into the darkened woods. He sensed that his pursuer seemed reluctant to leave the path, so Curtis strode deeper into the unfathomable blackness to escape. The further he penetrated the gloom, the more distant the cries of the phantom savage became. He pressed deeper still, until the eerie voice was a faded memory.

Once he felt securely beyond the reach of his tormentor, the boy halted his stumbling progress, peeled off his T-shirt, and wiped the redolent mucous from his face. His predicament had worsened immensely. Disoriented, off-course, sequestered by darkfall, and in the densest heart of the forest primeval, he was hopelessly lost in an alien corner of space and time. His quest for the safety and familiarity of the Fort was doomed without the direction that the path had offered. Desperation crept over his emotional state, and a mournful whine escaped his lips.

But at that very moment of the deepest sense of hopelessness, providence, in the form of sound, floated to him from across the fathoms of blackness. Two brassy quarter notes followed by a lifted whole note that seemed to hold for an eternity split the night, providing newfound hope and guidance. A bugler at the walls of the Fort was blowing "Taps." The haunting melody was bittersweet—they had played "Taps" at his father's military funeral—but familiar, and it harkened the location of Fort Grant to Curtis through the darkness of the woods. The boy pondered the words from memory as the bugler continued his unerring, twenty-four-note solo.

Day is done; gone's the sun,
From the lake, from the hills, from the sky
All is well; safely rest,
God is nigh . . .

Reciting the lyrics to himself reminded him of his father's bravery. It greatly heartened the boy, and he started toward the source of the brassy tones.

"Not that way; you'll never get back!" a voice admonished from the darkness.

"Who's there?" Curtis bleated.

"A friend indeed!" the voice sang out.

"Well, I'm a friend in need, no doubt about it!" Curtis returned. "Where are you, Randy?"

"Over here," Randy answered. "Over here," he repeated.

Curtis directed his sight toward the direction of the sound and caught a glimpse of motion in the dark. Randy was waving his arms.

"Hurry this way," he continued. "The portal is shifting again. You don't want to get caught out here on this night—no way, pal."

"I'm with ya on that, buddy. But exactly where is 'here'?"

"No time to explain—just haul ass while there's time."

Randy was beckoning to another of the arboreal tunnels so prevalent in these woods. They reached the opposite end just as the final note of "Taps" faded into echoes in the night. They were standing in front of the portion of the Fort's wall that was riddled with faults, the place where they'd scaled to reenter before. Oddly, the orange light of sundown lit the white plaster quite radiantly. Darkness seemed to have retreated.

Curtis turned to face his friend and gasped at what he saw—or rather, *didn't* see. Behind and beyond lay a desert wasteland, devoid of any vegetation save a few creosote scrubs.

"What the hell?" Curtis murmured.

"Not exactly hell," Randy chuckled, "but it might have been if you'd stuck around any longer. And by the way, how does it feel to be back in 1963?"

"I feel like I've been rode hard and put away sweaty."

"Well, you stink like you've been swimming in a chum-bucket," Randy observed. "Now, we better get you back inside before you're missed."

"They're probably already looking for me, for as long as I've been gone."

"What makes you think that? It's only been about thirty minutes."

"You messin' with my mind again?"

"As always," Randy grinned. "Now start climbing!"

The Mag and the Moon

O ld Mr. Osgood was in rare form the morning that Randy paid
an unexpected visit to Curtis in World History class. The
ancient pedagogue was droning on and on in his usual mind-
numbing style, chanting the day's lesson on Hannibal's campaigns
against Rome in the third century before Christ. In spite of its vast
chronological distance from the early 1960s, Curtis had initially been
fascinated by the subject: first because of the whole novelty thing with
the elephants; second because the fabled Carthaginian general was from
Africa (and Curtis assumed that that meant he was black); finally,
because the term *strategy* was associated so frequently with Hannibal's
name that they seemed almost synonymous. Randy had planted the seed
with Curtis that strategy was something that a winning boxer had to
know. Therefore, strategy was something that Curtis was eager to learn
everything there was to know about it.

And so it was singularly unfortunate that old Mr. Osgood happened
to be the only teacher on the Fort Grant faculty whose concept of
lecturing was to read directly out of the textbook in a quiet monotone
that would sedate a coffee-drinking Jack Russell terrier. His one saving
grace was a comic countenance: he sported a nose that was a dead ringer
for Karl Malden's own great bulbous snout, a feature that captured
immediate visual attention and netted him a number of clever, if
unflattering, monikers.

Curtis had made a dutiful effort to follow along in the book at the
beginning of the lecture, but the text had little to say on specific strategies. And after ten minutes of the decrepit teacher's humming litany of
endless dates and places—the numerical gravestones of prehistoric

power struggles among dead men with tongue-twisting names—Curtis wanted to scream to keep his leaden eyelids from slamming shut. He glanced around the classroom from his vantage point in the back of the room by the rear door and noted that a number of heads were resting on desktops. Some of his criminal colleagues were actually snoring, but old Osgood was oblivious, due to a serious hearing impairment. This and the fact that the old man's watery eyes were riveted on the page made it easy for Randy to enter the classroom unnoticed. He glided through the rear entry doorway—the door itself propped open to facilitate any bladder-related urgencies—then slipped silently into a vacant desk behind Curtis.

"Got something for you," he whispered as he reached over Curtis's shoulder and placed a magazine on the colored boy's desktop. It was a glossy copy of the latest issue of *Sports Illustrated*. The March 25th cover consisted of a shaded profile of Sonny Liston in what appeared to be a contemplative moment. But it was not the cover story that caught Curtis's immediate attention. The third feature article on the contents page promised a blow-by-blow critique of the less-celebrated Cassius Clay and his bout with Douglas Jones that had taken place at Madison Square Garden two weeks prior.

"You can read it later," Randy advised in a hushed tone. "And you can skip all the trash about Sonny Liston—what a thug!"

"Shhh—shut your face, worm," Curtis hissed under his breath. "You're gonna get me detention."

Randy cocked his head toward the chanting teacher. "Are you kidding me? You could bring a freight train through here carrying the Marine Band playing Sousa marches, and ol' Schnozzgood wouldn't so much as glance up from that book he's glued to."

"Shhh—I tell you no lie, Randy. You're gonna get me *swats* if you don't shut the fuck up."

The droning at the front of the room abruptly fell silent. Curtis realized with dread that he had inadvertently raised the volume on the word *swats* for emphasis, creating a ripple in the otherwise placid pool of silence in the classroom. His gaze drifted forward to the lectern, expecting Mr. Osgood's limpid stare to be narrowed on him. To the boy's amazed relief, those rheumy eyes were not only turned away from him, they were securely lidded. The old man's head was nodding, a symptom that he'd fallen victim to his own hypnotic droning. He'd actually put *himself* to sleep.

"Look at that!" Randy chuckled quietly. "He's off in the twilight zone. Let's go out in the hall where we can talk out loud."

"Okay, okay," Curtis whispered. "I could use a piss break anyway."

Adjourning across the wide hallway to the restroom, Curtis verbally accosted Randy while relieving himself into the long trough-style urinal that lined a long wall opposite the toilet stalls.

"Man, you got to quit poppin' in on me like this. You know, *you* might be a trustee and can get away with murder." The gushing sound from the stream he released reverberated from the bare institutional walls. "But *me*," he continued, "I'm just the henhouse spook that keeps causin' trouble. You and your surprise visits are gonna get me into a world of shit!" He zipped up on the final word to punctuate the completed event. "Aahh . . . good to the last drop."

"Don't sweat the little things, man," Randy replied coolly. "You've been as nervous as a long-tailed cat in a room full of rocking chairs lately, since that gang of Harvey's has been hunting for you."

"I just try to stay out of the corners, that's all—just like you taught me about the ring."

"Fair enough, but you ought to know by now that I'm just here to help you. I won't get you into a pickle. Anyway, you might have noticed that all of these teachers here avoid incidents like the plague. They don't want to get involved with discipline or punishment—least of all old banana-beak in there." The pale boy paused to let the logic simmer. "They just want to give their lame lectures, collect their paychecks, and go home—can't you see that?"

"I s'pose so," Curtis conceded. "So what is it you wanted to say that's so all-fired important that you make me miss one of old snoozy-snoot's prize-winning bedtime stories?"

"A couple of things," Randy chirped excitedly. "First, you gotta check out the moon tonight. It's still a gibbous, but it's waning fast and you know what that means."

"Oh boy," Curtis groaned, "here we go with the moon again. Can't we talk about whatever's *second*?"

"I can't say as I blame you for being a bit spooked. Things do get more bizarre around here during the half-moon phase, but look on the bright side: you might get another visit from that dusky, half-naked maiden you encountered last month, remember?"

"How can I forget? Please, tell me *how*!"

"Now come on, if you could dismiss her indisputably gruesome side, you have to admit she's pretty cute on her good profile. And you can't deny that she boasts a nice pert set of melons," Randy added with a wink. "I mean, they stand up pretty proud for a girl about to celebrate her hundred-and-tenth birthday!"

"Man, you are one sick puppy, you know?"

"So they tell me. But you should check out the moon, nonetheless. It will be half full before long. And when the moon is right, well, just about *anything* can happen around here."

"Listen, little bony buddy, all your talk about the moon makes me wonder about *you* sometimes. I think maybe you're just a bit touched by it all—you know, a little loony tunes, maybe?"

"Hmm, that's a tough one to dodge. But it's not just me," Randy mused. "When you think about it, we're all really under the lunar influence—the whole human race, I mean."

Curtis rolled his eyes. "Here we go, once again taking us *One Step Beyond*. Thank you, John Newland."

Randy shot him a look of contempt. "No, I'm serious here. The moon is really symbolic of the entire human condition. We sometimes live in complete darkness, sometimes bathed in light, and sometimes in between. We experience increasing and decreasing degrees of knowledge and ignorance, love and hate, war and peace, hope and despair, the corporeal and the spiritual, both collectively and in our personal lives—just like the waxing and waning of the moon."

"And here I thought you were gonna argue that you *aren't* a bit touched by it," Curtis muttered. "Seems like you're makin' my 'loony tunes' case for me."

"The moon has been historically significant throughout the ages," Randy continued in his usual precocious manner, oblivious to Curtis's dig. "You know, the moon's phases formed the basis for the earliest calendars. The thirty-day months imitate the twenty-nine and a half days of the lunar cycle pretty closely. In fact, the word *month* is a simple corruption of the English and Germanic word for moon."

"Please, professor, spare me the history lesson!"

"And of course there are the tidal effects caused by the moon's gravitational pull on the oceans," Randy persisted, "It's the same lunar pull that is said to cause insanity in some people. Did you know that that's why they call them *lunatics*?"

"Did I ask for this lecture?"

"But listen, in our own particular circumstance, we need to recognize that the moon's phases represent the tension between good and evil, enlightenment and superstition, fear and valor. The half-moon over Fort Grant is a celestial representation of the battle between the forces of darkness and the light of justice. And the fact that it's a *waning* half-moon," Randy declared, "makes me sad to say that it looks like the forces of darkness seem to have the upper hand here—at least for the time being."

"Enough already, Aristotle, you're hurtin' my brain!" Curtis protested. "I promise to look at the moon tonight if you'll just ease back on the philosophy."

"You know you're getting really bad at faking ignorance, Curtis. You should lose the Stepin Fetchit routine. You're smarter than you let on—which is smart in itself, I guess. I'll back off only because I know you know exactly what I'm talking about, and I've made my point. But you want to keep it all light and superficial because it frightens you. Can't really say as I blame you, though."

"Whatever you say, Einstein. Let's just get on to what's *second*."

"Huh?"

"You said there were a couple of things. A couple is usually two. First was the moon, so what's *second*?"

"Oh, okay. Second has to do with the article in that magazine I just gave you—the one about the Clay versus Jones fight last week."

"Two weeks ago, but who's keepin' track?"

"Apparently you are, and that's what I'm getting at."

"Meanin' what?"

"I'm saying that I've noticed that you seem sort of, I don't know, *fixated* on Cassius Clay—as a role model, I mean."

"Well, as a matter of fact, I *have* been trackin' his rise through the ranks, if that's what you mean. But I don't recall even so much as bringin' up his name around you. So where do you get off sayin' that I'm *fixated*, as you say?"

"Oh, let me see . . . by the way you train; by the way you talk; by your mannerisms; hell, by the way you *look*, even. I swear, you could be his younger brother, for God's sake, by the way you look. Just look at his picture in that magazine. You're a dead ringer for the man—especially now with your recent development of muscular definition. I mean, you'll be his fucking *twin* in five more years. Hell, you may wind up *fighting* him in five years, for that matter—that or maybe—"

"Slow down there, mister manager," Curtis interjected. "I got to go the whole amateur route before all that. You know, Golden Gloves, '68 Olympics—same way Cassius came into it."

"There you go, referring to him on a first-name basis, following in his footsteps. You see, I know how much you admire Cassius Clay, Curtis, and that is why I am going to be your host at a certain ringside event so that you can observe firsthand the pugilistic strategies of your ideal." He completed the phrase with an exaggerated flourish, like a game show host presenting door number one.

"Oh, so you're gonna take me to the *Garden*?" Curtis chuckled sarcastically.

"Next best thing: I'm going to sneak you into the Lieutenant's quarters to watch the replay of the Clay-Jones match on *The Wide World of Sports* this Saturday—to celebrate the next phase of the moon, of course."

"Yeah, *sure* you are. You're puttin' me on, right?"

"No, I am in earnest."

"Listen, I don't know no *Ernest*, you little weasel. I just want to know if you're serious."

"Serious as a heart attack."

Still skeptical, Curtis narrowed his eyes to ebony slits. "Just how the hell are you going to manage *this* little escapade, huh, toothpick?"

"That's what I do: *manage*. But you should leave the details to me."

"They say the devil is in the details, so I'm turning you down on your tempting offer there, Lucifer, until you tell me what the devil your plan is."

"All right, all right. I didn't want to gloat, but you forced my hand. I happen to have made our chief administrator an appointment to have his car looked at over in Safford this Saturday afternoon. It seems that it's been on the fritz lately—won't turn over sometimes, but not all the time. Quite mysterious, indeed. I imagine it's going to take some time to isolate the problem."

Curtis tried his best to stifle a grin, but failed. "You think you're pretty clever with that little coil wire trick, don't you?"

"Well, let's just say that some of us are exceptional boxers, and some of us are exceptional pranksters. In any case, I assume you will now accept my generous invitation to join me for a round-by-round analysis of Mr. Clay's boxing tactics, yes?"

Curtis's grin widened. "Hell, yes—count me in, by all means. 'The thrill of victory and the agony of defeat.' What time?"

"One o'clock to catch all the prefight hoopla. But I'll be seeing you before then for training, right?"

"Absolutely!"

"Okay, you'd better get back into class before the great proboscis wakes up and takes a head count."

Curtis strode to the open doorway and turned around. "Thanks, man. You have no idea . . ."

"Yeah, I think I do. Now go, and be quiet as a mouse sitting back down. You've been gone a long time. Better just slide into one of those desks closest to the door."

Curtis breezed across the threshold and eased into the first desk he came to. He would collect his magazine during the bustle that the bell would create. He looked over and located it on the desk he'd vacated, then glanced to the lectern to assure himself that he was not noticed. Mr. Osgood was still napping with a bit of drool running onto his chin. Still

301

snoozing, that is, until a familiar voice that sounded like it came from Curtis himself pierced the silence with the thunderous volume of a breaking tidal wave:

HEY, SCHNOZZGOOD! IS THAT REALLY YOUR NOSE, OR ARE YOU EATIN' A FUCKIN' TWINKIE?

The outburst was delivered from the back doorway just adjacent to Curtis's location, and there was a slight Louisiana twang to it—a pretty convincing imitation of the boy's own distinct accent. Curtis whirled around just in time to catch the backside of Randy's Converse tennis shoe disappearing behind the jamb. Turning back, he was shocked to see that every face from each of the desks in the room before him was now peering at him in awe. Mr. Osgood suddenly raised his own countenance, elevated his great proboscis like an inflated pointer, and aimed it directly at Curtis—or so it seemed. He cleared his throat, as if the impending pronouncement was to be a sentencing. The quaking colored boy thought he heard a distant fanfare blowing and the rattling of sabers floating on the breeze that blew through his skull.

"And so when Hannibal's proud pachyderms met their icy fate on those Alpine slopes," the old man croaked, "he lost a crucial dimension in his grand strategy."

With that, the bell rang to dismiss the class. Curtis collected his mag along with several congratulatory remarks from classmates on his excellent heckling effort. Somehow he knew that Randy could hear him as he swore beneath his breath.

"Just you wait 'til I see you again, you wormy little centipede. I'll crush you like a fuckin' bug!"

"*Don't sweat the little things, man,*" came a whispered reply from nowhere.

302

Interlude (the third)

"Sounds like they delivered pretty good on their promise down there at the Fort," I broke in without thinking. I cringed right then at the instant I'd clumsily let loose with that outburst, knowing too late that I had just broken my promise to restrain myself from interrupting the tale again without good cause.

Curtis went quiet for what seemed like an hour, but was probably less than sixty seconds at most. Our noisy comrades had long since left the area with their serpent captives, ceding the otherwise soundless night to crickets and coyotes. I do believe it was only the distant howling of those coyotes that coaxed him back into communication with me—a needed distraction for him from the wild desert dogs' mournful song playing out across the darkness. He seemed to really detest that sound.

"What the hell are you talkin' about, *promise*?" he hissed, evidently displeased by my unwelcome intrusion into his story stream.

"Um, I guess I was talking about the motto," I explained, though I'm sure I was unconvincing. His resumed silence clearly stated his need for a better accounting. "You know, 'the first mission is to educate'!"

"Oh, *that* motto," he recollected. I think he was impressed with my ear for such minute details, as his tone softened. "Yeah, Fort Grant was an education all right. Hell, I got a whole lifetime of learnin' from that place."

"And I didn't just mean Mr. Osgood's history lessons; I meant the kind of understanding about good and evil that you got from your talk with Marcus when you were supposed to be pulling weeds—that sort of thing."

"Yeah, but my education didn't all come from Marcus neither, not by a long shot. Oh, it came from him and Randy too, and the Lieutenant and a kid named Leon. But I gotta say I owe the biggest part of my schoolin' to good ol' Harvey Huish."

"Harvey—your archenemy? You're kidding!"

"No shit, Vince—if ever there was anybody to learn from about pure evil, just watchin' him had to be like gettin' a fuckin' college degree in it."

"Oh yeah, I get it now—the prince of darkness, sort of."

"Somethin' like that. See, once I gave up the whole plan of keepin' to myself and turnin' a blind eye, I started noticin' all kinds of monkey business like I never imagined—all of them directed by Mr. H himself."

"Monkey business—like what?"

"At first it was just little things. I'd notice some rooster or other coppin' a smoke in some out-of-the-way corner. I wondered where the cigarettes came from, but didn't give it a whole lot of thought. But now and then I'd catch a whiff of a really sweet kind of smell in the air, and I knew somebody was smokin' a joint. That really made me wonder, so I asked Randy about it."

"And just what did Mr. Kartchner reveal to you?" I asked.

"A lot. He told me that Harvey used a little seed money that he got from his lawyers and in no time at all built up a racket inside the walls of the Fort that would put Joe Bananas to shame."

"What do you mean, *racket*—like some kind of illegal activity?"

"Activities, Vince—several schemes, all going on at once, and all hatched by Mr. Harvey Huish."

"What kind of schemes are you talking about, Curtis?"

"Well, first of all, he bought off one of the guards, that asshole Jeb, and sent him on monthly 'errands' down to Nogales to buy kilos of marijuana for hawking joints to some of the roosters at a huge profit. He had one of the roosters on his payroll who specialized in rollin' five-paper numbers. No lie, Vince, this guy would roll cigars that would keep three tokers suckin' smoke for an hour. Yardbirds paid dearly for one of those magic stogies."

"But I thought inmates weren't allowed to have spending money. Where did the cash come from?"

"That was Harvey's scheme too. He convinced most of the roosters to write their parents and beg for 'insurance' money on the QT, which most parents understood to be the kind of extortion that goes on in the slammer. It was no surprise that they coughed up the bread to protect their kids from getting' gang-raped. The cash, which was really to buy dope, came through the mail."

"But how did they manage . . . ?"

"Well, get this: the guard assigned to screen the incoming mail was—you guessed it—Jeb, the rooster dorm guard who made Harvey's south-of-the-border weed runs. How's that for covering all the bases?"

"Pretty slick," I conceded.

"Oh hell, that's only one of the scams. It gets worse—dirtier, that is."

"How so?"

"Well, you remember the Doc?"

"Sure."

"Okay, he turned out to be some kind of serious pervert—liked young boys and such. So, in exchange for the Doc's 'friendship,' every couple of weeks, Harvey and his boys would strong-arm one of the hens or chicks, knock him out with an ether rag, and deliver him to the Doc for a cozy little sleepover in the infirmary."

"That's disgusting!"

"I told you it gets worse."

"Yeah, you did. So, what kind of 'friendship' did the Doc extend to Harvey for his trouble?"

"Somethin' like with the guard, only the Doc had official authority to buy better dope, legally."

"Better dope?"

"Yeah, morphine pills—better, and a lot more expensive."

"How do you mean, *better*?"

"Better for controllin' people, and that was always Harvey's big goal—slippin' into the driver's seat and runnin' the whole show. This was one of his favorite scams. He would get one or two of the chicks hung up on the pills. Then he'd sell the stuff to several of the roosters, who used it to trade to those kids for a ride on the magic mattress, if you follow my drift."

"That's sickening!" I exclaimed, nearly shouting.

"Look, Vince, people adapt. Besides, I told you before that some of this stuff ain't exactly fit for Disney, but for some reason I feel sorta like I should tell the whole story, or nothin' at all. What ol' double-H was into was disgustin' all right, but I've got a better word for it: *evil*—pure and simple."

"You got that right," I agreed, then fell quiet for a moment, letting the impact of his simple statement weigh on my mind.

Curtis broke the short silence. "So, Vince, you got any more questions before I go on with my story?"

"A few."

"I figured."

"First, I wonder: How did Harvey keep up all of this activity without it getting back to the Lieutenant?"

"Because he kept it all pretty well held down to the roosters' dorm, where Jeb was the guard, so it was really no sweat to keep a lid on it," Curtis answered without hesitation. "Besides, the Lieutenant trusted his guards and pretty much turned a blind eye to things goin' on in the yard—at least, for a while."

"Okay, but why do you think Harvey went to all the trouble to set this all up in the first place? I mean, the guy really didn't need the money. He was filthy rich to begin with, right?"

"Right. Like I said before, Harvey's biggest aim was to be in control. The money was a way to lord it over everybody. Any profit he made he used to keep buildin' up the rackets—tunin' up what he had, or startin' new ones. He had it all happenin'—cigarettes, booze, cards, dice, drugs, and perverted sex. Whatever the weakness, Harvey would use it to gain and keep control over the other inmates. And hell, he had a leg up over everybody just by bein' who he was."

"You mean by being from a rich family?"

"That didn't hurt his plans, but no—I mean his evil nature. See, I believe that all of us, no matter how bad, have some sense of right and wrong. But . . ." He hesitated.

"But *what*?" I pressed.

"But I think there are special cases like Harvey who have no sense of decency whatsoever. I call that pure evil, and if evil is your aim, that gives a huge advantage over anybody with even a trace of goodness."

"How so?"

"'Cause, for an evil body, any goodness is weakness. And in a way that's true because anybody with even a lick of goodness has a hard time believing that anybody can be pure evil. So pure evil plays that doubt for all it's worth. And Harvey, he was the master at playing people," Curtis stated, and paused again. "Then there's somethin' else I never thought of 'til just now."

"What's that?"

"Well, just recallin' all of that makes me see it clear now. I think he was practicin'."

"Practicing for what?"

"For bigger and better rackets on the outside. It was like the Fort was a trainin' ground for Harvey—an Erector Set of crime. He sharpened his skills as a minor league mobster, all the time with an eye on the big league—aimin' to be a tycoon like his daddy someday, I imagine, only with a darker side than even the old man."

"Makes sense, I guess. But you said he had all of these schemes up and running in no time at all. I still wonder how he got so much going on so quickly and so completely."

"First, just think about the membership list in our little club. Fort Grant inmates are not exactly the Mouseketeers to begin with. Mix that together with the whole thing about Harvey being pure evil, and put it all in a spot where evil really does haunt the grounds and the walls—a place so cursed that a river refuses to run over its ground. Well, that seems to me like the perfect garden for growin' a little vice, now doesn't it?"

"I suppose that's true," I conceded.

"Now, Vince, can I get on with it? There's still miles of ground to cover. And try to hold the questions until I'm done, will ya?"

"I'll do my best," I assured him. I looked at my watch again. It was still stuck on 11:15. "Say, Curtis, have you noticed it's getting sort of chilly?" I observed with a little shiver.

"Try to hang in there, pal," he sniffed. "It's about to get a whole lot chillier."

The Event

awn broke on Saturday with the promise of unfolding into a momentous day, and it would not disappoint Curtis in that regard, although some of the events that were about to emerge were not even remotely anticipated. He blinked the sleep from his eyes as the early morning light streamed in through the grated dorm windows. The now-predictable baying of the desert dogs had awakened him several times during a night of fitful sleep, and the young man rose only partially refreshed. Between that howling reminder of his circumstances and the pale light of the waning moon, the after-midnight hours had been particularly disquieting.

He dressed himself mechanically, snagged the *Sports Illustrated* magazine that Randy had given to him, nodded to a few fellow sleepwalkers, and drifted to the mess hall in a daze. He was seated at his regular solitary place browsing the articles, but he did not become completely animated until he was halfway through a helping of scrambled eggs and fried potatoes. Then, complete awakening came abruptly and unwelcomed. A hulking shadow fell across the boy's steaming plate.

"I haven't seen you out on da field lately, spook. Where ya been?"

It was Gerd "Noodles" Brinkerhoff, Harvey's colossal toady. His immense presence evoked the analogy of a big dumb battleship—a slow but overbearing force, heavily armed.

"I found a friendlier playground, Noodles," Curtis muttered without looking up. "But I'm touched to hear that you missed me."

"Whatcha readin' daht's so intrasting, spook?"

Curtis was constantly amazed and repulsed at the grating way that Gerd combined the heavy Germanic accent from his native country with the hayseed colloquialisms that he'd picked up in the stir and during his formative years in the lower social strata of the Great Southwest. He sounded like Himmler astride a horse.

"It's just a magazine, Noodles," Curtis returned, becoming annoyed. He couldn't resist a poke at the dull, gargantuan oaf with the jutting brow. "You know, someday you too may enjoy the information boost of *Sports Illustrated*, Noodles, once you learn how to read, that is."

"*Sports Illustrated*, huh? Well, it just so happens daht Mr. Harvey Huish iss missing hiss latest issue of dat makaseen. How dah hell did you get your hands on daht, anyways?"

"I got it from a friend, as if it's any of your business."

"A friend, you say? Dah way I hear it, your only friend iss yawr happy-hand."

"Man, Noodles, you're about as funny as a game of tavern darts with Stevie Wonder—you know that?

"Daht may be," the burly boy leered, entirely oblivious to the humor in the simile, "but I wouldn't want to be in yawr tennies when Harvey Huish finds out daht you stole hiss fucking makaseen. I tink you might be cruissin' for a bruissin'."

"I told you, I got it from a friend," Curtis repeated, now sounding less convincing. "And make a note to yourself, Adolf, that I don't bruise easily—not like some of the fruits I know."

"We'll just see about daht, spook." With that, the German immigrant boy lumbered off.

Troubled by the exchange, but not so troubled that he lost his appetite, Curtis polished off the platter of eggs and spuds, and washed a second one down with a carton of milk as well before reporting for Saturday morning duty at the laundry annex.

Curtis's shift didn't start until nine, and his internal clock told him it was barely past eight-thirty when he ambled over to the annex building.

"You're fifteen minutes late, son."

It was Marcus. He was the assigned overseer for the six boys in rotation to perform the loading and unloading of the previous week's soiled clothing and bedding for the entire school into and out of the industrial-sized washers, extractors, and dryers. Without responding, Curtis began pulling wet sheets from the huge cylindrical washer and packing them into a large, drum-shaped extractor when Marcus eventually approached him.

"You okay, boy?"

Just to hear him talk with the old man's Huckleberry Hound drawl tickled Curtis's insides.

"Sure 'nuff am, Marcus. Why do you ask?"

"I don't know—you've made yourself pretty scarce lately. Then you show up late. And now there's this rumor about a magazine that . . ."

"Jesus Cheez-its, Marcus! I can't even believe how fast the bullshit spreads around here! You don't believe what you hear from Harvey's camp anyway, do you?"

"Well, let's just say I subscribe to the old adage that a lie can travel twice around the world before the truth even gets its pants on," Marcus chuckled. "Don't get me wrong; I'm just lettin' you know what's out there, that's all."

"Much obliged, as always."

"You watch your back, boy. There's folks out there that would do you harm," Marcus whispered, "an' they ain't all young-uns neither."

"What do you mean by that, Marcus?" Curtis wondered aloud.

The aging guard put a finger to his lips, then turned away and proceeded to direct another boy in the process of folding dry sheets.

Curtis worked hard all morning, gripping the sopping mounds of wet clothes from the washer and loading the extractor. The work was physically demanding enough to distract him from dwelling too much on what Marcus had said about the magazine, but it was not a substitute for a workout at the sandlot. Just the same, he did work up a sweat, and by lunchtime he was hungry again—hungry enough that the thought of skipping a meal to avoid trouble never entered his mind. He rushed over to the mess hall early in observation of the first-come-first-served rule and noted with some satisfaction that only a few other inmates had queued up ahead of him.

His dorm buddy, Leon Hawkins, had pulled KP duty and was ladling scoops of a hearty-looking brew into melamine bowls. The aroma of stewing chicken, picante, and lime permeated the air, and the smell of hot flour tortillas wafted from a warming oven.

"Hey, Leon—what's cookin', man?"

"Hey back at ya, Curtis," Leon grinned. "We just rustled up about fifty gallons of chicken posole and a truckload of tortillas for lunch, that's all."

"Well, dig down deep into that vat and bring me up some bodacious chunks of poultry, 'cause I am famished!" Curtis declared with gusto.

Leon obliged and passed Curtis a steaming bowlful with extra hominy and chicken, all perched on a plastic tray with two piping-hot tortillas wrapped in onion-skin paper.

"So, Curtis," Leon inquired in a lowered voice, "that magazine that you're totin' under your wing there—is that the one you lifted from Harvey's collection?"

"Man, what the hell you doin' tossin' out such a vicious rumor like that?" Curtis fumed.

"Hey, jump back, Jack. I'm only passin' on to you what the grapevine told me. Like they say, *Don't kill the messenger.*"

"Yeah, well you can go back and tell the grapevine that I got the mag from a scrawny little white kid whose mutilated body will be found in the dumpster out back after I get through with him!" Curtis declared.

"Too late, I'd say, for alibis, bro. The buzz is that Harvey and his boys are already gunnin' for you."

"Well, that don't cut no ice with me, man. Let 'em take their best shot. I'm feelin' pretty bulletproof these days, anyways."

"The offer to back you up is still out there, you know," said Leon. "You can lean on us if you need to."

"Thanks, man, but this ain't your beef."

"Then you might oughta think about flyin' under the radar for a while, bro."

"I've about had my fill of that too. But hey, my food's coolin'. Thanks for the news update, and be cool, Leon."

"Later, tater."

Curtis carried his tray over to his usual table and chowed down, glancing up at odd intervals to possibly catch a glimpse of Randy's perpetually imminent approach. He placed the purloined periodical on the bench seat next to him, concealing it from plain view. The chow line grew and dwindled at length, but no sign of the pale boy materialized. Curtis grew impatient. His irksome companion's failure to appear only fueled the smoldering anger he felt over the magazine fiasco.

Before long, Gerd Brinkerhoff strolled in, took a tray, and sat down with his soup, thankfully oblivious to Curtis's presence across the hall. Without Harvey or his other minions to egg him on, the Bavarian bruiser didn't seem to pose much of a threat, mean reputation notwithstanding. Still, the likelihood that he would be joined by his cohorts before long generated enough discomfort in the atmosphere to prompt Curtis to an early exit.

He'd no sooner cleared the side doorway to the verdant yard adjacent to the Administration Building, when a hushed voice halted him in his tracks.

"Where you headed in such a hurry, mister?" It was Randy, stealthily emerging from behind the out-swung door.

"Lookin' for *you*, ya little rat-bastard," Curtis returned hotly while wagging a meaty forefinger in the smaller boy's dumbstruck face.

"What the hell kind of thanks is *this* that I get for treating you to an exclusive viewing of the boxing event of the year?" Randy squeaked at length. "I'm really offended, Curtis."

"Oh, you're offended, huh? Well, I'm so totally pissed I can't even see straight. You set me up, you little weasel-neck!"

"What *ever* are you talking about?"

"Don't play dumb, Randy!" Curtis produced the rolled-up magazine from under his arm and struck Randy on the top of his head with it, accentuating the first word of his next statement. "*This* is what I'm talkin' about. You stole this fuckin' magazine from Harvey Huish and gave it to me without cluin' me where it came from. Now him and his goons are out to get me again. That's what I call a setup if there ever was one. Why don't you just shove a goddamn broom handle up my ass and break it off while you're at it? Hell, that'd be less painful than a blindside haymaker from that Nazi, Gerd Brinkerhoff."

"I . . . I . . ."

"Don't even try to worm out of it. *You* set me up, pure and simple—just like you set me up in old Schnozzgood's class yesterday with that stupid prank. Hell, Randy, *everything* isn't a fuckin' joke, ya know. Some things are *deadly serious*—get it, ya goofy little prick?"

A palpable silence ensued as the accusation festered. At some length, Randy cleared his throat, as if to signal that he'd arrived at a tack for his counter.

"Well, *there's* a fine thank-you for my thoughtful generosity," he retorted with mock indignation. "I risk life and limb to appropriate a nice gift for you, and you repay me with accusations and name calling. Now I'm doubly mortified." He folded his arms Jack Benny–style to express his annoyance.

"Let's see," Curtis fumed, "I'm the one who's takin' the fuckin' fall for this, and *you're* mortified? How the hell does *that* work?"

"First of all, you ought to know by now that nearly every item that comes into my possession is boosted. How many times in the past week have you called me a klepto? You ought to have known better than to be flashing that magazine around like a fucking flag. What, were you born yesterday, Curtis?"

"Sure, I guess in the back of my mind I figured you'd probably pulled your usual five-finger discount somewhere. But oh my, what a strange coincidence that you happened to snatch it from the one sicko who loves to hate me. Then, to top it off, you just incidentally failed to clue me in on that info."

"Man, I thought you'd just take it back to the dorm to read it before lights-out. How was I to know that you'd drag it all over the countryside like an announcement? Do you think it makes you look somehow intelligent to walk around with a magazine tucked under your arm?" Randy paused to let the point sink in, then continued. "Listen, Curtis, if I wanted to 'set you up,' there are more certain ways of doing it than giving you a hot mag on the chance that someone might spot it. Besides, I'm the one who's been hiding you away until things die down. Why would I suddenly change tack? Face it, you've jumped to the wrong conclusion, and I think you owe me an apology."

"Don't hold your breath," Curtis muttered.

"Listen," Randy offered after a pause, "if you still want to watch the match, we'd better stop wasting time with this and get over there. It's almost one-thirty, and I think we're probably already going to miss all the prefight gab."

While Curtis was still unconvinced of Randy's innocence, he had to concede that he'd blown off some steam with the tirade, and Randy had deflected some of his accusations with a sort of tortured logic. But it was mostly the strong lure of watching the fight that broke Curtis's inclination to hold a grudge. He incidentally wondered where the time had gone, since the noon meal had seemed to be only minutes ago.

"Okay, show the way," Curtis muttered with some reluctance in his voice. "But take this off my hands." He offered the purloined magazine and Randy took it, rolling his eyes.

The pale boy glanced around now in an exaggerated sort of clandestine fashion, and beckoned Curtis to follow him along a twisted path through the Lieutenant's leafy glade, into a breezeway that bisected the Administration Building. He pushed open a heavy wooden side door inset to the interior plane of the thick adobe wall. It was a recessed portal that led them directly into the inner sanctum of the Lieutenant's quarters.

The two boys stepped into a darkened, spacious room of about twenty feet to a side. The only source of light was a recessed casement window adjacent to the right of the entry, which was nearly smothered from the outside with a thick curtain of cat's claw—a veil of lush greenery that barely allowed any natural illumination at all.

The somber cast of the subdued light might have been the most distinct aspect of the setting, were it not for the period furnishings. The antique atmosphere gave Curtis the disquieting impression that he'd stepped through the adobe portal and across the threshold of some time warp—one that had instantly spirited him and his companion into a retrogression of some seventy or eighty years.

Left of the entry stood an antique combination dresser/washstand—a dark-walnut chest of drawers accessorized with a framework of scrolled columns that rose from either side of the rear and supported a pivoting mirror and towel rack. A white porcelain pitcher matched a recessed white-enamel bowl for washing. Just beyond, a wooden coat-and-hat stand offered residence to a leather belt and holstered revolver; the pearl grip of the pistol-butt seemed to wink from its perch.

315

Curtis continued to scan his surroundings in awe as Randy disappeared into an alcove in the southeast corner. "I'm going to turn on the swamp cooler—it's really stifling in here," he called over his shoulder.

Across the room stood a Queen Anne–style walnut sideboard bearing several bottles of different brands of bourbon, a glass tray containing four barrel-shaped drink glasses, a pewter ice bucket, and a burl-wood desktop cigar humidor. Immediately to the left was crouched a double-pedestal rolltop desk, its slatted cover rolled back to reveal a seriously cluttered work top. A bankers' desk lamp with the traditional green-glass shade and pull-chain switch squatted to the rear of center, its brass base besieged by a tide of loose yellow and white leaves of paper.

What enchanted Curtis most were those plain white sheets, unlined, that contained pencil and charcoal sketches of a face—dozens of replications of the same subject at different visual angles. The distinctive facial features, the boy surmised at once, were hauntingly familiar as he scanned a frontal aspect. A skull-tight edging of ebony hair defined a high forehead, perfectly devoid of line or worry. The oval curve of the mask outlined an exotically alluring visage etched with pronounced cheekbones, a fleshy aquiline nose, and full lips. A series of carbon lines and shadings accentuated a pair of black almond-shaped eyes that stood against a bleached pulp background—an ivory-white paper that deepened their appearance. But their gaze seemed to be cast not directly into the eyes of the beholder, but somehow beyond, as if they were directed slightly over the shoulder of the appraising party, or perhaps even *through* the onlooker.

Then, the boy's eyes fell on another rendering, a left profile, and the hair on the back of his neck prickled. It was the same face, but unmistakably the lovely aspect of the phantom Indian girl he'd encountered in the dormitory corridor in the middle of the night many weeks ago—the one whose right profile was not nearly so attractive.

A sudden whirring sound overhead signaled Randy's throwing of the switch that activated the swamp cooler. The movement of air was instantly amplified and immediately cooler as the room filled with positive pressure that escaped slowly through the slightly opened casement window with a characteristic moan.

"Hey, don't mess with anything on that desktop, Curtis," Randy warned as he reentered the main room.

"Randy," Curtis gasped. "It's *her*. It's the girl I saw that night last month, or the month before, I guess—the one with the tore-up face."

"Oh, you mean his drawings? Yeah, he sees that face quite differently than you or I do."

"Does he see her too?" Curtis wondered aloud.

"I don't know about now . . . I suppose now and then he does. But once upon a time, he would see her almost every night."

"What do you mean?"

"Never mind. It doesn't matter, and we're going to miss round one if we continue to gab. It's already one-thirty." He strode across the room and drew aside a drape that Curtis had not noticed before. It revealed a small nook that housed a tabletop Philco television perched atop what appeared to be a console hi-fi. "Ta-dah!" Randy sang out in mock fanfare as he clicked on the set. "Grab yourself a ringside seat while this baby warms up."

"Oh man, this is so cool!" Curtis exclaimed, as he snatched a straight-back chair from the desk and planted it in front of the still-dark TV. "I didn't know you could get any reception way out here in *Nowhere Central*."

"Marcus rigged a directional antenna up on the roof that catches the Tucson signals," Randy explained as the set hummed to life. "Luckily, the clearest channel is the one that carries ABC."

"It's takin' *forever* to warm up," Curtis complained.

As if in response, the gray tube flickered and lit up with a cavalcade of streaming black-and-white images of sports figures, performing at the peak of their various chosen challenges. A brassy fanfare and a familiar voice suddenly boomed from the set.

Spanning the globe to bring you the constant variety of sport . . . the thrill of victory . . . the agony of defeat . . . the human drama of athletic competition . . . this is ABC's Wide World of Sports!

"I love the part where he says 'agony of defeat,' and the ski-jumper crashes into the snow like a truckload of wet bird shit fallin' outta the sky!" Curtis chattered merrily.

Good afternoon, sports fans, and welcome to another presentation of ABC's Wide World of Sports.

It was, as always, Jim McKay announcing—his rugged good looks and baritone voice were always a good complement to the athletic theater.

This week, we have a stellar lineup of events to present. We will bring you live from Churchill Downs an in-depth preview featuring the eighty-ninth running of the Kentucky Derby to be presented next month, here on Wide World of Sports. *We will cover the favorites and the long shots, probing the facts behind the question that racing fans the world over are asking: Who are the horses and what are their odds of winning this most prestigious of all horse races?*

"A fuckin' horse race *preview*? What the hell is up with this, Randy?" Curtis demanded.

"Sssh! Be patient—just listen!"

We will also bring you from Mexico City the pinnacle of that nation's sport world, the Mexican National Jai-Alai Tournament. It's an exotic blend of skill and endurance that is sure to capture the imagination of our viewers at home.

"Jai-alai? What about the fight?" wailed Curtis.

"Settle *down*, Curtis. You're like a little kid!"

But first, we take you to Madison Square Garden for a recap of last week's heavyweight bout between the self-professed contender for the crown, Cassius Clay, and his native New York challenger, Douglas Jones.

"A *recap*, Randy—really? I thought they were gonna just show all ten rounds—the whole fight. What a gyp!"

This time Randy kept a diplomatic silence. McKay chattered briefly on the follow-up to the fight—how Clay had taunted Jones at the weigh-in and how he'd predicted knocking the veteran challenger to the mat in the fourth round.

And now, we take you to that most renowned of all boxing venues and to my esteemed colleague, Howard Cosell, who will provide the blow-by-blow commentary. Howard?

"Oh, that does it," said Curtis. "I *hate* Howard Cosell. He's the most puffed-up windbag in all sportscasting."

"Then he'll be a fitting complement to your hero, Curtis," said Randy. "Cassius Clay is no shrinking violet himself, you know. Besides, I rather like the way Cosell has injected his lofty vocabulary into the otherwise crude level of discussion among sportscasters."

"You would," Curtis muttered.

Thank you, Jim McKay, and good afternoon, ladies and gentlemen. Howard Cosell coming to you from this most storied arena of sport and entertainment, Madison Square Garden, where just last week, a brash young fighter from Louisville, Kentucky, Cassius Clay, took on the more seasoned opponent, Douglas Jones, to present further irrefutable evidence of his readiness and his right to challenge the holder of the heavyweight crown, Sonny Liston.

"Oh brother," Curtis groaned, "this guy can top even ol' Schnozzgood at putting a roomful of people to sleep."

To the boy's relief, the cameras cut from Cosell to the filmed footage of the event, beginning with the fighters' entrance into the ring. The booing from the crowd as Clay climbed through the ropes was over-whelming. Curtis watched steely-eyed as his young hero waved to the audience, flashing a defiant grin that provoked the unruly crowd all the more. Cosell's voice-over broke in:

I should remind our television audience that Clay's swagger and out-spoken manner have earned him no small measure of contempt from this audience. True to form, the young fighter has predicted to reporters that he would knock the hometown favorite, Jones, onto the mat in the fourth round. But audacity notwithstanding, it behooves me to be punctilious regarding the Louisville upstart's punching proclivity. His speed, his strength, and his ro-co-co style have skyrocketed him to the upper levels of pugilistic stardom in just a matter of months. Some would call him supercilious—I just call him super. But let's watch what happens in this first round.

"Turn down the sound, man," Curtis told Randy. "I can do without the noise from Howard's mouth."

Randy complied reluctantly, but quietly.

The fighters came out with the bell and, as Curtis already knew from reading the magazine article, Jones out-boxed Clay in the first round.

Perhaps fueled by the crowd's scorn for the younger, more vociferous boxer, Jones fought aggressively and landed a near-fatal right blow to Clay's head early in the round.

Curtis shook his head in dismay. "He's not fighting up to par," he moaned.

As if answering Curtis's lament, Clay came roaring back from the next two bells, tagging his opponent several times to net him the decisions on those rounds. His young protégé, glued to a black-and-white TV behind the walls of Fort Grant, became visibly buoyed. But when the decisive fourth round came and went without a knockdown, the younger fighter seemed to lose his timing. A lackluster performance over the next three rounds left Curtis somewhat disenchanted with his idol.

"He's losing the snap in his punch and the spring in his step!" the boy cried aloud.

"Not for long," said Randy. "Keep watching."

Indeed, and as was related in the magazine piece, Clay's performance in the final three rounds was stellar. His split-second timing returned; his dancing style came back; the familiar snap and spring were there as well. But most telling was the intensity in his facial expression. The younger fighter was unmistakably confident for the remainder of the bout—Curtis could see it in his smoldering eyes.

"Well, you know the rest of the story," said Randy. "But what did you learn about strategy, Curtis?"

"Three things," Curtis replied. "First, if you've got a strategy, don't share it with the world."

"Good. But with Cassius Clay, the predictions tend to stoke the gate, so it's more theater than anything with him."

"Yeah, right. And second, if a strategy fails, adapt and form a new one."

"Yes!"

"And third, if all else fails, endurance can carry the day."

"Perfect. You're smarter than you let on, Mr. Jefferson."

Curtis's gaze returned to the set in time to see the referee raise Clay's arm in victory. "Turn the sound back up, Randy," he ordered.

The apparent outrage from the 18,000-plus fans came across in waves of booing, and missiles in the form of beer cups and bags of peanuts flew from the hands of the angry crowd into the ring. Cosell's voice-over was a verbal redundancy of the audio-visual.

This crowd is apparently quite unhappy with the unanimous decision by the judges, but I think they have lost all objectivity, as any replay of this fight unmistakably demonstrates that Clay clearly had the superior performance, although Jones put up a valiant effort, no question.

Once again, Clay waved to the crowd, then strode to center ring. He reached down and picked up one of many peanut bags that littered the canvas mat, took one of the peanuts into his mouth, cracked the shell between his teeth, spit out the husk and chewed the nuts with a triumphant smile. He was on his way.

Randy rose to turn off the set, but not before Howard Cosell pitched his signature closing remark:

This is Howard Cosell, telling it like it is.

"Okay, so how did you like it?" Randy asked, as the picture vanished from the tube.

"Well, I was disappointed that it was just a recap. It was sort of like the *Reader's Digest* version of a fight."

"Ah, c'mon, Curtis. You know what the format is on *Wide World of Sports*. How could you expect anything different?"

"I dunno. I just did, that's all."

"What else?"

"Well, I *hate* Howard Cosell."

"You said that, and we turned down the sound on him."

"Okay, but you asked."

"Fair enough. Anything else?"

"I hated to see him boxing half-heartedly. That was discouraging. But most of all, I hated the way the crowd treated him afterwards. It wasn't fair—Clay was the better boxer, overall. It really pissed me off!"

"I agree, but what can you expect of a New York City crowd? He was lucky to escape that mob with his skin."

This reminded Curtis of his own precarious circumstances. "Are you going to put Harvey's magazine back?"

"Sure, as soon as the opportunity presents itself."

"I got a bad feeling about what's waiting for me out there," Curtis murmured, almost to himself.

"Which reminds me," said Randy, "we better clear out of here before the Lieutenant comes back. It's almost three o'clock."

"You're full o' shit if it is!" Curtis declared. "We just watched a twenty-minute recap that started at one-thirty. It can't even be two."

"Okay, in case you haven't noticed, the time does funny things around here—especially when it comes up on a half-moon," said Randy. "Anyway, we just need to get the hell out of here pronto!"

"Great," Curtis remarked drily. "First you frame me, then you run me out into the danger zone."

"Oh don't whine, Curtis. It doesn't become you," Randy admonished as he ushered his friend out the side door and up the garden path. "Besides, these things have a way of blowing over. Harvey's pretty occupied with his escape plans. I'll bet he hasn't given the magazine thing a passing thought."

"I don't know . . . I guess you're probably r—"

"Hey, *spook*!" As if there were some cosmic cue to dispel any hopeful notion of a pass, a grating voice boomed from just behind. It was Noodles Brinkerhoff with a half dozen of Harvey's other cohorts. "Weef been looking for you."

"A Fight! A Fight!"

Gerd "Noodles" Brinkerhoff strode forward and stood spread-legged before Curtis at the narrow bottleneck in the path where it passed between the mess hall and a utility building. His half-dozen minions spread out across the path at the colored boy's rear. No escape route appeared. Randy vanished like a snowflake dancing in the flames of hell.

"Listen, spook, I spoke wit Harvey Huish a while ago, and he tells me to brink back dat magazine auf hiss or bring him awl of yawr front teeth."

Smoldering heart notwithstanding, Curtis kept his distance. Noodles Brinkerhoff stood more than a head taller than Curtis, in shoes the size of aircraft carriers, jeans of circus-tent proportions, and a white T-shirt that might easily double as the mainsail of an island schooner, like *The Tiki* from *Adventures in Paradise*. His bear-like frame and early facial hair demonstrated an abnormal physical maturity that was well beyond his seventeen years. Either that or the bureaucracy had bungled the birth date on his immigration papers. Even the burliest guards seemed to tread lightly around Gerd. A Boris Karloff jaw, sunken eyes, and a Bela Lugosi pallor further enhanced the almost supernatural aura of intimidation that lit the way of the young behemoth's every path.

Hoping to avoid a clash, Curtis chose a diplomatic response. "Tell Harvey it was just an honest mistake, and that he's gonna get it back . . . soon."

"I'm not your messenjah boy, boy," Noodles grunted. "Just give me dah makaseen, dat's what Mr. Huish wants."

"You can see, Noodles, I don't have it on me."

The big German boy stepped forward into the zone of confrontation.

"Daht suits me just fine, becawss I'm really pahshal to Mr. Huish's second choice." He grinned malevolently, revealing a mouthful of gray teeth.

Curtis took a careful step backward to remain just outside the Bavarian bruiser's apelike reach. He sensed that the rest of Harvey's entourage pressed close behind him, but he resisted the instinct to avert his eyes from his antagonist, even for a split second.

"Listen, man," he proposed, "I got no beef with you. Why don't we each just go our own way and let Harvey Huish fight his own fights—how 'bout it?"

Gerd's scorn shone in his azure eyes, and Curtis instantly knew that no amount of reason would appeal to this boy's better side. There simply was no better side there to implore.

"I guess iss just my day for getting my hantz dirty on a little Mau Mau's snotty face," the huge boy sighed theatrically as he shrugged a pair of mountainous shoulders.

As if some internal switch was thrown, partly from the epithet but mostly from the sense of no retreat, Curtis's tone immediately reversed. He looked his opponent up and down.

"Just how tall are you anyway, Gerd? You're quite the big boy, aren't you?"

"Six-three," the big German boy responded proudly, unaware of the imminent verbal snare. "Why do you ask?"

"So's I know just how far to step back when you fall at my feet!" Curtis chuckled with delight. Present company would not know that he'd just shamelessly plagiarized his hero, Cassius Clay. In fact, he was now *channeling* the "Louisville Lip," and starting to love every brash second of it.

"Why, you smaht-ass little pawch-monkey!" Noodles retorted, now apparently steamed. He strode forward catching Curtis off guard. They came face-to-face, close enough that the big boy's bitter breath rolled noxiously into Curtis's face. But instead of seizing on the element of surprise, the Teutonic titan opted for more posturing, poking the front of Curtis's collarbone with a right forefinger the diameter of a giant-sized

Payday bar. "I'll haff you crying for your chocolate mammy in just a few seconds," he boasted crudely. "Or maybe she's too busy with dah milkman, eh?" he taunted while punctuating with the finger pokes to the chest. "Maybe daht's where you got dah light brown skin, eh? Maybe yaw dah milkman's whelp—a little white cream mixed with dah chocolate, eh?"

Convinced now that a clash was inevitable, Curtis, in a lightning move, seized the wagging candy bar appendage and bent it back hard, meaning to break it. But Noodles jerked it back before it snapped and in a flash returned with a freight-train blow from a left hook that tagged Curtis on the right ear and nearly took his head off. Aided by an instant adrenaline rush, the German boy stoically folded his sprained finger into a clenched right fist, which he immediately fired off at the staggering Curtis's head. But the young Negro boy recovered his wits at that very split second and managed to dodge the deadly blow with a quick sideward duck of the head. He heard the wind from that swipe, in spite of the loud ringing in his injured ear.

Now Curtis assumed his fighting stance and began to backpedal. The lumbering Noodles advanced flat-footed and took alternating futile left and right swipes at the bobbing and feinting colored boy. Streams of sweat from Gerd's broad Frankenstein brow began to sting his eyes. Curtis commenced with a barrage of left jabs at Gerd's poorly defended face but could not land a solid tag. The German kid's towering height made the smaller boy's attempted blows to the head fall short, and Curtis didn't dare move in closer where those deadly haymakers might connect. Now searching for a strategy, Curtis spontaneously changed tactics and began to work on the torso, landing solid whirlwind combinations to the ribs on the seconds between Gerd's poorly aimed punches, then withdrawing just out of reach of the wild recovery swipes. Curtis's phenomenal speed and agility enabled him to launch these maddening sorties at will and retreat with a minimum of risk.

"Where'd you learn to fight, kraut-breath," Curtis taunted between heavy exhalations, "from your mother—from the fat hausfrau?"

"Hold still, you little pygmy, and I'll split yawr nappy head like a melon!"

Gerd growled as he lunged forward and swung wildly like a mobile windmill.

Curtis ducked and dodged the flailing giant whose wild lunge now sent him stumbling headlong into his company of supporters. Curtis circled counterclockwise a quarter turn, briefly facing due west. The lowering mid-afternoon sun blazed bright, and the glare flash-blinded the boy for a split second. An impulse-driven tactic—like an epiphany—dawned on him at that instant, and he shifted another quarter turn, now facing south, opposite his opponent who'd spun in recovery from his wayward charge. Curtis was now peripherally aware of a small gathering of onlookers who began to ring the area. The German boy's allies were no longer at the colored boy's back, which was no small relief.

"Where'd you go, schnitzel-face? Come back and fight!"

Now Curtis was thinking in broader terms. He knew he could easily win a contest of endurance, but yardbird fights like this rarely lasted long enough for that. They either degenerated into all-in ethnic brawls, or were broken up by the guards. Neither alternative was acceptable to the young protégé of Cassius Clay. It had to be a decisive victory; nothing else would do. For that, he would have to dispatch his adversary in short order. But a knockout punch was out of reach, and continuing to fight inside to score body blows was a tactic that would soon be anticipated. The sorties were becoming riskier with each performance. A scheme was called for, and the boy's wits were working overtime.

"I'm going to *kill you*, spook," Gerd roared.

"You have to catch me first, *turd*," Curtis chirped, delighted with himself for the spontaneous rhyming corruption of his opponent's name. "Yessir, Gerd the turd—hope you had your Cheerios this mornin', 'cause you're gonna need 'em!"

A throng of spectators, idle yardbirds starved for excitement and summoned by the commotion, quickly encircled the ongoing slugfest, forming a human ring about thirty feet in diameter. A spontaneous chorus of youthful voices chanted a familiar fanfare that reminded Curtis of previous backstreet battles—a common and crude schoolyard announcement of an interracial clash:

A fight! A fight! A nigger and a white!

The sting of the taunt subsided though, as Curtis acknowledged shouts of encouragement from his own swelling contingent of supporters with a nod. Noodles apparently hadn't won any "Mr. Congeniality" contests among his fellow inmates. They hooted and hollered as Curtis bobbed and weaved, ducking wild swings from Gerd, tagging the German giant's board-hard ribs, then retreating in a flash. The colored boy's bunny-quick maneuvers dazzled and bewildered the dull-witted Gerd, as Curtis slowly but surely side-shuffled to position himself with the afternoon sun at his back, forcing his opponent to peer into the glare. Without hesitation, the big German boy stupidly raised his hands to shade his eyes. Curtis had, of course, anticipated this opening and lunged, throwing all of his might into a powerful, straight-right blow at the solar plexus.

"Big dummy!" he hissed through clenched teeth, as he withdrew from the perfectly executed attack.

Gerd folded like a deck chair with a windless groan, head lowered, where his smaller adversary could now easily reach the downturned face with a right uppercut. Curtis could feel the cartilage in the German boy's nose yield under his taught bare knuckles. He backpedaled away from Noodles to assess the damage. The colossal boy stood stationary, feet spread apart, eyes closed, holding his bleeding nose with both hands. This defenseless stance was too tempting to resist, and Curtis was feeling no mercy for his tormentor. A well-placed punter's kick to the testicles brought Gerd to his knees with a groan.

"How's *that* for a boot to the bratwurst, huh?" Curtis sang out merrily.

Now the head was in easy reach, and "Curtis Clay" launched a salvo of combination punches to the eyes and forehead. Gerd's sketchy grasp on consciousness began to slip away, and the towering German boy presently teetered and fell forward like a tree in the forest, smacking his forehead on the hard-packed gravel on impact.

Gerd's support group began to advance, menacingly, but their threatened intrusion was quickly intercepted by Leon Hawkins and his own group of colored toughs.

"You boys best leave it be, unless you wanna see some more of the same," Leon's voice trumpeted above the din.

Pumped up with adrenaline, the swaggering Curtis now danced around his fallen victim. "What's the matter, kraut-breath—taking a little nap?"

The dust that the scuffle had kicked up was still settling, and it collected on the young colored boy's sweaty countenance like face powder, creating a sort of thespian mask.

"Get up, schnitzel-face," Curtis taunted as he circled the fallen Goliath. "I'm not finished with you."

But Noodles lay still as a cadaver, save the heaving of his labored breath. A little wisp of dust rose and fell where his mouth and nose pressed against the hot gravel of the pathway.

"Get up, you filthy Nazi pig, and take another poke at the milkman's boy! How did all those milk bottles feel crashing into your thick fuckin' skull, huh?"

A spate of chuckling issued from the onlookers. Noodles did not stir. Curtis stopped circling and stood facing his vanquished foe, flat-footed for now, hands on his hips. Now he was performing for the crowd, even more reminiscent of his pugilist idol from Louisville than ever.

"What's the matter, Franken-hoff? Are you hurt? Shall we go call your mama? Shall I go and find the fat old Fraülein? Oh, but maybe she's busy with the milkman herself—what about that, huh? Getting some free cream to go with her blubber muffins, maybe?"

A chorus of laughter erupted from the spectators. Now Gerd groaned and rocked his torso slightly.

"Look, it's still alive!" Curtis cried in mock surprise. "Shall I finish it off? Shall I kick its Nazi ribs in before it gets up?"

"Kick the shit out of him!" someone from among the crowd shouted out.

"*Oye, Vato Negro!*" came a cry from the Mexican contingent. "*Hágalo! Mátalo!*"

The triumphant Curtis had worked himself up into an irrational frenzy, and the unruly crowd that apparently felt no love for Noodles was egging him on. He found himself approaching the fallen hulk to make good his threat of finishing Gerd off with a few swift kicks, when a familiar voice came nagging from behind and caught him short.

"As your trainer and manager, I'd strongly advise against that!"

Curtis spun around, took a well-aimed swing at Randy, and missed, as always.

"That won't do you much good either," the pale boy advised.

"Where were you when I needed you, and why shouldn't I settle this score?" Curtis shouted. "This big Bluto deserves whatever I dish out."

Randy grinned. "That may be, but if he's playing 'possum,' and he gets a hold of your leg, you'll be down on the ground in a heartbeat." He now chuckled. "In a wrestling match, I'd bet good money that 'that big Bluto' would break you like a stale cigar."

Curtis took a couple of discretionary steps away from the still-quiet Gerd at the thought of this possibility.

"Besides," Randy continued, "you'd do well to melt into this crowd now before a guard shows up."

This was good advice, and it immediately sobered the adrenaline-intoxicated Curtis. He moved to the outer edge of the ring of boys, as Randy suggested, and no sooner had he concealed himself in the crowd than Marcus emerged from the mess hall and strode over to the center of activity, leather sap in hand.

"What the hell's going on here, a clown convention?" he boomed. "Or is it just a 'happy Fizzies' party?"

Spying Noodles on the ground, he crouched and carefully rolled the fallen mountain of flesh over. The German boy surprisingly sat up with something like a whimper. Marcus brushed the gravel from the big kid's red face, and Gerd began to sputter and spit. His forehead was riddled with inch-long cuts. One eye was swollen shut and he was bleeding profusely from both nostrils.

"Here," said Marcus, offering a clean white handkerchief, "pinch this over your nose, and keep your head up. The bleeding will stop."

Gerd did as he was told.

"What happened?" Marcus inquired.

"Nuh . . . nuh-ting," Noodles stammered.

"*Nothing*? Well hell's bells, boy, I'd hate to see your condition if *something* happened!" Marcus looked up and glanced around the circle of onlookers. "What the hell happened here?" he repeated to the shrinking crowd.

"He fell," someone called out, anonymously.

"He fell," another repeated.

"I fell," Noodles parroted the blatantly false alibi.

"You fell, huh? You look like you fell from the Empire State Building."

Marcus stood up and stretched out a hand. "C'mon," he said, "try to get up."

Again Noodles complied and with some assistance rose shakily to his feet.

"If I help you, do you think you can make it over to the infirmary?"

Gerd nodded cautiously.

"Then let's go, son. Forget about this and let's go get you cleaned up and checked out."

The two began to lumber off toward the infirmary like a couple of clumsy waltz partners, but someone could not resist one last verbal dig.

"Yeah, go home to your fat-ass mama, you Nazi snot-bag . . ."

The voice, the phrasing, and even the inflection belonged to Curtis, but his lips did not move. Once again, his ventriloquist comrade had framed him.

Marcus turned and held his hand up, shooting the dissipating crowd a look of annoyance. "Enough, already! The rest of you—break it up! Go about your business!" he barked.

Curtis turned and glared at a grinning Randy, just as Leon and his colored boys ambled past.

"Man, I got to hand it to ya—you got balls, my brother," Leon chuckled as he breezed by.

"*Tienes el poder, Vato Negro*," one of the Mexican boys added.

"Well, so much for your low-profile approach to things," Randy mused. "Henceforth you'll be known far and wide as 'Vato Negro,' and Noodles will be known as 'Gerd the turd.'"

"Yeah, thanks to you, I've got a serious reputation—and one I could do without," Curtis groused. "I'm a world away from the loner Sergeant Joe wanted me to be."

"Could be a good thing," Randy offered.

"Yeah, maybe now Harvey will back off of me."

"Don't count on it," Randy returned, gravely. "Gerd Brinkerhoff was nothing more than a coal-mine canary for Harvey. More than likely he was testing you. That's a pretty good indication that he is preparing a strike of his own. You'd better watch your back for the next couple of days. His power is greatest during the half-moon phase. Take it from one who knows."

"Then what possible good can this sudden yardbird popularity be for me?"

"Probably a mixed blessing. You've got allies now, and that can't be bad. They could help even up the odds when the chips are down, like they did just now."

"I suppose you're right," Curtis agreed, "but right now all I can think about is gettin' a drink of water. I'm dryer than a popcorn fart on a desert hike."

"You've been hanging around Marcus and his folksy similes too long. But you might as well head over to the mess hall for refreshment. It's nearly time for the early dinner bell anyway."

"What the hell are you talkin' about, fool? This fight lasted about four minutes, tops. It's got to be about three-fifteen, three-thirty at the latest."

Randy beckoned toward the lowering afternoon sun. "I told you before, you can expect some skipping effect from the clocks around here, especially during this time of the month."

———————

After chasing down two heaping helpings of macaroni and cheese and three buttered rolls with four tumblers of ice water, Curtis was ready to sit back and review the upshot of the day's events.

"You know what, Randy?" Curtis belched, patting a swelling belly. "I ought to get in fights more often. It's better exercise than runnin' in circles over in sand-land. That little exhibition match gave me a hell of an appetite, I swear."

331

"Like I've said before," Randy warned, "don't get too cocky. You're not wearing the crown yet, and if you let your guard down while you're here, you might not stick around to get your shot."

"Look, I didn't go asking for it, but I whipped that big boy's fat white ass pretty up-an'-walkin' good, and I don't mind sayin' I feel pretty stoked about it. Besides which, I'll just bet you that Mr. Harvey Huish will be backin' off of this grudge he has against me, now that he knows what a tough hombre he's dealin' with," Curtis gloated.

"I told you already, don't count on it," Randy countered. "Noodles Brinkerhoff might have been Harvey's advance charge, but that snake is not one to retreat. Once again, you just dealt him a crippling blow in front of the whole inmate population. By defeating his number one toady, you've unwittingly challenged his place at the top of the heap. If he doesn't retaliate now, he loses face and his entire trumped-up front of superiority is deflated. It's not a matter of *if* he strikes back; it's a question of *when*."

"You may be right," Curtis observed, "or you may just be stirrin' the pot again."

"I hate repeating myself," Randy sighed as he rose from the table, "but your victory this afternoon was a mixed blessing at best. Try to remember what Shakespeare said about this sort of circumstance."

"Oh, brother . . ."

"He said, 'Discretion is the better part of valor.'"

"And what the hell does *that* mean?"

"It means watch your back," Randy called over his shoulder as he breezed out the side exit.

"Discretion . . . the better part of valor, my ass," Curtis muttered under his breath. "After this afternoon, Harvey Huish maybe ought to be quotin' Shakespeare's chicken-shit poetry."

Suddenly aware of his solitary status at the table, he glanced around, nervously. Across the hall, Harvey's minions, absent their leader and his second, ate in silence. Whether this was a defeated brooding or a quiet buildup before a storm of vengeance, Curtis could not determine.

Nor was he inclined to, as a tantalizing aroma broadcasting through the air of the hall teased out a tugging yen for yet another helping of macaroni, and it leaped easily to the top of his list of considerations. He scanned the darkened serving station for some sign of life, and found one. Marcus, who had apparently pulled KP duty tonight, was loading ravaged chafing trays onto a cart. The leftovers would be saved for side dishes alongside tomorrow's lunchtime fare.

"Can a poor, hungry inmate who's late for the line still get a serving?" Curtis pleaded as he approached. "I need some nourishment."

"Late for the line, my ass," Marcus scoffed. "More like your fourth time through," he observed as he spooned more cheesy yellow goo onto Curtis's plate.

"Really only the third," Curtis corrected. "I don't know what it is, but I've got the appetite of a grizzly bear this evenin'. More hungry even than my usual starvin' self."

"Small wonder," said Marcus. "So, Curtis," he continued, "I don't suppose you know anything about what happened to that big German kid they call Noodles, do you? That kid's in an awfully bad way. Looks a bit like he tried to jack off a mountain lion with a pair of vise grips."

"What happened to who?"

"That's what I thought. Seems everybody around here is blind, deaf, and dumb."

"Well, you know, you have to be pretty dumb to wind up here in the first place, Marcus—myself included," said Curtis. "Hell, the dumb stunt that put me in here ought to go into the history book of dumb stunts."

"History . . . that reminds me," said Marcus, "I'm supposed to substitute teach for Mr. Osgood on Monday. I'll need to bone up on the Roman era."

"You—teach history?" Curtis grinned, skeptically.

"Sure. You might not know it, but I'm quite the history buff—especially when it comes to warfare," Marcus gloated. "I'm especially keen on the Civil War, but I'm fascinated by military tactics and strategies in general—makes for great storytelling."

"No kidding, Marcus? 'Cause I'm kind of interested in tactics and strategy myself."

"No kidding, kiddo—I'm a military-strategy fanatic," Marcus smiled. He stroked the graying stubble on his face thoughtfully. "For instance, there was this famous German pilot, Oswald Boelcke...are you familiar with the aerial war during World War One?"

"I know they flew those double-wingers—like the crop dusters."

"*Biplanes* is the correct term. Anyway, this German ace, Boelcke... his favorite tactic was to place himself between the sun and the enemy plane."

Curtis began to get the uncomfortable feeling that this was something more than a history lesson.

"Yeah," Marcus continued, "the whole idea was to put the glare of the sun in the opponent's eyes so he couldn't strike back with any accuracy."

Curtis squirmed, but mustered enough courage to probe Marcus further. "So what do you think of that tactic...or someone who uses that tactic, maybe?"

"I think it's just slicker than deer guts on a doorknob," Marcus chuckled.

A beam of pride lit Curtis's face.

"You know," Marcus observed with a contrived faraway look in his eyes, "I didn't just fall off the turnip wagon, boy. I *do* know a thing or two—and I can guess the rest!"

Resistance

"Curtis, can you tell me if you still know the way down to the gravesite?" Randy wondered aloud at the close of another Sunday sandlot training session.

It was the end of the third week in April when nature traditionally hints at the approach of another infernal summer with a couple of premature heat waves. Such was the case, and each afternoon the mercury was climbing higher than in the day previous. At that moment, Curtis was thoroughly absorbed in cooling himself through the ritual dousing of water at the close of each session. Between the clank of the pump handle and the shooshing sound of the water pulses, the soft-spoken inquiry was muffled.

"Goddamn it—I asked you a fucking question!" the younger boy railed.

Curtis perked up from his pump-spout shower and shook the residual droplets from his wiry hair.

"Whoa, simmer down there, twig-boy," he grinned. "I must've missed that for all the water in my ears. Can you just say it again, please?" It seemed to Curtis that his slender counterpart had been somewhat distant and moody through the duration of the day's workout, and he had completed the regimen more from memory than from the younger boy's fragmented direction.

"I asked you if you still know the way down to the gravesite," Randy repeated. "It's very important."

"Sure," Curtis replied. "No need to get all bent outta shape. I've got this picture-map stuck in my head, and I don't think it will ever go away." In fact, though the daily visions had gradually subsided, the images of the various mile-markers that Curtis had observed on that first and only journey to the site had indeed etched themselves into his brain. "What brought that up anyway?" he asked with some trepidation.

"The Rubicon."

"Come again?"

"Julius Caesar's crossing of the Rubicon—that's what brought it to mind."

"Oh brother, somethin' tells me I'm gonna get pounded with another lesson from Professor Pomfritt," Curtis chuckled.

"And it's a lesson that I know you've already learned in old Schnozzgood's World History class," the boy retorted, "so I won't repeat it now except to remind you how his crossing of that river has come to symbolize passing a point of no return. Once a decision is made, and a line is crossed, there is no turning back."

"So what the hell does any of that have to do with the path to the gravesite? There's no river." He spat on the ground. "That river bed's been dry for almost a hundred years. Besides, the Schnoz said old Jay Cee had a horse and an army. I got neither. None of this Rubicon crap cuts no ice with me. You know, last time I crossed a line it wound me up here. I'm real skittish anymore about crossin' any goddamn lines."

"You're playing dumb again, Curtis, and you're not fooling anyone— least of all yourself. You and I both know that there's a deadline looming, and you need to make a commitment to joining the plan—a commitment that you can never renege on. I assume that by now you've moved beyond that indecision you were struggling with before."

"What makes you think so? Nothin's changed. Like I said before, I'm not signin' on to no *scheme* of yours until I know all the details," Curtis sniffed. "Like they say, the devil's in the details."

"You want details?" Randy retorted. "I'll give you details. I've penetrated Harvey's veil of secrecy, and I know what his plans are."

"Don't stop there," Curtis coaxed after a long silence. "I could get interested."

"Well, it's pretty much what I figured before. Next Friday or Saturday, Harvey is going to fake a case of the mumps."

"How the hell do you fake the mumps?"

"Easy—with a few cotton balls between the cheek and gum. He'll look just like a squirrel in a walnut tree. Anyway, Doc is going to quarantine him in the infirmary to get him out of sight for a while. Then, on Sunday night—well, after midnight, so technically Monday morning—he'll go over the wall, which will give him a day and a half of cover while he makes his way over to the coast. That's where he'll assume the new bogus identity that his shyster lawyers have concocted for him."

"Hmm, pretty slick. Just one thing I don't get."

"What's that?"

"You say his court date is on Tuesday, right?"

"Right—the day after he turns eighteen."

"Then why do you think he'll wait until after midnight on Sunday to go over the wall? Why not Saturday night? It would give him a longer head start."

"Well, because thirty-six hours is plenty of time for him to make it across the desert over to Los Angeles and blend into the city. But mostly, Monday morning is symbolic to him."

"How's that?"

"It's his *birthday*, Curtis. It's a historic event for him—the momentous occasion of his long-awaited emancipation. I'm sure he'll hear a fanfare blowing in his ears as he's going over the wall."

"Man, it's hard for me to imagine how that giant hamster-head of his could get any bigger."

"Nevertheless, he does seem to have all his bases covered, ego notwithstanding."

"Well, I'm happy for him. He should fit right in with all the other nutjobs over there in the land of LA. And just think, he can go to all the Dodgers games this summer and watch that showboat Sandy Koufax choke on a regular basis. It's perfect!"

"About as far from perfect as you could get, is what I'd say," Randy countered. "If he manages to escape, his evil practices will be unleashed on innocent people. He'll be free to rape and murder and enslave people at his pleasure. You, Curtis—you have the power to block his path to supreme wickedness."

"Man, I don't know how or why I got picked for this mission. I sure don't recall volunteerin'."

"It shouldn't be difficult for your part. Just lead him down the path to that place. Lead him to the gravesite, then get the hell out of there. It's simple."

"Ah, there it is—there's the one detail that you've been dancin' around like Bojangles Robinson: What happens to ol' Harvey once he's gotten down to the gravesite? Does the ground open like the mouth of a goddamn whale and swallow him up? 'Cause that seems completely possible with all the other loony stuff that happens around here. So, what is it, Randy? Does a flock of harpies drop down out of the sky and carry him off?"

"Nothing quite so dramatic as that."

"What, then?"

"Let's just say that Mr. H is rendered harmless at that point and leave it at that."

"Oh, thanks. That really clears things up for me."

"Listen, Curtis, you just need to make your decision now and stick to the plan. Trust me, you're better off not knowing about Harvey's ultimate fate."

Curtis drew in a great draught of air through his nostrils and scrunched his face like he'd just inhaled the concentrated essence of a vast poultry farm. "Well, if I ain't knowin', I ain't goin'! How's that for a smack-you-upside-the-head decision, Mr. Toothpick?" he said bluntly.

Randy seemed dumbstruck by the conditional statement. His mind raced to find a way to evade the finality it conveyed.

"You know what I think?" he returned at length.

"Like I care what you think," Curtis huffed.

"I think you're afraid," Randy opined, pointing an accusing finger to punctuate the charge. "I think you're balking at this because you're scared shitless of Harvey. Deep down, you really doubt that you can prevail in a one-on-one with him. You're struggling with a little lack of confidence right now—am I right?"

Curtis stroked the pump handle a couple of times and splashed the spurts of water onto his perspiring chest with a cupped hand.

"Hmm . . . let's think about this one," he droned, attempting a façade of serious deliberation. "You know, ever since I whupped ass on that Nazi snot-bag goon of his, I haven't seen hide nor hair of Mr. Huish or any of his playmates. Yep, not so much as a glimpse of that stupid Dodgers ball cap at a meal. Matter of fact, it could lead me to believe this whole scene is the other way 'round. Maybe it's not the mumps ol' Harvey is fakin'. Maybe it's really a case of *chicken* pox. Maybe he's just pissin' his pants over the now-famous Curtis Jefferson right fist—the fearsome widowmaker blow that put away his bad-ass *numero dos*. I'm sure old kraut-breath has told him about the downhill-kickin' mule by now, doncha think? Maybe I oughta just meet ol' double-H face-to-face and tell him to back off, *or else*."

"Oh, brother—have you got it a hundred and eighty degrees wrong."

"Uh-huh. Here we go. Now *you're* gonna set *me* straight, 'cause you got it all figured out. But really, you're just guessin', and your guess is no better or worse than mine."

"Listen, Curtis, my theory makes more sense than yours. Harvey is laying low while he sets up his escape plans. That's the reason and the only reason he's made himself scarce. But make no mistake, he's not about to forget about you in the meantime. You've humiliated him before the entire inmate population more than once. I hate to say it, but my guess is that the final farewell message that he sends to that audience will be through your dead body."

The gravity of that pronouncement precipitated a prolonged silence. Nevertheless, Curtis rebounded in due time.

"Man, you're confusin' me, pencil-pal. First you tell me I'm balkin' 'cause I'm scared. Then, when I tell you I ain't, you tell me I should be. I swear, the way you pivot's gonna give me a case of whiplash."

"All I'm suggesting is that you keep a low profile over the next week," Randy sighed, apparently growing weary of the argument, "then launch a preemptive strike to ensure your own survival. Like they say, the best defense is a good offense."

"Oh, I see—a *preemptive strike*, and I can guess what that is. That's your advice for me for my safety and my survival. Oh, Randy, I'm really touched by your concern for me."

"Of course I'm concerned for you—we're friends," Randy replied, dismissing the sarcasm entirely.

"Trouble is," Curtis countered, "I just can't help noticin' that your 'concerned' advice also just happens to satisfy your oversized hunger for vengeance. Quite a coincidence, isn't it? Does make me wonder, though: What did Harvey ever do to you to get on your shit list—did he piss in your Wheaties?"

"That doesn't matter now," Randy muttered. "What does is keeping you safe and keeping Harvey from escaping. Can't you see that?"

"The way I see it is this: Harvey flies under the radar for the rest of the week. He won't rock the boat by messin' with me for fear of drawin' unwanted attention to himself. Then, when he goes over the wall, he's so stoked on freedom, he doesn't pay ol' Curtis Jefferson another thought. All my troubles are goin' over that wall with him, and I can go back to sleepin' with both eyes closed."

"And you think he's going to drop the whole vendetta just like that, eh?"

"If he's anywhere near as smart as you say he is, he will. Look, if he just turns up missing, the county cops will stumble around looking for him for a while, then give it up when the trail grows cold. But if he leaves a corpse—even a black corpse—behind him and crosses a state line, he'll have J. Edgar Hoover and every G-man in the country crawlin' up his ass before he gets as far as Indio. No, in my book, Harvey skates and I dodge a bullet. Simple as that."

"Think so?" Randy replied. "I know Harvey Huish pretty well, and when he's got an axe to grind, he doesn't let go quite that easily. But even so, are you really so uncaring as to let him run loose among innocents, knowing the heinous crimes he'll commit—the misery and murder he'll inflict upon good people?"

"Not my concern. Listen, I'm not a cop and I'm not a fortune-teller. I can't be sure what he will or won't do once he's free," Curtis reasoned. "But whatever it is, it's not my responsibility to stop him. Last time I checked, they don't deputize inmates. I don't have the authority to make a 'preemptive strike,' or whatever you call it."

"So bottom line is, you're refusing to commit to my plan—is that it?"

"Sure sounds that way, doesn't it?"

"Then if that's the case, don't look for me to help you figure any of this out anymore. In fact, don't look for me anymore at all. I'm done with you, Mr. Jefferson."

Curtis blinked. "What're you sayin'—just because I won't jump right in to your creepy-ass scheme, you're *bailin'* on me?"

"Sure sounds that way, doesn't it?"

"But what about our boxing partnership?" Curtis began to plead. "There's no reason to give up on bein' my manager."

"You're such a *chump*," Randy smirked. "All of this manager crap was just a ruse to get you in shape for the final confrontation. When I think of all I've done to get you on board—man, what a worthless waste of my time."

Curtis fell silent again, until the full weight of the stinging remarks sank in.

"Well, maybe you can scrounge up some other *chump* to do your dirty work before next Sunday," he finally retorted. "Sorry, but it ain't me."

"Sorry? You'll be sorry, all right, when you find out that Mr. Huish loves nothing better than to settle a score," Randy warned, as he turned to walk away.

"Far as I can tell," Curtis answered, regaining his composure, "You're the one with a score to settle. Man, you say you're just hungry for justice, but it's truly vengeance that's eatin' you up. And like my mama used to say, 'When you dine with the devil, you best have a long spoon.'"

Randy turned and backpedaled his exit to make fast his parting remark: "Well, you're gonna wish you had your mama to hide behind when the waning moon catches up with you next weekend." He turned away and strode out the open gate.

Curtis shouted his last retort: "You can take that wanin' moon and stuff it up your whinin' ass, Randy. Yeah, and you can go take a flyin' fuck at a speeding truck, weasel-boy!"

He wondered if he imagined the faint phrase that wafted on a warm afternoon breeze: *I can't hear you anymore.*

Interlude (the fourth)

"You heard me, I said 'Take a flyin' fuck at a speeding truck, weasel-boy!'" Curtis shouted again.

At that, the telling broke off so abruptly, it was startling. A hush fell over the surrounding landscape like the entire night was holding its breath. I waited, thinking this was a dramatic pause, but the silence lasted well beyond mere effect. Still I waited, wondering and anxious, but not daring to break the stillness that seemed to go on forever, for fear of interrupting yet again.

At last, I could no longer hold my peace. "Hey, Curtis—you okay?"

He failed to respond at first, and I thought I actually heard an audible gasp, or maybe even a sob float through the darkness.

"I had a dream," he uttered at last in an unusually strained voice, "and it kept me alive."

"I know what you mean," I said sort of mechanically, trying to be sympathetic.

"Do you, Vince? I mean, do you have a full-bore, pie-in-the-sky, fantasyland, lifetime hope of *something*?"

"Sure, I do," I replied proudly. "I'm going to be a best-selling novelist someday."

"Is there some kind of grand prize or something like that for writers?"

"Well, I guess the Pulitzer Prize for literature would be the grand-daddy prize for writers."

"So, don't you want to win that prize?"

"The Pulitzer? Sure, I'd love to. That would be outstanding!"

"Yeah, it's good to have an *exact* goal in mind. You know . . . like I was gonna be the heavyweight champion of the world!"

"What do you mean 'was'? Aren't you still shooting for that pie?"

"Sure, but now I think I do have to lower my aim a little. I have to get real, you know?"

"I don't think you have to lower your expectations to be real, Curtis," I said. "You're a phenomenal athlete. You really could be, or *will be*, a contender."

"Oh hell, I know that," he huffed. "It's just the size thing that's doggin' me."

"Huh?"

"Yeah. It's like if my growth spurt doesn't kick in real soon, I'm gonna have to settle for *welterweight* champion of the world."

"Oh," I sighed, relieved. "That's different. There's no shame in adjusting your aim to meet the conditions on the ground," I reasoned. After another silence I asked, "So, are you still training these days, Curtis?"

"Oh, sure I am," he chuckled in a sort of self-conscious way. "What about you—are you scribblin' your way to fame and fortune?"

"I guess you could say that. I mean, I've written a couple of short stories—nothing that would ever really sell. I've never even shown them to anyone."

"Okay, but I mean do you have a *routine*—like a daily exercise program where you write like a thousand words a day or something?"

"No, not really—but I guess that's not a bad idea. Actually, Ray Bradbury—he's my favorite author, kinda like my own Cassius Clay—he writes *ten thousand* words a day," I stated to a dark silence. "So, Curtis, I take it you still work out every day?"

"Pretty much, but I gotta confess, I really don't have that same enthusiasm that I had back then during those sandlot sessions. It's pretty much gotten to be drudgery."

"Why's that?"

"Dunno. Guess maybe I'm just waitin' for my second wind," he said sort of wistfully. "Now, let me see—where was I?"

"You just finished telling Randy to take a flying fuck."

"Oh yeah. Hey, you know somethin', Vince?"

"Yeah, what?"

"You really ought to be careful about who you share your dreams with."

"Why's that?"

"'Cause doubt can creep in, and then those dreams can sorta lose their shine, ya know?"

"I'll take that as good advice."

pivot point

It was nearing dusk, the time when long afternoon shadows reach toward evening. Harvey Huish was making his way from the infirmary toward the mess hall, his head still buzzing from a huffing session with Doc. Halfway through his trek, a strange darkness suddenly fell across his path cutting off his forward march abruptly. In fact, the sudden onset of the shadow was so startling Harvey let a little yelp escape his lips as he blocked the glare of a westering sun with an outstretched palm. "What the f—"

"What's the matter, Harvey—spook give you a little fright?"

"Curtis?" Harvey nearly gasped. "Is that you?" Still partially sun-blinded, he found himself talking to a dark, rather menacing apparition silhouetted against the solar globe.

"In the flesh, Mr. H—which is more than I can say for a lot of the people around here."

Harvey sidestepped to the left to gain a clear view of this human obstacle.

"You got a lot of goddamn nerve . . ."

"That's right—I really *do* have a lot of nerve, don't I?" Curtis chuckled wryly. "Here," he continued as he stretched out a roll of glossy paper with his left hand, "I brought your precious magazine back as a peace offerin'. Cost your deputy-dog a serious ass-whuppin', no lie."

Harvey snatched the mag from Curtis's grip and let it fall to the ground. "That rag isn't gonna buy you shit from me, coon. Your days are numbered."

"I was sorta hopin' you wouldn't feel that way anymore. I figured with the big plan and all, you'd just kinda drop any beef you think you got with me."

"What the hell are you talking about—*big plan*?"

"You know, the *escape plan*, Harvey." Harvey's mouth went agape as Curtis continued. "The whole phony mumps quarantine, the over-the-wall on your birthday, and the rendezvous in Bonita Springs. That plan."

"Well, you little wise-ass. How the hell—"

"Doesn't much matter *how* I know. Fact is, I *do* know, and that oughtta make you pretty uneasy. That is, unless you want to kiss and make up. I don't know why you don't just lay low and let bygones be bygones."

"This doesn't change anything, Curtis. In fact, this just makes me more determined to throttle the life out of you!"

"If you were gonna do that, asshole, you'd be doin' it right here and now. No, you don't work your magic in the daylight. Your power has weak spots that I'm learnin' about fast. And after the poundin' I gave that goon of yours, you might wanna be steppin' lightly around ol' Curtis Jefferson your own self."

"Listen, spook, don't get too uppity. You might know a thing or two about boxing, but when I get you in a neck-lock, all that thrashing around won't do you much good."

"Like you'd ever get that close. Man, I guess I gave you too much credit for havin' good sense," said Curtis, shaking his head dismissively. "But there's a couple of things you need to know before you go sneakin' up behind me in the dark again like the chicken-shit that you are."

"Yeah—and what's that?"

"First off, it wouldn't be too bright to murder somebody right before you bust out. Hell, they probably won't even raise a posse for you just escapin'. But you go leavin' a corpse behind and there'll be horses and helicopters and bloodhounds swarmin' all over the desert between here and Blythe, and tha's a fack, Jack."

"So, what if I don't leave a corpse? What if you just vanish off the face of the earth like you never existed? Why wouldn't people just think you escaped too?"

"That brings me to the other thing."

"Other thing?"

"Yeah, the other thing that covers *that* thing. See, one of the things I picked up in this wacked-out school is how to write a good letter. So I wrote this letter to a friend on the outside—a cop, as a matter of fact—tellin' him the whereabouts of a note, and if he doesn't hear from me again in a week, that he's to contact the Lieutenant to retrieve that note. But hey, I don't wanna snitch you out unless I have to. I'd just as soon see you leave and leave me be."

"And I suppose that note tells all the details of my escape plan," Harvey growled.

"To the letter," Curtis gloated. "From the cracks in the wall, to Bonita Springs, to the back roads to Californ-I-A. See, I'm just full of surprises, Mr. Huish."

"Okay, so that gives me a week to make you disappear and maybe just move my plans up. So don't get so smug. You're not so smart after all—or safe."

"Well, I'm hopin' not to have to use my emergency backup plan."

"Oh, I can't wait to hear this one," Harvey smirked.

"Just this," Curtis snapped. "If I so much as get the slightest clue that I'm threatened—just an inkling—then I go over the wall ahead of you, right then and there. They may catch me sooner or later, but the minute that I turn up missin', the night watch will triple, and they'll patch all the cracks in the walls. You'll be shit outta luck there, double-H. They'll haul you up to Florence, and you'll do hard time where they just love young boys."

"Well, you little bastard! You wouldn't . . ."

"Ah-ah-ah—best be careful, Harvey," Curtis mock-admonished. "I'm already starting to feel uneasy. Best back off before I bolt like a bunny—you know, *a jungle bunny*!"

"Well, it sounds to me like you've got all the bases covered, Curtis," Harvey grumbled at last. "I gotta hand it to you. Looks like you got yourself a truce."

He extended a hand and Curtis reached out to shake, but retracted at the last split second.

"Are you *shittin'* me?" Curtis shouted in disbelief. "Do you think I'd trust *your* word? I'd rather shake hands with a jellyfish. No thanks," he continued. "I'll take my chances. You just have to decide which is stronger, mister—your head or your hate. Whichever it is, a handshake won't tell me shit."

———

It was past midnight, though Curtis could not have known that when he awoke with a start. It was neither a sound nor any physical sensation that stirred him from a restless half-sleep. And it was not exactly a dream, but more a narcotic sort of vision that cut short his fitful triumph over insomnia. It was the image of a pair of blue eyes, large and lidless—eyes without a face—that haunted his every nocturnal compartment.

He sat up and blinked. The eyes had not vanished with awakening, as he had hoped. Instead, they settled in the windowpane facing his bunk—larger than life and tirelessly vigilant. There were several disconcerting features that named their owner—deep-set and closely placed. Curtis had stared into them many times before. But the most intimidating quality was the sheer emptiness behind them: shark eyes, but of human design. The combination assured that they unmistakably belonged to his nemesis, Harvey Huish. Small surprise.

Curtis sighed and threw the top sheet aside, weary, but committed to defying this intrusion. His feet hit the cold concrete floor and he quickly pulled his jeans and T-shirt on over his moist brown body. Slipping into his Chuck Taylors, he glanced up to see that, yes, the eyes were still watching.

He padded on cat's feet out to the common hall to find it as it often was—unguarded. Marcus's presence had been sketchy of late. He hesitated at the doorway for a moment. The only movement outside was the swarming of a dozen or so moths, flirting with the glare that beamed from the mercury vapor lamp. He stepped across the threshold.

He had to do this; there was no choice in the matter. His enemy was calling his bluff, and quite rightly so—it *was* a bluff, in some respects. There was no letter and no note. Given his alliances in the administration, Harvey might already know this. What he didn't know was whether Curtis would actually go over the wall if threatened. Truth be known, Curtis was not certain either. He did know, however, that he would have to take it to the limit before making that fateful decision.

Keeping within the shadows cast by the dormitories, Curtis made for the secluded section of parade ground where the familiar cracks in the wall would provide the means of escape. He noted that the haunting pair of eyes followed along, jumping from window to window as he advanced along the bunkhouse perimeters, dogging his movement with an unrelenting surveillance.

Upon reaching the end of the row of dorm buildings, Curtis halted to take stock of the next leg of his supposed exit. The stretch of open parade ground between the wall and his present furtive position was dauntingly wide. He reckoned the distance to be about a hundred yards, a gap he could easily close in less than fifteen seconds on a dead run. Scanning up and down the parade ground and along the row of dorms, Curtis registered no movement. He'd come this far undetected. No one was astir, and the glare of the mercury vapor light had diminished to a glow at this distance—a faint blush that barely tickled the walls and skimmed over the graveled ground. The only eyes that watched him were those that settled in the end window of the last dorm.

Curtis stared momentarily into those lifeless pools of blue nothingness that seemed to probe his intent. They would take this hesitation to be a falter. He moved slowly toward the edge of the building's shadow and noted that the faceless eyes remained in the window, imprisoned, it seemed to him, in those reflective panes. They could not follow, but only gaze. Curtis took some encouragement in the eyes' apparent constraint—another limitation to Harvey's dark art. Spurred on by those watchful orbs, Curtis began to canter across the wide opening toward the wall.

Sprinting now across the parade ground where, on his first day here, he'd seen the vision of the triple hanging, he suddenly arrested his run and froze at the sound of crunching gravel. A moving mass of utter darkness like some hell-born black cloud glided toward him from his left side. He reflexively backpedaled out of the apparition's path. What passed before him forced an intake of breath like it was his last. As he gaped in disbelief, the Lieutenant's dark blue Impala, top down and lights doused, floated past and disappeared into the darkest pockets of shadow at the far end of the parade ground—its mesmerized pilot apparently oblivious to Curtis's errant presence on the field.

Shaking his head in utter incredulity, Curtis resumed his run for the opposite wall, reaching it without further incident. The adobe blocks and stucco radiated the heat they had retained from the afternoon sun. It was a strangely pleasant warmth that Curtis accepted as a sort of welcoming to a now-familiar place. He grasped the broken stucco fissures and quickly vaulted to the top of the rampart. Scrambling onto the ledge, he lay prone there for a moment, searching the parade ground below for any sign he'd been sighted. Once again, no one or no *thing* was astir. He pushed his torso up with piston-pumping arms and stood up tall on the wide parapet, facing eastward up the length of the wall toward the administration building.

He wondered about his cryptic brush just now with the Lieutenant. Had the mercurial headmaster really failed to spot Curtis as he bolted into the path of his car, or was he just riding the crest of one of his notorious binges beyond the point of caring? The answer mattered, as it might weigh against his turning back and finishing the night in his bunk.

He turned 180 degrees and cast his gaze down the westward run of wall to where it disappeared into darkness. Bonita Springs lay sleeping just an easy six-mile hike away in this direction. Perhaps he could use a phone there and call a friend to come and pick him up. More likely, he'd be ratted out by a sleepy resident and returned to the Fort. Outside, the easterly route was more intimidating: twenty-five to thirty miles of sun-scorched desolation between the Fort and a few scattered hamlets that lay beyond. But east or west—that was a choice to be made outside the wall. The more immediate choice loomed large—whether to leap toward freedom and the great unknown, or jump back down onto the parade ground and face his nemesis.

Curtis turned his head to the left and stared into the utter blackness outside the wall, shuddering as he recalled how Randy had warned that the wall kept out the unnamed evils that lurked in the darkness beyond.

Yet tonight it was a silent darkness—no howling coyotes or demonic riders to contend with. All seemed peaceful without—and yet . . .

What of the alternative? The eyes without a face were a test, not really a threat—Curtis knew this from the start. Would jumping back inside intimidate Harvey as a countermeasure, or would failing to follow through with an escape embolden him? Had he lost his ally, Randy, for good? Could the Lieutenant be counted on to intervene in an all-out battle?

Outside or inside? As he strained for a decision, he watched the blue eyes in the window across the way, as they watched him. The immediate power that Curtis held over Harvey—the ability to bring down his escape plan—was intoxicating. Whichever way he chose, he longed to loiter there for a few minutes to tease his tormentor. But the windows of the dorm buildings reminded him of his exposure. He could not be certain that only one pair of eyes was watching. The risk of being spotted by a waking inmate or a dorm guard was too great a gamble to be tried in exchange for the passing thrill that teasing Harvey aroused.

Without further deliberation, Curtis made his decision, turned in the direction of his choosing, and deliberately stepped off the wall. In that same instant, the eyes without a face vanished from the windowpane.

A Bond

The night seemed to go on forever, but when Curtis's voice trailed off, we sat there, the two of us, in the cool and quiet of the dark air. Once again, I gazed up into starry depths, waiting for him to return to the tale. I took this to be a dramatic pause, which Curtis was famous for, but it went on a little too long for that. I finally broke the silence.

"Why is it we're stopping here?" I asked in the most indifferent tone as I could muster. I continued to stare up at that infinite nighttime canopy stretching out above us. The endless magnificence of it really began to steal my attention.

"Because that's what you usually do when you get to the end of a story, brilliance," he replied.

I knew I couldn't make out his face in the dark, so I didn't even bother to interrupt my upward gaze. Still, I could easily imagine that devilish grin he most certainly was wearing.

"Oh, I rather doubt that," I muttered.

"Doubt what?"

"I doubt that we're at the end of the story."

"Listen, it's my story, and I get to end it where it ends," he huffed, sounding more than a little peeved.

"A little while ago you told me that the story is bigger than you."

"Yeah, so what?"

"So that means you don't get to end it wherever you want," I said with an air of authority. "Besides," I added, "you're just jivin' me. This story isn't done—not by a long shot."

"What makes you so damn sure?"

"Several things. For starters, you didn't just escape and come back to Jacobs Well like nothing ever happened. You'd be a fugitive."

"So what if they just stopped lookin' for me?"

"Not likely."

"What else?" Curtis growled.

"Lots of loose ends."

"Like what?"

"Like what finally happened between you and Harvey? I know you jumped off that wall and back down inside that night."

"Who says so?"

"Yogi Berra."

"Huh?"

"You know: *'It ain't over till it's over.'* Get it? It wasn't done between you two."

"Now you're just guessin'," he grumbled. "What else you got?"

"Plenty."

"Like what?"

"Like what's with all the weirdness about the Lieutenant? And by the way, who killed Kenny's wife, Primrose? And what about the old judge—where does he fit in? And then there's that shaman, Ezra? He seems like more than just an off-the-wall character."

"You're a pretty smart guy and a good listener. You should be able fill in the gaps on some of this stuff, Vince. You got anything else?"

"Lots of stuff, Curtis, we're wasting time with this little performance. Why don't you get on with it?"

"Like I said before—what makes you so sure that's not the end of the story?"

"Well, I saved the strongest clue for last."

"And what might that be?"

"My watch still says 11:15."

"I think maybe you just need to wind that thing, Vince," he chuckled. "But you're right about one thing. This story is way bigger than what I've told you so far. And it is *way* bigger than me—that ain't no lie. I'm just pretty well spent for one tellin'."

Still, I had to bait him into revealing at least one more turn of events.

"So I guess after all that waffling on top of the wall, you just jumped back into that snake pit after all, huh?"

"No way, José. What I did was jump to the outside. I just waited a while, then snuck back over where I remembered those climbin' cracks bein' in the outside of the wall."

"You didn't!"

"Sure 'nuff did. I couldn't resist havin' ol' double-H pissin' his shorts all night, thinkin' that I'd gone fugitive. He was sweatin' like a whore in church right up until breakfast when he seen me in the mess hall."

"That's hysterical."

"Oh yeah—you shoulda seen his face light up when he laid eyes on me. It's like I was his long lost buddy, suddenly turned up. I 'bout busted a gut laughin'."

"I imagine his warm and fuzzy feelings for you cooled pretty quick with you all crackin' up at him like that."

"Yeah, but just the look on his face made it worth the trouble. Besides, I figured that whole performance might make Mr. Huish think twice about messin' around with ol' Curtis anymore."

"Something tells me that might have been wishful thinking."

"I don' know . . . I really thought he'd back off of me—what with his escape plans and all, not to mention that I beat his *numero uno* goon to a bloody pulp." An audible sigh drifted across the darkness. "So much more to tell," he muttered.

But Curtis did not resume the telling of his tale, and it was just as well. The prolonged silence afforded me a few more moments to let the weight of what he'd related thus far sink in. I continued to gaze dreamily upward into the infinite depths of the star-spangled sky above and reflect. The vastness of that jeweled canopy beguiled my mind, seducing it into places rarely visited. Peering into the immeasurable distances made me ponder an eternal flight on an endless path to oblivion. The very idea attempted to place eternity into the present—a curious notion that Randy had hinted at. In fact, for all the storytelling of this night, I'd felt the clinging tentacles of time loosening their constricting grasp on my well-conditioned notions of it. Slipping into a reverie, I began to sense time as a more fluid construction than before, one that might, under certain conditions, allow past events to spill over into the present as more than just frozen memories—a sense that conformed well with Curtis's several references to the monthly recurrence of the Fort Grant atrocity. I recalled then what Kenny Armenta had repeatedly remarked: *all things are possible.* In my hypnotic state, that simple jewel of wisdom seemed nothing less than astounding.

We were still sitting cross-legged on that cultivated mound, and it was starting to get a little chilly out there in that melon field where Curtis had begun the saga of his reform school experience. But the enchantment of the stars and the slipstream of the story kept my spirits alive and warm with wonder.

It might have been a minute, or it might have been an hour since Curtis had gone silent. I was facing east and became suddenly aware that the inky black of the night was giving way to a faint predawn glow at the horizon. The familiar outline of the Superstition Mountains loomed against a deep purple band where the sun would spill over the bluffs in a little over an hour.

"I'm done," Curtis announced with sudden finality, after his period of stillness.

We arose from the ground simultaneously and began a cautious march through the lifting darkness. My remaining questions were eclipsed by my friend's authority and by God's dependable order of things.

"Curtis, I just don't know what to say," I finally muttered awkwardly. "I just don't have the words . . ."

"Aw hell, don't sweat it, Vince," he waved me off. "I didn't tell it to get your take on it. In fact, I wasn't exactly tellin' it to *you* at all."

"Huh?"

"That's right. I was more or less recallin' it to myself because, up to now, I'd never put the whole thing together like that, and I needed to hear it that way—in order of the way it happened and in spoken words. The bits and pieces that were comin' to me sort of hit and miss since it happened—that just wasn't cuttin' it."

"Because?"

"Because it's been naggin' my poor nappy head for almost a year now that I was supposed to take somethin' away from that whole nightmare stay—somethin' important—and I still wasn't gettin' it."

"So, do you 'get it' now?"

"Not exactly—I don't think it's somethin' that happens just like that!" He snapped his fingers to emphasize his point, and then completed the thought. "But hey, I've gotten a better grip on a big chunk of it, and I've planted some seeds in my mind now. I'm sure the messages that fit where I need them to will dawn on me just at the right times."

"For instance?"

"Well, for instance, I got a better sense of who is a true friend when I meet one. In fact, I can judge who's gonna be best of buds within a couple of hours now."

I knew he was referring to himself and me, as I too had sensed an unmistakable bond building between the two of us during the telling of the story. It was an indirect validation of a new friendship, and it set me aglow.

At the end of the field we hopped over the ditch and searched for the glint of chrome that would be our bikes.

"Makes me wonder," I mused as I mounted my trusty Huffy in the predawn gray.

"Wonder what?"

"I don't know. It all just makes me wonder."

"I guess I know what you mean," Curtis allowed. "Hey, Vince, you know what I wonder?" He suddenly laughed.

"No, what?"

"Aren't your parents going to have the sheriff's posse out looking for you about now?"

"I don't think they'll miss me if I can sneak in before they get up. They always sleep in on Saturday and they usually go to bed before I come in on Friday night, so there's no bed check or anything."

"Lucky."

"Well, I sure *hope so* anyway," I gasped.

"Why's that?"

"Because if they catch me gone, they're liable to get fed-up and have me shipped off to *Fort Grant*!"

"Yeah, and now you know that's no place to spend the night, my friend."

Book club Discussion Questions

1. The sporadic suspension of restrictions of time plays a large part in the premise of *Path of the Half Moon*. How does the storytelling method enhance the relaxation of time limitations for the reader?

2. The symbolic image of the moon is prevalent throughout the book. Randy cites a number of facts about the moon that refer to dualism. What other more subtle metaphors regarding the moon might be involved with the story?

3. There is a strong suggestion that several of the characters are not subject to our normal understanding of life and death. Who are they and what might explain this phenomenon?

4. One of the story's themes suggests that there is a fine line between justice and vengeance. Does the story resolve this dilemma?

5. In the case of the Lieutenant, "indecision leads to tragedy." How does the Lieutenant's indecision differ from that of Curtis?

6. The story cites a historic animosity between certain Native American tribes. It suggests that the enmity predates the massacre and is perpetuated by it. Do you think the animosity still exists in the present day? Why or why not?

7. Does Harvey's family background explain or justify his evil bent?

8. Randy comments that intelligence and wisdom are two very different facets of the mind. How does this apply to the character of Will Farnsworth?

9. There seem to be some similarities between Randy and Vince, the narrator. Does this affect the relationship between Curtis and Vince? If so, how?

10. Who is the old judge, Natchez Mendoza, and why is his relatively minor role central to the story?

About the Author

Vince Bailey grew up in Central Arizona, starting in the late nineteen-fifties. His youthful experiences there contribute significantly to the nostalgic aspect of his fiction writing. *Path of the Half Moon* is his debut novel, and winner of the Arizona Authors' Association Literary Award.

Vince has also been published in several college and local newspapers, and for the past ten years he has penned a column for a nationally distributed trade periodical. Mr. Bailey currently resides in Peoria, Arizona with his wife, Rita. He's currently working on the next book in the *Path of the Half Moon* series.

uncommon publishing

We delight in publishing the non-traditional, unconventional, and
alternative, including:

Fiction
Metaphysical
Professional and Nonfiction
Romance
Young Adult
IE Snaps!

Review our list of themes and topics, and perhaps they will inspire
you to consider writing for original genres and audiences.

www.ingramelliott.com

www.ingramcontent.com/pod-product-compliance
Lightning Source LLC
Chambersburg PA
CBHW051218120726
47905CB00004B/1166